Jennie Jones has been professionally involved in the arts for most of her life. Theatre by theatre, stage by stage and later book by book, from Wales to London to Auckland to Australia. Jennie lives in Perth, Western Australia, and remains a countryfied girl at heart. She has a passion for stately homes and rustic cottages, is fond of collecting too many vintage wares, has numerous pot plants she's learning how to keep alive, and is happiest when writing stories about life, love, and everything between.

Also by Jennie Jones

Swallow's Fall Series
The House on Burra Burra Lane
The House at the Bottom of the Hill
The House at the End of the Street

Daughters of Swallow's Fall Series
The House on Jindalee Lane

The Rangelands Series
A Place to Stay
A Place with Heart

A Dollar for a Dream Series
Last Chance Country

DAUGHTER
of the HOME
FRONT

Jennie Jones

FICTION
HQ

First Published 2022
First Australian Paperback Edition 2022
ISBN 9781489270757

DAUGHTER OF THE HOME FRONT
© 2022 by Jennie Jones
Australian Copyright 2022
New Zealand Copyright 2022

Except for use in any review, the reproduction or utilisation of this work in whole or in part in any form by any electronic, mechanical or other means, now known or hereafter invented, including xerography, photocopying and recording, or in any information storage or retrieval system, is forbidden without the permission of the publisher.

This book is sold subject to the condition that it shall not, by way of trade or otherwise, be lent, resold, hired out or otherwise circulated without the prior consent of the publisher in any form of binding or cover other than that in which it is published and without a similar condition including this condition being imposed on the subsequent purchaser.

All rights reserved including the right of reproduction in whole or in part in any form.

This is a work of fiction. Names, characters, places, and incidents are either the product of the author's imagination or are used fictitiously, and any resemblance to actual persons, living or dead, business establishments, events, or locales is entirely coincidental.

Published by
HQ Fiction
An imprint of Harlequin Enterprises (Australia) Pty Limited (ABN 47 001 180 918), a subsidiary of HarperCollins Publishers Australia Pty Limited (ABN 36 009 913 517)
Level 13, 201 Elizabeth St
SYDNEY NSW 2000
AUSTRALIA

® and TM (apart from those relating to FSC®) are trademarks of Harlequin Enterprises (Australia) Pty Limited or its corporate affiliates. Trademarks indicated with ® are registered in Australia, New Zealand and in other countries.

A catalogue record for this book is available from the National Library of Australia www.librariesaustralia.nla.gov.au

Printed and bound in Australia by McPherson's Printing Group

MIX
Paper | Supporting responsible forestry
FSC® C001695

To friendship

PART ONE

Chapter One

Blueholm Bay—July 1942

'Emma!'

'Coming, Mum!' Pulling a cotton headscarf from the pocket of her shorts, Emma Hatton twisted it, wound the band around her head and knotted it at the top. She liked to think its bright yellow complemented her thick chestnut hair without overwhelming the paleness of her skin—an oddity, because her eyes were as brown as a nut too. But at least she didn't have freckles. Dad said she looked just like his mother and he told everyone she'd been a bonza-looking woman.

A horse neighing and women's chatter out on the street caught her attention. She threw open the frayed lace curtains of her bedroom window and studied her small town with a sigh. How she had got to fifteen without understanding that what she'd been waiting for all her life was the chance to use every scrap of her youthful energy and hope was a mystery. One day, she'd get out of Blueholm Bay and never come back. She'd see the world. She'd ride on trains, sail in ships and fly in aeroplanes all the way to Europe, or even America. She'd be free as a bird, not tethered to anything. Not the washing, nor the cooking. Not the cream and butter making. Not her brothers, nor her mother. Although she'd miss Dad.

She glanced over her shoulder at the bookshelf. Dad had given her a large atlas a few years ago. It had been a gift from a European settler back when Dad was a young man making his way in the world by felling trees and clearing weeds.

She'd been so proud that he'd not put it aside for his eldest son that she hardly dared turn the pages. She also had a novel each by DH Lawrence and Miles Franklin, a rather tattered copy of *Don Quixote*, two Dickens, and *Middlemarch* by George Eliot, which was a cracking good read. Her English teacher had given her the novels and they'd all go with her, wherever she went. She'd be sad to leave everything she'd known for so long but that was the way the world moved. It chugged and churned and seized people in its wake and Emma couldn't wait to be caught in the rip.

'Emma! For the love of God!'

'Coming, Mum!' She ran out of her bedroom and along the dark hallway, halting when she got to the kitchen, unable to hide the smile that had curved her mouth these last months as soon as she woke. No matter what chores were to be done or how long the day would be the war had changed everything and Emma's future beckoned with more opportunities than she'd thought possible.

'Sorry, Mum, I was just—'

'Gawping at yourself,' Mum interrupted, casting a disparate look at the headscarf in her daughter's hair. 'Here. Put these away. I've told you before they're like money and I'm struggling as it is.'

Emma took the tea and clothing coupons and returned them to the hole in the wall behind the food safe where her brothers wouldn't get hold of them, then pushed the safe back into place. They'd had the ration coupons for nearly three weeks. They were the most precious things she'd been entrusted with to date, apart from the boys, and she sometimes thought there was nothing precious about any of her brothers, although Danny was sweet at just turned five and Will still a little boy at seven and a half.

'Grab me the soap from the laundry,' Mum said.

Emma scooted out the kitchen, ducking her head beneath a patch of sailcloth that had come undone. Dad had nailed it to the beams he'd erected over the outdoor walkway so Mum wouldn't get wet when it rained on wash days. It was thoughtful of him but he didn't do the washing and Mum and Emma got soaked just from standing in the laundry with the copper boiling as though it was a volcano erupting.

'It's not much, is it?' she said as she came back into the kitchen.

'What isn't?' Mum asked, taking the soap and checking how many bars were left.

'The tea coupons. Two ounces for a week. Ten pounds for one person for the whole year.' Emma wasn't considered an adult but she liked a cup of tea and was mostly going without. Dad wouldn't have coped with such a small amount. He could drink up to ten cups a day. She wondered if he got tea where he was now. Surely the soldiers had enough for a brew?

'It's what we've got, it's what we put up with,' Mum said as she tied her apron strings. 'First clothing, now tea. They'll be taking the bread from our mouths soon.'

'But we make our own.' Being rural, they were better off than most who lived in Townsville. The Hatton yard wasn't big enough to grow many vegetables so Emma collected eggs for Mrs Jameson down the street in return for having a patch of land on her property to grow their veg. She tended it alongside Mrs Jameson's daughter, Janet, who was nineteen and had just started work as a typist in Townsville—unpaid mind you, but still. Working a proper job! In the city! Janet was talking about being trained for air raids and learning how to drive.

Everyone grew veggies or did their bit to help out and the Colsons provided milk for the town from their twelve cows. Mum took turns with one of Janet's younger sisters to milk them and that's how they got enough butter and cream for themselves. They used to get raw milk delivered but the Yanks didn't like it so now they could only get pasteurised. Not that Emma would be using any milk, raw or otherwise, to put in the cup of tea she wouldn't be getting.

'God help us one and all,' Mum said. 'We'll be bombed in our beds. Or worse, thrown out of our own house. Evacuated—but to where? That's what I need to know.'

Emma didn't respond straight away. Sometimes Mum asked questions then got mad when somebody answered. She often asked God for His blessing too, although she wasn't religious, not like the Catholics who actually went to church, but since Dad had gone to war, Mum spoke to God a lot, whether to ask for His help or to blame Him for something she thought was His fault.

'Bombs!' her mother said. 'How many more and what's to become of us?'

The bombing last Saturday and two more scares after that—the latest just yesterday—meant worry about being blown up in the middle of the night had taken pride of place in Mum's bag of concerns. Being over an hour's horse and cart ride north of Townsville, they hadn't heard the bombing or the planes. Nobody had, as far as Emma could tell, but panic had struck. The stories flying around were thicker than fruit flies on a bruised mango. If they were all true, they'd be blown up, displaced or starved within the week.

It was scary though, especially without Dad home. Dad was just down the road—the 51st Battalion had been in Sellheim at the start of March but were now at Mount Louisa—yet he hadn't contacted them or even replied to Mum's letters. 'He's sorting himself out,' Mum would say when she was feeling generous. 'He wasn't very well before he went.' Other times, she called him all sorts of names.

'Aunty Doris isn't worried,' Emma said, hoping to calm her mother. 'She was chipper when I saw her yesterday.' Dad's sister lived on the city side of Castle Hill and she hadn't heard the bombs either.

'Doris hasn't got money worries, has she?' Mum said. 'She's a woman with the telephone. No wonder she's chipper. She's likely charging people a shilling to use it.'

Emma tried to look contrite and hoped she hadn't failed or else she'd be the one to bear the brunt of Mum's displeasure about her sister-in-law having a lot more than the Hattons would ever hope to have. She always visited Aunty Doris when she was in Townsville because Aunty Doris was family and even Mum said it would be unseemly not to pop in on family. Mum probably said this because Aunty Doris often gave them a fresh pineapple, or sometimes—much better—a tin of biscuits. They hadn't had biscuits for a while but yesterday, when Emma visited to get some old jumpers to unravel and knit socks for soldiers, her aunt gave her six pork chops, a string of sausages and a bundle of last week's *Daily Bulletin* which Emma pored over whenever she got the chance. She enjoyed reading about what was going on in the world practically more than munching on a biscuit.

'Evacuation is only a threat if conditions deteriorate,' she told her mother. 'That's what they said in the *Bulletin*. We likely won't get evacuated, but I read that if it does get worse, some people might be ordered to specific evacuation centres and won't be permitted to exercise any option.'

'Specific? Exercise an option? You can put a stop to your fancy words and your reading, young lady. Without your father here everything's landed on my shoulders—if you haven't already noticed.'

'I'm just saying we won't be thrown out of our house.'

In February, the police and ARP wardens had been door to door, counting how many women and children they might have to evacuate. Dad said he wasn't bloody going anywhere and neither were his wife and kids. Mum said that was because they had no bloody money and nowhere to go.

Doris looked like someone had stuffed a dead rat in her mouth when Mum told her they might be turned out on the street. Probably because she could suddenly envisage her lovely house in the city being overrun with the Hatton lot. Half of Townsville had already gone of their own free will, packing the trains and heading south, leaving their front doors wide open and their worldly goods to the mercy of thieves or the Japanese. Although there was good money to be made renting houses out to the Yanks, according to Aunty Doris.

Aunty Doris didn't have much to complain about but she always had a good story to tell. She'd told Emma she wasn't allowed to make a trunk-line telephone call to her parents-in-law in Brisbane without getting permission from the military authorities, and she said a friend of a friend's neighbour had to watch his house burn the other night because he couldn't get hold of the telephone exchange for nearly thirty minutes.

The Hattons didn't know anyone they might need to call, but Mrs Jameson three doors down had the telephone if it was necessary, and it would only cost sixpence—not a shilling. They might have to telephone about Dad one day, so Emma kept a sixpence under her mattress in case Mum had run out of money when the time came. She'd stolen it out of Mum's purse and hoped this wasn't a bad thing because sometimes needs must.

'They'd probably forget about us anyway!' Mum exclaimed. 'We're fending for ourselves out here, and all of us women.'

There were close to a dozen men still in town who were either disabled in some way or too old to be called up, but Emma chose not to remind her mother.

'I'll need you at Mrs Cosgrove's today,' Mum said. 'Get yourself ready.'

Emma flew out of the kitchen and down the wood-panelled hallway for the front room. This was the news she'd been hoping to get. It meant she wouldn't have to watch her brothers after school. Mrs Jameson would take them in with her brood.

'Come on, you lot,' she said, clapping her hands to get the boys' attention. 'Time for school. You've got ten minutes to get yourselves ready.'

'Too many rules,' Joe said, eyes on the board game he'd been making out of bits of cardboard he'd secreted away. He was twelve and the worst of the four, but she forgave him because he suddenly had a lot more chores and was expected to be the man. He wasn't quite ready for it.

'You can blame the Japs for that,' Simon said. He was nine and getting to be as bossy as Joe. 'When I'm old enough, I'm going to join the air force and shoot them all down.'

'Not if you don't go to school,' Emma said. 'You have to have learning to get good jobs or fly planes.'

'Says you, who doesn't go to school.'

Emma ignored him. She'd loved every moment in the classroom and wished she was still at school, but obviously being the only daughter that would never have happened.

'Ack-ack-ack-ack-ack!' Will mimicked firing a machine gun at their youngest brother and on cue, little Danny hit the floor, spreadeagled, eyes and mouth wide open, tongue sticking out.

Emma stifled a laugh. It wasn't good to encourage him.

Schools had been closed from January to March after Pearl Harbor was bombed. Some schools had been shut completely, already taken over by the Americans for their many needs. Having the boys home seven days a week had been a handful. Will and Danny had been home all day until just recently, doing whatever schoolwork their teacher sent round.

Simon snatched the cardboard Joe was working on.

'Hey! Give that back!'

'What is it?' Simon asked as he held it up and stared at the drawings and squares. 'It looks like Tank Attack to me. That's not new and you've got snakes but no ladders.'

'They're flying tanks, idiot, and they're not snakes, they're firemen's hoses.'

'I want to finish it with you.'

'You'll bodge it,' Joe said, raising his chin. 'I'm going to sell it to the Americans. I'm a games inventor and I'm going to be rich.'

'Don't go thinking your blood's worth bottling just yet,' Emma told him. 'Simon, put it down and go get the sandwiches from the kitchen.'

'Emma! What are you doing in there?'

'Nothing, Mum. It's all under control.'

'Be quick about it.'

'I'm going to invent a tank that can fly,' Joe told Simon as he cleared away his pencils. 'And it'll drop bombs on you.'

'I've already been bombed. All week.'

Joe huffed. 'They were nowhere near us and I heard there was only one stick dropped on the first raid. Anyway, you have to wear glasses and you would have missed the bomber planes even if you'd been right under them.'

'I would not!' Simon pushed his glasses further up his nose, his expression full of outrage.

'Does a bomb have a stick?' Danny asked, pulling on Emma's shorts. 'Like mine?' He held up his precious stick which he used to make a tremendous racket with by running it along all the picket fences in town. He called it his musical instrument. He said he made it himself because Dad wouldn't buy him a violin like the one he'd had as a boy.

'You know you can't take your stick to Mrs Jameson's after school, Danny,' Emma said. Mrs Jameson was a good sort but

Danny's music-making gave her a beastly headache and they all had to be nice to her because she helped Mum out an awful lot. 'She's got mandarins for you and Will.'

'Don't want mandarins. Want watermelon.'

'No chance of that happening, they cost too much.'

'We'll grow some,' Simon said.

'Don't be daft,' Emma responded.

'I'm not daft. You're daft.'

'Too right,' Joe said.

'Yeah, you're just a dumb daft girl,' Will chipped in.

'And you lot are three terrors waiting to feel the back of my hand.'

'Aren't I a terror too?' little Danny asked with a hopeful expression.

Emma ruffled his hair. 'Not yet, but I expect you will be soon.'

He jumped in the air and whooped, then Will joined in and Emma clapped her hands again. 'Go get your shoes! All of you! Mum and I have important war work to attend to.'

'Since when is washing the Yanks' uniforms war work?' Joe said sarcastically as he marched out of the room. Simon and Will followed, marching out of step while saluting their leader.

Emma bent to help Danny tie his shoelaces. While he was distracted, she pushed his musical stick behind her. 'I've put your peg in your bag,' she told him. He was the only one who took a peg. His best friend at school came from a family who had less than the Hattons, so he only got a peg to bite on in case he got scared during a bomb raid and Danny wanted to be just like his friend. Emma made sure her brothers had cotton wool for their ears and sticking plaster and disinfectant in case they got hurt and now the younger two had gone back to school, she made sure Danny had a little extra cotton wool to give to his friend.

He scrambled up from the floor and wiped his nose with the back of his hand. Emma caught him by the scruff of his jumper and hugged him close.

'Get off!'

She smiled as he shook himself away, mad as a cut snake. Please God, none of them got hurt. Little monsters though her brothers were, they were her blood and she'd been looking after them since their births in one way or another.

'Emma!'

'Coming, Mum.'

Chapter Two

An hour later, Emma was already perspiring. She'd had to sit on the floor of Mr Jameson's wagon, squashed between the legs and the smelly shoes of the other women. Mr Jameson would go on to the city and do odd delivery jobs then come back and pick them up at the end of the day. There wasn't any air on the floor, no matter how much she fanned her face with a newspaper during the twenty-minute ride and now she was waiting for the wives to move so she could get off the cart and get to work.

The wives made quite a bit of money doing washing at Mrs Cosgrove's three days a week. Mrs Cosgrove had installed fourteen new concrete coppers once she'd understood how viable the business was, although she was as old and rickety looking as the bridge that crossed the creek in Blueholm Bay and hardly ever did the washing herself. There were plenty of women in and around Townsville doing Yanks' washing, plenty of Yanks needing the service, and Mrs Cosgrove had cottoned on to the enterprise when the Bohle River airfield construction had got underway. The Blueholm Bay women took turns doing the washing because otherwise it wouldn't be fair that some got the income and others didn't, and anyway, they also had households to run and their own washing to do.

'The man's got a full load, I'll give you that,' Katy Wheaton said as she passed a lit cigarette to Betty Soames. She was talking about one of the Americans and it wasn't about the size of his wash bag.

'I reckon he's got just the same as what my Bill's got,' Betty replied after taking a drag of the cigarette and handing it back.

'Yeah, but you haven't been able to make use of what your Bill's got for some time.'

'Doesn't mean I'm desperate for it.'

'So how come you stare at your Yank's load so often?'

'My eyes are only on his crotch because I'm sitting down and he's standing! And he's not mine.'

Katy Wheaton laughed as she pushed her hair back and tied a scarf over it. 'I'm not blaming you, I'm just making an observation.'

'Well, keep it to yourself or my name will be mud.'

Emma was sure her blushes were visible as she waited for the cart to empty. They often forgot she was fifteen and she had every intention of making sure it stayed that way. There were valuable life lessons to be learned from the wives.

Once she was off the cart, she gathered the sack of wash sticks and tucked three of the metal scrubbing boards under her arms. She'd come back for the glass ones. Mrs Cosgrove said she wasn't forking out good pounds for more equipment than she already supplied only to have it stolen from under her nose, so the women had to bring their own wash sticks, scrubbing boards and irons. Emma's job was to help set up and then spend the day going from one woman to another, seeing if they wanted a hand, so long as Mum didn't need her. Generally, she could do anything they did, as befitted a girl her age. She'd been doing it all at home since she was eight anyway.

'What do you want me to do first?' she asked when she joined her mother, who was studying a sheet of paper: a list of whose clothes they'd taken in for washing yesterday.

'I've got seven loads of ironing to do and you can do the folding and bagging.'

'Righto.' Wednesday was a good day to help out because the new lot of washing wouldn't get started until after lunch. Tuesdays were for washing and drying. Wednesdays for ironing, folding and bagging plus taking in the next batch of washing, which would be hung to dry overnight, undercover, on the long lines strung up for the purpose. Thursdays were only for ironing and bagging and was the least hard work. Hopefully, Emma would be back tomorrow too.

'Here they come!' someone shouted, and all the women turned.

Two military vehicles spilling over with Yanks drove through the paddock gate. The women waved and some whistled with their fingers in their mouths.

'They're early!' Mum called. 'They'll have to wait until the irons are on!'

'Don't worry, Miriam, we'll keep 'em entertained,' Katy Wheaton said with a grin.

'I bet you will,' Mum muttered.

Emma's stomach rumbled as she tied her apron around her waist, so she pulled it more tightly. It wouldn't do to be hopeful of getting something nice to eat but the Americans often came bearing goods that were outrageously expensive or unattainable to the likes of the locals. They got hold of anything and everything, but they could afford it. They were kind though, and didn't mind sharing. They were always smiling and telling jokes nobody understood. Betty Soames's sister told them one Yank asked her to go to a restaurant on Flinders Street and get him steak and eggs because he couldn't stand the chow, as he called it, being served at base. He'd given her his tin dixie pan to put the food in. The restaurant chef had cooked the meal and Betty's sister had taken it back to the Yank, who gave her ten shillings and told her to keep the change. Ten shillings for a meal that cost little more than two-and-six! Joe said some boys in the Townsville schools had been given ten shillings just to deliver a message. Emma couldn't imagine getting all that money for doing practically nothing.

'Stop gawping and get going!' Mum yelled, pushing a sharp elbow into Emma's back.

Emma made her way to the old barn that was now the washhouse, scrubbing boards beneath her arms and the sack of wash sticks in her hand. 'Morning, Mrs Cosgrove!' she said cheerily.

'There won't be anything good about it once these are lit,' Mrs Cosgrove answered, staring at the row of coppers. She turned her attention to the barn doors. 'The war is on our doorstep, Emma, and look at that lot.'

Emma looked over her shoulder to the wagon where some of the women were still lingering, chatting to the Yanks. The women liked the friendly humour bandied about by the Americans. Some of them liked the flirting too, but surely none of them meant it? It must be a relief to smile and laugh, with all their men gone and some not likely to return.

'I don't think they mean any harm.'

Mrs Cosgrove grunted. 'You remember this, Emma—we women ought to make of the war what we can without making fools of ourselves.'

'Yes, Mrs Cosgrove. That's good advice.' Emma put the scrubbing boards and sack of wash sticks down since her arms were aching. 'You've got one of the coppers on the go already,' she said when she noticed it.

'Had a couple of them come over yesterday evening since they couldn't get their wash here earlier. Thought I'd help them out a bit this morning, since they brought me a watermelon.'

'Lucky you! Watermelons are going for eight shillings each at the moment.'

'That won't be the last price rise we see,' Mrs Cosgrove said with a grimace. 'Pineapple and paw paw will soon be things of the past for the likes of us, you mark my words.'

'I'll keep an eye on the copper for you if you like,' Emma said.

'You're a good girl, Emma. Don't go forgetting how important that is in life. Have you heard from your dad?'

'Not recently.' Not at all, but Emma knew not to say anything about this. Mum had discovered his whereabouts with the help of Aunty Doris and both said he'd likely write soon.

Emma wasn't sure why her dad hadn't already done so. Unless Mum was ordering him about even in her letters. Dad hadn't been unwell before he left, that was something Mum had said to one or two neighbours. He might even be happy to be gone after putting up with Mum's complaints all these years and maybe that's why he wasn't writing back.

'He was a good sort as a young man, your dad,' Mrs Cosgrove said, bending to push a log further into the fire beneath the copper. Dad had worked at the Cosgroves' poultry farm, but that was before he married Mum and before Mr Cosgrove died. 'He was never in his cups. Always had a tall tale to tell. Used to make us laugh, he did.'

This was the dad Emma remembered from when she was little and before Will and Danny had been born. He'd been raised in Bohle, but his parents had died in a house fire when he was twelve, so he left school and went out to work. Aunty Doris was taken in by a neighbour until she moved to Townsville when she was fourteen and got a job in a big house. Dad met Mum in the Bohle Plains in late 1925 at one of the get-togethers the CWA arranged so that women could meet up and have a chat, getting away from the monotony of day-to-day domestic and farming work. Mum had been visiting a friend and Dad had been around because he was clearing land for the settlers.

Emma couldn't picture what her mother had been like as a young woman, but she was a scary sort now, so something must have happened to make her this way. Being poor, probably. Not that her mother was in a much different position to any other wife in town now that all the men had gone. Apart from the Colsons. They were as posh as the king and queen. They had a live-in housekeeper and a girl who went in daily, and a car and enough influence to get petrol to run it while there was a war on. They'd lost their gardeners and labouring men to the war, though, so Emma supposed even the Colsons were doing it hard.

'Best get on with things.' Mrs Cosgrove wiped her hands on her already dirty apron and shuffled to the far corner of the barn in the boots that had once belonged to her husband. She liked to sit and smoke after she'd checked on everyone.

Emma picked up the sack of wash sticks and the scrubbing boards and put them in an empty stall.

'Come on, ladies!' Mum yelled in the yard. 'Or else I'll be thinking about changing the rosters next week.' Being the one to approach Mrs Cosgrove about the work, Mum was unofficially in charge of the women.

'Bitch,' Katy Wheaton said as she walked into the barn with her irons.

'Don't let her hear you,' Betty said, picking up a plank of wood she used as a tabletop.

Emma stepped further into the stall so they didn't see her.

'Betty! Get that table sorted. We're keeping these servicemen waiting.'

'Yes, Miriam!' Betty called. 'Just sorting it out now.' She slid the plank onto crates piled one on top of another for table legs. 'Yes, Miriam,' she said in a low tone meant only for her companion. 'No, Miriam.'

'Three bloody bags full, Miriam,' Katy Wheaton replied.

'Just jump when she yells,' Betty said. 'Like her kids have to.'

'I reckon there's only one of them who does the jumping.'

'Too right, and she jumps the highest.'

'Whatever Mummy says.'

Emma sank against the wall of the stall. She had no idea why they would talk about her this way unless it was because they disliked Mum so much. But why take it out on Emma?

She gathered herself and came out of the stall casually, as though she'd just turned a corner from somewhere else. 'Can I give you a hand, Mrs Soames?' she asked with a smile.

'No thanks, love.' Betty cast a cautious look her friend's way.

'You're a good sort, Emma,' Katy said.

It was a bit hurtful to think they were passing some sort of judgement on her but Emma kept her smile in place. It wouldn't do to stir up trouble.

'I'll take the irons for you, Mrs Wheaton,' she said, holding out her hands. 'I'm just about to light the stove.' The old irons most of the women used were heavy things and you had to clip on a separate handle so you could pick them up and not get burnt. Everyone had two irons because the heat from the first didn't last long and they'd be here until midnight if they only had one iron each.

'That would be really helpful, Emma, thank you.'

'Mrs Soames, can I get you anything?'

'No thanks, love. I'm fine.'

Betty was now set up by the large barn doors, which were flung open to let some air in. She would take the soldier's name and tag his bag of clothing and whatever else he wanted washed so it wouldn't get lost. Then Mum would hand out the laundry bags to the wives, ensuring each woman had the same amount or there'd be arguments.

'All sorted, Miriam!' Betty called. 'Send those lovely fellas over here and we'll keep them smiling while the irons heat up.'

The other women were already organising their ironing stations. Mrs Cosgrove supplied four mangles and six ironing boards. The first job this morning would be to flick the dry clothes with water then wrap them up in towels to help get the creases out.

Emma bent to check the wood stove. They'd need to keep it going not only for the irons but for the kettle so they could have a cup of tea with their sandwiches. 'About seven hours to go,' she murmured, and flung another log into the stove for good measure.

Four hours later, the new washing was bubbling in hot soapy water. The ironing and bagging had been done and handed over, apart from three kit bags not yet collected. They'd had their lunch and Emma had been rewarded with a cup of tea by Katy Wheaton. Probably because she felt guilty for saying Mum was a bitch as well as mocking Emma in some way and hadn't been sure if Emma had overheard.

Emma stirred Mum's wash. The Hattons didn't have a proper wash stick like most of the others, just half a broom handle Joe had sawed for them. Emma didn't mind. A lot of people were poor and it didn't mean they were any less worthy as human beings.

'It's all very well being nice to the Americans,' one of the women said as she stirred her load, 'but they're taking all the food and water.'

'And no bugger is doing bugger all about it!' another woman called out.

'Someone ought to give those blokes in Canberra a backhander,' Katy said. 'Or knock their heads together.'

There was a lot of talk in the newspapers about the poor North Queenslanders and their depressing plight, with not enough food and not enough security for their very lives. Everyone blamed the government. 'Gross negligence' and 'dereliction of duty' were words Emma had read over and over in the last week.

'Got a smoke, Betty?' Katy asked. 'I've run out.'

'In my bag, by the table.'

'Smash them politicians on the head with a block of ice, I reckon,' Irene McDonald said. 'That'd get 'em moving.'

'If you can get your hands on the ice.'

'My Lyla is delivering ice now,' Irene told them proudly. 'Driving around with two other girls, she is. In a van.'

'Does she get to suck on the ice chips?'

'Or bring a block home?'

'No such luck.'

Driving. All of the girls Emma knew could drive a horse and buggy or even a cart with two horses but imagine being at the helm of a real motor car. That had to be better than being a typist like Janet Jameson, stuck in a smoky office all day with dozens of others. Especially when you were volunteering your time and not getting paid for it. Not that Emma would say no to a typist's job if she were offered one. She'd run at it.

She went back to the stirring. Mum hated doing this part and no wonder. Emma was hot and sticky all over. Mum was talking to Mrs Cosgrove in the far shady corner where the steam didn't reach. They were probably discussing how much money they'd made and working out a time when the cash would be divvied out.

Emma put the wash stick down, pulled the headscarf from her hair and wiped the sweat from her forehead.

'Don't know what your mum's going to do without you next year when they call you up for war work,' Katy Wheaton said.

The government had introduced conscription for single girls and married women without children who were between sixteen and twenty-four. In just over four months' time, in January 1943, Emma would be sixteen and she'd have to find gainful war work. She wasn't sure what Mum was going to do about this. Joe wouldn't be able to handle the cleaning and washing like Emma did. But there was an age to go before January.

'I expect we'll get along,' she said to Katy.

'What are you thinking about doing?'

Emma shrugged. 'Whatever they tell me.'

Katy dropped her cigarette butt and ground her heel into it. 'That's right, love, you just keep doing as you're told. Don't want to annoy your mum, do you?'

She moved on, leaving Emma feeling out of sorts. She'd been ridiculed before, but only by Mum or her brothers, especially as they didn't understand how much Emma loved reading and learning, and she'd got used to all that. But Katy Wheaton was making her feel inadequate in a new way. Did she think Emma was the sort who always said yes? Someone who lacked judgement and sense of her own? Is that why she'd been talking about her earlier?

Maybe it was because she was no longer a girl but not yet a grown woman. Perhaps there was a gulf during these years between longing for dolls and pretty things and recognising the reality of life as it was, and these years were a bridge that had to be crossed.

'Come on, Emma,' Mum said as she strode across the barn. 'Time to get this lot out. Go fill the rinsing tub with water.'

Emma pushed Katy's comment behind her and went to do her job. She enjoyed this part of the washing routine. All the cold water right up to her armpits, cooling her down while the heat and humidity swarmed around the barn.

'Bugger it, this lot's still grubby,' Betty said, staring at a pair of steaming trousers hanging off the end of her wash stick. If the clothes were still stained after the boiling they got a good scrubbing with Sunlight soap then into the hot tub they'd go again. At home, if they were washing Dad's work gear, his trousers and shirts would get soaked overnight first, but there wasn't time for that out here. 'Grab me my scrubbing board, would you, Emma?'

'Just filling Mum's tub.'

'The soap, Emma!' Mum said. 'Where did you put it?'

'It's in the stall. I'll get it in a minute.'

'And fetch my scrubbing board too,' Mum said. 'I've still got three dirty shirts here.'

'Righto!'

'Where's Betty?' Mum said when Emma handed her the soap and scrubbing board.

'Loo break.'

'Get those soldiers their bags. They're by her table.'

Emma picked up a rag to dry her hands. There were three Yanks waiting in the open doorway. She hadn't heard their vehicle drive up with all the noise going on.

'Tick them off on her list,' Mum said. 'They should have already paid, but check.'

When Emma got to the table, her heartbeat just about skyrocketed. It was him. The Yank with the hazel eyes. She'd seen him before and he'd even winked at her the last time she'd been at Mrs Cosgrove's.

'Hey, I remember you,' he said, stepping away from his friends. 'Let you out of the factory for a moment, have they?' He nodded over her shoulder at the washhouse.

Gosh, he was good-looking.

Emma swallowed hard.

The three soldiers were now regarding her and she went hot all over, but they probably didn't notice her blushes as she was already flushed from being in the hot barn. The Americans weren't different in size to any other man, but they were somehow bigger in stature and bolder than any men Emma had met. Although not being allowed to go out on her own, except for visiting Aunty Doris, meant she hadn't met many young men.

'Are you here to pick up your laundry from yesterday?' she asked the good-looking one, not brave enough to meet his eye.

'If it's not inconvenient.'

'It's all ready for you. Name?' she asked.

'That's what I was gonna ask you,' he said quietly.

She glanced up. He was still smiling and it was a smile that sparkled. Being gazed at in this manner was like supping from a glass of fizzy champagne—however that might taste.

'What's your name?' he said softly.

'Emma,' she said, then had to clear her throat. 'Emma Hatton.'

'You're a pretty little lady, Emma Hatton. It's a pleasure to meet you.' He held out his hand. 'Private Frank Kendrick, USAAF Engineers.'

The United States Army Air Forces … it even sounded glamorous.

Emma took his hand. His engulfed hers with strength and warmth.

'Combat?' she asked. He was ever so tanned and his uniform fit him to perfection.

'No, but it sure feels like a war zone around this town sometimes.'

'It does get busy, doesn't it?' A lot of Yanks thought Townsville a hot, dirty, lousy troop town. Emma tried not to listen when she heard that type of comment but it certainly felt like Townsvilleans were in the front line too, their city overrun by military. 'Do you work with the fighter pilots?'

'Supply,' he told her. 'Armament, construction, maintenance, repair. Whatever I'm called to do. Without me and the guys I work with, the pilots wouldn't get far on their bombing missions. Not without someone on the ground.'

'It's nice to meet you, Private Kendrick,' she said, remembering to take her hand back.

'Girls as beautiful as you can call me Frank.'

If she'd been red before, she must now be the colour of the watermelon she hadn't tasted in a long while.

'Leave her be, Frank. She's just a kid.'

Private Kendrick peered at her. 'How old are you?'

'Nearly eighteen.' She didn't twitch as she said it, not even a blink.

Frank gave her a wide grin. 'That's a good age to be. I'm twenty-two but I remember turning eighteen. My folks threw me a humdinger of a party.' He gave her a contrite look. 'I was even allowed a drink, although I'm ashamed to say the beer got the better of me that night. I watch myself these days. No more than three drinks in an evening. When I get time off, that is. Do you get to the Roxy much?'

Emma brushed a hand over the top of her head, thankful she'd taken off her wet headscarf. 'We rural girls tend to stick at home, but I'm hoping to get into Townsville in a few months' time. I have to help with the war work.' Too late, she realised her mistake. 'I mean, I am doing war work already. Obviously, at my age, I have to. But I'm hoping to get away from home and into the city to do more meaningful war work.'

'Instead of washing our uniforms?' Frank laughed. 'What would we do without you? Up until we found you ladies, we'd been doing our washing in the shower.'

Emma frowned. 'How?'

'Well, we kind of put them on the floor of the ablutions block and turn the taps on.'

Emma drew a startled breath. 'That's an awful waste of water! Didn't you think?'

'About what?'

'Water is a precious commodity around here.'

'Heck, I'm sorry.'

'It's not just food that's rationed, you know, it's water too.'

He stepped back, grinning, hands in surrender mode.

'You getting a scolding there?' one of his buddies asked.

'I think it's just a minor adjustment to my usual mode of operation,' Frank said while grinning at Emma.

'Emma! What are you doing? The copper fires have to be put out.'

Emma spun around, mortified at being caught talking to a Yank. 'Just telling this soldier about the water shortage,' she told her mum. 'You'll never guess how much water they were wasting before they found us to do their washing.'

'Aw, come on,' Frank said in a low voice. 'That's below the belt.'

Emma turned her head. 'I have to tell her something. Trust me, I know what I'm doing.'

Frank grinned again and looked over her shoulder. 'My apologies for keeping your daughter occupied when you've got work to do, Mrs Hatton. I'm about to pay up right now. All you women are doing such a grand job and we thank you.'

Her mother paused, eyeing them both with a creased brow. Then her attention was taken by a shriek and a clatter that sounded like a pile of ironing boards falling over and she headed back into the barn.

'Thanks,' Emma said, turning to Frank.

'You're welcome. I like a woman who knows how to handle people.'

A woman. She supposed she was, almost, but how wonderful that her virtues had been noticed by this mature and confident man in such a short amount of time.

Emma checked Betty's list. Frank was the only one of the three who hadn't paid. 'Your washing comes to five shillings.'

He dug into his trouser pocket, pulled out a wallet and held out a ten-pound note. 'You keep the change. Go buy yourself something nice.'

Emma's jaw dropped. Keep the change?

'For God's sake, Frank,' his buddy said, bemusement on his face.

Frank shrugged. 'A guy has to do something for these lovely Australian women now and again.'

'Yeah, but ten pounds?' his other friend said.

'You bet. It'll be worth it, wait and see.' He turned to Emma. 'I'd best be going, Emma Hatton. You've got chores to do and I have a war to fight.' He picked up his kit bag, slung it over his shoulder and gave her a lazy salute, his hazel eyes boring into hers. 'I'm hoping I'll see you again. Real soon.'

Emma smiled, spellbound, her insides melting as she clutched her ten-pound note.

She would do everything in her power to make sure Private Frank Kendrick saw her again.

So long as Mum didn't know about it.

Chapter Three

September 1942

'Twenty pounds,' Aunty Doris said, staring reverently at the two banknotes she held in her fingertips as though they were fragile pieces of antique silk.

Mum snatched the ten-pound notes off her and tucked them back into her purse. 'I'm not saying we're not grateful for it. I'm just saying it's a little odd.'

Emma had been helping Mum at Mrs Cosgrove's three days a week since the end of July but Frank had only been back once in early August.

'What does he do?' Aunty Doris asked, choosing a biscuit from the tin on the dining table. Biscuits she had brought over this afternoon, having heard about the second ten-pound note episode from someone in Townsville who had relatives in Blueholm Bay. The Wheatons, probably. They were as nosy as the earth was round.

'US Engineer,' Mum said. 'Army Air Force.'

'What's his rank?'

'Private.'

'Well,' Doris said. 'I know they're paid well but perhaps this one comes from a wealthy family since he's flinging ten-pound notes around.'

'That's what I thought.'

Doris sucked in a breath then skimmed a look at Emma, who averted her gaze and pretended to straighten the tablecloth. 'What did he say to you? The first time he gave you ten pounds.'

Emma looked up. 'He said he used to do his washing on the shower floor. I told him that wasn't acceptable.'

'Acceptable—hark at her,' Mum said.

Doris never commented when Mum spoke about Emma in that stingingly demeaning way. Emma wasn't sure if it was because her aunt didn't agree with Mum or if it was because she couldn't make up her mind one way or the other.

'And the second time?'

'He didn't speak to her,' Mum said. 'He spoke to me. Emma was in the back of the barn as usual and he says to me how lovely I was looking, and then asked me where my daughter was because he had something for her.'

'Cheeky one, then.'

'I told him Emma was busy. I wasn't going to put up with his sauciness.'

'Of course you wouldn't, Miriam.'

Mum thrust out her bosom, pride at her knack of knowing how to put a person in their place making her swell. 'He pulled out his wallet, handed me a ten-pound note and told me to use some of it to pay his bill then share the rest with my daughter.'

'How much was his washing?'

'Five shillings. I had to give Cosgrove twenty per cent of that, but I took it out of my own purse and kept the note. Betty Soames and Katy Wheaton had their ears flapping the whole time.'

'It was Katy Wheaton's sister who told me about this second ten-pound note,' Doris said.

Emma rolled her eyes but fortunately neither woman saw.

'I nearly fainted in shock when I heard. I thought I'd best come out here to see what was what.'

'Nice of you to make the time, with you being so busy and all.'

'This happened last month, Miriam, and I'm only just hearing about it! Of course I came over.' Doris stuck out her pinky when she picked up her cup from its saucer. 'Twenty pounds!' she said to Emma. 'You have brought some luck to your family, haven't you?'

'She's too young.'

Doris threw an exasperated look at Mum. 'I'm referring to a proper relationship. A courtship. A lot of our girls are getting involved with a Yank.'

'And mine isn't going to be one of them.'

'But think, Miriam, just think a moment. He's a wealthy lad.'

'He'd take her away! She'd be off to America and we'd never see her again.'

Emma tried not to cringe. It was excruciating being talked about as though she wasn't in the room. All she'd got out of Frank were two or three winks, plus that splendid smile and two ten-pound notes—and here was her family discussing her as though she were a prized mare to be auctioned off.

'He hasn't been back since anyway,' Mum said, frowning as she noticed Doris's pinky.

'Where's he gone?'

'No idea.' Mum took hold of her teacup with both hands and leaned her elbows on the table, showing her disregard for her sister-in-law's snobbish ways.

'Probably just as well,' Doris said, and took another biscuit from the tin. 'As you say, she's too young. I can't see our Emma coping with a grown man. They can be nice, these Yanks, but men are men after all. If you get my meaning. She'd get her heart burned.'

'She'd get her backside burned if anything untoward happened.'

A momentary silence ensued but it was filled with nuance that made Emma's stomach churn. Mum hadn't overheard the flirting between her and Frank, nor that she'd told him she was eighteen.

'Our Emma wouldn't do anything untoward on purpose,' Doris said in a placating manner, and Emma squirmed for real. Two weeks ago, one of Frank's buddies had turned up and Emma had found the courage to sneak out of the washhouse through the rear doors and grab his attention without anyone seeing her. When she'd asked him where Frank was and if he would be turning up to get his clothes washed again, the buddy had said, 'He's up at Mareeba.'

'Oh.' All the way up by Cairns.

'Looking for another ten-pound note, are you?'

'No! I just wondered where he was. He was very kind.'

'Don't take what Frank says or does to heart, honey.'

'I'd give the money back if I could,' she'd said quickly. 'But my mum took it.'

'Oh, he meant you to keep it. Don't worry about that.'

'Have you written to Doug to tell him?' Doris asked, bringing Emma out of her thoughts about whether she'd ever see Private Kendrick again.

'I'll tell Doug when I see him face to face. Don't you go writing to him either,' Mum warned.

'I won't breathe a word. Our men aren't exactly happy with the Americans being all over our country, showing off the way they do.'

'Doug wasn't all that well before he signed up.'

'I remember you saying so.'

'I don't want him bothered or worrying about his daughter. Nor about my reputation, because let's face it, Doris, it's me who's in the firing line if anything unfortunate happens. I might not be rich like some, but I've got my pride. I pray hard, I work hard.'

'You're a martyr, Miriam. That's what you are, having to deal with what God's given you.'

'Thank you,' Mum said.

Emma kept her focus on the tablecloth. Poor Dad. He was never told anything for real. He was mostly just scolded. No wonder he never wrote back.

'Where is Doug now?' Doris asked.

'His battalion has gone up to Cairns. I happened to hear it from Irene McDonald. Her brother is with the 51st too. Obviously,' Mum said, lowering her voice, 'Irene knows nothing about Doug not having replied to my letters. If she did I'd tell her I don't write to him often because I don't want him concerned about us all at home, working our backsides off.'

'I expect Doug's working his off too.'

'I tell you, Doris, my day is a long hard slog and none of us know how long it's going to go on for.'

Doris nodded in sympathy.

Emma sighed. Sometimes she wished she had a friend. Someone her age or maybe a bit older. But she was always so busy doing chores or minding her brothers that she hardly ever saw any of the girls she'd been at school with. Most of them lived in the Bohle Plains anyway. Janet Jameson came to mind, but they'd never been more than acquaintances since Janet was nearly four years older. The last thing Emma wanted was for Janet to tell her mother about Frank, because Mrs Jameson would be shocked to hear Emma enquiring about an adult man. And a Yank at that. Mum's face would turn puce if she found out. *Emma Hatton, you have let this family down. You have let your father down. You have let me and your brothers down.*

What she'd really mean was that Emma had humiliated her mother, who would then have trouble holding her head up at Mrs Cosgrove's and keeping her authority over the wives.

Maybe this was what Betty Soames and Katy Wheaton had been having Emma on about. Perhaps they did see her as the sort who was always a goody two shoes.

'How's Harry Colson doing?' Doris asked.

Mum shrugged. 'Getting on as best he can. He's been out of hospital some time.'

'What a thing to happen.'

'We all went to the funeral to pay our respects to his parents,' Mum said.

'I heard it was well attended.'

'Mr and Mrs Colson were the decent types, given their class and position. Cynthia came. Looked wretched, the poor woman.'

Emma wondered if Harry Colson's sister, Cynthia, was as wealthy as her brother. She lived in Melbourne. She'd married a few years ago but her husband had been at war most of that time. She probably had servants and a number of friends but she must be lonely.

'I imagine she would be wretched,' Doris said. 'I doubt she'd inherit anything, it would all go to her brother. Was she given any of her mother's jewellery?'

'Ivy Williams didn't know. But Maud Colson's engagement ring was quite the thing to see. Platinum with diamond clusters. She had matching earrings too. Mrs Colson was always properly dressed in her jewels.'

'They wouldn't have buried her with any of it, and it would have gone to Harry, that ring. I expect his parents imagined their son would be married long before this. The best thing for him now is to get that done or his mother will be turning in her grave with worry.'

'I doubt anyone would have him,' Mum said, glancing Emma's way briefly then lowering her voice again. 'Some say he's not quite right.' She tapped her head.

'He's an assistant bank manager, Miriam, not just a clerk. He's got to have some brains.'

'He's a quiet one.'

'I agree, but I'm still surprised he's not already married. How old is he now?'

'Coming up to twenty-nine.'

'Fancy having to have another operation on his gammy leg, though. How unlucky is that?'

Everyone in Blueholm Bay knew a bit about Harry Colson's past. He'd been in a fishing boat accident when he was in his early twenties. He used a cane to get around and although his injury hadn't stopped him from driving, it had kept him out of the armed forces.

'The motor car is wrecked,' Mum said. 'Harry was in the back seat and that's what saved his life, because it was the front that bore the damage from the runaway team.'

'How terrible.'

'The wagon driver lost control when the Colson car came around the bend. The front of the car caught the rear of the wagon, which dragged it halfway down the ridge. All four horses went over the escarpment along with the wagon. One had to be shot.'

'Never! Mr and Mrs Colson must have been practically crushed!'

'Probably not even recognisable,' Mum said, eyes glistening.

'I don't want to even think about it,' Doris said with a shudder. 'What was the wagon carrying?'

'Ice.'

Doris tutted. 'Such a waste.'

Emma wasn't sure if she was referring to the Colsons or the ice.

Mum lowered her chin, indicating she was about to impart a secret. 'Ivy Williams told Mrs Jameson he's bought another motor car.'

'You'd think he'd have had enough of driving.'

'That's what I said. But he has to get himself to the bank every day and his gammy leg can't be giving him too much bother now he's had it operated on. It's not a brand-new car, obviously, with the war on, but Ivy said she thinks it cost three hundred pounds.'

'Three hundred pounds!' Doris shook her head in disbelief. 'Do you think he'll stay on here in Blueholm Bay?'

'Ivy says so. She said he would never consider living anywhere else even though there must be more for him in Brisbane or even Melbourne with his sister.'

Ivy Williams was the Colson's housekeeper and according to her, she knew much more about the wealthiest family in town than anyone else would ever know.

'Mark my words,' Doris said, 'he'll get himself married. It's not as though he hasn't got anything to offer. Even with …' She tapped her head.

'It'd take a strong woman to put up with any eccentricities he might have, Doris. The quiet ones are usually the shifty ones.'

'Yes,' Doris murmured. 'But all that money would help, I'm sure.'

'Another cup?' Mum asked, lifting the teapot. She poured and added milk and half a spoon of sugar to each cup.

'Has Cynthia heard from her husband?' Doris asked. 'She must miss him dreadfully. Especially now she's lost her parents.'

'Ivy said it's her understanding she isn't taking too well to the fact her husband is overseas.'

'Most of our men are overseas!'

'But not in Britain, Doris. Robert Allen is in Britain.'

'Oh, well, forgive me for forgetting that,' Doris said as she checked her nails, which were painted a vivid rose pink. 'What's he doing over there anyway? That's what I want to know.'

'He's fighting the—what is it, Emma?'

'Luftwaffe.'

'Yes, that one.' Mum turned her attention back to her sister-in-law. 'He and other Royal Australian Air Force diggers are doing wonderful things with the Bomber Command lot.'

'They should be over here fighting for our lot. Britain have got their share of Yanks now so why do they need our men?'

Mum clearly didn't have an answer for this so she simply pursed her mouth. For a moment, neither woman spoke.

'Anyway,' Doris said, replacing her cup in its saucer. 'What I also wanted to let you know, since I'm here unexpectedly, is that I've rented out three of my bedrooms to American servicemen.'

Emma glanced at her aunt, then her mother.

'Is that right,' Mum said, straightening her spine in a manner which told Emma she was holding on to herself before making a further statement. She was counting the pounds Doris would be bringing in. All the while staying in her own home and not having to work to pay the bills, like the Hattons had to do.

'I don't need the money,' Doris said. 'It's a kindness.'

Mum didn't answer but her expression said it all.

'I've got five bedrooms, Miriam. All empty except mine.'

'What about the fourth empty bedroom? Why aren't you renting that out too?'

'Well, that's what I want to discuss.'

Doris and her husband didn't have children and, as far as Emma knew, they weren't too upset about it and were perhaps even hopeful none came along. Uncle Raymond worked in the mining industry but he'd gone to war and was already a sergeant. Doris had never had to work except between the ages of fourteen and sixteen when she met her future husband. They got married a few months after. Mum said Aunty Doris had always known a good thing when she saw it.

She might be right about that. Doris hadn't made anywhere near the sacrifices some had. She had a girl who came in every day to do the cleaning and washing plus all the cooking. There had always been food in their pantry, and not just ordinary foodstuffs but special things: tinned or packaged items that would be a luxury for Emma's family. Doris didn't have a food safe because she had a refrigerator. She also had an electric iron and she never even used it. The girl who came in daily had asked if Doris would upgrade to a steam iron—the very best thing going—but Doris said she didn't think there was any need to splurge on unnecessary items.

'The thing is,' Doris continued, sitting upright on her chair and mirroring Mum's rigid spine and no-nonsense expression. 'My girl has turned sixteen and she's gone back to the family farm for her war duties.'

'I see,' Mum said, her features not altering although Emma detected a spark in her eyes that might be enough to light the range without a match.

'You know how busy I am with my volunteering, Miriam. I'm run off my feet with the Red Cross.'

Mum pursed her mouth again.

'So what I was thinking is that with Emma about to be forced to come to Townsville when she turns sixteen next January—there won't be anything here in Blueholm Bay that can readily be called home front war duties, Miriam—and given that my time and energies are going to volunteering for our dear men fighting for King and country ...'

'And?' Mum asked, her expression now set like stone.

'Well,' Doris said, raising her hands in the air. 'That's just it. How can I possibly care for these homesick souls when I'm inundated with my volunteer work?'

'I suppose you could have thought about that before you rented out three of your bedrooms. How much are you getting?'

Doris waved the question off. 'Not as much as you're imagining.'

'No,' Mum said, and rose to stand.

'No what?'

'You're not having Emma.'

Doris pushed her chair back and stood. 'I think you're being too hasty, Miriam.'

'I think what you want, Doris, is someone to do all the cleaning and cooking while you make money from the Americans.'

'You're taking it the wrong way. She has to be registered for voluntary work when she turns sixteen. It's the law. There's the home front to think of.'

'It's your home front you're thinking of,' Mum said sternly.

Emma kept as still as a mouse while this arrangement was being discussed. Neither woman appeared to have remembered she was in the room. They were eyeing each other up as though they were in a boxing ring. Emma was glad her aunt hardly ever visited and that Mum hadn't been to the city for ages. Being around the two of them was exhausting.

'Who do you know in Townsville who would be willing to take her in, house her and feed her and care for her except me?' Doris said. 'I've kept a room for her, and I could be getting good money for it.'

'I thought renting out your rooms was a kindness.'

'There has to be an exchange of money, Miriam. The Americans would insist.'

Emma wasn't so sure. It probably wouldn't be up to the Americans now since the Australian Army Hiring Service was in operation, sourcing buildings suitable for the Americans' needs. Thirty houses on Chapman Street had been requisitioned for a hospital. People had simply been evicted from their own homes. The Americans built walkways between the houses. One of Doris's many acquaintances knew someone who'd been evicted, and she said number twenty was now being used as an X-ray theatre, all the walls painted black, and apparently number sixteen was a mortuary. People were still complaining about not having been recompensed for their losses, even though they'd put in a claim, and some were saying even though they'd been paid, they hadn't been given anywhere near enough. Neither had they been given an alternative place to live. They'd had to fend for themselves. Some had moved out of Townsville altogether and would likely never return. Who'd want to go back to a morgue? Or a house with all its rooms covered in black paint?

'You know you'll have to think about it soon,' Doris said, taking her jacket off the back of her chair and slipping her arms through, buttoning it up as though donning armour. 'Better to have her living with family than with some other bugger, which is why I'm offering her my spare room now.'

'Better for you, you mean,' Mum said, hands clenched at her sides.

'You can't keep her hidden here, Miriam. They're raiding the shops and cafés, looking for girls and women who aren't pulling their weight.'

'Like you said yourself, I've got three months before I need to let her go.'

'She could be doing her bit now; it's not like she's incapable of hard work.'

'And where would that leave me?'

'Exactly where you'll be left in three months' time!'

'I need Emma here,' Mum said. 'Not breaking her back at your place.'

'That's unfair! I'd look after her.'

'She's staying here.'

'They'll arrest you!' Doris said, sticking her chin out.

'They wouldn't dare!' Mum yelled back.

Doris slammed the lid on the tin of biscuits she'd brought and Emma flinched. Her aunt had a point. Emma couldn't valuably do war work in Blueholm Bay. There were plenty of wives with plenty of children to do the veggie growing and egg collecting. Janet Jameson hadn't been able to stay. She'd had to go and live with one of her many cousins in the city and was only home occasionally when she wasn't on shift at the typists' office. The problem was, if Emma was given a choice, she knew exactly where she'd prefer to be breaking her back.

'Who does she think she is!' Mum exclaimed once she'd seen her sister-in-law to the door.

Emma gathered the teacups and the teapot and strainer from the dining table and carried them into the kitchen. Doris had taken the biscuits with her, even though Emma had thought them a gift.

'There'll be no more helping out at Mrs Cosgrove's,' Mum said, following her.

'But you need me out there.'

'I'm not having you noticed more than is decent.'

'What do you mean?'

'There are things you don't understand. You're only a girl. I've already heard Katy Wheaton talking about you.'

'What is she saying?'

'Never you mind.'

'Shouldn't I know so I can stand up for myself?'

'Will you please stop with your answering back! You're giving me a headache.' Mum put her fingers to her temples and took a few breaths, eyes closed.

Emma bit her tongue. There had to be more coming.

'Right,' Mum said as she came out of her contemplation. 'From now on, you're going to be doing chores at home. I've decided to take on some extra work at Mrs Cosgrove's. I expect a few of the wives wouldn't say no to working five or six days a week, especially as it keeps the job here, with us ladies in Blueholm Bay. We all need the money.'

Emma swallowed the moisture in her mouth and waited for her mother to announce her fate.

'From now on you can do the milking up at the big house.'

'The big house?'

'I'll let Ivy Williams know. She'll keep an eye on you. You can start tomorrow morning.'

Emma had milked cows before, but it would take a bit of time. And Ivy Williams was an old bat.

'You'll come home when you're finished and do all the work we need done in the house,' Mum said. 'I'll be working hard, I won't have time to do everything. You can do the late afternoon milking as well. It'll free up one of the other Jameson girls. I'll get Mrs Jameson to keep the boys after school until you've finished up at Mr Colson's.'

Emma put the teapot on the drainer. She was dying to ask what would happen when she turned sixteen and desperately worried her mother might hide her after all. Then she'd never get out of town. She'd never get away.

'But Mum, the boys—'

'They'll have to start looking after themselves.'

'Danny's not even six.'

'Will you stop with your backchat! I can't think straight.'

'Knock, knock. Did I hear our name mentioned?'

They turned as Janet Jameson stepped into the kitchen from the hallway.

'The front door was open so I just came in.' Janet put a parcel onto the table. 'Mum said to bring these over. Veal chops. We got a stack of them from a cousin in Townsville who's a butcher. The Yanks like it, apparently.'

'The Yanks like what?' Mum asked.

'Chops for dinner. Just serve them with potatoes and minted peas. Anyway, we have enough to share them around a bit.'

'That's very kind of your mother, with beef so scarce,' Mum said, her voice less scornful. 'We'll have it tomorrow.'

'Tomorrow's Friday,' Emma said at the same time Janet said, 'It's a beefless day tomorrow.' Two days a week had to be beef free. They couldn't buy, sell, cook or eat anything that had beef in it. Not even sausages or tins of beef. It was a way of ensuring the armed forces got enough.

Mum didn't appear too keen about having been reminded. 'I'm so worked off my feet, I don't know what day it is,' she said to Janet. 'We'll set the chops aside for Saturday then.'

'You're quiet,' Janet said to Emma.

'Emma has a lot of contemplating to do,' Mum said.

'About what?'

Mum didn't answer, and neither did Emma.

'Well, if she's not busy, I don't suppose I could pinch her off you for a half-hour, could I, Mrs Hatton? I have to prune the roses for Mum and could do with a hand since I'm not much of a gardener.'

'I'd be grateful if you did take her out of my sight,' Mum said as though Emma wasn't in the room, which made her feel like a worm on a hook. 'I've got a heck of a headache and all she does is nag. You,' she said, turning to Emma, 'start pulling your weight, girl, and while you're at it, think about your manners. Mrs Williams up at the big house won't put up with what you get away with here.'

Emma fumed. This was so unfair! She did pull her weight. She wasn't a nag. She was a yes girl like Katy Wheaton and Betty Soames clearly thought.

'Let's get going then,' Janet said to Emma. 'When there's work to be done, it's best to get it done.'

Emma tried not to stomp out of the kitchen.

Janet followed. 'I hope the wind doesn't change. You've got a face like a squashed monkey.'

'How droll,' Emma said, still stinging from Mum's words.

Janet simply smiled.

Emma continued down the hallway. It was always embarrassing having one of the Jamesons in the house. Not that Emma noticed the peeling wallpaper Dad had so carefully put up in the front room when Emma had been a little girl, toddling after him with her kiddie's paintbrush. She hardly gave a glance to the chipped woodwork all over the house or to the garden picket fence with its cracked and warped posts. She usually ignored it all, but at this moment she saw it, even though she was near blinded with frustration.

Outside, the spring sky was pastel blue and the palms on Herring Corner by the Osbornes' grocery shop rustled in the breeze like crinkled paper. All the streets in Blueholm Bay were named after fish. Herring Street, where Emma and Janet lived, Whiting Court, Snapper Crescent and the John Dory track, which led to the rickety bridge over a shallow creek that wound through seven miles of sandy shore like a pale blue ribbon until it reached the ocean. And it was all so ... boring!

'I heard you got yourself into trouble at old Cosgrove's,' Janet said as they turned for her place, three houses down.

'I did not.' Emma stopped walking.

Janet paused and stuck her hands in her trouser pockets. She'd said only last week that the best thing about the war was that she got to wear pants, as the Americans called them. When she wasn't in the office, typing. 'Something to do with a Yank and a ten-pound note,' she said, her smile now filled with delight.

'I didn't ask him for it!'

'Not saying you did. He took a fancy to you, though, didn't he?'

'He might have.'

'Look.' Janet pulled her hands out of her pockets and walked back to Emma. 'Just be grateful you didn't have to do anything for it.'

'I did his washing.'

Janet spluttered a laugh. 'Boy, you're an innocent.'

Emma hauled in a breath. 'If you're referring to sex, then no. Obviously, I didn't do that for him.'

'Well, when you do get to do something for a man, make sure you want it too.'

'Have you done it?'

'None of your business. But I've seen girls throw themselves in the path of any GI they came across. What was your mum talking about in the kitchen?'

'I can't go to Mrs Cosgrove's any more. I've got to work up at the big house.'

Janet whistled. 'That's a punishment, all right. Going to be the new fetch-and-carry girl for Ivy Williams, are you?'

'I have to do the milking.'

'Watch your step. The old bitch will make you do all sorts of jobs if she gets the chance.'

Emma sighed.

'Cheer up, Hatton. You'll get out of here soon. No-one can make you stay, not even your mother. You'll be sent to Townsville next year to do real war work.'

'Do you think so?' Emma felt a fool asking but her mother might come up with any number of excuses to have her daughter stay in Blueholm Bay.

'I don't think so, I know so.' Janet pulled off her wide-brimmed straw hat, which had seen better days. 'Here.' She stuck it firmly on Emma's head. 'With all that fair skin you're going to burn pruning the roses for me.'

'Who said I was going to do all the pruning?'

'That's the way it'll be if you want me to tell you all about the Americans and the Roxy, and how I have a boyfriend. A GI boyfriend,' Janet said and carried on walking, hands in her pockets again. 'And anyways, I'm crap at pruning roses and you've got a green thumb so we can barter. You prune and I'll tell you dozens of stories about living in the city.' She looked over her shoulder. 'Don't be a tortoise, keep up.'

Emma let out a bemused breath and ran to catch up. 'Don't go thinking just because you're four years older than me that you're better than me.'

'There you go, nagging and nagging. It's going to get you into trouble, Emma Hatton.'

'I'm already in trouble,' Emma said, but somehow she didn't feel as bad as she had ten minutes ago. 'So what pictures have you seen at the Roxy?'

'I've seen them all. Whatever they're playing, I go see the picture. I've got a friend who's an usherette.'

'Gosh, you lucky thing.'

'Aren't I?' Janet smiled as she pushed open her front gate.

Emma went into the garden feeling lighter of heart. Even the thought of getting up at four tomorrow morning didn't feel so onerous. She'd get along with Ivy Williams somehow. It wasn't as though she had to sit and chat to the housekeeper—or to Mr Colson. She couldn't imagine how that might go, with him being so posh and her being a little nobody from the town. Especially if he was a bit funny in the head.

'I'm thinking of joining the AWAS or the WAAAF,' Janet said, handing Emma a pair of gardening gloves and the shears she'd picked up from the pathway next to the bed with all the roses. 'I want to do something meaningful where I get to wear a uniform.'

'Will your mum allow it?'

'Why wouldn't she? I'm already doing my bit for the war, but I want to do more.'

'So do I.'

'You will.'

Emma made a face.

'Really,' Janet said, sitting on the bottom step of the staircase that led up to the house, elbows on her knees. 'You'll be able to do what you like. Just wait and see. You'll find out for yourself next January.'

Emma could only hope so because being around Mum was a lot like being in a battle she didn't have a chance of winning.

'Free,' she said to Janet. 'That's what I want to be.'

'Well then, you've got to aim for it. You've got to make it happen.'

'Too right,' Emma said, and pulled on the gardening gloves. She would make it happen. She damn well would.

Chapter Four

There was something uniquely relaxing about milking cows. Their gentle lowing and chewing as they stood patiently in the stalls in the Colson barn was almost a lullaby at five thirty in the morning. Emma leaned her forehead against the cow she was milking, inhaling the smell of country and grass that emanated from it and liking the velvety feel of its hide. The cow moved but Emma kept pulling on the teats in a rhythmic squeeze, tug, squeeze, tug.

After she'd got the first few cows back in the paddock, she made her way to the house. She had two full pails of milk which had to be poured into dishes to set for twenty-four hours so it could be separated for cream. Other women would be up at the big house during the day to make butter and cheese from yesterday's lot of milking. Emma would have to drag a churn of cream down to the front garden gate later, after she'd finished the afternoon milking, so Mr Jameson could pick it up and distribute it among the families in town.

When she turned the corner by the shed, she paused. Up at the house the kitchen light was on plus another downstairs and one upstairs. Ivy Williams was up and getting breakfast on the go. It wasn't as dark now, the orangey sun creating a golden ray on the horizon. Only one star twinkled, as though it had been left behind. Emma had always loved looking up at the stars and the crowded constellations. As a child she'd thought of them as her friends because they wouldn't chide her for getting things wrong or for wanting to immerse herself in a book, relishing the story and adventures as though they were her own. As she'd grown older she wanted to shine as brightly as the brightest star. Wanted to stand out with all the others and be seen as normal and part of the crowd, yet all she'd felt like recently was the little star left behind.

Would she ever find the other stars? The ones happy to have her in their midst?

She took her gaze back to the horizon. If it had been full light, she'd have seen the ocean and Colson Beach. She could hear the water lapping, and salt from the air lingered on her lips in the flavoursome dusting she'd become accustomed to as a baby.

Treading carefully on the paved pathway, she reached the edge of the gardens and stared in astonishment. She'd only ever seen the garden close up once when she'd been here with Dad, who'd come up to do some carpentry work on the shed door. She'd passed it often enough though, on her way to the beaches further north for a swim or a picnic with some of her school friends.

There was no grass; it was all gravel. So many topiaries. Nobody in their right mind would have such a formal garden this close to the ocean, which was one of the reasons they all thought Harry Colson a little odd—he'd been the one to encourage his father to develop the garden about ten years ago. The geometric topiary shrubs and hedges were creepy. Even more so in the shadowy dawn. The sight made her think of a cemetery, the shaped trees like tombstones.

The Colsons had arrived in Queensland from Britain with their then twelve-year-old son and eight-year-old daughter in the 1920s, well before the Great Depression when all the banks closed, and moved to Blueholm Bay in the thirties once they'd built the house. Why they'd chosen to settle here, Emma didn't know, but talk around town informed her it was because they'd come from the English countryside and enjoyed the sense of withdrawing from the hustle to somewhere quiet and rural. The family had three men working full time on the garden before the war; now Harry Colson just had women who came in to help whenever time allowed.

If it was up to her, she'd pull up all these topiaries and sow a lawn and plant daisies, her favourite flower.

'Hello. Good morning.'

Emma nearly dropped the pails, slopping milk over the rims and onto the brick path.

Harry Colson held up a hand. 'Please don't be alarmed.'

She put both pails down since her hands were suddenly shaking. 'I didn't see you there!'

'Who are you?'

'Emma Hatton.' She almost bobbed a curtsy but stopped herself in time—he wasn't actually a king. 'From the town. Number eleven Herring Street.'

'Hatton,' he said as he hooked his cane over his arm and held out his hand.

He wanted to shake her hand! She wiped hers on her shorts first.

'A pleasure to meet you,' he said. 'I don't think I've met the Hattons.'

'You have. At least, some of us. My mum milks your cows, but now I'm doing it. And my dad has done some work for you.'

He tilted his head. 'Yes, I do recall the name. Something about chickens?'

Emma swallowed. 'That would be my brother, Joe. He let your chickens out. My dad brought him up here to apologise. He didn't mean it, Mr Colson. I mean—he did mean it, otherwise he wouldn't have done it, but he just wasn't thinking.' She was gabbling, so she closed her mouth and clasped her hands in front of her.

'Now I remember. No harm done, except for those who had to run around catching the chickens. I believe it took them over two hours.'

'I'm sorry about your parents,' Emma said, purposefully changing the subject. What was Mum going to say when she found out Emma had met Harry Colson under such terrible circumstances? Sneaking around his garden!

'Thank you.'

'Are you better now?' she asked, trying to keep her eyes off his leg, which might have been shorter than the other one but she didn't want to stare. He was quite tall though. Much taller than Dad and far more imposing.

'I'm getting there,' he said. 'The garden reminds me of my parents. It has offered me solace in the last saddening months.'

Emma turned to look at the green-leaved statues, precisely trimmed. 'I'm sure it has.'

'I was pleased when my father took up the idea of gardening, although I admit I had no idea it would run to topiaries.' He smiled a little. 'Do you like them?'

What could she say? They were grand and ugly. 'They're sophisticated and they look a bit isolated, but there's certainly an artistic flair about them.'

'Undeniably,' he said, with the shadow of a smile. 'What are you intending to do once you finish school?'

'I've already finished my schooling.'

'That's a shame. Do you like reading?'

'I love it.'

'You might like to take a peek in my library while you're here.'

'Oh, no, sir. I couldn't do that.'

'Why ever not?'

Why not? Mum would have a fit if she discovered Emma had snuck into Mr Colson's garden, let alone browsed through his book collection. No matter how wonderful it would be to have a full library all to oneself, even if only for ten minutes.

He shifted slightly, then winced and used his cane to steady himself. 'May I ask how old you are?'

'I'll be sixteen on January the twelfth.'

'Sixteen?' He looked away for a moment, studying his father's prized topiaries. 'That's certainly a lot younger than me. I'm an old man.'

'No, you're not.'

He snapped a look her way, his expression wry. 'You're not far off being half my age.'

'That doesn't mean you're old. It means I'm young. It'd balance out when we're both ten years older.'

'Wisely put.' He offered her a bow of his head. 'I like you, Emma Hatton.'

'Mr Colson!'

Emma turned at the sound of Ivy Williams' voice but Harry Colson didn't move a muscle.

'What are you doing out here?' Ivy scolded Emma, stomping down the stairs from the verandah, her skirts and apron whooshing around her shins.

'We were discussing the garden,' Mr Colson said, smiling at Ivy. 'Emma here thinks my topiaries look a little isolated, but she likes the overall artistic flair.'

'They're very smart, sir, as I've often said.'

'There we are,' he said to Emma. 'You're in agreement.'

Emma almost huffed a laugh.

'Well. My day awaits.' He nodded at Emma. 'Very nice to meet you. Thank you for being a diligent worker and helping us out.'

'It's not help, Mr Colson. We have to do it. It's the war effort.'

'Nonetheless, I'm sad to say I would have no idea how to handle a cow.'

Emma shot a look at Ivy and reckoned he'd just managed it nicely. As soon as she thought it, a smile popped out. Harry Colson caught her eye and she knew he'd understood what had gone through her mind. She quickly turned her gaze to the ground.

'There is nothing better than a good witticism before breakfast,' he murmured.

Emma felt her cheeks heat up.

'A what, sir?' Ivy said. 'I thought you'd be wanting a boiled egg. Is there something else I can get you?'

'An egg will be sufficient. What time is breakfast, Mrs Williams? I find myself ravenous this morning.'

'It's ready when you are, Mr Colson. I've already got the water on to boil the egg.'

'Thank you.' He turned back to Emma. 'Good luck in three months' time when you turn sixteen. The world will open up for you. Meet your freedom with relish, will you? For me.'

He made his way across the garden and through the rows of topiaries in the dim of the morning light like he could have done it blindfolded. He might have had a bit of a struggle with the stairs up to the verandah but he didn't pause. Not for a second.

Emma liked him. He reminded her of her English teacher, a kind, studious man, softly spoken but with enormous intelligence he used sagely. He'd never castigated any of the children if they came last in a test and sometimes offered them a little joke or a funny story about things that had happened to him or people he knew.

There was nothing remotely wrong with Harry Colson's mental capacity. He was bound to find some woman to marry him. If he wanted to get married.

'Don't let me catch you out in this garden again,' Ivy hissed.
'Don't worry, Mrs Williams. You won't.'
'It's his private space. Not for the likes of you.'
'Yes, Mrs Williams.' *Three bags full, Mrs Williams.*

'Get those pails up to the kitchen, girl, and get back to the other cows. Be quick about it.' The housekeeper folded her arms beneath her ample bosom and stared at Emma with a look of disgust.

Emma went around the side of the shed to the stairs that led to the kitchen verandah, walking steadily so she didn't slop any more milk. There was no way she'd get caught like that again, and no way she'd be back at the Colson house after she turned sixteen if she could help it. If she could only have one desire in life, it would be to never return to boring old Blueholm Bay at all, and if the last star in the night sky had still been around she'd have taken a chance on it and cast her wish.

Freedom. Come get me.

Chapter Five

Townsville—May 1943

It might be servitude, but Emma was loving every second.

She had been in Townsville for nearly four months and had settled into her routine. She had her own room, the smallest and more of a storage space than a bedroom, but she didn't mind. The Yanks who boarded didn't want an evening meal because they dined out, and they were never around for lunch, nor did they need their washing done because the US forces had that organised, so it was just breakfast Emma had to deal with, along with her and Aunty Doris's washing and ironing and keeping the house clean.

Mum had stuck to her word and kept Emma in Blueholm Bay until mid-January, milking cows, then feeding the pigs and chickens up at the big house and working hard at home too, all the while ensuring her brothers behaved themselves and did their homework while Mum went to Mrs Cosgrove's six days a week and had one day off at the weekend so she could rest and put her feet up. But once she turned sixteen, Emma had had to sign up with the Women's Voluntary National Register and tending veggies and animals at home wasn't considered crucial when there were others to do it and so much more that young women of Emma's age were needed for.

Emma was also working for the Red Cross as part of her home front war duties, although Doris had said what Emma was doing for the Americans in the house was also a duty. Emma supposed it was, and she didn't mind what she did, whether it was cooking the Yanks' breakfasts or toiling in the halls and canteens for the Red Cross.

She happily knitted socks and more for the diggers, packed POW parcels with the utmost care and occasionally got to see the soldiers at the wharf and hand out some goods they might need during their recreation leave. Towels, writing paper, cigarettes— and tea.

When she saw other women write notes and stick them in a sock or a glove, she started doing the same.

These gloves [socks/balaclava] were knitted with pride for what our brave diggers are doing for all of us back home.

Dad hadn't left Australia yet. His battalion had joined with the 31st last month. The new 31st/51st Battalion was doing amphibious landing training. He'd been in touch with Mum at last, just one letter, but it was two pages so he must be feeling better about life even though he was at war.

As Emma only went home to visit every two weeks on a Sunday afternoon she had only seen her mother and the boys a handful of times since February.

It felt odd to be away from them. There was a bit of homesickness involved but on the whole it was a relief to be away from her mother. When she left Blueholm Bay, Mum hadn't said goodbye or wished her luck, she'd just said, 'You get on with life. You don't complain.' It had felt like there were a hundred complaints contained in that one sentence.

Women supplemented their home front work with other jobs now open to them since the men had all gone, although a lot didn't actually get paid. The government called it voluntary self-sacrifice. It didn't feel right to Emma that the government was now getting women to do for free what had previously been a man's paid employment. If there was a scrap of luck out there, Emma would prefer payment for her work. It wasn't as though she wouldn't still be doing her volunteering with the Red Cross.

She'd broached the idea of a paid part-time job with Doris, who'd agreed, saying she wouldn't have to dip into her own pocket in order to let her niece have a little treat now and again if Emma was earning her own money. What Emma wanted was to start saving money for her future. Like Mrs Cosgrove said, she had to make of the war what she could.

The war was still terribly close to home even with most of their men away. Just two weeks ago, the Japanese torpedoed a hospital ship off the coast of Brisbane. Two hundred and sixty-eight lives had been lost.

It made it all so very real.

The click-clack of the needles as Emma knitted another balaclava was the only sound at sundown in her aunt's house, the table lamp giving more than enough light, even with the brownout. All of Doris's windows had been covered in brown paper. They took the paper down in the kitchen and living room during the day so they could see what was what out on the street.

Emma also had books to read when she got the chance, thanks to Uncle Raymond liking a good yarn. She'd just read an Arthur Gask, followed by a Nevil Shute and was now well into *Under Capricorn* by Helen Simpson. There were hardly any marks on the pages of that book so perhaps her uncle hadn't been interested in Australia's history, but Emma found the contrast of romantic alliances back then fascinating. A convicted groom marrying an English lady. A son of a lord with an ex-hangman's daughter.

A noise in the hallway made Emma look up.

Doris came into the living room, her handbag over her arm. 'Right, love, I'm off out with Lucy and Peg tonight. You know what to do.'

'I've got the breakfasts prepared. They gave us eggs this morning,' Emma said with a smile. 'Plus a pound of strawberries and we've still got a pile of ripe tomatoes. So I thought I'd make them a potato omelette with tomato slices and we'll save the strawberries for a tart.'

'Omelette it is then, so long as there's enough left for us.'

'There'll be plenty.' The three Yanks who boarded were good sorts and grateful to have a real house to live in. They weren't the same soldiers who'd boarded when Emma arrived; there had been two changes since then. The newest lot arrived only last month but had continued their countrymen's tradition of adding to the pantry.

'Have you put the billy out for the milkman?' Doris asked.

'Did it half an hour ago. Where are you going?'

'The Regent.'

Emma went to the Regent to catch a matinee if she had a chance, and if Doris slipped her a little money. There'd be heaps of soldiers there with their girls.

'I expect you'll be in bed before I get home,' her aunt said. 'I'll try not to wake you.'

When Doris left, Emma put her knitting onto the side table and picked up the *Daily Bulletin*. She had the whole evening to fill. She couldn't listen to the radio because, after Pearl Harbor, all the stations had been ordered off the air at sunset.

She turned to the positions vacant column. Women who worked in factories were getting nearly five pounds a week. Emma wouldn't get that much but there were plenty of other jobs she could consider.

> FEMALE employees, with or without experience, wanted immediately by the US Army Quartermaster Laundry.

'No, thank you,' she said out loud. Anything but more washing.

> SMART Girl, between 16 and 20 years, good knowledge of bookkeeping, suburban shop, good girl, good wage.

That would be full time though, and she didn't know anything about bookkeeping, although she could probably learn if someone gave her the opportunity.

> WANTED: a Girl or a Woman; no washing, little ironing. No. 12 Blackwood Street.

Ideal! But they'd likely want her for most of the week and all Emma could really put aside, given her other duties, was two days.

She ripped out the page so she could scan the rest of the positions vacant later. She'd keep the page in her handbag since there was little enough else to fill it. She had her near-empty purse, a handkerchief and a pen with some paper so she could write the notes and stuff them in the socks. She also had a lipstick and a powder compact that Janet had given her as a birthday present. They were used but it was still a joy to have them. The lipstick was a natural colour, so not terribly noticeable, and as there was only a tiny bit left, Emma didn't wear it every day. The powder compact wasn't full either, but it was enough to be going on with.

If only she had somewhere to go in the evenings to warrant using them.

The handbag was also new. New to Emma, anyway. It had belonged to the girl who'd worked for Doris but she'd left it behind when she went back to her family farm. Emma had polished the leather and could hardly see the scratches on the base. She'd never had a handbag before so was extremely proud of it.

'Hi there.'

Emma looked up. 'Evening, Lieutenant Bill. Is there something I can get you?' She put her handbag down and stood.

'No, nothing, Emma. I'm off to meet the other two. Just wanted to let you know we might be late.' He grinned. 'As in, we might not be back until the early hours of the morning.'

Lucky things. 'Enjoy yourselves! You deserve it.'

'We sure do.' He stepped further into the living room. 'Where's your aunt tonight?'

'She's out with a few friends.'

'Looks like everyone's out for a good night except you.'

Wasn't that the truth.

'Surely you're not going to sit in here all evening?' the lieutenant said, eyeing the basket of wool at Emma's feet.

'I thought I might meet up with some friends later then I changed my mind.' She smiled through the lie. None of the boarders had asked how old she was so she'd never told them. She was growing her hair and styling it a little differently, trying her best to look and act like a real adult. 'They've probably already hooked up with others now. They'll be a gang, having fun.'

'That's no good.' The lieutenant paused a moment. 'Why don't you come with us? We'd be happy to have you tag along. There'll be other women.'

Emma really ought not to, but Katy Wheaton came to mind. What would she say if she could see Emma now? Cowering in her aunt's living room with her knitting.

'Come on, Emma. Say yes and let me shout you a good time. It'll be my way of thanking you for the lovely words you wrote for my girl back home.'

Emma had found the lieutenant chewing on the tip of a pencil at the kitchen table one evening, frantically trying to write something romantic for his fiancée back in America, who had written to say she thought he might not love her any more and could he confirm it. He'd been horrified.

So Emma wrote down the poem 'A Red, Red Rose' by Robert Burns, which she'd memorised at school, it being so beautiful.

And fare thee weel, my only Luve!
And fare thee weel awhile!
And I will come again, my Luve,
Tho' it were ten thousand mile.

Which it pretty much was from Townsville.

And if the lieutenant was going to shout her it put a different slant on the situation, since she didn't have any money of her own. Not that she wanted him to spend his money on her but the thought of getting out …

'All right!' she told him. 'You're on.' Why not? She could always walk home if she wanted to get back before Doris. 'Could you give me a few minutes to get changed?'

'Sure. I'll wait in the hall.'

'Where are we going?' Emma asked less than ten minutes later as she closed the front door behind her, making sure it was locked. She'd changed into her lilac satin blouse—again, courtesy of Janet, who'd had it for a couple of years until her bust got too big—and one of the two versatile oyster-grey linen skirts she owned, which were good enough for going out in if dressed up with the blouse. The skirts had been Doris's, no longer wanted because they'd already been let out twice. Emma had to take them in quite a bit, being much less heavy at the waist and far slimmer in the hip. She was going to use the cut-off fabric to alter an old pillbox hat she'd found stuffed in the back of a wardrobe which Doris had said she could have. She'd put on her makeup and tidied her hair, tying back the top part with a ribbon and rolling her fringe. Soon it would be long enough to pass her shoulders, which would look really grown up.

'We'll check in with the other two in a sec,' Lieutenant Bill said. 'Not sure where we're meeting their ladies. Up for a bit of a walk?'

'You bet!' Emma said, her smile wide.

'There are the other guys!' the lieutenant said when they reached the end of the street, waving to catch the attention of the other two servicemen who boarded at Doris's house.

'Hey, Emma. How's the day treating you?' Lieutenant Hadley asked.

'Pretty good right now.'

'You're looking lovely,' Lieutenant Floyd said. 'New blouse?'

'Not quite.' She was probably blushing, but she didn't care. They were all so kind.

'Where shall we head?' Lieutenant Bill asked Floyd.

'We're picking up the ladies on Flinders. We'll have a bite to eat then head to Denham Street. After that, we'll see where the night takes us.'

Lieutenant Bill glanced down. 'Okay with you, Emma?'

'Absolutely splendid!' The American Red Cross and Recreation Hall Canteen was on Denham Street. She'd been dying to go to one of the dances.

'Then off we go.' He offered her his arm and she took it, all unease about being out for the evening when she shouldn't be flown away on a breeze of elation.

Flinders Street was packed. Australians, Americans, all in uniform. It had been a long time since Emma had seen any young man wear civvies. The women looked utterly glamorous too, with or without a uniform. Those without were dolled up in their finest, looking radiant and ready for anything good.

Anything happy. Anything that took away the blues, and the Americans certainly provided on that front.

There were soldiers and armed forces vehicles everywhere, with guns and searchlights at strategic points. All the vehicles were in brownout, their headlights masked.

'How are you doing?' Lieutenant Bill asked.

'Enchanted by it all,' Emma said, arm still tucked in his.

He patted her hand. 'It's good to get out for a bit of a fun time, eh?'

'I should say.'

The noise, the throaty laughter and high-pitched giggling, the smells, the chatter. It was like being in a Hollywood film with an orchestra underscoring all the exciting parts. She'd never seen her city so busy. So bustling. So full of anticipation and expectation, even with all the shortages. It was almost mayhem, but everyone seemed to know where they were going—or didn't give a damn where they ended up.

'We're a bit late,' Lieutenant Hadley said as he checked his watch.

'Where are the girls?' Floyd asked.

'Athol's,' Hadley said, then crossed the street, everyone following.

Concrete air-raid shelters lined the centre of Flinders Street. Hanlon's Hideouts, they were called. Emma had never been in any shelter under serious worry of a raid but there had been plenty of practice drills. Back home, Mr Jameson had a shelter made out of old water tanks laid on their sides and covered in dirt. He'd dug steps to get down to it and kept it stocked with supplies but had to constantly re-stock because every time it rained, the tanks filled up with water and took days and sometimes weeks to drain. He'd rebuilt it dozens of times but in the end he told his family, 'I think we'll just leave it to chance.'

Aunty Doris had a small shed in her backyard which was banked and topped with sandbags, but she never went into it if the siren went off. She sat in the kitchen with a cup of tea and told Emma if they heard an explosion, they were to duck under the table quick smart.

'Cooee! Over here, gentlemen!' Two women were waving and smiling from a table.

'Thought you'd stood us up,' one of them said as she accepted a kiss on the cheek from Hadley.

'No chance of that happening. We got waylaid. Hey, ladies, this is Emma. Emma's the young woman who lives at the house we board at. It's her aunt's place.'

Emma took a decidedly brave breath and beamed at the women, both of them at least six years older than her and both wearing bright colours, not oyster-grey linen.

'Nice to meet you, Emma,' said one, holding out her hand over the table, which was already piled with cutlery and glasses.

The women were nice enough, but more or less ignored her after the initial introductions, though Hadley's girlfriend kept glancing at her. Emma sat up straighter, thankful she had her makeup, her blouse and her smart hairdo. The woman was wearing a green rayon dress with a high neckline and short sleeves and she'd pinned a large red fabric flower to her shoulder. It was so big the petals were flopped over. With her hair so blonde, the pea green dress made her look a bit sickly.

It was a woman's patriotic duty to keep up appearances. Even Mum agreed on this but only ever used her compact and lipstick on her day off. She said it would all melt off her face anyway if she wore it to Mrs Cosgrove's. But a lot of the wives took their lipstick with them and regularly reapplied.

As if on cue, Hadley's girlfriend opened her handbag and produced a lipstick and a hand mirror then stretched her lips as she painted her mouth. Red was the colour of the day. Auxiliary

Red. Fighting Red. Commando Red. One woman Doris knew said her Yank had written home to his 'mom' and asked her to send an emergency supply. She'd sent two dozen tubes. Doris had got her hands on one, but Emma hadn't liked to ask even when the woman said her Yank was sending for more.

'Enjoy that, Emma?' Lieutenant Bill asked when she put down her knife and fork.

'It was delicious!' She'd opted for a Venetian salad with baked ham, apple rings, lettuce hearts, shredded carrot and mayonnaise.

After they'd finished their meal they all trooped out onto the street, which was just as packed as before.

'Are we going to Denham Street now?' she asked Lieutenant Bill.

'You bet, sweetheart. Having a good time?'

'The best!'

While the gang she was with queued up to get inside the American Red Cross Canteen and Recreation Hall, Emma had a sudden thought that she might be found out once inside, especially if they were checking ID cards. Would they bother, with so many queuing to get in? They might. It was a bit of a worry and she didn't want the lieutenants to know she'd deceived them by not telling them her actual age.

She turned so she had her back to the others, opened her handbag and took out her compact. If she put a little more lipstick than usual onto her lips, that might help. She'd need to keep her wits about her too, so she drew herself up, shoulders back, and wished her shoes had higher heels.

'Move it, love, they're letting us in and you're holding us up.'

Emma jumped when a woman patted her arm in a get-going manner. She turned back to the queue and discovered a number of people had pushed in front of her. The tops of the lieutenants' heads were now three or four groups in front, about to enter the dancehall.

Should she simply join them, or would people think she was pushing in? She glanced around. Perhaps she'd better not try to get into the recreation hall at all.

But she couldn't let Lieutenant Bill think her lost.

She opened her handbag, pulled out a pen and a sheet of paper and wrote him a note.

'Excuse me! Would you do me a favour?' she asked as she ran to the front of the queue.

'What's up, sweetheart?' an officer asked.

'I was with a group of lieutenants who have just gone inside and I got distracted for a moment.'

'There's a queue, sweetheart,' the woman with the officer said as she held more firmly to her man's arm.

Emma shook her head. 'I don't want to go inside. I just need to get a message to them so they know I'm all right and I've gone home.'

'I don't know,' the officer said. 'There'll be plenty of lieutenants in there …'

'His name is Bill O'Connell. He's with officers called Hadley and Floyd. They're with two women and one of them is wearing a bright green dress with the biggest and ugliest red fabric flower pinned on it—you can't miss her.'

The officer took the note off her and pocketed it. 'Okay, I'll do my best.'

'Thank you,' Emma said. 'And thank you, too,' she said to the woman with him. 'I appreciate it. He'll be worried.'

The woman shrugged and shifted her focus. 'Here we go, darling, the queue's moving again.'

Emma turned and got her bearings. With a confidence she wasn't sure was real now she was on her own in the dark of the night, she strode down Denham Street heading for Wills Street.

She hadn't got further than a few hundred yards when a group of Aussie diggers fell onto the pavement, followed by two

Yanks. They barrelled into her, the boozy breath and sweaty shirts circling her as she got twirled around in the middle of them.

'Say that again and you'll get my answer!'

'Go back to Uncle Sam, why don't you?'

'I'm here fighting your damned war, buddy.'

'I'm not your bloody buddy!'

Emma's handbag got knocked out of her hand and she bent to grab it. She pushed at the legs of one man as another kicked her bag. 'Hey!' she called out and straightened, ready to give him a mouthful, only to see a fist flying towards her face.

She ducked.

'Watch where you're putting your fists!' a woman said, pushing through the men. 'There are women here, you morons!'

Emma stumbled but righted herself by holding on to the woman's arm.

'You okay?' the young woman asked.

Emma nodded.

'What's your problem?' the woman asked the digger.

A few others had now circled them and the Yanks were making their way across the street.

'That glamour boy!' The digger pointed at the Yanks. 'We're sick of them. Glamming it up and giving their money away to our women.'

'We're not *yours*,' the firecracker at Emma's side said. 'Why don't you go bag your head? I see you haven't got a woman with you. Nor are you likely to get one if you carry on like this. Go back to base and get some sleep.'

'Stupid cow,' the digger said, but he walked away, pulling at his shirt as he went, tucking it back into his trousers.

'You all right?' the young woman asked when everyone had gone back to whatever they'd been doing before.

'Shaken, but satisfactory, considering,' Emma said.

The woman grinned. 'He was a bit rough, that one. Too much booze.'

'I thought it was rationed.'

'They know where to get it when they want it.'

Emma's attention was taken by the two Yanks who'd had the blue. They'd joined the group across the street. Something about one of them distracted her.

Gosh, it was him! Private Kendrick. It was Frank.

'Frank!' she called. 'Frank!'

He turned, and his eyes lit up. 'Hey, wash gal!'

'Hello!'

Emma's breath caught as he dashed across to her. He was so much more good-looking than she remembered.

'What's your name again?' he said, taking hold of her hand.

'Emma.'

'That's right! Hi, Emma,' he said and bent to kiss her on the cheek. 'So you got out of the washhouse.'

Emma's skin tingled from the warmth of his lips.

'What are you doing out here?' he asked. 'Where have you been all these months and why haven't I seen you?'

'I came out with a group … I got separated.'

'Their bad luck, my gain.'

'Frank!' a woman called. 'Come on, mate.'

'Put her down!' a Yank shouted. 'We've got four here already. Plenty to go around.'

Frank laughed. 'Look,' he said to Emma. 'My guys are heading off so I'd better go.'

'Yes, of course.' For some crazy reason she'd expected him to stay with her.

'Frank, come on!'

'It's so nice to see you,' Emma said.

'We'll meet again, yes?'

'That would be lovely.'

'Okay, beautiful Emma.'

This time when he bent his head, he kissed her on the mouth. It wasn't a peck either, it was a proper, full kiss that sealed her lips to his for at least four seconds.

'Next time we meet, it'll be just you and me,' he told her when he lifted his head. 'I promise.'

'How do I get hold of you?' she asked, stepping forwards as he jogged backwards.

'I'll be around.' He smiled, then gave her a wink.

Emma put her fingers to her lips as he ran across the street, darting between others. When he reached his friends, a woman linked her arm in his, smiling up at him and pressing herself against his side. He said something and she laughed, a trill that carried above the noise of chatter all around her.

Emma lifted herself to tiptoes to better see him, although Frank didn't look back.

'Is that your boyfriend?'

Emma turned to the young woman who'd helped in the scuffle. 'No,' she said with a laugh as Frank disappeared, still in some shock that she'd just had her first kiss. 'I know him though. I met him back home when I was doing his washing. He gave me ten pounds.'

'Did he now?'

'Twice,' Emma said, still smiling. 'Private Frank Kendrick. Do you know him?'

'I've seen him here and there.'

'You wouldn't happen to know how I could get in touch with him, would you?'

'I could find out.'

'I'd be ever so grateful.'

'Happy to help.' The young woman straightened the collar of Emma's blouse and did up the top button, which had come undone. She wore a lot more makeup than most other women, but she had the type of friendly gleam in her eyes that made Emma smile back.

'Are you out on your own?' Emma asked.

'Just finished my stint at the canteen. I'm a hostess. Making the boys feel welcome. I also sing.'

'You're an entertainer! How marvellous. I couldn't sing for my supper if I tried.'

'With your looks you wouldn't have to do much singing,' the woman said with a laugh. 'And actually, I'm only in the chorus. I'm probably tone deaf but they haven't got wind of it yet.' She smiled brightly. 'Don't let on though. Being in the chorus means I get driven out to the different bases. I wouldn't get to any of the dances otherwise.'

'Good on you.' Her new acquaintance would no doubt get a lot of attention whether she was singing or just standing around doing nothing. Her hair was much richer in colour than Emma's, almost auburn, and she wore a sunflower yellow dress with shoulder pads, short sleeves and a belt in matching material. The yellow made her green eyes pop.

'Thanks ever so much for helping with those diggers,' Emma said. 'I thought I was going to get punched in the face.'

'Yeah, it got a little crowded there for a minute or two. Hey, is this yours?' She bent and picked up Emma's newspaper page from the *Daily Bulletin*, which must have fallen out of her handbag when it got kicked to the ground.

'I'm looking for a part-time job. I can't do full time because I want to continue with the Red Cross work I do, and I have to be around to help my aunt. I live with her.'

'Not much here,' the woman said, scrunching her nose as she studied the newspaper cutting. She folded the sheet and handed it back. 'What's your name?'

'Emma Hatton,' Emma said, tucking the cutting into her handbag and snapping it closed.

The woman held out her hand. 'Cassie O'Byrne. Nice to meet you.'

'You too,' Emma said, accepting Cassie's handshake.

'Well, come on, Em. Let's go get ourselves a coffee and a toasted sandwich to celebrate. I'll pay.'

'Where will we go?'

'Dunno. We'll find somewhere. Come on.' She linked her arm in Emma's and pulled her along.

'What are we celebrating?'

'Meeting each other,' Cassie said, her eyes twinkling. 'We're going to be friends, you and me. I can feel it in my water. Hey, I just had a thought. There's a job going at Gibson's Cafeteria on Flinders Street.'

'Really?'

'Two days a week for a pound and six shillings. I know the owner. Want me to put in a word for you?'

'Oh, yes please!'

One pound and six shillings a week. All Emma had was the sixpence she'd pinched from her mother's purse in case they had to telephone about Dad one day—although that was still under her mattress at home—and a few pennies saved from whatever Doris gave her.

'How old are you?' Cassie asked as they sat in a café, toasted sandwich in front of her.

'Eighteen and a half. How old are you?'

'Twenty.'

'Twenty?' Emma said, lifting her coffee cup. She hadn't wanted anything to eat, not after that big Venetian salad, and neither did she want her new acquaintance to have to pay for anything but the coffee.

'Don't I look it?'

'Yes! Of course, I just—'

'Put it this way,' Cassie said, dabbing her mouth with a paper napkin. 'I'm as much twenty as you're eighteen and a half.'

Emma smiled, not worried about having been found out. 'I'm coming close.'

'Baloney.'

'What's that?'

'Not sure. Something about bullshit, I think.'

Emma nearly choked as she laughed and had to put her cup of coffee down, which had not only milk in it but two sugars, courtesy of Cassie making eyes at the old man who'd served them.

Cassie giggled. 'I reckon you're seventeen.'

'Sixteen and a bit,' Emma said, instinctively knowing she was safe with this girl.

'I'm seventeen, just turned.' Cassie took another bite of her sandwich.

Emma's eyes widened. 'You actually do look twenty.'

'I know. I make sure of it.'

'Where's your family?'

'There's only my dad, and he's not much cop.'

'What about your mum?'

'Died nine months ago.'

'Gosh, I'm sorry. Did your dad kick you out of the house or something?'

'No way! I left.'

'How come?'

Cassie dabbed her lips with the paper napkin again. 'Three months after my mum died, my dad tried to kiss me on the mouth.'

Emma stilled. 'Like, as in …'

'Yeah. Very much like as in.'

'God. That's horrible.'

'I packed my suitcase that same day and left. Never been back.'

'And you're coping all on your own?'

Cassie's eyes shone with pert wickedness. 'A girl like me knows a thing or two.'

'How can you be buoyant after something so atrocious happened to you?'

'Buoyant? What do you mean? As in—floating?'

'As in capable and happy.'

'Oh!' Cassie laughed, shaking her head. 'Gee, I can be a dummy sometimes.'

'You sound just like the Yanks.'

'I mostly stick around them. Not too bothered about our Australian men, not after my dad. My uncles weren't too keen to keep their hands to themselves after I turned thirteen, either.'

'They're not all bad, our men.'

'True, but the Yanks are more thrilling.'

'You're telling me. That's why I'm hoping to see Frank again sometime.'

'They're around, then they're not, then they turn up again.'

'Like bad pennies?'

Cassie leaned forwards with a grin. 'Like a lot of pennies!'

She carried on eating but Emma had lost her sense of taste, even for the coffee. How did this young woman manage after what had happened to her? Out here in the city, all on her own?

'What shall we do next?' Cassie asked when she'd finished her sandwich and they had returned the plate and their cups to the counter. 'I live in a boarding house for young women and the doors are locked at midnight, but I've found myself in possession of a key.' She winked. 'Which means I can stay out till whenever.'

'I have a key too. But I should get back to my aunt's place.' It was close to one in the morning and Doris would be home by now although she wouldn't have checked on Emma, who should be fast asleep in her little bedroom.

'I'll walk you back,' Cassie said. 'Where does she live?'

'The city side of Castle Hill, heading for the cemetery and West End—but you can't walk me back.'

'I'll have to. You're my new friend and you might get lost.'

'I'm not entirely stupid.'

'There's nothing stupid about you, Em. I can tell. I could tell immediately, especially when you opened your mouth. You talk like an educated young lady. It's all those fancy words you use.'

'Like what?'

'I don't know. Like—atrocious, when I would say bloody bad shit.' She paused. 'Can you spell it?'

'Of course I can.' Emma smiled, then spelled 'bloody bad shit' for her new friend.

Cassie laughed, doubled up, Emma following suit until a digger stopped to ask them if they were ill and could he be of assistance. They assured him they were fine and thanked him for his kindness.

It was only a half-hour's walk to Doris's house and they filled the time by talking about everything: Life. Love. The Yanks. Emma told Cassie all about her mum and how she'd come to be in Townsville and how she'd met Frank.

'How will you get home yourself?' Emma asked when they reached her front door.

'I'll find a Yank to escort me. Look,' she said, pointing to the end of the street where a group was wandering along with a number of women. None of the women were in uniform. The uniformed women would have had to scarper back to base or the YWCA before the doors got locked at the stroke of midnight.

'All I have to do is look a little lost and bothered and they'll help me,' Cassie said. 'They're good sorts, most of them. I'll be fine. How can I get in touch with you again?'

'My aunt has the telephone but it might be best if we kept our friendship a secret for now.'

'No worries. How about we meet at Gibson's Cafeteria tomorrow and I'll introduce you to the owner. What time suits?'

'Around three? I've got Red Cross work to do and that will likely take me up to two o'clock or so.'

'Three's good for me. I usually make sure I get some rest after lunch.' Cassie squeezed Emma's hand. 'It's been a lovely evening, Em. Much better than spending it with a Yank.'

'I've loved it too. Much better than crying over Frank Kendrick, who practically abandoned me. But you will try to find out where I can reach him?'

'I promised, didn't I?'

They hugged.

Emma smiled as she watched Cassie walk to the end of the street and wave at the GIs, who turned and waited for her to catch up.

Her smile was still in place when she crept into her bedroom and quietly closed the door, leaning against it for a moment and catching her breath.

She'd received her first kiss, she had a new friend she already adored and now there was also a possibility of paid employment. What a splendid, splendid day!

Chapter Six

August 1943

A number of splendid days later—nearly three incredible months' worth to be exact—Emma turned her back to the counter at Gibson's Cafeteria where she now worked two days a week and took the latest letter from Frank out of her apron pocket.

OPENED BY CENSOR

Dear beautiful Wash Gal

Cassie had kept her promise and found him. Emma wrote her first letter, which reached him via some GI Cassie knew, and Frank had written back almost immediately.

It was unbelievable. Emma mailed her letters addressed to him via his unit, but his went to Cassie's address so Doris wouldn't find out. Frank had only answered four of Emma's seven letters since early June but that wasn't unusual. There was a war on.

I can't say a lot about where I am but we're working hard and I miss you so much! I'm still so sorry I didn't stick around with you after the last time we met. But we can make up for it—

The rest of the sentence had been blacked out but Emma felt sure he was up around Lockhart and Claudie Rivers where two new runways had been built.

> *I dream of you all the time, Emma Hatton. You're so different to the other girls I've known. You're sweet. You're beautiful! And I think perhaps my heart is yours.*

Emma wasn't sure how she had earned Frank's heart when they hadn't actually had a date and had to remind herself constantly not to get carried away. But it was so easy to be swept up in delight. No-one had ever spoken to her this way. Nobody had ever thought her worthy of their heart.

Except for Cassie.

'Hello, wash girl.'

Emma laughed. Speak of the devil …

She quickly folded Frank's letter and pocketed it before turning to Cassie, who eased onto a stool on the other side of the counter. Cassie teased her relentlessly about Frank. Emma wasn't able to fully explain what knowing him meant. Something about feeling grown up, probably. But she could easily describe what having Cassie O'Byrne as her friend meant.

Everything.

They cared about each other. Truly cared, like sisters might. Emma was no longer a lone star in the night sky. She had a friend.

She also had Frank. Or would, once he returned to Townsville. Given the sweet words he wrote and everything she'd read in the newspapers about new runways and other infrastructure, she was sure of a wonderful reunion sometime soon. Although she was a little nervous at the prospect, never having had a boyfriend before, and Frank was a man.

Cassie pulled her cigarettes out of her handbag, along with the gold-coloured lighter some soldier had bought her. 'I haven't received another letter from Frank yet if that's what you're hoping I'm here for.'

'Don't be daft. I hardly care.'

'You're the daft one,' Cassie said, lighting her cigarette. 'You care too much.'

'No, I don't.' Well, she tried not to.

'It's quiet in here today,' Cassie said, glancing around.

'It wasn't earlier.'

'You got a minute to chat?'

Emma leaned her forearms on the counter. She always had time for Cassie. She'd changed Emma's life as much as the war had. From her thoughts to her actions, Emma's world was entirely different to anything she'd imagined possible let alone known before.

'So long as we don't get raided. There were a couple of young girls in here earlier. One of them flew behind the counter and ran into the kitchen when two old men in suits walked in.'

Cassie giggled. 'Shame on them. Not pulling their weight for the war. So come on, own up. Why the soppy expression? No! Don't tell me, I can guess. You're thinking about Frank and all the kisses you'll get when he comes back.' She took a drag of her cigarette and blew out the smoke.

'I might be.'

Cassie tapped ash off her cigarette into an ashtray, a look of distaste on her face. 'Can't get used to these things.'

'So why smoke them?'

'It makes me look sultry and sophisticated.'

'Not when you're grimacing.'

Cassie laughed. 'I'll keep going until I can't stand it any longer. Are you sure you don't want to try one?'

'No, thanks.'

'What's your job schedule for the rest of the week?' Cassie asked.

'I'm helping at one of the ACF canteens. We're decorating a hall for a get-together next Saturday afternoon.' Emma didn't work at the Red Cross any more, she'd moved on to help the Australian Comforts Fund. Cassie volunteered too, on the afternoons she didn't have to entertain the troops in the evenings, so they saw a lot of each other. Emma sometimes volunteered to serve the food at the Comforts Fund events too, either in the daytime or the evening. Doris didn't mind. Hopefully by the time Frank returned, Emma would be able to easily get out of the house and go on a date. A real date with a real man. Mum would go off her head if she knew.

'How are things in Blueholm Bay?' Cassie asked.

'I missed the last visit so I haven't seen them for weeks.'

'I don't blame you for not wanting to go.'

'I've sent Mum a bit of money to help out. Our neighbour Mr Jameson is in Townsville most days so I give it to him to give to her.'

'Does she write a thank-you note?'

Emma spluttered a laugh. 'Last visit all she did was shout. The boys are trying to wriggle out of any work sent their way when they're not at school. She hasn't got time to write to me.' Her mother had hardly even spoken to her on any of the visits.

'Sometimes you're far too considerate, Miss Hatton,' Cassie said.

'Well, I always try to be, Miss O'Byrne.' Emma stuck out her tongue and Cassie grinned.

She drew on the cigarette and exhaled a perfect circular puff.

'Who taught you that?' Emma asked.

'This new guy I'm seeing. Eddie.'

'Put it out,' Emma said. 'You loathe it. I know you do.'

Cassie ground out her cigarette in the ashtray. 'I do actually hate it and I think trying it for a whole month is enough. Don't you?'

'Absolutely. So who's this Eddie? A Yank, I presume.'

'Lieutenant Eddie Shea,' Cassie said, eyes sparkling.

'You're seeing another officer?'

'I told you I was the lucky sort.'

'Shame it only took you two dozen GIs to find the best.'

Cassie choked on her laugh. 'You're growing up, Em.'

'Says you, the seventeen-year-old.'

'I'm nearly twenty-one to everyone else, thank you for mentioning it. Anyway, we'll both be one year older soon.'

'Have you just met this Eddie?'

Cassie nodded. 'I'm not sure he'll work out but I'll give it a bit longer. He's ever so sweet.'

'Where's he from?'

'Wiscon—Wis-con-sin. I think that's how you pronounce it.'

'Where is it?'

'Dunno.'

'Somewhere wonderful, I bet. I'll look it up in my atlas when I'm next home. Want a lemon squash?'

'Yes, please.'

Emma got them each a drink and paid with her own money. 'Is this Eddie army, air force or navy?'

'He's an army medical officer.'

'Good heavens!'

'I reckon. He's a radiologist. Works with all the X-ray equipment and makes diagnoses and whatever for the patients.'

'Which hospital?'

'Thirteenth Station.'

'Gosh, he's at Aitkenvale. That's not far.'

Cassie smiled. 'I met him at a dance. They've got a movie screen and a stage out there.'

The music played at the dances was absolutely the best. And Emma loved being part of it, even if she was only there to serve the food and drinks.

'We can go together when Frank comes back,' Cassie said. 'We can have a double date.'

Emma frowned. 'What if Frank doesn't ask me on a date?'

'Of course he will. That's why he's writing to you.'

'It's just that I'm nervous. How will I know how to act?'

'You just have to stand there. He'll do all the acting. He's bound to fall in love with you.'

'Do you think?' He did make her feel terribly grown up with his beautiful words. 'I hardly know him, or him me.'

'It can happen at first glance though.'

'Love? Do you think so?'

'Eddie said it probably can.'

Emma considered this. It explained a lot about what she felt. Like the enormous trembling throughout her whole body when Frank had first winked at her at Mrs Cosgrove's and everything inside her had quivered. Like the sensations whooshing through her when he'd kissed her on the mouth. He'd been telling her a bit about his life in some place called Kernville in California in his letters. Writing about his parents and his brothers and sisters. He wouldn't do that unless he thought Emma was special.

But they still didn't know each other. Not properly.

'Nice dress,' Emma said to Cassie, popping straws into the glasses of lemon squash. 'New?'

'Do you really like it?'

'Love it! You look the bee's knees.'

It was a mint-green short-sleeved shirtwaist dress with a thin fabric belt and pointed collars. It made Cassie look at least twenty-two. She'd finished it off with peep-toe beige sandals and a dark green fabric handbag—both also new.

'But there is a war on, you know,' Emma said, noticing that Cassie had caught the eyes of the five Americans at the table by the door.

'How do you think I get money to wear a dress like this one?'

Emma wasn't keen on hearing the particulars. She was too shy to be a hostess even if she'd been allowed to, but she loved the dances.

'Want a new dress, Em?'

'No, thanks.' It would be nice to have a brand-new dress but she had enough clothes to be going on with. She'd made over a few more outfits, and her new going-out frock had been a cobalt-blue tablecloth with little white daisies on it. She wore it to serve food at the dances but one day she might actually get a chance to wear it out with Frank.

'I'll buy it for you,' Cassie said.

'Where would you get the extra money and coupons?'

'That would be telling.' Cassie's smiles were always full and open. So unlike the rare smiles in the Hatton household. A person couldn't miss the delight within Cassie. She made others feel wonderful, and even women liked her for her pertness and quick way with words.

'I think you ought to start being more careful about who you go around with and what you take from them,' Emma said. 'Those soldiers by the door are looking at you like they want to eat you.'

'Let them. I don't mind.'

'Don't you feel funny when they look at you like that?'

'No,' Cassie said as she picked up her lemon squash. 'Some of these Yanks are an easy touch. I feel sorry for them. Certain kinds of women take them on a merry-go-round. Me? I like to look after them in whatever way I can. If that means letting them talk about the girl back home or letting them hold my hand and buy me dinner or a new handbag, I don't have a problem with it. Why would I?' Cassie folded her arms on the counter. 'How many men have you known, Em? I don't mean sex, since neither of us have done that. Although it's on my mind quite a lot sometimes.'

Emma had learned to ignore Cassie when she spoke like this, trying to force a reaction out of her. 'Do you think Frank's an easy touch?' she asked.

Cassie shook her head. 'Not him. I reckon he knows what he wants and what he's doing. He'll be good for a laugh though, once he comes back to shower you with kisses and ten-pound notes.'

Emma grinned. There was a secret thought inside her that she might soon fly the nest completely. Up and away like a balloon and across the ocean to a faraway place in America. But she didn't often let the thought drift into her mind in case she jinxed it.

'So how many men have you known?' Cassie asked again.

'Not many. My dad. My uncle. The other husbands and dads in Blueholm Bay.'

'Not those men, silly!'

'Oh, you mean unmarried men.' Emma thought about it. 'Apart from the officers at Doris's house and the military personnel who come into the café, just one, really. But not in the way you mean. He must be about thirty years old now.'

'Is he at war?'

'No. He's got a bad leg.'

'What else has he got?'

'A big house and twelve cows.'

Cassie crumpled to the counter, her laughter sputtering, which made Emma smile, even though she knew the joke was on her.

'Twelve cows and a big house,' Cassie said. 'Honestly, Em, I love you to bits and pieces.'

Emma chewed on her smile and diverted her gaze.

Three women from the Australian Women's Army Service had come in and she went to serve them. They were pleasant as they placed their orders but more intent on their conversation and Emma unashamedly listened to their plans for the evening as she mixed one ginger and two strawberry ice-cream sodas.

'Ninepence each,' she informed them and they scattered the coins on the counter after digging into jacket pockets. Their uniforms were marvellous. They had epaulettes on their shoulders with a badge on each, and another badge on their hats, and they wore shirts and ties. Their work was important and probably secretive, but they didn't seem worried or scared. They laughed all the while they drank their sodas. They probably danced most nights of the week over on Magnetic Island, which had a recreation centre run by the Australian Comforts Fund.

'Girls from sixteen to eighteen are considered too young for full-time employment, but not for unpaid skivvying,' she said to Cassie when she left the glamorous AWAS women and reached the far end of the counter again.

'Are you complaining?'

'Absolutely not. Although I do think women doing a proper man's job should be paid the same.'

Cassie blew out a breath. 'That'll never happen.'

'It might.'

'You're always so optimistic about this stuff.'

'I just think if a person wants something done, they should jolly well fight to get it done.'

'Aye aye, Captain Hatton,' Cassie said as she straightened on her stool and saluted.

'Stop teasing me. I like it here and I love getting my one pound and six shillings.'

Emma had a sudden thought about her father. He'd been sent from Cairns to Merauke in Dutch New Guinea in June and she hoped he was getting enough tea over there. Somehow, knowing he might be getting his tea made her feel better about whatever else he was having to do, or see, or fight against.

'You should be doing that when you turn eighteen next year,' she said to Cassie, nodding at the AWAS ladies. 'You'd look fantastic in a uniform. You've got the figure for it.'

'So have you,' Cassie said. 'Are you thinking about doing it?'

'Dear Mama wouldn't let me. Good job she doesn't know I'm writing to an American when I'm not volunteering or earning my one-and-six.'

'Two kisses and four letters from Frank have gone to your head.'

'It's nerve-racking imagining more!' Emma said. 'When are you next seeing Eddie? Do you think he's likely to turn into someone special?'

Cassie shrugged. 'I might like this one. He makes me feel … well, I'm not sure yet. Sort of … comfortable.'

'You wouldn't want to be with a man who doesn't make you feel lovely,' Emma said. 'Does he have a girl back home?'

Cassie stirred her lemon squash with her straw. 'He says not.'

'Do you believe him?'

'I might.'

'Make sure he treats you right.'

'I will.' Cassie reached over the counter, taking Emma's hand. 'Friends forever?' she asked, an earnest expression on her face. 'No matter what?'

For someone so bold, there was a lot of hurt going on inside Cassie. Probably something she was covering up with her feisty behaviour and her outrageous flirting. But it was more likely something to do with the way her father had treated her.

'Forever and ever,' Emma said, and closed her fingers reassuringly around Cassie's.

'Will we always help each other if we need it?' Cassie asked. 'If we're in trouble.'

'Always.'

'You know me. I'm likely to get into all sorts of trouble.'

'Not if you're careful.'

Cassie smiled her impudent smile but there was gratefulness there too, and Emma willingly returned it.

'Whatever you need, I'll always be here for you, Cassie.'

'Same. But you'll get along fine all by yourself.'

'I'd rather have you with me.'

'I do love you, Em. With all my heart. You're brave.'

Emma laughed. 'How come? I haven't done anything!'

'But you would be brave if you needed to be. Smart women like you always are. They always find a way to pull through the troublesome times. And we're still young. I bet so much is still going to happen.'

'Let's hope we're brave enough to do whatever we need to do whenever we have to do it,' Emma said, raising her glass of lemon squash. 'And if one of us gets into trouble, the other will always be around to help.'

'Abso-flaming-lutely!' Cassie said as she chinked her glass against Emma's. 'Here's to us! Here's to our friendship!'

'Whatever happens.'

Chapter Seven

Blueholm Bay—December 1943

It was two weeks before Christmas and Emma put a smile on her face as soon as she pushed open the back garden gate. She hadn't been home for a month and wasn't sure what kind of reception she'd get.

'Mum!' she called. 'It's me!'

There was no answer. Her brothers ought to be around somewhere and Emma was pretty sure Mum wasn't going to Mrs Cosgrove's on a Sunday. Emma had been lucky, getting a lift with Doris's friend, Peg, who had family in Blueholm Bay. Peg had a motor car, which put her on top of Doris's list of people to know.

Stepping inside the Herring Street house, Emma closed the door and carefully took off her revamped pillbox hat, putting it on a chair under the kitchen table, suddenly nervous about what Mum might say when she saw it. She plonked her handbag and the parcel Doris had sent onto the table and put the cotton bag with her Christmas presents for everyone onto the floor next to the chair. The door to the walkway was open and there was a pile of clothing on the ironing board in the laundry.

Emma turned at the sound of a door opening and smiled when her mum came into the kitchen. 'Hello!'

'I was having a lie-down,' Mum said, not even looking at Emma. She did a double take when she saw the package on the table. 'Doris sent this?' she asked, picking it up and unwrapping the newspaper. 'Four sausages and enough ham to feed only your father if he was here. There are five of us in this household or do you expect me to go without?'

'Sorry. That's all Aunty Doris had.' It wasn't true but when Emma had tried to explain to her aunt that the older boys were big eaters and that the sausages were rather small, Doris had huffed and said, 'I can't look after every soul under my care!' She didn't like it when Emma made her visits home, saying it was inconvenient since the officers might take a sudden fancy to afternoon tea and who was going to serve it?

'All she would spare, you mean,' Mum said, rewrapping the meat and putting it in the food safe.

Emma opened her handbag, took five pounds out of her purse and put it on the table. 'I've got this for you.' She'd been trying to save as much as possible to help out and mostly survived each week on six shillings, putting five shillings from the pound into a box for her own savings and keeping the remaining fifteen shillings for her family. Of course, if Mum ever needed more money, Emma would hand over her savings box. But if it wasn't asked for or necessarily needed, surely it was all right to keep it.

Mum scooped the money up and shoved it in the pocket of her apron. 'Working hard, are you?'

'You bet.'

'So am I.'

Emma wasn't going to enquire about Mrs Cosgrove's since it might bring up a reminder of the two ten-pound notes Frank had given her, and that would make Emma blush, since Frank was back in Townsville and she was seeing him fairly regularly.

A date with a real man was no longer something to be wished for or worried about. They were getting along so well. Like good friends, except they kissed, which was heavenly.

'Any news from Dad?' she asked, trying to get over the sense of not belonging, as though she'd walked into someone else's kitchen without knocking.

'Not a word since before he went to New Guinea. I don't know how he thinks I'm supposed to cope without him and now without you.'

'They have to do what they're doing, Mum.'

'Don't start,' Mum said, holding up a hand. 'You have no idea what it's been like here. Not since you got yourself out. Why can't you think about me for a change?'

'I am thinking about you. I know how difficult it all is …' It was hard pretending to be cheery when all she wanted to say was, 'Everyone's doing it hard. There's a bloody war on!'

'Where are the boys?' she asked.

'Mrs Jameson has them. I've had one of my headaches. Can you get any more days at the cafeteria?'

'Sorry, no. I tried. They can't pay me for more hours.' She picked up a knife from the table and pulled a chopping board piled with carrots towards her. 'I'll finish off the veggies, Mum, and I'll do the ironing. Why don't you lie down again? I'll make you a cup of tea in half an hour if you like.'

'That would be something.'

Mum trudged down the hallway, shoulders stooped. Emma gave a sigh and got on with the carrots. She hadn't felt this timid in forever. She was fine in the café and quite competent when chatting with the diners or her cafeteria coworkers. And she never felt awkward when she was with Cassie. Or with Frank.

He'd been injured when he'd got his hand caught in some machinery up at Mareeba, so when his unit had been sent back to Townsville he'd been transferred to the USAAF technical supply unit at Base Section 2 in the city. He'd visited her in Gibson's on a few occasions to begin with. He was busy so she didn't expect to see him all the time, but it was glorious when he walked through the door, his smile wide and given solely to Emma. She'd had to remind him to treat her like he would any other waitress in case the cook or one of the regular waitresses noticed the attention he threw her way, but Frank said he treated every woman he met with the same cordiality and Emma couldn't disagree. He was popular with everyone.

It was wonderful to go out with him, although he didn't like the idea of a double date with Cassie and Eddie. Frank said he wouldn't like being with an officer all evening, but one night, kissing her in the dark beneath Castle Hill after walking her part of the way home, he said he'd think about it, for Emma's sake.

Except the next time she'd asked he refused again.

She jolted when the kitchen door thudded against the wall as her brothers trooped in.

'Quiet!' she told them in a hissy whisper. 'Mum's lying down. She's got a headache.'

'We know,' Joe said, pulling off his cap and launching it in the air. 'It's why she sent us to Mrs Jameson's place. We're not stupid.'

'What's for tea?' Simon asked.

'I'm very well, thank you for asking. How are you?' Emma enquired of her second-eldest brother.

'Did you bring us something?' Will, now eight and a half, said, followed quickly by six-year-old Danny's gleeful, 'Is it chocolate?'

'It's sausages.'

'Bum, bum, bum.'

'That's enough from you, young Daniel.'

'We say bum all the time now you're not here,' Will informed her.

'And worse!' Joe said, staring Emma down. 'Much worse.'

'Arsehole,' Simon said, pushing his glasses up his nose. 'That's just for starters.'

Emma bit her inner cheek. 'Don't let Mum hear you.'

'We're not idiots, we're boys,' little Danny said, then stuck his nose in the air and turned to walk out of the room, the others following. Joe gave Danny a slap on the head as he pushed him to the back of the line.

'Ouch! What was that for?'

Emma picked up the cotton bag she'd put under the kitchen table and followed them to the front room.

Mum had got the Christmas tree up and despite it being an austerity tree made out of bare branches and twigs tied and knotted together with string—Joe had designed it for Christmas 1942—it looked quite lovely. All their glass baubles and tinsel had gone to the war effort but the younger boys must have made the newspaper chains and the fringed paper hanging from each branch. The old star was lopsided but had been newly coloured with a bright blue pencil.

'That looks gorgeous!' she said to the boys.

'I coloured the star for the top,' Danny said. 'That's the best bit.'

Emma made a move to ruffle his hair but he ducked, grinning at her before pulling a face.

'Manners,' she scolded.

'We don't have to do what you tell us,' Joe informed her. 'Not any more.'

'And how are you getting on being the man of the house?' Emma enquired.

Joe sank into the old armchair and put his feet up on the tapestry footstool, but not before kicking his boots off. Even Joe wouldn't dare Mum's wrath if he got mud on her family heirloom. All he needed was a mug of tea at his side and a newspaper in his hands and he'd look just like Dad. Although Dad was much quieter a personality than Joe.

'I'm doing quite fine, thank you.'

'Is there anything interesting happening in your boring life?' Simon asked.

Emma noticed he had sticking plaster on the frame of his glasses. He must have broken them. Easily done and probably an accident but she imagined their mother would have had something to say about it. 'Yes,' she said with no intent to tell him anything about what she was getting up to.

'I expect she gets all mushy and weepy when she goes to the pictures,' Joe said. 'All girls do is cry.'

'That can't be true,' Will said. 'How can they cry at pictures that have lots of dog fights and hero diggers doing absolutely marvellous deeds like capturing the enemy before they kill a whole brigade of our soldiers? They're the best pictures,' he informed Emma. 'I bet no girls even go to them.'

'John Wayne is here in Queensland!' Simon said. 'And Cary Grant was here before.'

'I know, I heard,' Emma said. 'They're entertaining their countrymen.'

'Why can't they entertain us?'

'Because they're looking after their own.'

'The bummer bloody Yanks,' Joe said.

'Joe Hatton!'

'Yeah,' Simon added, taking his glasses off and spitting on the lenses before polishing them with his shirt tail. 'Arsehole bloody bummer Yanks.'

'Simon, stop it this instant or I'll—'

'You'll what? Just try it!'

'Hey, what's that?' Joe asked, leaning forwards and nodding at the cotton bag in Emma's hand.

Emma let the swearing go. It wasn't worth arguing with them because she wouldn't be here long enough and she didn't want to ruin the few hours she had with them—although she was already wondering why she was bothering. 'Your Christmas presents and if any of you touch them your hands will drop off, because Santa is watching.'

Danny looked up, eyes fraught with worry. 'He can't see everything we do, can he?'

'Absolutely everything.'

Joe and Simon sniggered and Emma shot them a warning look.

'Including when you go for a piss,' Joe said, making Simon laugh again.

'Good job I've been extra special good then,' Danny said, sticking out his scrawny chest and offering his sister a brightening expression. 'What did you get for me?'

'What did you get for me?'

'Nothing.'

Typical. If she'd still been living at home she might have given them a few hints regarding a decent homemade present but it was what it was.

She pulled out the two parcels she'd wrapped in some worn red rayon material that had been one of Doris's old blouses. Emma had sacrificed green hair ribbons to tie around them so they looked festive. 'Then I expect this parcel for all of you is stuffed full of nothing too,' she said with a smug smile as she held up the larger of the parcels.

All the boys' eyes were on the presents and it warmed Emma from the inside out. It was a lovely thing to get a present. She was pleased she'd been able to buy some with her hard-earned money and she hoped she'd done well with her choices.

She'd bought the boys Cambric playing cards, two pocket novel westerns, and had managed to get hold of a bottle of lime juice cordial. But she'd had no idea what to buy her mother. A nice, colourful scarf seemed unnecessary out here.

Stockings couldn't be found, although Cassie said she'd get some. But when would Mum wear stockings? Doing the laundry? Pulling up veggies? In the end she'd settled on a tin of biscuits one of the officers at Doris's house had got for her—Emma had insisted on paying for it since it was going to be a gift—a copy of the *Women's Weekly* and a little book about embroidery. Not that Mum had time, but she'd once harped on about all the darning she had to do when she could be embroidering a nice handkerchief for herself so perhaps the book would go down well.

'I'm going to do the ironing so no more noise!' she told her brothers as she put the presents beneath the tree. 'Tea will be ready soon.' Not that Emma was staying, she had to meet Peg.

She left the boys to it and once in the kitchen felt a little let down, but what had she expected? She'd been gone for so long and perhaps it was normal that her family didn't feel like it was hers anymore or that she belonged.

Two hours later, having done all the vegetables and the ironing and got tea together for her family, Emma said her goodbyes. Her brothers jutted chins or murmured cheerio in acknowledgement but didn't get up to hug her. Her mother said, 'Next time tell Doris we need more than a few slices of ham and four sausages to keep us fed.'

Emma made her way down Herring Street towards the grocer's shop where Peg would pick her up. The street was a little busier than it had been earlier.

'How's it going, love?' someone called.

'Not bad. How about you?'

'Can't complain, although I'd like to.'

Emma smiled and carried on, not wanting to reflect on her visit home and the sad note it left inside her. Maybe she'd make it a monthly visit from now on. Probably nobody would even notice, and perhaps there was some way she could stay in Townsville after the war. A full-time job so she could pay rent to her aunt or even rent one of the rooms in Cassie's guest house, which would be fabulous, and she could send more money home, which Mum would be grateful for.

A motor car came around the corner from the bridge over the creek and Emma halted, wondering why Peg was coming from that direction. But it was the Colson car and Harry Colson was looking directly at her. He must have recognised her too, because he was slowing the car.

'Good afternoon,' he said as he wound down the window. 'It's Emma Hatton, isn't it?'

'Yes, sir,' Emma said. 'Good afternoon. What a lovely day.'

He leaned an elbow on the window frame. 'I'm afraid not for some.'

Emma was sure a thousand eyes were jabbing her in the back. Curtains would be moved aside from windows, women in their yards would have paused in their work and the children would be gaping at the motor car. Hopefully, Mum was in the kitchen at the back of the house but it wouldn't be long before she heard about this.

'I'm off to Melbourne for a visit,' Harry Colson said, and Emma noticed the luggage on the back seat. A suitcase and a briefcase. 'It's my sister, Cynthia.'

Emma raised her brow, not knowing what to say but not wanting to appear impolite.

'She's a bit low,' he continued. 'It's her husband. He's been missing for some time.'

'Oh, I'm so sorry.' Emma forgot all about her own concerns.

'He was shot down a few months ago.'

'I had no idea.'

'I haven't informed anyone here in town. I didn't want to start some rumour before we knew whether he had survived or not.'

'Your sister must be beside herself with worry. I'm sure he'll be found.'

'Sadly, he already has. He's a prisoner of war at a camp in Germany. We heard yesterday.'

They'd heard terrible stories about POWs in Japanese camps and Aussie diggers had been captured in North Africa and in Greece too. But Emma had never heard of any digger being in a German camp, although she knew a number of bomber crew had been shot down over Germany this year and some of them must be Australians.

'I'm so sorry to hear that, sir.' Imagine if she and Mum and the boys got the same news about Dad. It would be unbearable.

'Please don't "sir" me. I get enough of that at the bank. May I call you Emma?'

'Of course—Mr Colson.' She berated herself for almost curtsying once again. How ridiculous of her to feel the automatic need to do so every time she met him.

'Well, Emma. I'll trust you with my secret, if I may.'

'I won't say a word about anything you've told me.'

He smiled gratefully. 'Thank you. I'm hoping to discover more information on Allen from a few associates I have in the war cabinet. Not that there's anything we can do. The poor blighters must be in hell. He'll be held in one of the Oflags.'

'I'm sorry, I'm not sure what that is.'

'Officers are held in different camps to the ordinary enlisted men, as they are here. In Germany they're called Oflags and Stalags.'

'I see.' She made a note to read up about it when she got the chance, but she felt for both the officers and the ordinary men. They were all diggers doing their bit, after all. She just hoped the enlisted men were treated as well as the officers because otherwise it would surely contravene the Geneva Convention. She knew about this—she'd read about it in case Dad got captured so she'd be able to explain it to Mum and the boys.

'How is your world?' Harry Colson asked.

'I'm in Townsville with my aunt,' Emma said, thinking it kind of him to take the trouble to ask. 'She's boarding some American officers so I help out. I work in a cafeteria two days a week but I also do an awful lot for the Comforts Fund.'

'Well done, you. Doing your bit and beyond, I suspect. How's your reading?'

'Marvellous.' She bit her lip. Was it justified to use the word marvellous in a conversation that also held the words prisoner of war? 'I mean, it's educational to suddenly have the daily newspapers to read and a lot of women at the Red Cross and the Comforts Fund swap books. That's also been—' *Marvellous.*

'Is your father faring well?'

'He's still in New Guinea.'

'Ah, yes. Good luck to him. Well, I'd best get along or I'll miss my flight.'

His flight. How the rich and mighty lived.

'It's been a pleasure to see you again, Emma. You've crossed my mind a few times in the last year. I'm glad you're doing well.'

'Goodbye, Mr Colson. Please take my best wishes to your sister for a positive outcome.'

He gave her a small smile. 'It's all we can hope for. Thanks again for keeping this news to yourself.'

The car's engine thrummed and Emma backed away as he drove off. Without looking at the women who were still staring, she walked hurriedly to the Osbornes' grocery shop, figuring out an entirely fake conversation between her and Harry Colson in case anyone asked. She'd say he was simply enquiring after her father which she felt sure he'd done with any of the women he might occasionally bump into, wishing their husbands and brothers and sons well.

But she was dizzy with shock. The esteemed Harry Colson had charged her with a family secret. She bet even old Ivy Williams didn't know what had happened.

Chapter Eight

Townsville—February 1944

Frank had been popping into Gibson's much more often than he had before Christmas. It was wonderful, as though Emma was suddenly the most important person to him in the whole world. He'd taken her out tonight and was spoiling her rotten. Emma didn't mind that they were celebrating her seventeenth birthday nearly three weeks late. There *was* a war on.

Frank had been ever so generous, giving her two pairs of nylons and a new lipstick and they'd gone to the pictures at the Roxy, so as not to bump into Doris, who preferred the Regent. Emma's head was still spinning from the sound of the orchestra and the tapping of dancing feet in *Girl Crazy* as Mickey Rooney won back the heart of Judy Garland.

'Enjoy that?' Frank asked when they got out onto the street.

'Oh gosh! It was superb!' The part where Judy sang 'But Not For Me' had brought tears to her eyes and a pang to her chest. 'Thank you so much, Frank.'

'Hey,' he said, pulling her hand to rest in the crook of his arm. 'That's what guys do for beautiful women.'

Women. It always made Emma's heart flutter when he called her a woman. Although he still thought she was two years older than she actually was.

Doris had been giving Emma sidelong glances in the last few weeks. 'You're growing up,' she said as though surprised by the sudden evaluation.

Emma had smiled politely and said nothing. Doris hadn't given her a birthday present, and she hadn't got anything from home either.

Frank, on the other hand, had showered her with much more than presents. He'd given her his full attention. He hadn't even talked about the other friends he often went around with. He'd said he was all Emma's tonight.

She ought to tell him the truth about how old she was. But why change anything? They got along so well and she'd seen him far more than usual recently. It was easy to get out behind Doris's back because she thought Emma was helping serve the food and drinks at the dances.

'How's your hand?' she asked. Frank sometimes asked Emma to massage his injured hand, groaning in pleasure as she kneaded and rubbed his palm and fingers, saying she was better than any of the nurses he'd known. It was such a big, strong hand and hers looked so delicate next to his.

'Come on, angel,' he said now, grinning down at her. 'Let's go look for some more fun.'

'I ought to get back. It's quite late.'

'I know,' he said with an easy assurance. 'That's where we're heading. I've got a surprise for you.'

'Another one?' Emma said with a laugh.

He gave her a wink. His dark blond hair was cut so short it made his ears look like they were sticking out, especially when he wore his cap, although that was how most men looked these days. But even when he was grimacing or pulling a serious face, there was a natural ray of high-spirited mutiny in his expression, a tongue-in-cheek boldness that suggested he was looking for fun no matter what his mood. He always stood tall and those around him would lean into him when they were having a conversation, never the other way round. There was a defiant insouciance about him that almost everyone liked.

They walked towards Castle Hill and Doris's street, the silence between them calming and reassuring. He didn't usually walk her all the way up the street, he normally left her at the end then watched to make sure she got inside safely.

'So what's the surprise?' Emma asked when they reached the house.

He pulled her hand more firmly into the crook of his arm. 'We're going to steal a few minutes together. Just you and me.'

'Where?'

'How about your aunt's air-raid shelter?' he whispered in her ear. 'We can be alone there and I can tell you how much you make my heart burst with pride when I'm out with you.'

Emma's face heated up. It was part pleasure, part—she wasn't sure what. 'It's not an actual shelter, it's just a shed.'

Frank brushed a hand down her back, pulling her in closer. 'Come on. For me.'

Emma was hesitant, because going out with Frank to the pictures or somewhere in town Doris would never go was one thing. But there wasn't only her aunt in the house, there were three other servicemen too and they came and went at all hours.

'I want to be alone with you,' Frank said. 'I didn't even want to share you with the folk in the picture house.'

Emma giggled. 'Don't be silly.' But she knew they ought to move before someone saw them. 'Come on then.' Ten minutes would be all right. No-one would know and Emma had a hankering to be kissed some more.

Nobody used the air-raid shed but at least it was dry at the moment, although a bit musty and cobwebby.

Frank closed the door and turned to smile at her. Emma waited expectantly, knowing he was going to kiss her thoroughly, the way he did if they were in a really dark, secluded spot.

He shuffled two large sand sacks together so they had a seat.

'Frank, can I ask you something?' Emma said as they sat, his arm draped around her, heavy and warming.

'Anything, angel.'

'Would you reconsider a double date with Cassie and Eddie?'

'Aw, come on!' He pulled his arm from around her shoulders and turned his head away. 'I've told you, I'm not going to stand around saluting all night. I don't hang out with officers.'

'You wouldn't have to do that,' Emma said, already missing the warmth from his arm. 'Eddie's a lovely man.' She'd only met him a handful of times but he was a perfect gentleman.

'He's a damned officer. I'd have to be on best behaviour.'

'I honestly think it might be fun.' Cassie had asked about this so often and this was really Emma's last shot.

'I wouldn't be having fun, let me tell you,' Frank said, leaning his elbows on his knees, looking for all the world like a drowned man.

Emma moved closer and put her head on his shoulder. 'Sorry I asked. I don't mean to be a pest.'

'Aw, come here!' he said amiably, turning and embracing her.

Emma held her breath. She knew next to nothing about dealing with men but she was learning. How odd it was for Katy Wheaton and Betty Soames to come to mind. She hadn't given either of them a thought since leaving Blueholm Bay yet now her demons were flying back as though they'd tumbled out of an old suitcase. What would they say if they knew little Emma Hatton couldn't get her boyfriend to do one simple thing for her?

They'd say she wasn't trying hard enough. Wasn't able to hold onto a man.

She dare not ask again though. Frank cared for her and he looked out for her. He must love her, just a little. She had to give him time.

He gave her a rueful smile after their next kiss. 'I guess I'd better get going.'

'I thought …'

He tilted his head. 'Angel. You thought I wanted more? Of course I do. But only if you want it too.'

He moved in close for another kiss, and Emma let him put his hand up her skirt—just above her knee. It felt mean not to give him some hope. He might be deployed somewhere else one day soon. Nobody knew what was going to happen.

'See me out, would you?' he asked, a smile in his voice as he took her hand. 'Then I can kiss you again at the gate. One last kiss for our special evening.'

Out at the gate, his mouth was firmer than usual against hers. 'I won't be around for a little while,' he told her.

'Oh? You're not getting billeted somewhere else, are you?'

He shook his head. 'Just got a few things I need to attend to. I know so many people, and they're all clamouring for my attention. I've been neglecting them recently. Because of you!' he added, pushing a fingertip onto the tip of her nose.

'You're too popular.'

He shrugged. 'I have some buddies who need a favour, that's all.'

She didn't ask what with but she felt as though she'd created a problem. One she didn't have the first clue about getting out of. 'You're a good friend to have,' she told him, hoping to appease the situation.

'Will you miss me?'

Of course she would. Not that he was actually going somewhere, he was just saying … What? Was he punishing her for asking about the double date?

'Will you be gone long?' she asked, after swallowing a lump in her throat.

'Long enough for you to think about kissing some other guy!' He pulled her in tight and swung her around, his hand cheekily on her bottom. 'Don't let that happen or you'll break my heart.'

Emma wanted to laugh out loud with relief. But she had to remain quiet since her aunt's bedroom window faced the street.

'I tell you what,' he said when he let her go, 'I'll find a way to see you again soon. Would you like that? Because I sure would.'

Emma nodded. She would love it. And next time she'd keep her mouth closed about double dating.

Chapter Nine

March 1944

Emma and Cassie had found a patch of parkland off Flinders Street and were sitting on a bench, legs to one side and ankles crossed, with ham and tomato sandwiches and straws stuck in bottles of lemon squash, gazing across Ross Creek. The air was thick, the day overcast and muggy, but at least they were outside and could chat without being overheard.

'Would you like to see the world?' Cassie asked, dabbing the corners of her mouth with a handkerchief which she then used to fan her face. She wore a light blue chambray dress with a dainty collar and short puffed sleeves and hadn't even got a crumb on it let alone any perspiration marks. Cool and collected even in the heat, although Emma had a feeling there was something bothering her friend.

'I plan to one day,' Emma replied, flicking a bug off her brown shirtwaist work dress. The cafeteria owner had coughed up the coupons for the material and Emma had made it herself from a pattern the other waitress at Gibson's had lent her. Unlike her going-out frock, it was plain, but she'd stitched it with care and had added a fabric belt even though no-one saw it because of her apron. 'When I'm earning more than one and six a week,' she added with a smile. 'What about you?'

'I'd like to but it would be a bit scary.'

'We'll go together!'

'I'm quite happy to stay in Australia, actually.'

'What's wrong?' Emma asked when she caught sight of her friend's worried expression.

'Nothing.'

'Something is. Come on. Tell.'

Cassie rested the bottle of squash on her lap. 'Are you dying to get married, Em?'

Emma's eyes flew wide open. 'What's brought this on?'

'Can't a girl ask what her best friend thinks about things?'

Emma shifted position, crossing her legs as it was far more comfortable than keeping them in line, knees together. 'I don't intend to die waiting for marriage but of course it'll happen one day.' Maybe sooner than later, if Frank did have proper feelings for her. He hadn't indicated anything permanent but he had kept the promise he made at her birthday celebration date to find time to see her while helping his buddies. They'd gone to the pictures again. Twice. He'd told her they were a team and she was his girl but he hadn't looked her up since then and hadn't been into Gibson's either. She had no idea what he was doing and it felt like a betrayal not telling Cassie about it. She already had a dread within her that perhaps her friend didn't like him.

Strangely enough, the other thought bothering her was that even though it would be marvellous to go to America, she wasn't entirely convinced she wanted to get married to do it. Would she enjoy being an American wife, raising American children?

The thought was part tantalising, part worrisome and she wasn't sure which was sending the tingles down her spine.

'I'd like to get out of Blueholm Bay.'

'You're already out,' Cassie reminded her.

'I meant out of the vicinity of everything that keeps me tied here. Parental rule, poverty. Because of the war, my life is suddenly worth living.' She uncrossed her legs and put her hands on the bench. 'Is that a terrible thing to say? I don't mean I'm not worried about our men or that I want the war to go on for years.'

'It probably will though.' Cassie folded the paper their sandwiches had been wrapped in and Emma took it off her and put it in her handbag to reuse. 'Wouldn't you miss your brothers if you left Queensland?'

It was odd that Cassie imagined Emma leaving the state when Emma was envisaging leaving Australia altogether and seeing France and Britain and plenty of other countries in Europe and beyond. Like America.

'Honestly, they hardly look at me when I go home for a visit, let alone speak to me,' she said. 'I'm just a girl and girls can't do anything, according to Joe.'

'Do you feel grown up, Em?'

Emma shot her friend a surprised look. 'How could we not be with everything going on around us? We'll likely never experience this sort of adventure again in our lives.'

'God, that sounds extreme.'

'You said it yourself, we don't know what trials and troubles life will throw at us—but this has got to be one of the best times. Apart from all the losses and worrying about our diggers.'

'I'm beginning to wish I could stay young forever,' Cassie said and sucked on her straw again, making a gurgling noise.

'I'd like to think I was a valuable addition if I did get married,' Emma said. 'You know, useful, not just loved. I want to be valued.' Of course she wanted to be loved but maybe there was more. More than what she'd seen between her parents, where love must have been at the start but hadn't lasted and neither had any bond or rapport they might have shared.

'You'll always be valuable,' Cassie said. 'You're that type. The clever kind of girl, not the silly kind like me.'

'There's nothing silly about you, Cassie O'Byrne! I won't have you say so.'

'Oh, I don't mind. Not one bit. I love myself and I respect myself. Although I do like pretty things, I won't deny it, and that can lead some to think I'm a bit selfish or greedy.'

'But you're not. I know you're not.'

'Eddie doesn't think so either.'

'Well, there you are.'

Cassie looked away and sighed.

'What is it?' Emma asked. 'There's something wrong, I know it.'

'I'm wondering if I ought to stop seeing him.'

'Eddie? Why, for goodness' sake? He adores you!'

'That's the problem.' Cassie turned her head, her expression solemn. 'I don't want to leave you, Em, if it comes down to having to leave.'

'Oh, Cassie!' Emma put a comforting hand on her friend's knee. 'I'd miss you too. But of course you'd leave if he asked you to marry him. You'd go to America.'

'Yes—without you! I'd be sad but I'd also feel lost. You've done so much for me, Em.'

'I have not. It's you who's done the good for me.'

'You don't understand,' Cassie said plaintively. 'You're smart and I'm just ordinary. I'm a girl wishing for more sparkly things. You, on the other hand, are so good.'

'A goody two shoes?' Emma said, appalled that Cassie might see her that way, just like Betty and Katy.

'Lord, no! You've got too much gumption for that. If you got into trouble you'd stand up for yourself. But me? I'd need support.'

'Well, don't get into trouble. And if you do, I'm here for you.'

Cassie smiled. 'I knew you'd say that. This is what I mean. You're content with what you've got and I'm always longing for something more.'

'I long for things too.'

'Like what? You won't even let me buy you a new going-out dress. I'd never willingly wear a tablecloth.'

Emma burst out laughing. 'Oh, Cassie, you're too funny.'

Cassie smiled, albeit reluctantly. 'All I'm saying is you're brave and I'm not.'

'I'm not brave, I just make do.' Emma shifted so she was fully facing her friend. 'You'll break Eddie's heart if you drop him. He's got an absolute crush on you; you can see it in his eyes. I bet he's already over the moon in love with you.'

Cassie blushed. 'I think he might be. He probably is. I guess.' She shrugged it off as she perked up. 'Can't blame him.'

'No,' Emma said with a laugh. 'Can't blame the man.'

'Anyway, this is all silly. He hasn't asked me to marry him and perhaps he won't, so I won't have to make a decision.'

'Wouldn't love play a part in your decision?'

'I guess.'

'Do you think you're falling in love with him?'

Cassie frowned. 'Don't know.'

'Well, like you say, it's a problem you may not have to worry about. And anyway, I didn't think you'd want to tie yourself down to a kitchen sink until you were at least properly twenty-one.'

'I don't want to be anywhere near any kitchen sink no matter what age I am! Honestly, Em, don't you know anything about me? In my dreams I have servants.'

Emma nudged her good-heartedly. 'Can I borrow one?'

'Of course! I'd give you anything that was mine.' Cassie licked her finger. 'Cross my heart and hope to die.'

'Me too. Whatever I have that you need, it's yours.' They smiled at each other, Emma happy that she'd been able to reassure her friend about her worries.

She said nothing more about the repercussions of Eddie proposing and Cassie accepting but the notion was now in her head. Cassie might leave Australia and Emma would be without her.

Unless Frank proposed and they could somehow meet up in America, or at least be closer to each other. Except she had visions of writing letters from America to her parents and brothers and not one of them writing back. They might forget about her completely and then she'd lose her family—such as it was. Blood was thicker than water. Dad used to say so all the time.

Cassie bumped her elbow against Emma's, catching her attention. 'Can we make the double date sometime soon? You and Frank and me and Eddie. I'd love you to really get to know him.'

'I'll have to check with Frank,' Emma said cautiously. This was another thing she was keeping from her friend. It was as though Frank had somehow overpowered all her senses.

'You mean get his permission.'

'I mean I have to check with him about when he might be available. He's a busy man.'

'Isn't he?' Cassie said sourly. 'It's funny how he can't find time to take you out more.'

'He says he has to share himself around.' Emma felt ghastly. This was yet another thing she'd kept from Cassie: the fact that Frank was off helping others and they were having some sort of break from each other—if that's what it was that was keeping him away from her. It would be heartbreaking if they split up since they got along so well. Like buddies, not just a guy and his girl. He made her feel loved. But maybe not valued.

She didn't know when she'd next see him. But he'd turn up. Like a bad penny. Although he was a decent sort, really. Except she now understood not to ask too much of him or push him for more than he was happy to give.

Maybe this was growing up. All the changes and emotions. She'd have to learn to live with it all and get on with things.

Emma took her friend's hand and made a pointed effort to cheer herself up. 'I'll come out with you and Eddie if Frank can't make it, and I'll even double date with a man who's a friend of Eddie's if you like.'

'Would you?'

'I said so, didn't I?'

'We'd better not tell Frank though.'

Emma shrugged. 'Frank who?'

Cassie's real smile returned, the one that shone, and Emma was grateful to see it. 'Thanks, Em. Love you.'

'Love you too. Always will.'

Chapter Ten

June 1944

Emma shivered and pulled her cardigan more tightly around her.

'Come on,' Frank said, putting his arm around her shoulders. 'Not far now.'

'Don't you have to get back? I can find my own way home.'

'I've got time. I've always got time for my girl.'

'How's your hand?' Emma asked as they walked towards Castle Hill. He'd said his wrist and his fingers stiffened as the weather got cooler.

He winked. 'Good enough to hold onto you.'

Emma was so pleased they were still together. Frank had been around, here and there, over the past few months, and they saw each other once a week. Most weeks, anyway. She had wondered if he was off seeing other women but didn't know how to ask. She felt like she had a right to know but there again, if he did see other women it might only be when he was in a gang. Everyone was intent on having as much fun as possible these days.

'I was hoping we might take a rest,' Frank said as they reached the end of Doris's street with only a slice of moonlight to light their way.

He meant the air-raid shed. They hadn't been there since the last time, ages ago.

'It's a little risky. My aunt is home tonight. She's got a cold.'

'Come on, angel. Just a few minutes. You and me. It's not as if we haven't stolen some time in there before.'

Emma pulled a face, unsure. The risks were monumental. How she'd managed to sneak Frank into the shed the first time was beyond her.

'Did I tell you I've written to my mom about you?'

'You have?'

'Heaps of times! I think she almost adores you as much as I do.'

'She doesn't have some American girl lined up for you?'

'She wants me to be happy.'

'And are you?'

Frank took her chin in his hand. 'You bet. You're my girl.'

He kissed her. 'You're so good to me,' he crooned, nibbling her earlobe. 'I need someone like you. A woman to come back to. A woman who understands me.'

Emma shivered. They might not have long together now. Maybe only months, if the war ended soon. D-Day had happened earlier in the month. Plenty were saying the landing at Normandy was the greatest amphibious military invasion ever and would go down in history. There was a sense of excitement in the air, as though momentum was finally building, as though the end was almost in sight if everyone kept their wits about them.

Emma was still patiently waiting for Frank to declare his love—or even just his dedicated affection and hopes for their future—so she knew where she stood. It was good to know he'd written to his mother to tell her all about his girl in Australia.

'All right,' she said. 'We can go into the shed. Just for a little while.'

'A little time together, angel.'

Emma let them into the backyard through the side gate.

Frank closed the door of the shed with a quiet click and bolted it. It was more musty smelling than before and there were a few more cobwebs. But they were safe inside, with only the night-time sky above them through the hole in the roof after a recent storm.

'Our secret place,' he said, smiling. 'Here.' He pulled a number of sandbags together so they had a kind of sofa to sit on, then took off his jacket and draped it over the sacks.

Emma sat and Frank hunched down in front of her. 'Can't we meet up one afternoon instead of only in the evenings?' She'd been asking for weeks and it hadn't bothered him like the double-dating issue had so she kept asking, delicately, when the time felt right.

'I don't want other guys eyeing you up in the daylight,' he said, planting little kisses on her neck. 'You're mine.' He lifted her face with his hands and kissed her.

Her eyes closed, and a rush of pleasure seeped into her bones when he put a hand on her shin, then slid it up, over her knee and under her skirt. Every pulse in her body throbbed but she didn't stop him.

This having a boyfriend business was a bit troublesome sometimes. She'd much rather have the ear of her friend than have to deal with Frank's hand on her thigh, which he tried to do every time they were in the dark or at the pictures. But she hadn't seen Cassie too much recently. She was out with Eddie all the time. Probably having sex. Cassie had dropped hints about what it was like although they hadn't spoken about it in depth. The waitresses at Gibson's did it all the time. Emma had heard them talking about it.

Such was life. People grew up, met someone special, got married and got on with it.

Emma wasn't convinced she was ready for any of it. But at the same time, she didn't want to get left behind on some dusty old shelf. Her mother would never forgive her if she ended up a spinster, and the idea of having to live in the Hatton house for the rest of her life was absolutely obnoxious.

She giggled at the thought.

'What are you laughing at?' Frank asked gently, nuzzling the corners of her mouth with his. 'Are you feeling good?' His hand was now on her upper thigh, curving around a muscle, warm and secure. He'd never gone this far before. 'Your skin is so smooth.'

'Frank, do you want to—' Emma stopped, unable to say the words.

He pushed her back gently until she was lying on the sandbags. 'Yeah, I'd love to. How about you?' He lay over her so his broad chest was flush against her breasts. 'Oh, Emma. Emma.'

Emma's head was filled with noise. The softness of his voice. A cacophony of crazy sounds, and she couldn't grab onto a solid thought.

'Frank, I don't think we should.'

'Don't deny me, angel. Don't make me beg. Don't make me go look somewhere else for what I need.'

When he pushed her skirt up and tugged at her knickers, she was almost breathless.

He shifted, moving down her body, and when he kissed the top of her thigh she nearly catapulted off the sandbags.

'Frank!'

'Emma, you're so damned beautiful. The most amazing woman I've ever known.'

'I'm nervous.' She had to admit this moment was terrifying and incredibly intoxicating at the same time.

'Don't be, angel girl. I'm here for you. I'm here with you. We're going to make beautiful music. I love you, Emma. I love you.'

Emma closed her eyes. He loved her, he'd just said it out loud.

But something in her brain was firing on all cylinders. *Don't do this*, it said. *Don't do it.*

Except she couldn't catch the thought and keep hold of it while his mouth played heavenly music on her skin.

'My mom is going to love you too. She's going to love you, do you hear me?'

She heard, and knew it had to mean he was going to propose.

God, it was actually happening.

She blinked a kind of mist from her eyes and as his hands wandered over her, she gazed through the hole in the roof at the darkened night sky. She needed to find her own place in life and if life was dictating she should be with Frank and become an American wife, then who was Emma Hatton to say it shouldn't be so?

Frank was no longer just her boyfriend. She was having an affair. And he loved her. He was going to ask her to marry him. Perhaps this very night.

As he stroked her, sliding his hand over her bare skin, for the first time in her life she felt beautiful. Glorious, even. A woman like no other woman in the whole damned world.

'Oh, Frank,' she murmured.

But somehow, she couldn't find the words to tell him she loved him.

Chapter Eleven

July 1944

'He's got a mouthful of a name,' Cassie said, slicing into a crumbed pork sausage on her lunch plate.

'Eddie?' Emma asked, trying to sustain the conversation while keeping an eye on the cafeteria customers and their needs.

Cassie lifted her fork in the air. 'You mean Edward George Charles Shea the third.'

'Strewth.'

'That's what I said. Eddie didn't get it and I had to explain what strewth meant.' Cassie doubled up in laughter. 'You'd think he'd know by now—he has been in Australia for the last two years! Tucked away in his X-ray laboratory far too often.'

Emma smiled. 'Tell me everything you and Eddie have been up to.'

Cassie laughed. 'I could tell you everything,' she said with a grin, 'but I don't want to shock you.'

Emma felt herself go hot in the face.

'Honestly though, Em, I'm falling hard.' Cassie looked Emma in the eye, her normally lively expression serious. 'I wasn't convinced before. It frightened me. You know, the thought of loving someone so deeply and of them loving me just as much.'

'And now?'

'I think I'm sure.'

'Goodness. This is a turn up!' Emma could hardly believe so much had happened to them since they'd had that chat about marriage and seeing the world as they sat by the river eating their sandwiches. 'Has he said he loves you?'

Cassie nodded, a true blush on her cheeks. 'You were right when you said love would play a part in my decision. I wanted you to be the first to know, Em. Eddie proposed and I said yes.'

Emma drew a breath, blinking through the happiness she felt for her friend and holding on to the incomprehension so it didn't show on her face. Cassie was going to leave. 'Good heavens! When did all this happen?'

'Last week.' Cassie beamed. 'Oh, Em! I can't begin to tell you how exciting it all is. I'm going to America! To Wisconsin.'

Emma swallowed, bewildered. Cassie and Eddie. In love. For real in love, not just some passing fancy.

'We'll be living with his family in Madison, which is the capital city of this Wisconsin place. Have you heard of it?'

Emma shook her head. 'Sorry, I forgot to look it up in my atlas.'

'Well, it's bigger than even Brisbane! Imagine that.' Cassie sighed, a decidedly content look on her face as she pushed aside her plate and leaned her arms on the counter. 'It's so dreamy being in love. I want everyone around me to fall in love! How about you?' she asked, perking up. 'How's your love life?'

Emma picked up the dirty plate and cutlery then darted a glance towards the kitchen doorway, a sensation of doom swimming inside her. The group of airmen who had come in ten minutes ago were still waiting on their food so both cooks would be stuck at the stove, frying up eggs and fillet steak. 'I haven't seen much of Frank recently,' she said, putting the plate into a crate filled with milkshake glasses and pudding bowls.

'Why not? Em, what's going on?' Cassie caught hold of Emma's arm. 'What is it? You're looking odd.'

Again, Emma glanced around to check they weren't being overheard. She lowered her voice anyway. 'He wants us to ...' This was so hard. She'd kept so much from Cassie. All her thoughts, her worries. All the things she and Frank had done. 'He wants us to do the everything bit.'

Cassie immediately sat upright. 'Don't let him.'

'I think I want to.'

'Doesn't mean it's right.'

'You do it.'

'I'm different. This is not for you, Em.'

'Why not?'

'Because I know what I'm doing.'

'Are you saying I don't? That's not fair.'

'I'm saying this is wrong for you. Frank doesn't love you.'

'You don't know that. And neither did all the other men you've been with say they loved you!'

'But I didn't sleep with them, Em! Only Eddie, and he knows all about everything I've done. Well.' Cassie paused, frowning. 'Almost everything.'

'Does he know you're only eighteen?'

'Not yet, but—'

'Does he know why you left home? Does he know you stole a key off your landlady? Does he know exactly how many men bought you dinner and a pretty handbag?'

'Em!' Cassie said, reeling backwards. 'What's got into you? Aren't you pleased for me?'

Emma stared at her friend, shocked at her outburst. At her sorrow for not having been truthful, and her envy of what Cassie was being given. There was no other word for it.

She swiped a hand over her face. 'I'm sorry. I'm not myself. Of course I'm happy for you. I'm utterly thrilled for you!'

Silence reigned for more than a moment, making Emma feel even more like a fool.

'What is it?' Cassie asked. 'What's wrong?'

Emma took a breath. 'Frank and I have already done it.'

Cassie's eyes flew wide open. 'When?'

'End of last month. In Doris's air-raid shed.'

Cassie's pallor turned from creamy rose to paper white. 'How many times have you done it?'

'Once.'

'Oh, Em, I wish you hadn't.'

'I'd like to do it again,' Emma said. 'I'm sure it would be better next time because I'd be prepared for it.'

'Did it hurt?'

Emma lifted a shoulder. 'A bit.'

'Could have been because you had your backside on the bare, hard ground.'

'I wasn't on the dirt floor! We had the sandbags!'

Cassie sat back on her stool, her frown still in place. 'Did he say he loves you?'

Emma shifted her stance. 'Yes. He said it. And he was gentle.'

'But is he trustworthy?'

'He told me he'd written to his mother about me. He said she was going to love me too.'

'Well, of course he'd tell you that. He wanted to get your knickers off.'

Emma tried to laugh off Cassie's words but couldn't. She hadn't seen Frank since that night. Nothing. No word from him at all. And he hadn't proposed. He'd left her to lock up the shed all on her own.

'I'm sorry, Cassie. I should have told you all this before. I don't know why I didn't! Can you forgive me?'

'I don't have to forgive you for anything! You're my friend.'

Emma nodded and willed herself not to cry. Cassie was more important than Frank, although she'd never given the relationship with Frank a proper distinction before now. She'd stumbled along, wishing for things that might not be the right things, hoping he loved her, believing he must, waiting for the inevitable marriage proposal. Which she wasn't sure she wanted anyway.

'I'm sorry about me and Eddie,' Cassie said softly.

'Don't ever say that!'

'But it's made you think about Frank and everything he's never done for you.'

'He hasn't been in touch with me since.' There was no point lying about it all. Not any more. He might have split up with her and hadn't even told her. There had been times she hadn't seen Frank for a fortnight or more, so perhaps he was just out helping his other gang of mates, but Emma didn't think so this time. 'I've been an idiot. Tagging along, waiting for him to turn up. He's probably had other women and I was just a girl there to be toyed with when he fancied something a bit different to the others, who probably gave him everything he asked for anyway.'

Cassie lunged over the counter and took Emma's hand. 'Are you going to be all right?'

Emma found a smile. It wobbled a bit but she shrugged it off. 'I guess.'

Cassie squeezed her hand. 'I love you, Em.'

'I know. I love you too. I'm going to miss you …'

'America,' Cassie said, her previous excitement about the adventure she was about to go on now filled with a little anxiety. 'Just think. Me, in America.'

'You'll be fine. Eddie's family will love you.'

'I hope so.' Cassie sat back on her stool. 'Will you visit? Please say you will.'

'Try to stop me.' Emma didn't want to lose Cassie, and one day soon, when the war was over, she'd be old enough to make her own decisions and earn a proper wage. Of course she and Cassie would meet again. Emma would never lose her friend completely. She simply wouldn't let it happen.

Chapter Twelve

August 1944

'At last!' Cassie said. 'I thought those women would never leave us alone and I've got so much to tell you.'

Emma paused in her task of untangling bunting for a dance to be held that evening in the recreation hall run by the Americans. 'I've got a bit to tell you, too,' she said. How two years could change a person, without a person even knowing. She felt she had ridden the waves somewhat blinded. No—wholly blinded. By inexperience and by ignorance.

'Eddie's parents have written again,' Cassie said.

Emma forced a smile. 'That's wonderful!'

'This getting married to a Yank business is complicated, though.'

'Why? What's happened now?' Emma had pushed thoughts of Frank behind her while she followed all the news about the wedding, but her nerves were stretched too far this morning and she couldn't think straight, could hardly remember anything Cassie had said about the marriage plans.

'You remember Eddie told his parents about me when he first wrote to ask for his grandmother's engagement and wedding ring?'

Emma nodded. 'Have they arrived yet?'

'Not yet, but oh my goodness, his parents sound absolutely lovely! I think the engagement ring is a diamond. An actual diamond, Em!'

'I'm so happy for you.'

'You might need to also feel sorry for me. We have to wait on the army getting themselves organised.'

'Why?'

'They're dragging their feet. Eddie asked for permission to marry me weeks ago. They don't want him to. They've refused plenty of other couples.'

'But that's absurd, you're in love.'

'Eddie's pushing harder now his parents have accepted it. His father is some bigwig, or he knows a lot of bigwigs.'

'Oh, that's right. I remember you telling me.'

'He's written to Eddie's CO to plead his son's case.'

'Gosh, you are a lucky girl.'

'Eddie's absolutely hellbent on marrying me. What an idiot I was to nearly let him go! When I think of it, I just shudder!'

'How is he doing?' Emma hadn't seen Eddie for ages. She'd hardly been out the last fortnight except to work at the cafeteria and was only here now because otherwise someone might ask her why she was shirking her duties.

'Remember his hospital in Aitkenvale was closed in June? He was at Armstrong Paddock for a while, living in a tent, but now he's at the 44th General Hospital in Black River. But I can't get to Black River without a ride, and it's at least a half-hour drive.'

'Surely they have entertainment?' Along with GI trucks to ferry the girls to and from the venues.

'This is the new bit I need to tell you about. I'm having trouble with my landlady. She's suspicious of me. God knows why, I've pulled the wool over her eyes so many times. I didn't even tell her I was engaged to an American until last week because it's none of her business. She told me I was a slut! Can you believe any woman would say that about another? She thinks I'm lying and she's threatening to throw me out. She discovered I'm a hostess and said she'd heard all sorts of appalling things about us. Bloody old cow. So I'm not taking any hostess spots any more. I've got to keep my reputation clean.'

Emma found a tremulous smile. 'When do you think the wedding will actually happen?'

'As soon as we get the rings—I hope. Eddie says he wants us to do this properly so we've got to wait. And he's been so busy. They had to take over a hundred injured soldiers by ambulance to get to the new hospital in Black River.'

'So you can't set a date.'

'Not yet. There are heaps of other girls in the same position as me. Everyone in charge is trying to stop their men from marrying an Australian girl. If they do let us marry, I've got to apply for permission to enter the United States and it can take ages to get a visa. But before we even get that far, the priest needs approval from Eddie's CO and he won't give it until he's thought about it some more. And the priest said he wants to see Eddie's baptism papers!'

'Why?'

'To prove he's Catholic. I'm not, of course, even though my dad is. But my mum never had me christened or baptised and I've never been to church in my life. So that's another problem. Eddie's going to see a Baptist minister as soon as he gets the rings from his parents to ask if they'll marry us instead.'

'But they have to allow you. You're engaged!'

'Apparently that doesn't matter. So in the meantime, I'm sitting around on my own and I'm not even going out to any dances, except to do this.' She picked up the bunting before flinging it across the table. 'It's utterly boring, Em.'

'What a nightmare.'

Cassie looked up with a cheeky smile. 'It won't be boring for long, though. I'm getting married! It's really happening. I've seen some lovely curtain fabric and I know you'd adore it. Will you let me buy you the material?'

'What for?'

'For a bridesmaid dress! And new shoes and a hat. I've got enough coupons for yours as well as all the accessories I'll need. I'm borrowing a dress from a girl I used to sing with. She wore it to her wedding, so it's not exactly new, but it's divine! She's lending it to some other woman after me. She's got a string of friends who want it. Honestly, she could probably start charging.' Cassie laughed. 'It's a silky material with the most beautiful sweetheart neckline, and I'm wearing a little white hat with a very short veil, so you can definitely wear a hat too. You ought to wear something light green, which will stand out against my white dress and my eyes. That colour will suit you too, with all that thick chestnut hair. I'll even put some daisies in my bouquet, just for you. And nobody will care that you're wearing curtain fabric. They probably won't even guess.'

Emma smiled but her heart was breaking. 'A bridesmaid?'

'My bridesmaid. What's wrong with you this afternoon? You didn't think I'd get married without you there, did you?'

Time stood still as Emma's thoughts shifted rapidly, one over the other. A wedding. A chance to smile. A joyous day she would miss.

'I can't,' she said in a shaky voice.

'What do you mean you can't?' Cassie paused, eyes fixed on Emma's. 'Em, what is it?'

Emma's cheeks burned as though she'd been slapped. 'I'm pregnant.'

Cassie stared at her. 'How do you know?' she said in a hushed tone.

'I'm sick every morning and I've got this weird metal taste in my mouth. I've heard enough from the women back home to know I must be. And I haven't bled and I should have last month.'

'You might be late.'

'I don't think so.'

Cassie stood, open-mouthed, eyes full of concern. 'Oh my God, Em.'

'You're not mad, are you?'

'Not at you!'

'But I might not be at your wedding.'

'Oh, Em.' Cassie took hold of Emma's arms.

'Are you shocked?' Emma asked. 'I know you are. You must be.'

'I should have expected it after what you told me. But I've been too bothered about myself. How ghastly of me. Really, I thought this would have happened to me, not you. Not in a hundred years did I think you'd get into this sort of trouble. Have you told Frank?'

'I wrote to him twice last week and the week before. As soon as I knew.'

'What did he say?'

'Nothing yet.'

'You haven't seen him at all since you did it?'

Emma shook her head. 'I came to the conclusion we'd split up. I was just trying to get on with life. But I have to see him now. I have to see him face to face.'

Cassie tightened her hold. 'Listen to me. You're not going to hear from him and you won't get to see him.'

'I'll go along to Base Section 2 if I have to.'

'Em—'

Emma pulled back. 'He's got to see me!' She wrung her hands as she gazed into her friend's eyes, filled with empathy. Or maybe it was pity.

'I'm so sorry,' Cassie said softly. 'But you'll get through. You'll have to, Em. You'll be right.'

How could anything possibly be right? Cassie didn't have a family but she had Eddie, who would become her new family. What did Emma have? A reluctant lover who must have received her letters yet hadn't answered. He must know she was pregnant but he hadn't contacted her. It didn't make sense. This was important news.

'Perhaps he's been deployed somewhere else,' Cassie said, as though hoping to produce an alternative reason from nowhere.

Emma shut her eyes but the darkness was peppered with spots of sharp grey and piercing white. She'd already gone through all the possible excuses a thousand times. 'I'm scared.'

'I'll help. I'll always help you. Remember our pledge? If one is in trouble the other will be there.'

But Cassie wouldn't be here. She'd be in America.

Emma hung her head. If this had happened to Cassie, Eddie would have been there to see her through and look after her. But Emma wouldn't get through this. Not without Frank at her side.

How stupid had she been? She hadn't wanted to be a Yes girl, a girl dancing to the tune of another's whims, and she hadn't wanted Frank to think her cold and unloving. Now Cassie would go to America while Emma stayed here, waiting for Frank, waiting for him to say of course he loved her, waiting for him to propose.

But it wasn't going to happen. She hadn't been special to him after all. She probably never had been. If he cared for her he would have found somewhere nice for them to do it. Somewhere with a bed and a proper bedspread, not a cobwebby old shed. He had enough money to rent a hotel room. He must know how to go about doing that. He had a lot of friends who would know, too, although she hadn't been allowed to meet many of them.

He'd kept her a secret, and it made her feel dirtier than she ever expected.

Her stomach churned and this time it wasn't because of the baby growing inside her.

'Em, we'll figure something out. I won't leave you.'

'You'll have to. You'll be off to Wisconsin as soon as you're married.'

'Not yet. It'll take ages to get everything arranged. I'm still waiting on my visa, remember, and I won't get that until we're married.'

'I'm going to miss it all!'

'No, you won't. You must come to the wedding! You have to, Em. You have to be there with me.'

'I can't.' Emma pulled her hands from Cassie's grip and covered her cheeks, shame overwhelming her. 'You said yourself it's going to take ages to arrange it all. By that time I'll be huge. People are going to talk about me.'

Cassie embraced her, the warmth of her cheek against Emma's real and comforting, the signature fragrance of her prized 7777 Eau de Cologne enveloping Emma's senses. 'Remember I told you how brave you are?'

Emma's chin wobbled so much she couldn't control it. 'I don't feel brave now. I don't think I'll ever be brave.'

'You have to be. This is it. One of our life trials.'

But it wasn't Cassie's, only Emma's. And Emma didn't want to bring up the differences between them, but the thoughts about what was going to happen kept tumbling. She might be thrown out on the street. She was going to be mocked and laughed at by everyone at the Comforts Fund. Thought repugnant by everyone who knew.

Cassie shook her. 'Em, listen to me. Wipe those tears from your eyes and get real. It's the only way you'll get through.' Her friend's gaze wavered, as though she was frightened about what she had to say next. 'You know what you have to do.'

Emma nodded. She knew exactly what she had to do.

She had to tell her mother.

Chapter Thirteen

Blueholm Bay—September 1944

'He's married!' Mum yelled, throwing Doris's offering of a pound of pork chops onto the kitchen table, scattering the knives and forks Emma had been cleaning to the floor. 'Bloody married!'

Emma moved backwards in case Mum picked up the carving knife and decided to throw that as well. She was used to her mother's ranting now, but still hadn't got over the terror of it. Mum had been exploding every few hours since Doris brought Emma home two days ago.

Doris was standing with her hand still on the knob of the open back door, looking like a rabbit staring at a trap, desperate to eat the food but scared it might snap her in two if she reached out.

'Close the door!' Mum hissed. 'Before the whole bloody street knows!'

Doris moved quickly, shutting the door and stepping further into the kitchen, but staying well away from the table, where any number of cooking utensils were within Mum's reach. 'I brought her home as soon as I guessed!' she said, clearly wanting the blame to be anywhere but on her shoulders.

After confessing to Cassie, Emma had waited another ten days for Frank to contact her. She'd even been up to base section, but his commanding officer had told some GI to tell her she would not be seeing Private Kendrick and she was not to go there again.

She'd cried so hard when she got back to Doris's house she'd been violently sick. Doris said she was calling for the doctor and as Emma didn't want that—knowing she had to tell Mum before anybody else—she'd begged her aunt not to. Doris had eyed her for a long while, her gaze darting between the sick in the toilet bowl, Emma's red-rimmed eyes and her hand, clutching her belly.

'Sweet Jesus,' Doris had said at last, blanching. 'Your mother's going to …'

She hadn't needed to finish her sentence. Emma knew Mum was going to kill both of them.

'I'm here to help in whatever way I can,' Doris said now, clutching the straps of her handbag in front of her. 'You said yourself he was a cheeky one.'

'But I kept her away from him, didn't I? You're the one who let this happen!'

Emma hardly dared to breathe. Being home already felt like an imprisonment. She wasn't allowed to help with the boys, who'd been told she was ill and to keep away from her. She wasn't allowed out of the house, not even into the backyard. The boys were sent to school as usual and Mrs Jameson had been commandeered to watch them after school until early evening, Mum citing the tiredness of having to look after a bedridden girl.

'What about Peg?' Mum asked. 'Has she asked any questions?'

Doris relaxed a little and put her handbag on a stool next to the range. 'Not a word. She knows nothing. She believed my story completely. She even sent her best wishes to the family this morning when she drove me out here. She hasn't got a clue.'

Doris had asked her friend Peg to drive them both back to Blueholm Bay. She'd fibbed and said Emma had been working so hard she was exhausted and the doctor was insistent the young woman have some vital family care. Emma had been instructed to whimper and cough during the journey. The whimpering hadn't been hard to conjure up. She'd been shaking so much her bones had practically rattled in the back seat, and her skin had gone ice cold at the thought of telling her mother.

Once Mum had been told, Emma stood stock still, waiting to feel the back of Miriam Hatton's hand. It took ten seconds, after the disbelief on Mum's face turned to burning rage.

Neither her aunt nor her mother had helped her get up off the floor, nor had either of them enquired about her in any way whatsoever. They'd just shouted at each other until Mum spun around to Emma and asked who the father was.

Frank had a right to know he was going to be a father, so she'd told them. At that point, she'd still harboured some hope that everything so far had been a misunderstanding. That he hadn't received her letters. That his commanding officer would speak to him and then he'd come find her.

'Let's give it some more thought,' Doris said.

'I've given it plenty, believe me,' Mum said, staring her sister-in-law down. 'I've hardly slept! A slut! My own daughter!'

Emma winced. It was awful knowing Mum loathed her so much. Despised her even. It was such a hard thing to take in that she rocked on her feet, dizziness overcoming her.

'I'll ask you again,' Mum said to Emma. 'Who knows?'

'Nobody.' They knew nothing about Cassie, and Emma was going to keep that friendship a secret.

'I have never been more humiliated in my life than I was yesterday!' Mum said to Doris.

'I know, Miriam. You told me. I was waiting for you outside, remember? I gave up vital Red Cross work to go with you.'

While the boys were at school, Mum had begged a lift into Townsville from Mr Jameson, stating she had to pick up some groceries from Doris since Emma was still bedridden. She'd gone to see the officer in charge of Frank's unit. She'd given him a mouthful when he refused to bring out the accused, then he told her the truth.

'Married—with a young child, too!' Mum said, spitting the words out before turning to Emma. 'You stupid girl.'

Emma swallowed the emotions that had built inside her, each one an ember of agony. Frank was married. It was still raw and unfathomable to understand.

'He knows what he's done,' Mum said to Doris. 'So does his commanding officer, but neither of them gives a damn.'

'Yes, Miriam. You said.'

'I was told to get myself gone and not make further disturbances. *Told*,' she repeated. 'Do not make further disturbances, Mrs Hatton!' she yelled. 'Do you know how that made me feel? How that made me *look*?'

Doris spread her hands. 'I didn't think they'd take this attitude and neither did I know he was married. I wouldn't have suggested you go there otherwise, would I?'

'What the hell am I going to tell Doug? You have to take some blame for this.'

'It's not Aunty Doris's fault,' Emma said. 'It's my fault.'

Mum scoffed. 'The Yank didn't play a part?'

'Can't you be a bit more empathetic?' Emma asked, knowing she'd get stung for speaking up but unable to hold back the words.

'Empath—? I'll give you a big word—prostitute. How does that sound? Delinquent—there's another. Whore!'

Emma was so stunned by the vitriol in her mother's tone she had to hold onto the meat safe in case she fell.

'I'm locking you up until I know what to do with you. We'll say you're still ill.'

'I've had an idea, Miriam,' Doris said, looking hesitant but more like her confident self.

'I don't care about your ideas, Doris. I have to find her a home to go to. How the hell am I going to do that, stuck out here surrounded by nosy neighbours and gossiping women?'

'That's just it,' Doris said. 'My idea.'

Emma closed her eyes and tried to mentally shut both women out. Whatever Doris's idea was, it wasn't going to be pleasant.

Chapter Fourteen

The sixpence Emma had hidden beneath her mattress was still there, which was a relief, because Mum had taken all the money she'd saved from her job at Gibson's, the whole eight pounds and a few shillings she'd hidden in the lining of her handbag. Mum had heard the coins rattling and had ripped the lining right out of the bag. She'd burnt the bag in the wood stove, along with Emma's lipstick and brand-new powder compact.

Emma stuffed the sixpence into her shoe and regarded her reflection in the glass on her bedroom window. She was wearing her ordinary clothes again. No more oyster-grey linen and smart blouses, no more going-out frock that was so pretty with its little white daisies. Mum had burned them all. Now Emma wore a serviceable shirt with the sleeves tightly rolled above her elbows, thick cotton shorts and sturdy brown lace-ups. Mum was out doing her stint at Mrs Cosgrove's and the boys were at school and if she didn't sneak out of the house now, she'd never get another chance—Mum had accepted Doris's idea and Emma was about to be sent to Brisbane.

They'd found her a home to go to. A Catholic place where the nuns ran an infants' asylum as well as looking after girls in trouble. But as far as anyone else was concerned, Emma would be doing her war duty volunteer work in Brisbane while also looking after Uncle Raymond's parents who apparently suddenly needed help around the house due to their age. Although Doris's in-laws hadn't been told what lies were being said about them in Townsville and Uncle Raymond knew nothing about the reality either.

Emma wasn't sure what to expect at this Catholic home, and she wouldn't remember any of the prayers she'd been taught as a youngster since they stopped going to church after Joe had been born. But she damned well knew she wouldn't be getting the use of a telephone.

She had to contact Cassie. Her friend would be worried sick.

There was no way she could ask to use Mrs Jameson's telephone, although if Janet had been home, she might have requested some help, but Janet was now in a proper paid job, working as a clerk with the WAAAF and they hadn't crossed paths in over a year. All that unpaid typing work in 1942 had clearly come in useful.

So the big house it was, the only other house in town that had the telephone.

Emma checked the clock on the mantle. Nearly two o'clock. Knowing Cassie, she would be at her boarding house, resting up in preparation for the evening having finished her volunteer work for the day.

As soon as Ivy Williams opened the kitchen door and saw Emma, she covered her mouth and nose with the end of her apron. 'What do you want? Aren't you sick?'

'I'm better now.' Emma held out her sixpence. 'I'm sorry to trouble you, Mrs Williams, but I was wondering if I could use the telephone. There's a person in Townsville I've met a few times and I heard that her brother has been injured. I'm quite worried about her otherwise I would never ask …' She trailed off.

'What's wrong with the Jameson telephone?'

'They're out.'

'What's all that?' Ivy asked, noticing the sheets and towels slung over Emma's shoulder. 'What are you doing to my washing?'

'There's quite a bit of it blown off the line,' Emma said. 'Not sure how, but I rushed to gather it since it was getting quite grubby on the ground—we had that spot of rain yesterday, didn't we? There wasn't a basket so I couldn't carry more than this.'

The housekeeper looked over Emma's shoulder, but she wouldn't see the washing line from here since the kitchen garden was beyond the big shed. 'I spent all morning on that wash!'

'I think the line must have broken. Or got caught or something.' The something being Emma loosening the line from its post and letting the wash trail on the damp, salty grass.

The housekeeper turned to the kitchen, rushed through to the laundry then scurried back towards Emma, a wicker basket in hand. 'Give me that!' she said and hauled the washing off Emma's shoulder, practically knocking Emma over in her rush.

Emma stepped to the centre of the doorway, blocking her path. 'Can I use the telephone quickly? Then I'll come help you with your washing. What a nuisance! You'll probably have to wash most of it again.'

'Just as well we've got a cupboard full of manchester or I'd be in trouble. Good quality linens, too. Not likely something you'd ever get your hands on. I'm not letting you get near it.'

'The telephone?' Emma said, offering the sixpence again.

Ivy grabbed the coin and stuffed it into her apron pocket. 'I'll be telling Mr Colson and I'll be telling your mother, too.'

Emma smiled. It didn't concern her that Mum might find out. Emma would be gone tomorrow, and whatever happened, she hoped to hell she never came back to Blueholm Bay. 'Mr Colson is such a kind gentleman. I'm sure he'd be obliging and wouldn't mind me using his telephone. If I ever see him again, I'll explain, and I'll let him know I paid the sixpence. I'll say I gave it to you for safekeeping.'

Ivy scowled, gauging Emma for a second or two. 'You'd better be done by the time I get back.'

Emma eventually got through to the exchange and the guest house where Cassie rented a room, then had to wait more interminable minutes while the landlady went to fetch her.

'Where are you?' Cassie said at last.

'Home. With Mum.' Emma kept her voice low and her eyes peeled. The telephone was in the hallway, a fancy area with expensive-looking rugs on the floorboards and highly waxed dark furniture. She felt like a thief in the night, even though the house was silent. Ivy's employer would be at the bank. He didn't usually drive through town until well after six o'clock, but she was still anxious in case she was found out.

'Strewth!' Cassie said. 'What has your mum done to you?'

'Do I really have to tell you?'

'Where are you telephoning from?'

'The big house belonging to Harry Colson. I bribed his housekeeper.'

'Oh, Em. I've been so worried. Does your dad know?'

'Mum wrote to him. He came back last month. His battalion landed on Thursday Island for leave but he didn't come to see us.'

'Maybe he's thinking kindly about you and doesn't know how to face you to say it.'

'Doubt it.' Not with Mum on his back, egging him on to see her point of view, and how much pain and humiliation she was going to have to put up with while he got away from the intense scrutiny by going back to Dutch New Guinea or wherever his battalion would be deployed next.

'How are you feeling?' Cassie asked.

Deathly. Ghost-like. A dark shadow cast on the ground at sunrise, like one of the Colson topiaries. 'Not bad. How about you?'

Cassie didn't answer.

'It's all right,' Emma said. 'I know it's different for you. I'm glad about that.' Cassie had Eddie, and he loved her. 'I'm leaving tomorrow.'

'What do you mean? Where are you going? I was planning to visit.'

'No! Don't. Nobody knows about you. They're sending me to Brisbane. To some Catholic place that looks after unwed girls.' She wasn't sure what the place was called because Doris had whispered it to her mother and then the women made their plans in lowered voices and Emma heard next to nothing. But it was a Holy something. There was a saint in the name too. 'The Holy something of Saint somebody,' she told Cassie.

'How did your mum find this place?'

'Doris found it.'

It had been a horrible moment, worse than any so far. 'They sort you out and then they get the thing adopted,' Mum told her.

'I don't want it adopted.' Dread had come to the fore. 'I want to keep it.'

'I can't begin to imagine what sort of married couple would want to take on someone else's trash,' Mum said, not having listened to her daughter's plea, 'but let's thank the Lord they do.'

'Mum—' Emma hadn't given too much thought about what might happen to her afterwards. She hadn't realised her mum wouldn't want another baby in the house.

'Nobody will take you on now,' Mum had muttered, busying her hands with beetroot, slicing through it so hard there were red stains all over the tabletop. 'You'll never have a husband.' She banged the vegetable pot onto the table as though angered more by the fact her daughter would be husbandless and under her feet forevermore than the fact Emma was a pregnant single girl, alone and frightened to death.

'Can I visit you at this place in Brisbane?' Cassie asked, bringing Emma around.

'I don't know. They haven't told me anything.'

'I'll visit.'

'You'd better not. You have to look after your reputation. How's Eddie?'

'I haven't seen much of him.'

Emma's heart rate shot off the scale. 'He's not—I mean, he still loves you, yes?'

'Yes! But it feels like he's busier than before and I'm sitting around doing nothing.'

Relief poured through Emma. She wasn't sure she'd cope if her friend's loving relationship had broken up. She didn't want both of their lives to turn to dust. 'How's your landlady? Is she treating you better?'

'Is she ever! Eddie visited her. He was so persuasive and you know how gorgeous his accent is. She nearly swooned. She even moved me into a better room. I have my own bathroom now. Well, I only have to share it with two other girls, not the whole household. Oh, Em!' she said. 'I dream about him at night when I'm not with him. I love him. I really do. I'm not making it up. I'd go live in a cave with him if I had to.'

'He's Edward George Charles Shea the third. I doubt you'll be living in a cave.'

'It's a figure of speech. You of all people should understand that given your intelligence. All I'm saying is that he is my life. My whole life.'

'And the wedding?'

'We've got the rings but I might have to get my dad to sign permission for me to go because I'm not twenty-one.' Cassie took a breath. 'He's got to promise he'll support me if need be, so the Yanks don't have to pay for my care if Eddie is moved back to America before we're married.'

'How on earth will you get your dad to promise something like that?'

'I'll have to blackmail him or something. At first I didn't dare tell Eddie what he'd tried to do to me after Mum died in case he went berserk. I thought he might tie my dad to one of his radiation machines and X-ray him till his innards fried.'

Emma covered her mouth with her hand as she snorted a laugh.

Cassie chuckled too. 'But I told him anyway, and also that I wasn't quite twenty-one and he was awfully good about it. We hope to get married soon.'

'Have you set a date?'

'Not yet. We've still got to persuade Eddie's CO then it'll be all systems go.'

'I'm happy for you, Cassie. Will you get passage on a war bride ship?'

'We're working on that as well as the visa permission to go to America. It's all so up in the air at the moment. I'm part ecstatic and part terrified something will go wrong.'

'I just know everything will work out.'

'Oh, Em, I'm so sorry. Here I am thinking about myself when you're in a rotten position. It's not fair.'

Life didn't feel fair, but Cassie's life hadn't been either up until now and she deserved what she was fighting for. She deserved the love being shown to her by Eddie.

'Can you forgive me, Em?'

There was a sadness in Cassie's voice that almost broke Emma. 'There's nothing to forgive.' It wasn't Cassie's fault Emma was pregnant and considered wicked and repugnant because she didn't have a fiancé. It was Emma's fault.

She put a hand on her stomach. The baby inside her had seemed almost unreal over the last solitary days. As though it couldn't possibly be there, growing. Emma closed her eyes and prayed she'd see Cassie again. Just one more time before she left Australia.

'I wish you could come with me to America, Em. I wish I could take you with me.'

'You finished?'

Emma nearly dropped the telephone receiver when Ivy Williams poked her nose around the hallway door.

She smiled, and nodded, then went back to the telephone. 'Of course I'll call again,' she said brightly. 'I'm terribly sorry about your brother but I'm glad he's on the mend. I'm sure you'll be fine too, once you get ... once you ...' Her throat felt so thick it was like she was swallowing mud. 'Once you get home.' To some place called Madison in faraway Wisconsin.

'Is there someone there?' Cassie asked.

'Yes.'

Silence. Emma struggled with her emotions and perhaps Cassie was also feeling desperate. Unable to help.

'I'll find you, Em. I'll see you soon.'

Emma had a gut-wrenching suspicion it would never happen. It was so hard to hold back the sobs she could suddenly hardly breathe. 'Take care, dearest friend.'

'I love you, Em,' Cassie said, choking through her tears.

'Me too. Always. No matter what.'

Replacing the telephone receiver, Emma turned to face Ivy, desperately hoping she could keep her own tears at bay. She hadn't thought it possible to lose everything. Her family. Frank. Cassie. Her baby. Yet it was happening.

But whatever was coming, she was going to have to cope.

PART TWO

Chapter Fifteen

Brisbane—October 1944

Up until the night in the air-raid shed, Emma had looked her problems in the eye, facing them with an untroubled spirit. But that had been youthful valour born of inexperience, because at the Holy something of Saint someone, she faced more difficulty than she'd ever believed it was possible to face.

'I hope you're ashamed,' Sister Hyacinth said. 'Putting so much dishonour onto your parents' shoulders. It's a disgrace. *You* are a disgrace.'

Emma concentrated on the light spreading around her feet from the sunshine pouring through the lead-paned windows of Sister Hyacinth's office.

'Whatever happens here, it serves you right,' Doris had said when she dropped Emma off. 'You're a stupid girl, like your mother said. You've upset your father and I just hope those boys of his never learn of your filthy ways. Under my roof!' she added, her usually accommodating expression pinched as tight as the skin on a drum. Her aunt hadn't spoken to her during the journey by train from Townsville to Brisbane. Not a single word until Doris led her through the back gates of the home, which was the only way in for a girl like Emma.

Emma hadn't answered, she'd simply turned and walked over the threshold of her prison.

The home was like living in a big house belonging to an affluent family, except the rooms were filled with pregnant unmarried girls and the corridors with nuns with folded hands and lofty piety, constantly on the lookout for disobedience. There were about ten or twelve girls at any one time and they never got outside the stone walls until they went into labour.

She wasn't even allowed to keep her own name. She was now known as Elaine Harper. Nobody had said if she was supposed to keep this new name for the rest of her life but surely not. Surely not …

'You are a despicable creature, Harper,' Sister Hyacinth said. 'The others are ready to have their babies adopted out yet you remain recalcitrant. If you are not careful, you will place us in a position where we have to take more desperate measures.'

Emma kept her eyes on the floor in case the sister saw rebellion in them. She could only imagine what those measures might be, and not every girl in the home was willing to give up their babies, they simply had no choice.

It was a half-hour horse and cart ride to the Brisbane Women's Hospital. Some girls said it was half an hour of agony if you went into labour before expected, and half an hour of torture learning how to live as a broken human being coming back, because you'd had your baby taken off you. Rebecca Wilson had sobbed so hard after she got back from the hospital—every night for five days and she was practically useless for work in the daytime too—that everyone got used to the sound and managed to fall asleep listening to it. One night, there was silence. They took Rebecca away on a stretcher, sheets and blanket and all, and nobody saw her again. She'd gone to God, Sister Hyacinth told them the next morning. Because of the steely glare in her eyes, Emma would never be sure if the sister thought Rebecca going to heaven had been a good thing for God or a bad one.

'Wipe that look from your face, you shameful wretch,' Sister Hyacinth said now. 'And I see a stain on the skirt of your dress. Wash it immediately. You will wear your petticoat and a fresh apron until it is dry. It will be an excellent reminder for the others that if we soil our lives, we live with the consequences.'

Like the other girls, Emma wore a uniform: a grey linen dress and a starched white apron, which had to be removed if summoned to the office. Her own clothes were stored beneath her bed in the dormitory in the small bag she'd brought. There would be no need of them until the day she left.

'Go about your business, girl. Consider your position while you work. You must pray for God's forgiveness and for the forgiveness of every married woman who is unable to have a child of her own.'

Emma let herself out of the office as the sister turned her attention to letters on her desk. She held onto the doorknob until her breath settled in her chest.

They'd got into her about having her baby adopted out practically before she'd unpacked her bag. They were going to take it off her as soon as they found decent, Catholic adoptive parents. It might be given away immediately after she gave birth or it might take a few days, in which case she'd have to wean it. She knew they meant feeding the baby. She had never been allowed to watch her mother feeding the boys, although she'd snuck a look on occasion. A few months after each had been born the boys had been weaned onto milk in a bottle, and Mum no longer had to hide in the bedroom ten times a day and Dad got to sleep in his own bed again and not on the sofa.

If Emma did get to wean her baby, it wouldn't be here, in the home. She'd have to stay in the hospital. One of the girls told her the unmarried mothers who still had their babies were put behind screens so the decent married mothers didn't have to look at them.

There wasn't any hope of keeping her baby but Emma kept refusing, not wanting to give up or give in. Not so soon nor so easily. It was her baby and she loved it and wanted to be its carer. It shouldn't be theirs. It *wasn't* theirs.

* * *

'Why aren't you wearing your dress?' Lorraine Freeman said, crossing Emma's path an hour later.

'I just scrubbed that!' Emma said in exasperation as she looked up from her position on the wooden floor.

'Sorry,' Lorraine said, stepping back. 'But what's going on? Where's your dress?'

'I soiled it. This is my penance.'

Lorraine's eyes flew wide open and she picked up the hem of her dress. 'Is mine dirty?' she asked, turning in a frantic circle.

'No. You're fine.'

She puffed out her cheeks. 'What a relief. It's the handout today and I want to be one of them who gets to the wall—but I wouldn't do it in my petticoat.' The girls fed the homeless on the weekends. The poor lined up outside the rear wall and the girls handed them food through two long slits. Not that the homeless had much better fare than the girls. Mostly watery broth made from the scraps from the girls' meals. Potatoes with the odd slice of sausage or a runner bean. How any of the girls didn't eat all their sausages was a puzzle. They only got them occasionally. Unless it was because they had upset tummies. Upset hearts.

'You're not doing the handout, are you?' Lorraine asked.

'Dressed like this? I'll be mopping or scrubbing floors all day I expect.'

Lorraine smothered a laugh. She was a bubbly sort of girl but in a nervous way. She slowed when turning a corner in the hallways or before entering a room, as though readying herself for something that might shock her. Lorraine wouldn't tell anyone her real name. It would get her into trouble with the sisters. None of the girls would tell.

'I'm on kitchen duty next,' Lorraine said.

'Well, you'd best get going if you want to do the handout.'

Lorraine went on her way and Emma checked the corridor to see if it was safe to rest for a moment longer, then left the scrubbing brush in a pile of soap suds on the floor and put both hands on her stomach. She'd been here six weeks, had shared dormitories and meals and chores with all the other girls with hardly a second to herself unless she was on the loo, and she'd never felt more alone in her life.

Wipe those tears from your eyes and get real. It's the only way you'll get through.

Her friend's words resounded in her head but in this place it was hard to imagine how a girl could possibly do it.

* * *

'So how often do they get this horse and cart out?' Sarah Powell asked a month later and only three days after she'd arrived. She and Emma were attending to the breakfast dishes in the big green porcelain sink in the scullery.

'It's the doctor who sends for the horse and cart,' Emma said as she dried another plate. 'The sisters fetch the doctor if they think our time is up.' She'd become accustomed to leading some of the girls through the ritual that was life in the home. Sarah—not her real name and she hadn't yet got used to answering when someone called her Powell—not only sounded posh she looked it. Even in her drab grey linen dress and scorched leather boots there was a refinement about her, but there was also a fearfulness that Emma recognised. She longed to know Sarah's real name. It wouldn't be something commonplace, it would be longer and melodic.

'How do they know our time might be up?' Sarah asked.

'Not sure. They don't tell us anything. But it hurts. The girls do a lot of moaning.' It wouldn't do any good to coat the truth with too much syrup. Sarah Powell had a lot ahead of her. They all did. 'The doctor's horrible, by the way. A real miserly sort. Stay out of his way and don't look him in the eye if you pass him in the corridors.'

'I don't think I've ever been so ill I moaned.' Powell stopped her washing up and looked down at Emma's stomach. 'How pregnant are you?'

Emma's hand went instinctively to her belly. She wasn't that big yet but she would be soon. 'Five months. You?'

'I suppose I must be closer to seven. I'm not sure.'

'Didn't you see a doctor when you were at home?'

'My parents sent me to live with my grandmother as soon as they found out. She lived in Mildura and said there was no need to inform a doctor.'

'Where are your parents now?'

'They live in Sydney, overlooking the harbour.'

'You have come a long way!' Emma was shocked. Most of the girls at the home were from Queensland.

'My grandmother was quite kind about it all but then she died and my father insisted my mother send me away. He knows a lot of people in New South Wales, you see. A lot of them are in politics, so he said it was best if Mother sent me to Brisbane.'

Emma gave her a smile. 'How old are you?'

'Just turned seventeen,' Powell answered in a tremulous quiver. 'You?'

'Eighteen in January—and Powell, don't let anyone catch you chatting about personal information. Be very careful about that.'

'Powell.' She sighed. 'It's not a bad name, I suppose.'
'I like it.'
'Do you like your new name?'
'Harper? It's all right.'

None of the girls asked who a baby's father was or what had happened. Even the new girls understood that. Nobody cared about the bugger anyway, but perhaps it was a way of keeping a little of their self-respect intact, because everything else they did was under scrutiny, whether it was their minds or their bodies. Neither belonged to the girls, according to the sisters.

'Did you have a thorough schooling?' Emma asked, knowing she shouldn't, but they were alone for the moment and she was eager to hear how a girl might have been educated on the better side of the tracks.

'Oh, yes,' Powell responded. 'I can embroider almost anything and I'm fairly excellent on the piano.'

Emma managed to hide her amusement. 'What about history and geography?'

'Didn't do much of either.'

'Art?'

Powell paused in her washing up and grimaced in a self-deprecating manner. 'I'm not too good but perhaps fair.' She looked up. 'To be honest, I'm absolutely useless at anything worthwhile except the piano. I'm not even good at drawing-room chit-chat.'

Emma smiled. 'I think you're marvellous.'

'Really?'

'Absolutely. You've got through so far and you've got a heavenly smile for all the other girls. You've got courage, I can see it.'

Sarah Powell's eyes shone. 'Gosh. Thanks.' She plunged her hands back into the water. 'At least there's not much need for drawing-room chit-chat here.'

Wasn't that the truth.

'You'll see the doctor soon,' Emma said. 'You'll also see the hospital nurse when she turns up to check on us.'

'They're a bit strict here, aren't they? I hadn't expected that.' Powell lifted the last plate out of the sink and pulled the plug. Yesterday, Emma had to teach her how to do the washing up. She was a fast learner and scared of what was to come but she was doing her bit.

'Can you tell me a little more about this place?' Powell asked. 'I'd hate to get anything else wrong. Sister Hyacinth has been quite displeased with me since I arrived.'

Emma stacked the dried plates in order of priority: those without chips for the sisters' dining room cabinet, those with for the girls and the orphans. 'We call her Sister H behind her back. She's in charge but the other sisters aren't too dissimilar. Sister Peter is the petite one but watch her. The others mainly just loathe us and order us about. The sisters are also in charge of the infants' asylum and we work for the children too.' The orphans lived in the house next door and the girls had to use the passageway on the top landing where a dividing hallway had been built years ago, carrying all the food and laundry up two flights of stairs and into the asylum. They had to clean and care for not only the children, the sisters, the servants and the gardening staff but also for themselves.

'Do the children get adopted?'

'Not often.'

'Why not?'

'Nobody wants them, I suppose. They're no longer babies. Some of them get taken to farms and places out in the bush but I expect it's not because the family wants a new son or daughter. More likely they need nimble, labouring hands.'

'Gosh, how sad. Are you getting your baby adopted?'

'We all are.' Emma might have refused to accept it in front of the sisters but she knew she had no choice.

Powell was distracted by footsteps behind them. 'Who's that?' she whispered, indicating a frail-looking blonde, shoulders stooped, head down as she assisted two other girls with getting the crockery to set the table for lunch.

'Garrett. She had her baby a week ago. Now she has to stay for a bit because she's got nowhere to go. I heard Sister Peter say they were going to get her employment as a servant.'

'Is that what she wants?'

'Her family don't want her back, so I don't think it'll matter what she wants.'

'That one?' Powell asked, nodding towards a young girl dithering in the doorway.

'Hetty. She's disabled.'

'She doesn't look it. She looks sweet.'

Hetty was usually on duty in the linen room because the nuns didn't trust her to not burn the house down if they put her anywhere near the kitchen and the stoves. She had to be supervised around the laundry coppers and the wood stove for the irons, and was only allowed to touch the wash in the cold tubs or hang the washing out on the line or bring it in. Emma gave her a hand if she had time—and if the sisters weren't looking. 'It's something in her head,' she told Powell. 'She has problems remembering things. She doesn't even know she's pregnant most of the time.'

'The poor thing! When is she going to have her baby?'

'I think she's only about three months pregnant so she's got ages.'

'What are they going to do with her after?'

Emma didn't know, and part of her didn't want to know. How were they going to tell Hetty she was in pain because she was in labour? She'd be scared, and she'd be on her own. The nurses wouldn't care. Nobody would care.

'Come on, you two!' Mrs Ross the housekeeper said. 'No dawdling, please. Put those dishes away and remember to wipe down the sink and the drainer.' She turned to Hetty. 'You come with me. You can help make the pastry for the apple pies.'

'I love apple pie,' Powell murmured.

'They're for the sisters, not us.'

'Oh, well. I hardly ever got one anyway. Mother says it's servants' food so I only got a slice when I managed to pinch it from the cook.'

'See?' Emma said, pausing in her work. 'I said you were courageous.'

The girl's cheeks flushed. 'I wouldn't dare pinch anything here.'

'No, and you'd better not!'

Powell sighed. 'What about Mrs Ross? I haven't had much to do with her yet.'

The housekeeper had eight children and was usually the one to advise the sisters when a girl's time had come or was almost upon them. Although the doctor was the law on that, sometimes things didn't go according to his schedule and a girl would need to get to the hospital sooner than he'd expected. Mrs Ross always knew. Before the doctor, the nurses or the sisters. Not that anyone gave her acknowledgement for it. Why she was forced to work here, Emma didn't know. Money troubles, probably. She was widowed and unlikely to get better employment. Or maybe she'd simply grown used to the place.

'She's good to the girls who return from the hospital without it being obvious,' Emma said as she picked up a stack of chipped plates. 'She gives them their tasks but doesn't harry them. If a girl can't manage it because she's sad, Mrs Ross makes sure another girl is there to help her.'

'That's terribly thoughtful of her. She's quite softly spoken for a housekeeper. Some of them are dragons.' Powell offered this in the manner of a young woman who knew all about housekeepers.

'I think she's secretly kind,' Emma said. 'But best not to test it.' Nobody knew anything about anyone around here. Nothing for certain, anyway.

* * *

'What happens when we get to the hospital?' Powell asked after lunch as they folded sheets in the large, windowless linen room.

Emma paused. 'I'm not exactly sure.' Some of the girls spoke of what had happened to them in the hospital, and others clamped their mouths and couldn't look anyone in the eye. Those were the ones who had to be given special lessons in how to be getting on with it and how to live with their shame.

'When do they take the babies off us?'

'Straight away. Unless they can't find a good Catholic family, then it takes a few days.'

Many of the couples were unable to have a baby of their own and there were other families where the wife was too old to have another child but they still wanted to add to their brood. Sister Hyacinth and a nurse were constantly on the girls' backs but a welfare lady would arrive towards the end and have what they termed a nice chat to any of the girls whose time was due to put a final stamp on the adoption.

'I think I'll let Sister H know my maternal grandmother was Catholic,' Powell said. 'She might be pleased about that.'

'Doubtful. If I were you I'd just stay quiet about anything and everything.' Emma gave the girl a look. 'Are you saying you're not Catholic?' She'd imagined only Catholic sinners would be allowed to walk the hallways.

Powell frowned. 'Not me, nor my mother once she married my father. I think they might have paid for me to be taken in here.'

'Really?'

'Quite a lot. About seventy pounds. Possibly more.'

'Goodness.' It was a surprise, although the money was surely put to good use. 'Well, I'm sorry you're here, I'm sorry we're all here, but it's lovely to know you.'

Powell smiled. 'You too, Harper. I couldn't have wished for a better teacher. I consider myself very lucky.'

That evening, after dinner, Father Anthony came into the living room, followed by Sister Hyacinth and Sister Peter. All the girls stood, bibles in hand since it was all they had to read between the evening meal and bedtime, while the priest gave them a talking to. He didn't often do this and hardly ever spoke to the girls or to the children in the infants' asylum next door.

He told them of the good the sisters and the church were doing and reminded them they should never talk about their time at the home to anybody. Not even to their families. They were to remember only the benevolence of the sisters and their humane charity.

Emma wondered why he'd suddenly decided to give them a sermon about their situation and if perhaps someone had complained—someone from the outside. But who? Who would know what went on behind these walls and would anyone actually care?

Then Sister Peter clapped her hands and the girls put down their bibles and moved in an orderly fashion out of the room to their dormitory, obedient to the last.

'Goodnight, Harper.'

'Goodnight, Powell. Sleep as much as you can. Remember, we're up at half past five.'

'Gosh, it even sounds early,' Powell said with a yawn.

The dormitory was quiet apart from the shuffling of sheets and the squeak of springs as the girls tossed and fidgeted, attempting to find a comfortable position on the thin mattresses.

Emma turned on her side and went through her ritual, sending good wishes to those she loved. She tried not to think of everyone during the daytime but at night, in the unnerving darkness, they came to mind, so she acknowledged them silently.

Her brothers. Her dad, who must loathe his daughter. She just hoped he wasn't so disappointed and humiliated he couldn't fight the war and keep himself safe.

She'd purposely chosen not to think about her mother so she moved on to Cassie, the forever friend she might never see again. Had she and Eddie set a date for the wedding? Was she planning a beautiful day full of kisses and love? Or were they already married?

Tears blurred her vision and she didn't bother blinking them away. Her world was crowded with troubles and even though Cassie would tell her to dry her eyes, perhaps sometimes it was best to let the tears fall. Maybe they would help wash away the injustice that ached in her heart and burned in her soul.

Chapter Sixteen

November 1944

Emma was on her knees scrubbing the girls' dining room floor as another girl held the mop, sopping up the water and suds. Powell was scouring the rough pine tabletop with a stiff brush, then she'd have to wipe it with a cloth. If the sisters found even a crumb let alone a wet patch they pretty much exploded.

'Sarah Powell. My office. Now.'

Powell jumped and the scrubbing brush landed with a clunk on the floor.

'Pick that up, you idiot girl.'

Emma kept her eyes down until she heard Sister Hyacinth's footsteps retreat from the doorway.

'How does she manage to make my new name sound like something dirty?' Powell asked, running her hands down her apron to straighten the creases.

'Because that's what she believes.' Emma stood, her knees sore to the point of being bruised. 'It's your turn to have a talking to,' she explained as she wiped her hands on her skirt beneath the apron. If they got their aprons soiled they were told off and had to change into a newly starched one. Why they were condemned for a dirty apron, she didn't know. How could they scrub floors without getting their clothing wet? Emma was doubly careful these days. She didn't want to be seen in the corridors wearing only her petticoat ever again. She pulled at the ties at the back of Powell's apron. 'You take this off when you're summoned to the office but don't forget to come get it afterwards.'

Powell sent a fretful look towards the door.

'Go on,' Emma said, giving her a push. 'Just be contrite about absolutely everything.'

Powell inhaled deeply and went after Sister Hyacinth.

Emma got back down on her knees.

'You're too *nice*, Harper.'

Emma looked up at the young woman with the mop. 'Good of you to notice.'

Wendy Stokes—or whoever she really was—was tall to the point of lanky, rosy cheeked and, at twenty-one, older than everyone else. But she didn't have a husband, so here she was. Her straight brown hair might be considered as plain as her looks but there was fire in her belly and all the girls watched out for her temper almost as much as they did that of the sisters.

Emma didn't mind working alongside Stokes. It was good to have someone to cross swords with. A way of letting off steam.

'She'll be a wreck when she comes out of that office,' Stokes said.

'Aren't we all after we've been in there?'

Stokes humphed. 'How did it go with you this morning?'

'The usual,' Emma said. 'You?'

Stokes didn't answer but her cheeks flushed an even deeper red.

'What?' Emma asked.

'Nothing. Bunch of bitches.'

Stokes didn't have long to go now, maybe seven or eight weeks, and Powell less than that. The four full months Emma had left felt like a life sentence. They'd started putting a lot more pressure on her about adopting out her child. Powell never questioned her position and didn't dare answer back so the sisters hadn't picked on her too much yet. But Stokes told them repeatedly she was happy to give up her baby. She said she couldn't wait to get rid of it because it had caused her nothing but anguish. Yet still the sisters found a way to punish her for her rudeness, for wanting to stir people up or for answering back.

Emma blew out an aggrieved breath. 'I'm sick of this,' she said. 'My name is Emma. Emma Hatton. You?'

'Winifred Sinclair. I prefer Wynn.'

Emma smiled. Wynn had answered without even taking a breath. 'Good to meet you, Wynn.'

'Oh, excellent, I'm sure. I'll still be calling you Harper. And don't tell that one we've swapped information,' Wynn added with a tilt of her head towards the doorway.

'Powell? What do you think her name might be?'

Wynn shrugged. 'Something posh.'

'Simone. Maybe Samantha.'

'She'll have a double-barrelled surname, I bet.'

'Do you think?'

'Bound to. She's classy.'

'Do you know where you're going afterwards?' Emma asked as she got back to scrubbing. She was keen to keep the conversation going since they were alone. It would be wonderful to have a friend, even a secret one.

'Back home,' Wynn said bluntly and a little scathingly.

Emma dipped her brush into the pail of soapy water. 'Is that a bad thing?'

'What's it to you?'

'Are you really content to leave without your baby?'

'None of your business.'

Emma felt sure Wynn behaved in this blunt manner simply to release the tension within but she was interested in why. It had to be more than just being here and working all day long. She was clearly fearful about going home. 'I haven't agreed to have my baby adopted,' Emma admitted, wanting to expose a little of her own fears.

Wynn paused and glanced at her, mop in hand. 'Do you have any choice?'

'No.'

'Well then, it's senseless of you to aggravate them.'

'I know it'll happen. I just don't want to admit it even to myself.' Emma guessed Wynn didn't want it to happen either and that's why she was belligerent. She was undoubtedly covering some anguish and showing the world a different persona to the real one. 'Is that how you feel?'

Wynn paled suddenly, her expression filled with distress. 'I don't feel anything. I just want to get back to normal.'

'Is home a nice place?'

Wynn mopped, gaze averted.

'Neither is mine,' Emma told her. But Wynn said nothing more.

Emma guessed Wynn would have as bad a time once she went back home as Emma would. Why else would parents send their daughters here and leave them, without word, without contact, without care? Perhaps Powell would have a worse time than any of them. Her family sounded strict and unrelenting.

'Did you know there are over a thousand fatherless babies out there?' Wynn said. 'Did you know there's a surplus of women and a shortage of men and that I'm going to be a spinster for the rest of my life?'

'Not necessarily.'

Wynn huffed. 'It won't bother me one bit. And you're not going to be a spinster, are you? You're far too beautiful. Some man will snap you up. Especially if you lie about all this stuff.'

Emma wanted to laugh. What man would want her if he saw her now, dressed like this, her hair scraped back in a tight bun, sweat dripping off her forehead and her knuckles as bruised as her knees. 'I'm soiled goods, Wynn. Same as you. I've got to pray twelve times a day for the other women. The ones who have lost husbands in the war and the ones who *will* lose a husband while the war's still going. They'll be widows.'

'That's not your fault.'

'Apparently it is. I've got to be ashamed forevermore because I'm having a child some other, more deserving woman might have had.'

'Is that what Sister H said?' Wynn grimaced. 'She talks a load of cobblers.'

'She said I was here because I'm concealing the fact I'm pregnant. Therefore the natural presumption is that I'm here to rid myself and my family of the shame I've brought them, and to do that I have to have the baby placed out. She said it's why they keep us girls out of sight. Because the sisters are thinking about our poor, wretched families.'

'Sanctimonious cow,' Wynn said.

'Yes, she is. But don't be too hard on Powell next time. She's got to go back home too after this.'

Wynn turned but not before Emma saw another look of disquiet in her eyes. There was nothing Emma could do to ease Wynn's pain until Wynn asked for help. Or at least companionship of a more robust nature. Perhaps Emma having admitted her real name would move things along, an unexpected event that might form a camaraderie between them. Like the one that had brought Emma and Cassie together out on Denham Street after the fight. When she'd seen Frank and he'd kissed her.

It felt like a decade ago.

At the sound of the sisters' subdued voices outside, Emma got back to work, dipping the brush into the pail of soapy water, thoughts of her friend infiltrating her mind.

Where was Cassie now? Already in America wondering about Emma?

It didn't matter. There was nothing Emma could do. Not about any of it.

* * *

A week and a bit before Christmas, Emma walked along the corridor towards the linen room with a slight spring in her step. It was more relief of monotony than actual joy but in this place, every small wonder was something to experience and today she had news to impart.

'Morning,' she said to Wynn.

'It's nearly lunch time.'

'How time flies when one is having fun.'

'What's got into you?'

'I've been given a new task.'

'Whose floor are you washing this time?'

'Well, that's the thing.' Emma hooked her thumbs into the pockets of her apron and leaned her bottom against the table. 'I've been told to get two girls to assist me.'

Wynn glared. 'You expect me to get down on my hands and knees at this stage in my hugeness? I am almost eight months along, you know. I can hardly lift a full pail of water without getting backache.'

'I haven't told you what the task is yet.'

'Get Powell to help you.'

'She's even farther along than you.'

'But she's younger. Fitter. More amenable.'

'Isn't that the truth,' Emma said with a grin.

Wynn mumbled something incomprehensible.

'No, really,' Emma insisted, 'it's a wonderful job. Want to do it with me and Powell?'

The girls had been put together a few times since the start of December and there was a tentative camaraderie building. Nothing had been set in stone regarding this new friendship and they were careful not to let the sisters know of it or they'd be split up, for sure. The sisters probably hadn't even considered there might be a problem with fraternising—something else that wasn't good for their souls—since each girl was as different as mustard, cream and chalk on the same sandwich: Wynn was the mustard, Sarah Powell the cream, which Emma supposed left her as the chalk.

'Do I have a chance to refuse this job?' Wynn asked.

Emma didn't answer.

'Of course I don't! So why bugger up my day with your nonsense? Whatever it is, I'll have to do it, won't I?'

'You won't regret it,' Emma promised with a smile, then halted when she heard Cook's voice. 'Shush.' She put a finger to her lips as she tiptoed to the doorway and peered down the corridor towards the kitchens. 'It's the gardener!'

'Old Tyrell? So what?'

'So he's talking to Cook. I want to listen.' Mr Tyrell hardly ever came into the house and Emma was hardly ever outside of it unless to hang up or bring in the washing. But she'd overheard enough conversations to keep her interest burning.

'He's after a snack, most likely.'

'It's the war. Don't spoil it for me,' Emma pleaded. 'I'm dying to know what's going on. Aren't you?' It was awful not to be given any news from the world. Not even of the war. Not much, anyway.

Wynn shrugged. 'I suppose.' She flung down her sheet and joined Emma in the doorway.

'They're fighting in frigid conditions,' Mr Tyrell was saying to his rapt audience of Cook, her two assistants and, in the background, young Ben the gardener's boy. 'The rain freezes as soon as it lands on 'em. They can't see nothing for the thick fog, it's heavily wooded forest and the Germans have already massacred soldiers *and* civilians. It's total devastation.'

'Christ,' Wynn whispered. 'I almost wish I wasn't hearing this.'

Emma squeezed herself tighter against the door frame. The Battle of the Ardennes had started nearly two weeks ago and it sounded brutal.

'This is it, I reckon,' Mr Tyrell said. 'The last push. It'll be bloody, mind.'

'It'll be bloody freezing, by the sound of things,' Cook exclaimed. 'And what's all this? *You* reckon? Since when have you been the brains of military intelligence?'

'I fought and lived through the Great War, didn't I?'

'But this one isn't the same.'

'I can read, can't I? I've got ears, haven't I? It's all over the papers and the radio broadcasts. I tell you, they're fighting their way through a snowstorm over there.'

'You ever seen snow?' Wynn murmured.

Emma shook her head. Neither was she likely to but it made her wonder about Squadron Leader Robert Allen and his fellow officers in a German POW camp. How were they coping in their Oflag? Did they even know there had been such a large push to win the war in the last year? They probably didn't.

'Does this mean the war will be over by Christmas?'

Everyone in the kitchen turned to stare at Ben.

'Don't be daft, lad. Christmas is only ten days away. It'll take months for the war to end proper. What are you doing in the house anyway?' Mr Tyrell said gruffly. 'Didn't I tell you to get the wheelbarrow out? Go on, out with you!'

Ben's face coloured and he looked like he wished the ground would open up and swallow him whole. He scarpered, dodging a cuff around the ear.

'Poor Ben,' Emma muttered.

'Poor sod,' Wynn agreed.

'I'm telling you, Cook,' Mr Tyrell said as he accepted a slice of warm bread just out of the oven from one of Cook's assistants. 'This is the last push and it's going to be a hard one for all of us.'

Emma pressed her lips together. She couldn't begin to envisage what it would be like to fight through such horror or what it would take to endure. But conquest, triumph and victory must be the forethought of every step taken by those in the front lines. 'I wonder how our diggers in the Pacific are getting on,' she whispered to Wynn. 'I worry about my dad.'

'My dad's out there too.'

'Life as we know it is about to come to an end,' Mr Tyrell announced, lifting a dirt-covered finger to swipe at the melted butter on his chin. 'And life afterwards ... That's anybody's take.'

Wynn sighed as she looked down at Emma. 'Why do I feel the same? Life before, life during, life after.'

'Because that's what it is.' The battle made Emma think about her own predicament. Not that she was putting herself on the same standing as those doing it tough, fighting and witnessing unspeakable things they might never get over. But in the ways of life, of growth of spirit and endeavour, of dealing with the trials and the troublesome times, she felt she was fighting too.

'Wonder what I'll be doing when the war ends,' Wynn mused, going back to her sheet after Cook began talking about more food deprivations and Mr Tyrell had politely requested the possibility of another slice of warm bread and perhaps a dollop of jam.

'I might still be here,' Emma said, aghast at the thought. 'I'm not due until the end of March.' She'd miss everything. Maybe not the homecomings, because surely it would take months for their men to return home, but the thrill, the relief. The dancing and laughter. The sharing of victory and the toasting for a better future, even if it was only with cups of rationed tea.

She looked at the floor she'd scrubbed so often she knew almost every grain and scratch, an unwelcome thought encompassing all the others. Her family wouldn't care that she was missing out by not celebrating with them once the end of the war came. They might not even allow her to go out once she got home. Or she might be sent to stay with Doris, who definitely wouldn't let her out. But apart from the lack of love or respect from her family, there was a new consideration in her head: Nobody, except her mother and aunt, knew the truth about what had happened to her. Nobody even knew where she was. She might as well already be dead. A vague memory in the lives of those she loved or cared about. Because nobody knew the truth. How was a person supposed to get real about that?

'What's wrong this time?' Wynn asked. 'You're scrunching your face. You'll get wrinkles doing that.'

Emma shivered in the coolness of the windowless linen room with the brick walls and stone floor. 'Nothing's wrong,' she said, trying to still the rushing of thoughts.

'So what's this new job I've got to help you with?' Wynn asked. 'And when do we have to do it?'

Emma drew a breath and returned to the table and the manchester. 'You're not going to believe it.'

'Try me,' Wynn said, not even glancing up from the sheet she was folding.

'There's some priest coming for a visit—'

'Oh, marvellous. Can hardly wait.'

'And because Mrs Ross will have her hands full of housekeeping duties for this venerable gentleman's arrival, Sister H has announced that I, and two girls of my choosing, so long as they're good, sweet, amenable girls,' she added with a grin, 'should dust the library twice a week.'

Wynn looked up. 'Every week?'

'At least until this priest arrives. That's happening in the New Year, so yes. Every week for the time being.'

'You're joking!'

'No word of a lie.'

'On our own? With the door shut?'

'Just the three of us, and I believe the door will need to be firmly closed. After all, the sisters won't want the other girls wandering in and touching the books with their dirty fingers.'

Wynn smiled, a real smile that reached her eyes. 'I knew you'd be worth knowing.'

Emma laughed, and it felt *so* good to laugh.

Chapter Seventeen

The three of them were in the library the day Sarah Powell admitted to her real name.

Emma swept her gaze over the crowded shelves. She was in awe as soon as she stepped into the room, flicking the duster over the plentiful books as fast as she could so she had a chance to pause and run an eye over the spines and the book titles. She hadn't been allowed to bring her own books to the home, and even though she had read each of them numerous times, she missed them. Books were like a silent companion. Always there, waiting to be picked up, offering insight or giving the reader a chance to question but never answering back.

Christmas had come and gone with no major difference to their normal working day. No presents. No word from family. Nothing to denote the day as being different from any other except for prayer, thankfulness and gratefulness for what the good Lord and the sisters were doing for them, along with another reminder from Father Anthony to keep their mouths closed about their life here at all times. Although he'd phrased it differently.

'That's it!' Emma exclaimed.

'What?'

'Father Anthony and his sermons. It's because the priest is visiting. The sisters must want to show themselves in a better light.'

'Oh, good,' Wynn said. 'Perhaps they'll feed us properly while he's here.'

'One can only hope,' Powell responded.

Emma turned back to the bookshelves, pleased to have deduced the reason for the Father's talks if nothing else in her life so far. There had also been a special service held on Christmas Day for the Allied forces and for every Australian and New Zealander out there fighting. The Battle of the Ardennes was ongoing, the bloodiest they had known, and Emma was still in a quandary about no-one knowing where she was. Of course her mother or Doris would come to pick her up afterwards—how could she think they wouldn't? They couldn't just leave her here. The only thing she had to consider was how to hold her head up when she got back to Blueholm Bay and how to stave off any gossip. But she had weeks and weeks to consider that and the new jobs they'd been given were genuinely to be thankful for. Dusting the library wasn't the only treat but it might be Emma's favourite. Or perhaps it was raking the leaves and the opportunity to inhale all the fresh air they wanted. The gardens had to be just so in case the priest fancied a walk before dinner or after prayers.

'I never thought I would enjoy dusting quite so much,' she said as she flicked the emu feathers on her long-handled duster over the spines of the books on the mahogany shelves. She was alive, she had friends, what more could she expect under the circumstances? It was no use having gumption, which Cassie had told her she possessed, when there wasn't an opportunity to use it. She was incarcerated.

'Wish we could do this dusting lark every day,' Wynn said dreamily. She was taking a break in the armchair and if one of the sisters walked in they'd have to pretend she'd fainted. At eight months along, her belly had grown huge. Bigger than Powell's and Powell was closer to her time than any of the girls in the home.

'We ought to be grateful for the two days a week,' Powell said.

'Oh, I am,' Wynn said in a saccharine tone. 'Very grateful.'

'It's better than washing up, Stokes. Those sinks are so deep I sometimes have to plunge my whole arms into the water to find a spoon.'

Emma smiled at the look of disbelief on Powell's sweet face, her bright blue enquiring eyes and tipped-up nose framed by fine golden hair that kept escaping its tight bun. The epitome of an upper-class young lady who ought to be home playing the piano and wondering what frock to wear for the afternoon.

'Like as not you'll think differently about your servants when you get home,' Wynn said. Emma glanced at Wynn to check if she was being snarky, but she was smiling.

'Oh, I will! Most certainly.'

'Have you seen the size of my ankles?' Wynn said, changing the subject as she lifted her feet off the carpet and rested them on a footstool that matched the armchair. 'Is it normal, do you think?'

Emma peered. 'It probably is.'

'Will mine get that big?' Powell asked with a frown of concern.

'Not now. I doubt it anyway.'

'Unless your ankles swell in the last few days,' Wynn said with a wink. 'They might get even bigger than mine. You might not get your party shoes on when you go home.'

'That's not nice, Stokes,' Emma scolded.

'Sorry, Harper.'

'I doubt there'll be any parties anyway,' Powell said, looking despondent.

'Cheer up,' Wynn advised. 'You're not gone yet. You've got another two weeks or so to torment me with your scolding.'

'I would never do that! Not to a friend.'

Wynn offered what might be the most affectionate smile Emma had seen her produce. 'Let's talk about that friendship, shall we?' Wynn said, spreading her fingers on the arms of the armchair.

'Yes, please!' Powell darted across the room and braced herself against the door, arms outstretched, hands on the door frame. 'I'll stand here and if anyone comes in, they'll hit me first so you get a chance to get up out of the chair.'

'Powell, there's no need for that—'

'No, really, Harper! I don't mind. Stokes is so much bigger than me. It must be tremendously difficult carrying that bulk around.'

'Thanks very much,' Wynn mumbled with an outraged scowl.

Emma chuckled at Powell's innocent and well-meant remark but halted when Wynn pulled herself upright in the chair and spoke again.

'I suggest we tell each other our real names.'

Powell gasped. 'Gosh! How daring!'

It would be best to put a stop to Wynn's playing around but Emma was also desperate to know the truth and at some point, either she or Wynn might stumble in front of Powell and inadvertently call each other by their real names.

'Are we really going to tell?' Powell said with a gleam of excitement in her eyes. 'How awfully brave!'

'You go first,' Wynn said.

'That's not fair!' Emma exclaimed.

'Oh, no! Let me, please!'

'Are you sure?'

'We've already told each other ours,' Wynn said, 'so you're the last to own up.'

'Now that really *isn't* fair!' Powell said, stamping her foot. 'How come I get to go last?'

'Because we didn't trust you.'

'Wynn, stop it!'

'Oops,' Wynn said, grinning.

Emma's shoulders sank. 'Sorry. I momentarily forgot.' She turned to Powell with a hand outstretched to Wynn. 'Winifred Sinclair but she prefers Wynn. And I'm Emma Hatton.'

Powell was gaping as she looked between the two. 'Wynn? Emma?' Then she beamed. 'It's wonderful to meet you both and I think you have splendid names.'

'So?' Wynn asked. 'What's yours?'

The silence in the room drew in on them as Powell took a breath.

'Susannah Poulson-Taylor,' she said with a look of circumspection, as though she were hopeful of a decent response after making the admission but not actually expecting one.

'Double-barrelled!' Wynn said as she thumped the arm of the chair. 'I told you!'

'Susannah,' Emma said, rolling the word in her mouth. 'It's a beautiful name.'

'Do you really like it?'

'I love it.'

Susannah clapped her hands in glee. 'Emma, Wynn and Susannah—the newest and bestest of friends.'

'Oh God, what have we started?'

'Remember now,' Emma said to Susannah, 'we're Stokes, Harper and Powell unless we're on our own.'

'Which is twice a week at least!' Susannah Poulson-Taylor said with a heavenly smile.

They eyed each other a few seconds more, creeping joy on their faces, clearly enjoying the moment.

'Right.' Emma turned to the bookshelves and flicked her duster. 'Let's get on with it.'

Wynn leaned back in the armchair and Susannah moved from the door to the drapes on the windows.

'Alice Walker went on the horse and cart this morning,' Susannah said not a half-minute later.

'I heard her yelling,' Wynn said, intertwining her fingers on the mound of her stomach.

'It must hurt, then.'

'I guess,' Emma said to Susannah with an apologetic glance.

It was the ignorance every girl here was kept in that angered her so much. It was unfair to let a young girl go through pregnancy and labour without giving her any idea what might happen to their bodies or what might go wrong. It wasn't only unfair—it was inhumane. She'd put a bet down that married expectant mothers were told a lot more than the unmarried ones.

The girls who came back from the hospital were willing to share some information but not straight away, they were too sad, and their bodies were bruised, too. Their arms and their ankles. 'Try not to fight,' one girl had told Emma, which scared her half to death. What would she be fighting? The pain? The moment the baby squeezed its way out? Or something else?

Alice Walker couldn't take much pain. She'd created an almighty fuss when she got a splinter in her thumb from collecting kindling for the wood stove.

Emma looked towards the window and the heavy drapes where Susannah was dusting the windowsill. They had to keep the blinds and the curtains closed so the sunlight didn't fade the book spines or the furniture. The air was heavy and still but if a slice of sunshine found its way in, the dust motes sparkled in the sudden ray, like tiny stars in the night. These days, Emma liked to ensure she found wonder in things she might have previously ignored. Like the motes and the shape of the clouds, or the aroma and the taste in the air, whether it be from dried leaves and grass clippings underfoot when bringing in the washing or the scintillating tang of a plum tart just out of Cook's oven that made a person's mouth water.

'Does your family have a library like this one?' Wynn asked Susannah.

'Quite a bit bigger.'

'Thought as much. Bet you don't have one like this either, Hatton.'

Emma looked over her shoulder. 'Not quite as spacious.'

Wynn laughed and Emma continued her dusting, moving to another bookshelf. She didn't dare pull a book from the shelf; she felt like a thief just reading the titles, which made her think of Harry Colson and the big house. Was he sitting in his library now, penning a letter to his sister or business compatriots? Had he ever ruminated on the secret he'd entrusted Emma with? He may have heard from Ivy Williams that Emma had been sent to Brisbane to supposedly care for her aunt's parents-in-law and that might settle any worry he may have that she'd open her mouth and blab. But he likely wouldn't care one way or the other and anyway, the whole of Blueholm Bay probably knew about Cynthia and her prisoner of war squadron leader husband by now.

'Have you seen any books about this Saint Philomena?' Wynn asked.

'Not yet,' Emma replied. She had discovered the name of the home on the letter paper in Sister Hyacinth's office: The Holy Refuge of Saint Philomena.

'I wonder what good things she did,' Susannah said.

'No idea,' Wynn murmured.

'Something self-sacrificing yet deeply beneficial to others,' Susannah said, then smiled at Emma. 'I'm glad I don't have to dust the office like you, Harper. I mean, Emma,' she corrected. 'I'd be a nervous wreck in case I knocked over some ornament or spilled the ink.'

'It's not so bad if you take care.'

Working for Sister Hyacinth had suddenly become a daily chore for Emma. She had to collect books and accounting sheets from drawers and cupboards, or take dictation for letters to bishops that Sister Hyacinth would later type up. Sister Hyacinth felt it was the best way to keep an eye on Emma because she was still refusing to have her baby placed out, even though she had no choice, especially now that she'd learned it was her mother, as her guardian, who had the final say.

With Mrs Ross so busy, Emma had also been dusting and sweeping in the office every afternoon. It was better than scrubbing floors and she was mostly left alone to do it. She enjoyed the peace and quiet even though she was only ever in the room on her own for ten or fifteen minutes at a time. There was a telephone in the office. She'd often looked at it and had once even lifted the receiver. Just to dust it, mind. It would be a crazy thing to try to use it. It would be downright stupid. Even if Emma pretended to be one of the welfare women who visited, the exchange operator would undoubtedly be suspicious and demand to speak to Sister Hyacinth.

It was a bitter disappointment, because it would be wonderful to hear Cassie's voice. If she was still in the country. Emma had no way of finding out. She'd made up so many stories about what might have happened to Cassie that she'd almost run out of imaginings. Was she in America being waited on hand and foot by Eddie's prosperous family? Or had they disliked her on sight and sent her back to Australia? But it did no good to dwell on her friend's new life, and Emma had recently begun using her brain for other things. Things that kept her mentally occupied.

'I read something the other day about girls like us,' she told the other two.

'Where exactly do you find your reading material?' Wynn enquired with a rise of her eyebrows. 'You don't even take a book from the shelves you're dusting.'

'Cook's assistant asked me to take some meat that had been delivered to the food safe. So I unwrapped it and snuck the sheet of newspaper away and read it. I take my luck where I find it. Anyway, it was an article in *The Northern Miner*.'

'That's Charters Towers. How did a newspaper from Charters Towers get here?'

'It's paper, Wynn. I expect it had been all the way to Cairns and back before it got to us. Now, can you please stop interrupting and let me tell you what I read.' Emma took a breath. 'It was an article about girls like us and how to lessen the likelihood of us turning to prostitution. Sorry,' she added as Susannah blushed, 'but it's important for us to know what they're thinking.'

'What who's thinking?' Wynn asked.

'The government and such. In this instance, some woman from the Commonwealth Health Department who reported to the National Health and Medical Research Council.'

'What a mouthful.'

'According to her, all the medical people testify that most prostitutes begin by having an illegitimate baby, and the consensus is that if we were rehabilitated and taught to care for our babies, as well as being found employment, the likelihood of us regressing to such a degrading position would be greatly lessened.'

Susannah was open-mouthed. 'What exactly does that mean?'

Wynn humphed. 'They're saying if we're brought into line they might find a way of making us proper human beings again.'

'They mentioned the possibility of a maintenance allowance. Say for a year, so the mother can get used to caring for the baby and also find work.'

'Gosh, that would mean we could keep our babies!'

'Don't get excited,' Wynn told Susannah. 'It's just talk in the newspaper. Nothing will happen for years, if it happens at all.'

'That's defeatist talk, Wynn. One day it might.'

'I'll remember you said that, Hatton.'

Susannah sighed and sat on the arm of the sofa. 'Do you know who's supposed to be getting yours?' she asked Wynn.

'Some woman who wants one ready made. She has two, but the second had something wrong with it so she gave it up.'

Susannah's eyes popped. 'Why?'

'Something about its heart not being good enough. It's going to die.'

'I don't understand why she gave it up.'

'Because she wants a perfect one.'

'Oh my goodness.' Susannah's hand flew to her chest. 'How terribly heartless.'

Emma met Wynn's eye, warning her they should change the subject. Wynn shrugged but didn't say more. Sometimes they overheard the sisters mumbling and any information about their unborn babies and where they might end up was a godsend to any of the girls willing to eavesdrop. Some girls didn't want to know but Emma was desperate for any information she could get.

'I think mine's going to a respectable family.' Susannah offered this with a look of fright in her eyes. 'They're probably in trade, but I'm hoping they're quite well off.'

Emma's baby was destined for a Catholic family too, which she'd recently discovered had now been chosen, so no chance of spending a few days in the hospital weaning. It was a baker and his wife and they already had five children. They wanted more but the woman couldn't get pregnant. Sister Peter called her Mrs

Houlihan and she called Emma's unborn child the Houlihan baby.

Emma let her duster drop to her side. Her baby was going to be one of a string of children getting fat from all the cakes their daddy baked. 'I don't want my baby to be a Houlihan,' she said, momentarily loathing her mother for not having given her half a chance.

'You're lucky to have overheard that much information in the first place,' Wynn said. 'And I don't know why you're so bothered. Look at me! I'm the size of a horse! If I had more strength in my limbs I could probably pull that cart all the way to the hospital.'

Susannah giggled. 'You're too funny, Wynn.'

'Aren't I?' Wynn responded, letting her head fall back on the chair.

'It won't be a Houlihan to you,' Susannah said to Emma. 'Not in your heart. It will always be yours.'

But only in her memory, and what if Emma died in childbirth? Who would be told, other than her mother? She and Doris would make up some story about her being hit by a motor car or knocked unconscious by a horse and cart outside Doris's in-laws' house, succumbing to death without ever waking up.

She put a hand on her belly and spread her fingers, always amazed that a child was within her, growing every day, every hour. If it was a girl, she was going to call her Grace, and if it was a boy, she'd probably settle for Douglas, after her father. Not that anyone would take notice of what she wanted. She could cling onto her child after she'd given birth and all they'd do was smack her around the ear and take little Douggie Houlihan off her.

She'd already begun to envisage the boy as he grew up and she wanted to picture him in a big flowery garden, maybe riding a pony. He'd have a toothy smile and he'd wobble on little chubby legs. Until he grew up to be a man. He'd be as handsome as his real father by that point, and his smile would sparkle. Or, if it was Grace, she would have a champagne-bubble smile, but she'd be gracious and refined and might even speak French. Except Emma had trouble picturing anything a Grace Houlihan might do except be taught how to bake and be covered in flour from dawn to dusk.

'Are we nearly finished in here?' Wynn asked.

Emma nodded distractedly. Every imagining of her child growing up surrounded by niceties and love was damaging in so many ways. If her baby was forced to toil and sweat for its new parents she would never know. She would never know her child and it would never know its mother or anything about her.

It was a heartbreaking thought.

'Wish I could fall asleep here,' Wynn said.

Emma turned, attempting to banish the gloomy mood she'd got herself into. 'Don't forget to straighten that cushion once you get off the chair.'

'You and I have got the raking to do next, so that's one good thing.'

'Fresh air!' Susannah said. 'Lucky things! I've got to go up to the asylum next.'

'You've got more energy than us to begin with,' Wynn said, pushing herself out of the chair. 'Those stairs don't worry you like they do me and Emma, but it doesn't mean we're about to have a picnic out there.'

'I still wish I was coming with you. It's creepy in the asylum. Not because of the children!' Susannah added quickly. 'I just mean I don't like the top floor.'

'It's where our dormitory is. You're up there all night,' Wynn argued.

Susannah gave a half-hearted smile. 'It's just something I keep having nightmares about.'

'What?' Emma asked.

'I don't know. I get a bad feeling sometimes.'

'You'll be fine!' Wynn said as she turned to plump the cushion. 'Stop complaining.'

Out in the hallway, Emma closed the library door and Susannah took all three long-handled dusters off Wynn while Wynn retied her apron.

'Powell!'

They turned at the sound of Sister Peter's voice, not having heard her footsteps on the carpeted stairs.

'Take up fresh sheets and a blanket to the dormitory,' she said to Susannah, her hands clasped gently in front of her. She was a small woman and although she hardly ever raised her voice or frowned, the sting from one of those petite hands could burn for an hour.

'I'm supposed to be up in the asylum next, sister.'

'Forget that. Ruby Forsyth soiled her bed during the night. Change the linen.'

Emma held her breath. The last time Ruby wet the bed, a number of girls had tried to hide it and sneak fresh linen upstairs but one of them had been caught and she and Ruby had been taken to the cellar, where they'd been locked in for the night.

Emma wasn't going to ask what punishment Ruby would be getting this time but knew she'd be monitored from now on. Every evening before she went to bed and every morning when she woke. It wasn't her fault. She was only fifteen. She was frightened.

'Yes, sister,' Susannah said and without a backwards glance at Emma and Wynn, she ran across the hallway as fast as her bulk would allow and up the stairs, forgetting to hand back the dusters she was holding, the emu feathers bobbing above the top of her golden head.

'Get on with your work,' Sister Peter told Emma and Wynn before making her way to the office.

Wynn stuck out her tongue behind the sister's back but Emma couldn't find a smile.

'What do you think they'll do to Ruby?' she asked.

'Don't know, but remind me to remind Powell she's got to put the dusters back in the linen room after she's finished in the asylum or there'll be hell to pay.'

'You're being kind, Stokes,' Emma said. 'Don't show that trait too often or people will start noticing.'

'I'm just looking after me!' Wynn replied, throwing Emma a grin. 'If she does forget I'm likely to get the same hell.'

Emma found a genuine smile at last. 'Me too,' she said, and followed Wynn. 'Don't forget me.'

'As if any of us could forget you, Harper.'

They might one day, but not today. Today the sun was shining and no matter how small the sense of liberty, Emma was going to enjoy every moment of being out in the garden.

Chapter Eighteen

The lower garden, where Emma and Wynn were working, was situated at the side of the house, running down a slope. At the bottom was a brick wall that ran almost the whole width of the garden. Behind it were old bedsteads and thin, stained mattresses and piles of junk that must have been there for years. Last week, Wynn had stolen two slices of pineapple before they scooted out to the gardens. They'd devoured them sitting on old crates behind the brick wall, thankful for the luxury of a five-minute breather but making sure they leaned forwards so the juice didn't stain their aprons. After the famine, it had been a feast.

Emma paused in her raking and waved at the gardener's boy. 'Hello, Ben!' Thirteen-year-old Ben was the laziest so-and-so known to humanity according to the sisters, yet Emma had never seen him do anything but work from the moment he woke until dinner time. He'd been brought up in the infants' asylum from a baby but nobody wanted to adopt him so he was stuck here, which was why the sisters had put him to work. Without pay, mind you. He got his board and lodgings and was supposed to be grateful for it.

Ben put his head down and ignored them as he trundled by with his wheelbarrow. Once the girls had raked a few pyramids he'd collect the leaves and take them to a burn pile.

'That little bugger looks like he could use half-a-dozen jam sandwiches,' Wynn said.

'He is a bit scrawny, isn't he? Perhaps I'll pinch him one.'

'He'd tell on you.'

'No, he wouldn't.'

Wynn looked up. 'How would you know?'

'I just do. I bet you a pound he wouldn't tell on me.'

Wynn guffawed. 'I'll expect it by mail once you get out of here,' she said. 'The whole pound, mind you.'

Emma grinned. 'I'll expect *your* pound by mail too, because I know I'm right. He wouldn't tell.'

'Where shall I send this pound?' Wynn said, leaning on her rake. '*If* I lose.'

Emma didn't know where Wynn came from and they hadn't asked each other much about their before lives, perhaps preferring to keep a part of themselves disconnected from the home, but the thought of Blueholm Bay and the consequences of Miriam Hatton finding a letter addressed to Emma Hatton put a halt to her amusement. 'Never mind. Let's not argue this afternoon.'

'Why? What's different about this afternoon?'

'We're out. Let's enjoy it.'

The occasional breeze blew over them, the sun shone on their faces and Emma wanted to ignore the gossamers of worries in her mind. She wanted to focus on the stirring of the leaves on the tall gum trees. The twittering of birds. The feeling of freedom when outside the confines of the cold, stone walls of the home.

'Do you think Mrs Ross likes us girls?' she asked as she began yet another pyramid of leaves.

'She's a housekeeper dealing with a full house. She's busier every minute of the day than we are. She probably hasn't got time to think about us.'

'I like her. I think she's kind.'

'I don't mind her,' Wynn said. 'She's good when it comes time to sort the girls out and she leaves them alone when they come back.'

'Her name is Helen.'

Wynn looked over. 'How do you know?'

'Mr Tyrell calls her Helen and she calls him William. She must have been attractive in her youth. You can tell, even now.'

'I suppose she is quite attractive, given her age,' Wynn said. 'They call her the housekeeper but really she's just a glorified charwoman. Is she having an affair with Tyrell, do you think? Perhaps they'll get married and she'll leave.'

'I bet not. He's a lot older than her, and she's already got a houseful.'

'You mean she's got more now than she'd have if she married again?'

'Don't you see?' Emma explained. 'If she married old Tyrell he'd make her give up her job so she could keep his house. Then where would she and all her children be? Reliant on him. It doesn't seem right when she's capable of earning her own wage.'

Wynn pursed her mouth. 'Quite the smarty pants, aren't you?'

'Thanks for noticing,' Emma said with a smile.

'If you think she's kind, why is she working in this place?'

'I expect it's because of the money, but don't you think it's also possible she wants to be here? To help in whatever small way she can? I've seen her let some of the girls get away with things the sisters would slap them for. Like pinching a slice of meat off their lunch platters.'

'Don't tell her I steal whatever I can.'

'We ought to pinch a jam sandwich for young Ben.'

'You're so *nice* all the time. It grates on my nerves.'

Before Emma had a chance to put Wynn in her place with some witty remark, Wynn spoke again.

'I suppose we could pinch something for the little bugger. I'll do it. I'm better at stealing than you.'

Wynn carried on raking but Emma paused a moment longer. Sometimes Mrs Ross glanced at the girls as they were huddled over hot irons or sooty grates, and Emma always felt the woman was looking into her soul. 'She *is* kind.' As was Wynn, although heaven help anyone who said it to her face.

'Mrs Ross? Why are we still discussing her?'

The sound of running footsteps on the path behind them made the girls turn.

'What are you doing out here?' Emma asked Lorraine Freeman.

'I have to get the mop!'

'They're not usually kept in the garden,' Wynn said acerbically. 'What have you done? And give us one good reason why we should help you.'

'Hush, Stokes,' Emma said, alarmed by the fraught expression on Lorraine's face. 'What is it, Lorraine? Why do you need the mop and what's the panic?'

'I have to get towels too. You have to help me! They told me I had to get old towels.'

'Why?' Emma asked, concern rising.

'It's Powell. And the baby,' the girl said, arms flapping at her sides.

Wynn dropped her rake. 'What's happened?'

'She fell down the stairs. The whole flight! Mrs Ross got the baby and Powell has to go to the hospital. I think there's blood everywhere!'

Terror shot through Emma. 'The baby?'

'I'm going to be sick,' Lorraine said, gripping her apron. 'And I haven't even seen the blood yet!'

'Oh, Christ,' Wynn said, and strode towards the house. Emma dropped her rake and ran after her.

Inside, the corridors were empty.

'What the hell is going on,' Wynn said in a shaky tone.

Emma's heart was thumping. 'I don't know.' The baby ... Susannah had given birth ...

'Girls!'

They turned at the sound of Mrs Ross's voice. She was walking calmly down the corridor.

'Please tell us,' Emma begged. 'What's happened to Sarah Powell?'

Mrs Ross herded them further down the corridor. 'Linen room. There's nothing you can do out in the entrance hall. Where's Lorraine?'

'I'm here!' Lorraine came charging in from outside, skidding to a halt, her leather boots squeaking on the floorboards.

'Calm down,' Mrs Ross told her. 'Amelia is waiting for you in the hallway. She has towels.'

'Don't make me go,' Lorraine said. 'I don't want to see the blood.'

'Don't be silly, Lorraine. There's hardly any blood. Now go. Do as you're told and stop this carry-on.'

Lorraine's face held an expression of abject misery but she went on her way.

Mrs Ross indicated Emma and Wynn enter the linen room then pushed the door to but didn't close it. 'Calm yourselves. Powell is going to be all right.'

Wynn's hand flew to her throat. 'Thank God.'

'She was carrying too much and tripped on the stairs from the asylum. She fell down a whole flight and that brought on the birth.'

'Did the baby die?' Wynn asked, sounding like she could hardly catch her breath.

Mrs Ross shook her head.

'Is it going to the hospital with Powell?'

'It appears to be quite well. It's being attended to by the nurse and the doctor has been called for. Then it will be handed over to its new family.'

'But Susannah hasn't even had time to get to know it!' Wynn complained.

Mrs Ross regarded her steadily. 'I remind you not to refer to Sarah Powell by any other name.'

'I don't care about that. Neither should you.'

'Was it a boy or a girl?' Emma asked.

'Did they tell her?' Wynn said. 'Does she know?'

Mrs Ross firmed her shoulders. 'You needn't concern yourselves.'

'Oh, sweet Jesus! They didn't tell her, did they?'

'She was hurt and bruised and almost unconscious due to the pain and the shock. It all happened quickly.'

'But that's not the point!' Wynn said, slapping the tabletop.

'Surely she could have been given a few minutes with her baby,' Emma said. 'It's unfair otherwise.'

'Are you saying they refused, Mrs Ross? Are you saying they took it off her as soon as it was born?'

Mrs Ross hesitated, but only for a moment. 'It is what it is.'

Emma's heart broke. What had sweet Susannah ever done wrong to anyone for this to happen to her?

'Can we see her?' Emma pleaded. 'Just quickly, so we can say goodbye.'

'You know that won't be allowed.'

'How did she fall?' Wynn asked, her voice now so constricted it was as though she'd had to drag a breath from her lungs to speak. 'What was she carrying?'

'The bed sheets, a pillow and a few other things. She tripped on a feather duster that fell out of her arms.'

'Oh, God, no!' Wynn cried, covering her face with her hands.

'She's mostly badly bruised, no breaks,' Mrs Ross said. 'There's no need to be alarmed.'

'But it's my fault!' Wynn turned an anguished expression Emma's way. 'She forgot to give them back to us. I had time! I should have followed her and got the dusters and I didn't do it.'

'No,' Emma said, moving to Wynn's side. 'It's not your fault.'

'It's nobody's fault,' Mrs Ross said. 'She'll be sent home from the hospital in a few days after she's been checked by the doctor.'

'She shouldn't have had them with her!' Wynn cried. 'She shouldn't have been trying to carry them along with everything else. She lost her baby!'

'Wynn, the baby's alive—'

'But she still lost it! She wasn't even given a moment to kiss it. I'm right, aren't I, Mrs Ross?'

The housekeeper's gaze, always so steady and unrevealing, suddenly filled with compassion. 'There's no need to worry about any of it.'

'But I do! I worry about Susannah and how she'll cope.'

'She'll be heartbroken,' Emma said. 'Surely somebody will tell her something about her baby?'

'We must not speak of these things. She will be taken care of by her parents and that's all you need to know.'

'They don't want her!' Wynn said, her anguish rising. 'They'll treat her like dirt!'

'Stokes,' Mrs Ross said steadily. 'Control yourself. For your own sake.'

Wynn took a deep breath and stood tall. 'My name is Wynn. Winifred Sinclair.'

'Stop it at once.'

'I'm Wynn. I'm Winifred Sinclair!'

'Wynn ...' Emma put a hand on Wynn's arm to halt her from saying more.

'Go about your business, both of you,' Mrs Ross said. 'Replace your dirty aprons and get on with your next tasks. It's all you can do.'

Wynn swiped a hand over her head when the housekeeper left, her cheeks as white as the folded sheets on the shelves surrounding them. 'I don't think I can take much more.'

'You can!' Emma said. 'You will. You have to.'

'You don't understand.'

'Yes, I do.'

Wynn's face crumpled. 'I'm sick of it!'

Emma took hold of her arms. 'Stop it, Wynn. Please stop.'

'I hate it here, do you hear me? I hate it!'

'I know, Wynn, I know.'

'These old women who run this place, they're nothing but petty, self-righteous, bullying cows—'

'That is *enough*!'

They jumped apart at the sound of Sister Peter's voice.

'Sister,' Emma said quickly. 'I'm sorry. We got a bit upset. We just heard about Powell.'

'None of your business.'

'We're just taking a damned moment to mourn her loss!' Wynn yelled. 'Can't you give us two bloody seconds to do that?'

'Stokes,' Emma said warningly.

'Wendy Stokes, you will remain in this room overnight.'

Fear replaced the distress in Emma's chest. 'Sister—'

Sister Peter's expression soured, her pea-like eyes turning as black as stone. 'Leave,' she told Emma.

Emma stepped forwards, hands pressed together in supplication. 'Sister, can I please speak to you? Can I please explain? We are so very sorry about what you heard. It was shock. Nothing more. We mean no disrespect. We promise.'

'Get out.'

'Sister Peter—'

'I said out!'

Emma glanced at Wynn, who'd frozen on the spot, panic visible on her face and in her darkened brown eyes. Emma moved to the doorway.

'Sister Peter,' Wynn said.

'You will stay here until morning.'

'But there isn't a window. There's no air in here, sister! I'll throw up if you lock me in.'

'Perhaps you should have considered the consequences before your outburst.'

Sister Peter turned and Emma blanched, scampering backwards and out of the doorway as the nun took the keys from a hook and closed the door to the room with a gentle hand, the lock clicking.

'Sister Peter!' Wynn called, thumping on the door. 'Please! I'll go crazy in here!'

Emma's knees were trembling so badly she had to put a hand on the wall to steady herself.

'Come away,' Sister Peter told Emma. 'There will be no dinner for any of the girls this evening. There will be bible reading then bed. Advise the others,' she said, before making her way down the corridor.

Emma stared at her retreating back, wanting to fall to her bruised knees and beg forgiveness for every girl in the home. For Wynn, for Ruby, for whoever was next. But what use would it do? Nobody would care, not one of them.

The girls would probably never hear anything about Susannah again but it wouldn't mean she'd be forgotten. Emma vowed to remember each of them. Every girl she'd met or worked alongside.

Wipe those tears from your eyes and get real. It's the only way you'll get through.

Emma covered her face with her hands, her body racked with anger. How had she fallen so quickly into the trap of acquiescing, of feeling oddly content, of being used to all this? The tiredness, the constant hunger, the worry about doing something wrong in front of the nuns or trying to see something pleasant in the bleakness. Looking for a rainbow, seeking out respite in its most minuscule form.

No more! No more.

She'd lost so much already. Her reputation, her freedom, the ability to help with the war work. It had all been ripped from her the moment she stepped into the air-raid shed with Frank. But she wasn't going to die. She was alive and she needed someone to know how she was faring. Someone who would care. She wanted Cassie to know where she was, who she was now, how she'd changed, what she'd already lost and would lose after she gave up her child, and how she was going to fight it. Fight injustice until she died. Even if fighting took her nowhere.

'What are you doing?' Sister Peter asked, her quiet voice resonating in the empty corridor. 'I told you to follow me.'

Determination swept over Emma, adrenalin flying through her system. She had to be strong now. Strong and resilient, so she could help Wynn, and Ruby, and anyone else who needed to feel loved and cared for.

'My apologies, sister,' she said, keeping her voice as contained as the nun's. 'I was wiping the tears from my eyes.'

Chapter Nineteen

January 1945

Emma had decided it was too risky to try to reach Cassie using the sisters' telephone but the seed of an idea of how to contact her friend had grown and she was running with it.

She glanced at the closed door of Sister Hyacinth's office. She'd moved an armchair in front of it and if anyone pummelled on the door, demanding she open it, she'd explain she'd been moving furniture in order to sweep beneath the rugs. There was paper and envelopes on the desk she'd just polished, after moving aside the correspondence tray, the pen and ink stand, the framed image of Mother Mary and an old stone Sister Hyacinth used to sharpen her letter opener.

Her heart was pounding but otherwise she was calm.

Dearest Cassie,

I'm unsure how I will get this letter to you but I have stumbled upon the opportunity to write and will somehow find a way to mail it.

Please do not reply. I fear it will get me into trouble. Not that I want to worry you—I loathe that you will be concerned about me—but life is not the easiest for we girls at this home and I want someone in my world to know what's happened to me and how I hope to get through.

They keep us inside day and night. We are used like unpaid servants. They despise us and, worse, they insist we should despise ourselves. We mostly don't, we get on with things, but I admit it is decidedly hard to feel like a human being and not a useless, unworthy creature.

They're going to force me to have my baby adopted out. I've been refusing up until now but I'm due to give birth at the end of March and time is running out. They have chosen a good Catholic couple and my baby will have brothers and sisters, however I fret that he or she may not have as good a life as I would wish for any child I have.

I will go home after this and life will somehow go on. My resolve to fight can only go so far—even I know that. I believe this is the worst trial I will face in my life but the security of my baby is paramount and if that means having it placed with an adoptive family, then that is what I will need to learn to live with.

How are you, Cassie? How is Eddie? Are you married? There is so much I long to know. But you may be on your way to America and might never get this letter.

How I'm going to miss you!

Think of me sometimes, darling Cassie, as I will always think of our precious time together and give thanks for it. You made me strong. You showed me how to live life and deal with it, come what may. You give me strength now, even in this dark place. You will never know how much.

Your friend forever,
Emma

Emma folded the letter, inserted it into the envelope and wrote the address of Cassie's boarding house, then paused. Surely it wouldn't go through the censors? It wasn't addressed overseas, nor was it addressed to or from military personnel, so if it was opened and read, there was nothing in its contents that would contravene censorship rules. Just the ramblings of a sad young woman.

Lifting the skirt of her dress, she tucked the letter into a makeshift pocket she'd sewn in her petticoat while on linen-mending duty.

Since there was no sound from outside, she quickly opened the top drawer on the desk, where she knew Sister Hyacinth kept her pencils and other office supplies.

She lifted folders and notebooks, moved boxes of thumb tacks and half-full bottles of ink, but there were no stamps.

She tried another drawer. Nothing. She had expected to find stamps, ready for use on the many letters to the bishops and priests, but presumably Sister Hyacinth didn't spend unnecessary pennies until she had to.

When she opened the larger bottom drawer, it was heavy and it squeaked on metal runners.

She held her breath and paused, listening for noise outside the door. Then she looked down and stared at the money box.

The box was unlocked, the lid not tightly closed. Emma lifted the lid. The box was full. Notes tied together in order of value, coins shiny or dull in slots in the top tray.

She took a sixpence and held it in the palm of her hand, staring down at it.

This was stealing. A sin. And she couldn't have cared less.

* * *

Two days later, the last thing on Emma's mind was her imminent eighteenth birthday. She was no longer counting the years. She was a woman with sense and fortitude and had no desire to recall the young girl she'd been. That was then, this was now. There were more important things to deal with.

'All right?' she asked Wynn. They were in the linen room folding freshly washed towels.

Wynn nodded. She hardly spoke when she was in this room. She managed her tasks, her lips thinned, and never caught anyone's eye. Emma always made sure the door was propped open so it didn't suddenly bang closed with a gust of wind. Wynn hadn't spoken about the night she'd been locked in here and Emma didn't push her to speak of it.

She glanced at her companion. 'Finished?'

Wynn nodded and levered herself from the stool she'd been allowed to sit on while folding the towels. She was due at the end of the month. 'I'm going to need a hoist soon.'

'You have rather blossomed suddenly,' Emma said with an encouraging smile. 'Come on, then. Next task. The new girls have stripped the beds and left the clean sheets. We just have to make them.'

'It's like carting around a donkey. I hope it's not bloody twins.'

The tragedy of Susannah falling down the stairs had been spoken of in hushed tones by the sisters. Not because of concern for Susannah, but for the possibility of what might have happened to the baby and how appalling it could have been for the adoptive parents if it had died. The sisters couldn't afford for anything to happen to a newborn baby—and the girl who was about to give birth to it—so Emma had been assigned as Wynn's chaperone.

'Sister H sent me to get boiling water for her teapot this morning before I had my little chat with the welfare woman,' Wynn said as they trudged down the corridor.

'What did you do?'

'What do you think? I spat in the jug.'

Emma was pleased to see a spark still flared in her friend. Maybe she'd found fortitude that night alone in the linen room, like Emma had found courage as she walked away from the locked door. The nuns had taken their dislike of Wynn further since her outburst and were consistently mean to her, regardless of how they looked after her baby's welfare. But Wynn got her own back. She made up stories for the girls at night, whispered tales of a group of nuns and welfare women being handed over to the Japs because they were mean-mouthed battle-axes and Australia didn't want them, and how they were made to cook for the deprived and unfortunate, and were chained up at night and didn't get to eat cake for another ten years. The stifled giggles from the girls in the darkened dormitory was balm to Emma's wounds.

A twinge in her side made Emma groan. 'Do you think the father is paying for his mistake like I'm supposed to be paying for mine?' she asked as she and Wynn reached the dormitory.

Wynn had lost the constrained look now they were out of the linen room and appeared almost her old self. She glanced at Emma as though Emma had lost her mind. 'What would anyone care about the part he played? It's you who's getting to be the size of a battleship, announcing your transgression to the world.'

Emma had told Wynn about how she'd been deceived, without mentioning Frank's name, and Wynn had reciprocated by saying she hadn't particularly fancied the bloke she'd been with but she'd wanted to try sex with a man so she could make future evaluations. Emma hadn't asked exactly what Wynn meant; it was enough that they'd shared snippets about the fathers of their unborn babies as it was.

'Sit down for a bit,' Emma said. 'I'll make the beds.'

'I've got to do the priest's bed after this. Bet you wish it was you getting your hands on his pillowcases. Don't get all jealous on me.'

'I'll withhold the need.'

'Honestly,' Wynn said. 'The nuns are so preoccupied by this bloke you'd think they fancied him or something.' She lowered herself to sit on the end of a bed in a row hidden from immediate view of the opened door.

'How did it go with the welfare woman this morning?' Emma asked as she began stripping pillowcases from their pillows.

'Well, I wasn't going to accept a cup of tea, if that's what you mean.'

Emma shook her head. 'You're too bad, Stokes.'

'They all got agitated with me,' Wynn said, plucking at the skirt of her dress. 'The nurse was there too. She told me I had to understand the predicament I'd placed myself in by getting pregnant while not married. She said if I kept the baby I'd become neurotic. She said I'd start feeling sex starved.'

'Sex starved?' Emma said, bug-eyed. 'Did she actually use those words or are you trying to shock me?'

'Sex starved!' Wynn said again in a resounding voice. 'The way all immoral women feel, according to her. As if I fit that category. I never want to have sex with a man ever again. I told her so, and she said I'll probably be put in an institution for being neurotic.' She looked at Emma, her cheeks blushing for the first time in days, and with a hint of a smile on her face that did everything but convince Emma she was contrite.

'What have you done?' Emma asked. 'What do you mean *if* you kept the baby?'

Wynn raised her chin. 'I made a stand. I said I don't want my baby placed out. I told them I'm going to keep it.'

'Wynn!'

'I know, it's quite unexpected. But I mean it. I want this baby.'

Emma threw the pillow in her hands onto the bed and joined Wynn. 'They won't let you.' Wynn's sudden defiance struck her to the core. This was much worse than spitting in a jug of water for the teapot.

Wynn firmed her expression. 'I've made my decision. I'm sticking to it.'

'They'll force you.'

'If it's a girl I'm going to call her Susannah.'

Emma's resolve softened. 'Oh, Wynn ...'

'I've got fifty pounds.' Wynn turned on the bed so she faced Emma. 'I brought it with me. It'll be a start, at least. I've got an aunt I can go to. I think she might help if I beg hard enough.'

'How on earth did you manage to hide so much money?'

'I stuck it in my knickers before I arrived. Figured they wouldn't look there. Not straight away. Then when I was alone, getting changed into my uniform, I shoved it up the hollow metal pipe of my bed.'

Emma slapped a hand over her mouth to muffle her laugh. 'Only you.'

Wynn smiled. 'I'm quite the card, aren't I?'

'You remind me of someone I know. Someone I miss.'

'Not the man!' Wynn said, looking down at Emma's protruding belly.

'God, no! Definitely not him. What will your mum do?'

'She'll try to stop me.'

'You don't think she'll change her mind once she sees your baby?'

'No chance in hell.'

'What if your aunt won't help?'

'I'll find somewhere to go. I'll change my name and say I've been widowed and struck by tragedy. Fifty pounds should see me through the first few weeks in a cheap boarding house until I can get a job and someone to mind the baby. I intend to do it, so don't try talking me out of it.'

'Dearest Wynn. Tough as the old boots on your feet.' Emma had every reason to believe Wynn would try to do as she'd stated and no reason to think anyone would help her. It was going to worry her every hour.

She took hold of Wynn's hand and squeezed. 'Talking about secrets,' she said, knowing Wynn would be distracted by her news, 'I've pinched some letter paper and an envelope from Sister H's office and I've written to a friend.'

Wynn turned her head. 'You have friends?'

'Shocking, isn't it?'

'It certainly surprises me,' Wynn said, then winced. 'These twinges are getting worse.'

'It's my friend Cassie,' Emma continued, hoping to distract Wynn from whatever pain she was in. 'She's engaged to an American officer. Possibly even married by now. She's going to be one of the war brides who sail to America, or perhaps she's on the ship as I speak.'

'Lucky bugger.'

'You'd like her.'

'I don't care about anyone but myself right now.'

'Try thinking about me for a change.'

'Oh, all right, Miss Bossy! Go on, then. Why did you risk stealing paper and an envelope?'

Emma lowered her voice. 'I need someone from the outside to know where I am. I want there to be just one person who knows what's really happened to me. Someone who knows me from before and who cares. I'd have used Sister H's telephone if I'd thought I'd get away with it.'

'She'd chop your flaming hand off!'

'That's why I wrote a letter instead. Except I've got a little problem.'

'You certainly have. Who's going to mail it for you.'

Emma glanced at the doorway to make sure they weren't being overheard. 'I thought I'd try young Ben. I'll bribe him with jam or honey sandwiches. I can easily pinch those.'

'I'll give you a pound so you've got money to pay for postage.'

'I don't need your money. I stole a sixpence from the money box in Sister H's desk drawer. She doesn't lock the tin.'

Wynn reeled back, hands on the bed to brace herself. 'They will *kill* you, Hatton.'

'Not if they don't know about it.'

'You're starting to sound a lot like me.'

'God, I hope not.'

Wynn gave a begrudging chuckle then flinched again and adjusted her position to put her hands on her lower back. 'I've taken my money out of the bed pipe and hidden it in the lining of my suitcase. It'll go with me to the hospital and nobody will think to look in it.'

'Just make sure no-one sees you touching that suitcase again. We've got the new girls here now and we don't know them well enough yet. If the sisters find your money, they'll take it.'

Emma was going to miss Wynn. She only had about ten weeks to go herself and she'd miss all the girls she'd met here. They hadn't heard anything more about Susannah. Amelia Morrison had gone just yesterday, going into labour early, and they had no idea how she had got on at the hospital, but Hetty, Lorraine Freeman and Ruby Forsyth were still here. Poor Ruby. She'd been hounded day and night and still wet the bed on occasions. She didn't lift her chin any more and hardly ever looked anyone in the eye.

'I've made another decision,' Wynn said.

Emma looked up, almost fearful of what it might be.

'I'm going to be someone,' Wynn declared, giving Emma a crooked grin. 'I'm not going to allow this episode to bring down my whole life.'

'Good for you,' Emma said, straightening.

'I'm not going to take any notice of fate or whatever people call the things that push us into our futures, because if you ask me, I reckon fate is up to the individual.'

Emma slapped the mattress. 'Bloody well said.'

Wynn nodded in agreement. 'One day people are going to take me seriously.'

'Me too.'

'Well, everybody knows *you'll* be someone, but they'd never dream Winifred Sinclair could be anything but bolshy, working in some shop somewhere to make ends meet.'

'How come I'm different? I might get a job in a shop too.'

'Yeah, but you're likely to launch a new line in lipsticks or frying pans and end up calling all the shots.'

Emma patted Wynn's hand. 'So are you, or so you say. You'll have to come good with this promise to be someone of note. Or I'm going to be disappointed in you.'

Wynn got herself up from the bed and took hold of the folded sheet left by the other girls, shaking it out and billowing it in the air to blanket the mattress.

Emma picked up the pillowcase from the bed where she'd flung it. Being in this place was so disempowering. It broke a person's confidence. It hammered self-belief and cracked trust, leaving a girl's soul wide open for others to perforate with their unkindness. Emma didn't want to be left in the dark ever again. She needed stars to light her path and at the moment the only star she could envisage following was that of her own self-worth.

Chapter Twenty

The sixpence and the letter were now secured in the secret pocket in Emma's petticoat. They were safe for the moment. The girls' undergarments were only washed once a week, apart from their knickers, which got a wringing out every Monday, Wednesday and Friday.

In the coming few days they would be told to rake the leaves as usual, and Emma would find Ben, bribe him, and keep everything crossed the young lad would manage to get out of the gates and mail the letter. After that, who knew? But at least she would have tried.

She paused on the top landing when she closed the door to the asylum, a metal bowl and a pair of scissors in her hands. She'd been charged with cutting the boys' hair and wasn't sure she'd done a good job but the boys probably didn't care.

Today was her eighteenth birthday. That joyous age she and Cassie had longed to reach and pretended to have already attained.

She crossed the landing to a small window at the head of the staircase and put the bowl and scissors on the floor. Placing her fingertips on the curve of the sill, she rose to tiptoes and looked out at innumerable clouds, chimney stacks and treetops.

The window had been leadlight once but one of the children had broken it with a bat years ago, before the war, and the stained glass had been replaced with a clear pane. She'd looked out of it any number of times over the months. Once, while on a mission for one of the sisters to assist with a boy who'd been sick, it had been after dark and she'd taken a moment to view the night sky, sprinkled with so many stars it was like someone had lit a hundred thousand candles way up high.

Today, thick white clouds hung in the sky like eiderdowns.

Turning eighteen made her wonder about home. She couldn't bring herself to think of the Hatton house as a comforting or secure place like the eiderdown blankets in the sky, but it was the only home she knew. Would she have joined the WAAAF and got herself a uniform? Would her mother have allowed it or would Emma have done it anyway?

Little Danny had turned seven, Will nine, Joe almost an unbelievable fifteen. Emma hoped twelve-year-old Simon hadn't broken his glasses again, because there'd be no money for new ones unless their mother was working seven days a week at Mrs Cosgrove's. She sent up a prayer for Dad, but didn't allow her mind to stay too long on thoughts of her mother.

She wasn't sure what she wanted to think about Doris. Her aunt had been harsher than necessary, borne, Emma supposed, of her own lack of education and inability to empathise with anyone who hadn't been as fortunate as she had been.

By comparison, and strangely enough, she wished Harry Colson well and hoped he was happy and that his sister was coming to terms with the burdens placed on her. She even gave a fleeting thought to Ivy Williams, who was getting older by the day and might be worried about what was going to happen to her once she retired.

How odd that Ivy would take a place in her thoughts. Ivy, whom Emma thought a cantankerous know-all. Contriteness swamped her, swimming through her veins in rivers of regret. If she was given the chance, she would look for ways to make amends with the woman. Maybe even with Doris. But she couldn't see how she might do the same with her mother. The person who had sent her to this fortress.

She turned when she heard footsteps on the wooden stairs and hurriedly picked up the bowl and scissors, readying herself for a telling off for dawdling and wasting God's precious hours.

But it was Wynn, coming up from the first floor. 'Taking a break?' Wynn said, a hand on her belly.

'What are you doing up here?'

Wynn took a deep breath and blew it out, then shoved her hand into her apron pocket and produced a chocolate-covered caramel. 'Happy birthday. It's not even melted. How good am I at nicking things?'

Emma gasped. 'How did you know? And who did you steal it from?'

'I heard you tell one of the girls last week. They've put a tin of toffees in the priest's bedroom. I didn't think he'd mind, and if he does, tough. He's probably so old the toffee will stick his dentures together anyway. Hurry up! Eat the damn thing. It's evidence.'

Emma stared at the rarity in her hand, shocked to have received such a welcome gift and already knowing it would linger in her memory as the best birthday present she had ever been given.

She chewed fast, savouring the creamy taste. 'It's soft,' she managed between swallows. 'Tastes like heaven.'

'Don't choke on it. I don't want to be responsible for your untimely death.'

Emma did choke. With laughter, but she managed to chew the last mouthful and swallow without succumbing to asphyxiation by caramel toffee.

'I've had some bad news,' Wynn said as they made their way down the stairs.

Emma halted, hand on the banister.

Wynn stopped a couple of steps down. 'The sisters telephoned my mother and it's been arranged that she's to collect me from the hospital after I've given birth. So long as I can walk, presumably, because otherwise she'll be dragging me.'

'Oh, Wynn.'

'I know. It's a bugger. I bet my mother is absolutely fuming about my wanting to keep the baby. She told the sisters she believed I was delusional and that the child must go to the family it's been granted to.'

'What are you going to do?'

'I'm not totally downhearted,' Wynn said. 'Not yet anyway.'

'What about your aunt?'

'My mother contacted her and warned her if she helps me she'll be banned from the family.' Wynn raised both eyebrows. 'My aunt won't care about that. They're sisters-in-law, you see. She's my father's younger sister and she and my mother never got along.'

Emma understood. She had the same in her family with the constant quarrels between her mother and Doris.

'I just need to get through the birth,' Wynn said, 'and make sure I don't let them take my baby, then I'll get up, get dressed and get out of there—they tie you down, so it could be tricky, but I'll figure something out.'

'They *what*?'

Wynn blinked. 'I thought you knew.'

'I hadn't realised …'

'Christ! Sorry, I honestly thought you knew.'

'I'd heard that it's best not to fight but I thought they meant the birth moment.'

'Who knows? That's got to bloody hurt too, but they shackle us to the bed.'

Emma grimaced, unbelieving. 'I know we're not allowed to see the baby ...' But being tied down? Shackled to the bed?

'For all I know they might put pillowcases over our heads,' Wynn said, and carried on down the stairs.

More than a little light-headed, Emma followed. 'Are you planning on fighting them off?'

'Too bloody right! I'm from strong stock. They're not dragging me around, nor are they tying me to anything. When I go on the horse and cart I intend to walk out the door on my own two feet. I'll do the same in the hospital. I'll walk to my own damned bed, or trolley, or operating table—wherever it is they put us—and I'm not walking out of the hospital unless it's with my baby.'

Emma had to cling to the banister all the way down the stairs, clutching the metal bowl and the scissors against her chest. 'Oh, God, Wynn.'

'Try not to worry about me.'

'How could I not?' The worst part was, she'd never know how Wynn got on. They were going to take Wynn's baby. Emma couldn't see any way out. And it was going to break Wynn's heart. 'Wynn!' she whispered heatedly, grabbing her friend's arm when they reached the corridor leading to the kitchen and laundry. 'Darling Wynn—'

'Don't get all emotional on me.'

'Do one thing for me. Once you're out, try to get a note to Mrs Ross.'

'Are you insane?'

'Let her know how you are and—and what happened.'

Wynn shook her off. 'The housekeeper wouldn't tell you even if I was stupid enough to write to her.'

'She would. I bet you a pound.'

'You haven't got a pound.'

'I will one day.'

'I'll think about it,' Wynn said begrudgingly. 'Now, follow me. We've got *you* to sort out.'

'Why me?'

'There's been more stealing,' Wynn said. 'I nabbed a honey sandwich before I trudged up two flights of stairs to wish you a happy birthday.' She stopped outside the boot room and grinned. 'We've been told to rake the leaves.'

'Ben!' Emma exclaimed, excitement making the blood rush to her head in an entirely different manner than before.

'Have you got the letter and the sixpence?'

Emma patted the skirt of her dress. 'In my petticoat pocket. I've had it there for days.'

Wynn took the metal bowl and scissors out of Emma's hand and plonked them on a bench. 'Come on then. Let's get it done!'

* * *

'There he is,' Emma said, indicating the far end of the lower garden where she and Wynn had been raking leaves for half an hour, panicking in case Ben wasn't going to turn up.

'Ben!' Emma called in a whisper. 'Ben!'

He looked across with a puzzled frown as Emma beckoned him over.

Both Wynn and Emma walked backwards, encouraging him to follow them until they were behind the old brick wall at the bottom of the garden and hidden from sight. Ben was shaking slightly when he stepped behind the cover of the wall. He had the demeanour of a scared puppy.

'Fancy something to eat?' Wynn said, pulling the honey sandwich out of her apron pocket and holding it tantalisingly up in the air.

'Where'd you nick that?' Ben asked, his eyes glued to the bread, with honey dripping through the sandwich seam. He rested the legs of the wheelbarrow onto the ground and wiped his nose with the sleeve of his shirt.

'Stole it from a pile meant for the cook's afternoon tea. Do you want it?'

Ben glanced over his shoulder, wiped his nose once more and snatched the sandwich. 'Ta,' he said as he bit into half of it, holding a hand beneath it, probably so he didn't lose any of the honey. For a moment, his eyes glazed. Then he scoffed the second half of the sandwich almost in one go.

'Good?' Wynn asked, as he licked his fingers.

He nodded. 'What did you give it to me for?'

'Ah, well, actually ...' Wynn looked at Emma.

'We wanted to have a little word with you,' Emma said. 'You know everything that goes on out here in the gardens and we were wondering if you might know how to slip out.'

'Slip out of what?'

'The front gate,' Emma said.

'Or the back gate.'

'Or any of the gates.'

'I'd have to steal the keys off the old man to do that,' Ben said, pausing to stare at Emma. 'Are you mad?'

'Believe me, that's a question I've asked a number of times.'

'It's important,' Emma said, hushing Wynn with a wave of her hand. 'Can you help us? I want you to mail a letter. I have sixpence to pay for the stamp and if it only costs three and a half pennies—and if you manage to mail it—you can keep the pennies left over *and* I'll make sure you get more honey sandwiches.'

Ben's eyes were full of wariness but he was clearly giving the notion of the sandwiches more thought along with a penny or two in his pocket. 'Too risky,' he said at last.

'But could you do it?' Wynn asked. 'If you decided you were going to?'

'I don't get to decide nothing.'

'All you'd have to do is steal a key, nip out for ten minutes and get back without Mr Tyrell knowing,' Emma said. 'We'll help steal the key if you tell us where it is.'

'Come on,' Wynn said enticingly. 'You can do it. I'll give you a whole pound.'

Emma lifted her head. 'Wynn.'

Wynn turned to face her. 'Look, I can mail your letter but I don't know when I'll be able to do it. I don't know for sure what will happen to me when I get out. Ben?' she said, looking back at the anxious young man.

He shook his head and stepped back. 'They're going to send me away.' He swallowed hard, his eyes filling with tears. 'They're going to get me a job somewhere. There's a young'un in the asylum who's almost ten now. They said he had to take his turn working for old Tyrell and I have to go.'

'Oh, Ben.'

'Those nuns are nasty enough as it is,' he continued, clearly defensive now. 'I don't know what they'd do to me if I snuck out of here. I can't get kicked out without anywhere to go and no reference for employment. Not even for a pound.'

'You'll do well, Ben,' Emma said encouragingly. 'You've got a good work ethic.'

Ben looked nonplussed.

'She means you've got the brains and the wherewithal to get yourself through life,' Wynn added kindly.

Ben shifted position. 'I hope to get a bicycle one day. I've always wanted one.'

'You will,' Emma assured him. 'Furthermore, I'm still going to steal honey sandwiches for you.'

'You don't have to. Not now.'

'But I will. If there's food to be stolen, you'll be getting it.'

He darted his gaze between the both of them. 'Are you having me on?'

'We would never do that.'

Ben took a step backwards, then another, either reluctant to believe them or bemused he was going to be rewarded after refusing a task. 'Sorry I can't help you,' he said, contrite, but still looking fearful.

'I understand, Ben.' It was not what she'd wanted, but Emma wasn't going to castigate the lad for being frightened half to death. She couldn't blame him. Not one jot.

'Well.' Ben regained his stiffened, boyishly stubborn stance. 'Anyways, if you tell on me about what I said about the nuns being mean, then I'll tell on you.'

Wynn caught Emma's eye, clearly thinking they should continue to try to persuade Ben.

Emma shook her head. It wouldn't do any good, and she didn't want the lad to be even more scared than he already was.

Back inside, unable to contain her disappointment, Emma pressed the heels of her hands against her eyes.

'Come on,' Wynn said, nudging her with her elbow. 'Give me your letter and I'll hide it in the lining of my suitcase along with my money.'

'No,' Emma said, dropping her hands.

'Why not? Honestly, you're starting to get on my nerves and in my condition, that's probably not a good thing.'

Emma put a hand over her heart. 'Wynn, I need this letter to go as soon as possible. Cassie might be about to sail and I'll never know where she is. She'll never know what's happened to me and she'll worry, I know she will. I can't wait for you to mail it. If she's still in the country, every day counts.'

Wynn looked away on a sigh of frustration. 'I'd go now if I could. I'd escape. The problem is giving birth.' She turned to Emma. 'What if it happened when I was on the train to my aunt's place? What if my mother's already at my aunt's, waging war? What if! What if!' She shook her head. 'Anyway, I just didn't want you to think I was lacking courage or something.'

'I'd never think that of you.'

'I should have told them I was going to keep the baby from the start.'

'We can't determine how we're going to feel or what we're going to do.'

Wynn glanced down at the floor. 'It feels like I'm useless sometimes.'

Emma stepped closer and put an arm around her shoulders. 'We're not, not any of us. We're imprisoned, Wynn.'

'I worry though. In case I can't get it done. In case I can't keep the baby. What will I do then?' she asked, querying Emma with a frown.

'You'll be someone.'

Wynn blew out a breath and took a step away, forcing Emma to remove her arm from her shoulders. 'So what now?' she asked, back to her normal get-on-with-it attitude. 'We've got to get you sorted. Maybe I can nick a gate key and you can nip out and post your letter. Or even telephone this friend.'

'I've got as much likelihood of getting out of here as you had.' Emma held up the skirt of her dress. 'We look like one of the poor! Ben would have been thought to be on an errand for his employers but nobody would sell me a stamp and no-one would allow me into their shop to request use of their telephone—not without first calling the police. Wynn, honestly. Look at us! We haven't even got coats, let alone hats and handbags.'

Wynn scrunched her face. 'I guess you're right.'

'But it's the purpose that counts. It's having gumption to attempt to do something others would see as reckless. That's what counts.'

'Uh oh,' Wynn said, peering hard. 'You've got the devil in your eyes. Why am I not going to like what you're about to say?'

'Because I'm going to ask Mrs Ross to mail my letter.'

'Holy Mary, Mother of God and all the angels! What is your obsession with the woman?'

Emma wasn't going to quarrel, neither was she going to change her mind. She *had* to mail her letter. There was a lot more to get through after the birth of her child. A lot more anguish to overcome and a life to rebuild. She'd need fortitude to back her up and Cassie knowing the truth would help.

'Are you sure about this?' Wynn asked, pinning Emma with one of her glares.

'Positive.'

Wynn grunted. 'On your head be it …'

Emma turned to find Mrs Ross heading their way from the scullery, carrying a large porcelain wash bowl and matching pitcher, plus a soap dish and a towel over her arm. They'd be for the priest's bedroom.

'Is there something I can help you two with?' Mrs Ross asked. 'Or are you dillydallying for a reason?'

'Sorry,' Wynn said, producing a bright smile. 'We're waiting for Hetty. We're going to help her fold the napkins and tablecloths. She's just in the loo. Dear little Hetty. Such a joy to be around.'

Mrs Ross's eyebrows rose. 'Having a good day, Stokes?'

'One of the best so far.'

Emma inwardly cringed at Wynn's poor interpretation of appearing content.

'It's nice to see,' Mrs Ross said. 'Just ensure you return to your usual behaviour soon or I'll suspect you've been at the honey jar. Too much sugar isn't good for the soul.'

Wynn blushed right up to her hair roots. 'No, Mrs Ross.'

The housekeeper went on her way and Emma turned to Wynn. 'This is my chance. Wish me luck.'

'I might even pray for you.'

Emma ran down the corridor but steadied her pace as she reached the entrance hallway.

'Mrs Ross, can I help with those?'

The housekeeper paused on the stairs and eyed Emma steadily. 'Take this and hold it carefully,' she said, handing over the pitcher. 'Where's Hetty?'

'Stokes will find her. They've only got the sisters' napery to sort out so they don't need me to help.'

Once they were in the priest's bedroom, Mrs Ross glanced out the door then closed it and turned to Emma. 'Out with it. I haven't been around all these years not to recognise a young woman who is up to something.'

Emma placed the pitcher on the dresser. 'I have a request of you.' She stepped away when the housekeeper moved to the dresser to deposit the wash bowl and the soap dish.

Mrs Ross stood squarely in front of Emma, waiting. 'There is nothing I can do to help you.'

Emma lifted the skirt of her dress, retrieved the letter and the sixpence from the secret pocket in her petticoat and held out the envelope. 'I need someone to know where I am.'

'Who might this someone be?'

'A friend.'

'A man friend?'

'No! Cassie O'Byrne. My best friend. She's engaged to an American medical officer and they're getting married, which means she will sail on a war bride ship to America and I'll never see her again. I need her to know how much I'll miss her. How much I love her.' Emma took a step forwards. 'I have a sixpence for a stamp.'

'Where did you get it?'

'I stole it.'

Mrs Ross inhaled sharply. 'I don't want to know where from,' she said before turning to stare out the window at the front garden, so neat with its beds of roses and its leaf-free stone path, the boughs of the lemon trees laden with fruit that was turned into jam or conserves, or sauces for fish or flavouring for custards. Everything the visiting priest would be sampling. Nothing the girls had tasted while here.

'Will you help me?'

Mrs Ross's eyes were now creased in concern. She wasn't modern in her dress but neither was her appearance unacceptable. Her dress was a sober beige, her hair still dark with the merest hint of grey, her face free of makeup and her fingers ringless apart from a gold wedding band. She was the sort of woman nobody would take a second look at as they passed on the street and Emma had a feeling this was the persona the housekeeper preferred. But she had hidden depths and kindness in her heart.

'What makes you think this friend is still in Australia?'

'I don't know that she is.'

'Where will this letter go if she's no longer at the address you have?'

'Maybe if you were to put your return address on the envelope someone might—'

Mrs Ross turned. 'Dear God, Harper! Have you lost your mind?'

Emma held her ground. 'My name is Hatton. Emma Hatton.'

Mrs Ross inhaled once more. 'You've only got a short time to go. Don't ruin yourself further, because the nuns won't care about you, only about the baby.'

'Sending this letter is my only hope.'

'You have no idea what you're asking of me.'

'I do. I swear I do.'

'It would be dangerous.'

Emma took another small step towards her only chance. 'I'll do anything you ask. Anything at all.'

The housekeeper's gaze wavered, holding the same light of sadness Emma had seen the day Susannah fell down the stairs.

'I don't want to take anything from you. You've had so much taken from you already. All of you.'

Emma nearly pounced on her, wanting to hug her. She was going to do it! 'Thank you! Thank you so much.'

Mrs Ross took the envelope. 'I hope I won't regret this,' she said, her reserve noticeable. 'But no more.' She held up a warning finger. 'Do you hear me? Nothing more.'

There was more, and it felt like an impossible ask, but she'd got this far ... 'Will you please add your address to the letter so that my friend can reply? If Cassie is still in Australia, she'll be gone soon. Will you give us a chance to say our farewells?' Emma held out the sixpence, the silence grating the air.

'Keep the sixpence but make sure you hide it well. Don't attempt to put it back from wherever you got it.'

Emma clutched the coin in her hand, suddenly aware of how tight her chest was. 'Will you allow my friend to respond to your address?'

'Once. I will do this for you once.'

Emma let out a sigh of relief. Now there was a real chance Cassie would get the letter.

'You mustn't expect anything from this friend,' Helen Ross advised as she moved to the door. 'People change. Their thoughts change, along with their intent. Your friend might already have forgotten you.'

'Never.' *Never*. She and Cassie were forever friends and had forged that bond with genuine love of each other.

'We'll see,' Mrs Ross said. 'But I suggest you keep your expectations low.' She folded the letter in half, lifted her apron and put the letter into a side pocket in her dress. 'Your friend is set if what you say is true. But you? Is there anyone waiting for you?'

Emma shook her head.

Mrs Ross nodded. 'You're strong. You'll survive. Time will help you heal a little. Believe me. Now let's get back downstairs.'

'You do care about us all. I knew you did.'

Mrs Ross halted, her hand on the door handle as she looked back at Emma. 'All I will say is that if this one act—foolhardy though I believe it to be—is in my charge, then I will perform my task. As you must perform yours. Your name is Harper while you're here. Don't forget it.'

Emma followed the housekeeper out of the priest's bedroom, the weight of the woman's words stinging. Emma's task was to hand over her baby. As all unworthy, unlovable unwed mothers must do.

But Cassie was proof that Emma had given and received love. Her unborn child was the proof of how much love it was possible to hold for another.

If it were in Cassie's power, she would respond.

Emma simply had to practise patience.

Chapter Twenty-one

Two fractious weeks later, Emma reached the entrance hall after running from the linen room and paused to catch her breath before climbing the stairs to the first landing. She had to get to Wynn, who was in another of the guest bedrooms, dusting the furniture and shaking out dead bugs from the curtains. One of the girls had left the window open all night after sweeping and there were mosquitos and flies everywhere, dead and alive.

Emma hadn't had time to fully contemplate what might be happening with her letter. The priest had been and gone but now the nuns were in a state of high excitement because they were expecting a bishop to visit after a commendation from the priest and every girl, regardless of how far she was into her pregnancy, had been ordered to scrub and polish everything twice. They'd been at it all week. It was best if she didn't dwell on her letter, as hope had a way of drifting like clouds which could accumulate at any hour and become a mighty storm.

'There's a colossal ruckus going on downstairs,' she said to Wynn as she stepped inside the guest bedroom at the far end of the first-floor landing, closing the door with her foot. 'Jemima Cartright is having her baby but the horse has gone lame. They're sending for another.' Emma dropped the towels on the end of the bed, then propped her hands on the mattress, leaning forwards, legs apart, to ease the twinge beneath her ribs.

'I've got a pain,' Wynn said.

Emma took a deep breath and exhaled it. 'Me too.' She straightened and pulled the top towel off the stack and shook it out, ready to refold it and hang it neatly over the towel rail next to the dresser. A scream rang out from below and her hands stilled. 'They've put her in the linen room,' she told Wynn. 'And guess what? It's not just Jemima. Cook's assistant—the one with red hair—scalded herself. She was putting a log in the wood stove and wasn't paying attention. She's burned her hand and half her arm. Mandy Smith fainted. Right in front of Sister H.'

'Where's Mrs Ross?'

'They told her to boil water and get some old sheets to put down. They've dragged another table into the linen room and said it would all need to happen right there. Apart from Cook's assistant—she's been taken to the laundry. Wynn,' she said in a hushed tone, 'I saw them take in straps. They're going to tie Jemima down.'

'Oh, God,' Wynn moaned. 'Have they sent for the doctor?'

'He's out on another visit so it'll be a while before he gets here.' Emma pushed back strands of hair that had escaped from its tight bun. 'What's wrong?' she asked when she realised her friend hadn't finished putting the clean pillowcases on the pillows.

'Where is everybody else?' Wynn asked.

'We've been told to stay out of the way. The other girls have gone to the dormitory, which is where we're to go after we've finished in here.'

'Is there a nurse?'

'On her way. There's only Mrs Ross until she and the doctor get here, but they don't want her help. They told her to leave. They said they were waiting on a proper nurse arriving.'

'The woman's had eight children. She's got to know what's what.'

'Well, they won't let her near Jemima. The baby's got new parents waiting on it. Sister H said it's imperative the birth goes quickly and smoothly.'

'She'd better start praying the nurse arrives soon.' Wynn lowered herself onto the bed, a strained look on her face. 'Because I think it's my turn too.'

Emma's mind went blank for perhaps a whole minute before it started whirling like a spinning top. 'Now?'

'Now. And it bloody hurts.'

Wynn collapsed back, and Emma ran for the door and yanked it open. 'I'm fetching Mrs Ross.'

'Don't leave me!' Wynn struggled to sit up. 'This is awfully painful.'

'I don't want you to have it up here all alone and I don't know what to do to help.'

* * *

'What do we have here, then?' Mrs Ross asked as she walked into the bishop's bedroom ten minutes later, a pail of hot water in her hands. Emma had found her in the infants' asylum so they'd been able to secure the water and also some of the children's towels, which Emma was holding.

Mrs Ross checked the hallway, then closed the door and turned the key in the lock. 'Strip the bed,' she said to Emma, then took hold of Wynn and got her to stand. 'Just for a minute. Then we'll get you back on the bed. Put the towels on the mattress,' she told Emma. 'Here you go, Stokes. Get on top of those towels so we don't make a mess on the mattress.'

'Christ, call me Wynn, would you? It'll make me feel more human.'

Mrs Ross ignored her.

'Is it happening right now?' Emma asked.

'We'll soon find out.'

Mrs Ross poured water from the pail into the bowl on the dresser and washed her hands, using the Velvet soap left for the bishop's use since there wasn't anything else. Then she pulled up Wynn's dress and put her hands onto her belly, moving them over her stomach, prodding and pressing. 'You need to open your legs and let me take a look. I'm going to have to feel inside you, so don't panic on me.'

'Is it happening as it should?' Emma asked. Her breath was hitched so high in her chest, she could hardly speak.

'Her body knows what it's doing.' Mrs Ross pulled Wynn's dress down and rose from her kneeling position on the bed. 'There's time. She'll have to go to the hospital.'

A door slammed downstairs and a torrent of voices rose in the air.

'I need to inform the sisters,' Mrs Ross said as she washed her hands once more.

'No!' Wynn exclaimed. 'They'll take the baby.'

'Mrs Ross, Wynn has refused to have her baby placed out. The sisters know it.'

'Your mother has made the arrangements,' the housekeeper said to Wynn. 'Everybody is aware of that. There is nothing you can do.'

'Not like this!' Wynn said. 'Please, not like this!'

'My task now, Stokes, is to concentrate on the present moment and that means getting you down the stairs.' Mrs Ross took a breath. 'Or Wynn if you like,' she said softly. 'Just for now.'

'Can't we wait?' Emma said. 'Just wait and let Wynn have her baby here. You can help, I know you can.'

'The sisters wouldn't allow it.'

'But they won't know until it's over,' Wynn said.

'It won't be over for a few hours. I can't hide you for that length of time and I may be dismissed if I were to attempt to do so. Now, please. Please, let me help you up. Jemima will be birthing here so the new horse and cart is available just for you and Cook's assistant.'

Wynn glanced at Emma, her expression raw and vulnerable.

'Emma, help me,' Mrs Ross said. 'Take one of Wynn's arms.'

'Hours?' Wynn grumbled as she was helped to stand. 'Surely it's on its way right this moment? It's *terribly* painful!'

'I know, Wynn, I know.' Mrs Ross tucked an arm beneath Wynn's. 'Come on, now, there's a good girl. I need you down the stairs before the contractions get worse.'

'How can they get flaming worse?'

'We each deal with the pain in different ways,' Mrs Ross said to Emma as they made their way down the stairs either side of Wynn, holding onto her, but it was mostly the housekeeper who was doing the heavy shouldering. 'There's no shame in crying out. Some cry louder, some hold it in. Some feel it more than others, that's all.'

'You know this is all wrong, don't you?' Emma said.

'Hush, now. Keep your eyes on the stairs. We don't want either of you falling.'

Wynn moaned and doubled over.

'Wait!' Emma cried. 'Mrs Ross, you have to wait for me.'

'Where are you going?' the housekeeper said as Emma flew up the stairs. 'I cannot wait for you, Harper!'

'Just wait, Mrs Ross! Please.'

Emma ran into the dormitory and straight to Wynn's bed.

'What's up with you?'

'Why is Jemima screaming so hard?'

'What's happening?' another girl asked as Emma dragged Wynn's suitcase from beneath her bed.

'Nothing,' Emma said, turning on her heel, the suitcase in her hand.

'It's a contraction,' Mrs Ross told her as she arrived next to Wynn who had only managed to get down another three steps and was doubled over once again. 'What's that for?' Mrs Ross asked. 'Why the rush for it?'

'It's Wynn's. She needs it.'

Voices rang out from downstairs. Then Jemima yelled, her screams echoing up the staircase. Emma shivered but focussed on Wynn and tried to forget that this was going to happen to her too.

'Mrs Ross, I've told Wynn to write to you when this is over. I need to know how she is and what happened. I told her to address it to you here.'

'You had no right to do that.'

'I had to. It's the only way I'll ever know. Wynn will cover her tracks. They'll never guess it's from Wendy Stokes. I promise. She'll just give you a telephone number or an address to contact her.'

'You will get me into serious trouble.'

'Not if they don't know!' Emma stared at the housekeeper, silently begging for her cooperation.

Then Wynn caught enough of her breath to speak, although her eyes were glassy. 'How many more flaming contractions will I get?'

'Come on, now,' Mrs Ross said, pulling Wynn upright. 'Just a bit further. You can do this.'

When they reached the bottom of the stairs they eased Wynn down to sit on the second step so she wasn't crouched too low to get up again.

'I have to inform the sisters,' Mrs Ross said. 'Say your goodbyes and do it quickly.'

Emma put the suitcase down and sat next to Wynn, putting an arm around her, cradling her head against her shoulder and stroking her hair, which was wet with perspiration.

'I'll find you, Wynn. After. I'll find you.'

Wynn huffed a laugh that turned into a gulping sob. 'My mother will send me away. I know it. She'll never tell you where, even if you found her.'

'Where is home?'

'Right here in Brisbane. About a mile from this place. My parents and brother hate me for what I've done to them— Oh!' Wynn ground her back teeth. 'Sweet Jesus, this hurts!'

Emma held onto her. 'Have faith, Wynn.'

'In bloody what?'

'In everything you do. It's going to hurt. All of it. But you can do it because you already are someone special.'

'You drive me insane, woman. You're so damned thoughtful all the time!'

'Thanks for noticing.'

Wynn gazed up, her eyes full of pain. 'Emma,' she said, her voice wobbling with emotion. 'You know I actually love you, don't you?'

'Yes, Wynn. I know.' Emma leaned in and pressed a kiss on Wynn's forehead, ignoring the sweat and the smell of fear. 'I'm going to miss you so much. You're my friend and I will always be yours.'

A hand grabbed Emma's shoulder and Sister Peter shifted her to one side. Her knee cracked on a banister rail and she winced but by the time she'd steadied herself, Wynn was being supported by Mr Tyrell and a coachman.

She struggled in their grip. 'I can walk. Get your hands off me!'

Emma suddenly remembered the suitcase and bent to pick it up. 'She needs this!' she said, running across the hallway.

'Stay back,' Sister Peter said. 'Stokes! Do as you're told. This is for your own good.'

Sister Peter grabbed the suitcase then gave Emma a backhanded slap across the face. Emma stepped backwards, skin stinging from the force of the woman's knuckles.

'Mr Tyrell, please get the stretcher if you and the coachman cannot manage her between you.'

'We'll be right, sister. Come on now, young lady, stop your silliness and let us get you to the hospital.'

Wynn burst into tears, stilling between the two men. Then she looked at Emma, her cheeks rosy and wet. 'One day, I'm going to do something. I'm going to show them.'

'I believe in you!'

'This is not fair.'

'You'll do it, Wynn. I know you will.'

'I'm not useless. I'm not stupid. I'm not!'

'You'll show them all, Wynn Sinclair.'

'Quiet!' Sister Peter said hastily.

Wynn was turned by the two men and dragged out the front door, followed by Sister Peter with her short, careful steps, her dignified countenance—and Wynn's suitcase.

'I love you, Wynn!' Emma called, raising a hand in salute. 'I will find you one day. I promise.'

Wynn might not have heard. Not with the pain and the noise and the confusion that must be resonating in her head, along with the voices of the coachman and Mr Tyrell telling her to hush with her crying, and the stomping of the horse's hooves.

Emma collapsed onto the stairs, the walls of the entrance hallway closing in on her and the light from the old lamps blurring her vision. Life in the home without Wynn would be empty. A void she had to endure on her own.

Wipe those tears from your eyes …

She dragged herself up, clinging to the banister. She would soon be on the horse and cart herself, and after that, she'd be sent home. Just like Susannah and Wynn. Regardless of what she'd said to Wynn, she might never know how either of the girls fared. She might never have the means to search for them.

How did you find a person who was lost? A person you knew next to nothing about yet understood within your soul you were meant to meet?

Chapter Twenty-two

February 1945

It was three weeks since Wynn had been taken away and over four since Mrs Ross had mailed Emma's letter. Emma's hope had frayed further, like someone plucking at a thread, unravelling a beautiful shawl until it was nothing but a heap of used yarn. Every day Emma made the same silent enquiry of Mrs Ross: *Has Cassie replied to my letter?* Each time, the housekeeper gave an almost indiscernible shake of her head.

Emma looked around the empty corridor, lips compressed, wanting to yank her hair from its bun and shake her head until she'd got rid of all the thoughts tumbling through her mind. It couldn't possibly take over four weeks for a letter to travel 800 miles from Brisbane to Townsville, even with a war on. Victory of the Ardennes Counteroffensive had been claimed in late January, and Mr Tyrell had been beside himself with admiration and pride. Thankfully he'd had a lot to say about it to Cook, so Emma had overheard bits and pieces. The Allies had headed for Berlin, but even Mr Tyrell couldn't say when the war might end.

As far as she could tell from the gardener's constant war chat, her father's battalion might have been sent to Bougainville last December. She no longer hoped her dad was getting enough tea because the reality was, he likely wasn't.

She continued down the corridor to the sisters' dining room, their neatly folded napery in her hands. There had been no note from Wynn either, which was troubling. Mrs Ross had reiterated her concern that Emma's interfering would get them all into difficulty with the sisters. Wynn would chide Emma for being so wretched when she'd known all along what the end results would be. Susannah would offer sweet words of comfort.

What would Cassie say?

'Harper. My office. Now.'

Emma retained a bland expression but felt sure her pain and anger was burning in her eyes. She turned them to the floor as Sister Hyacinth led her into the office and closed the door, only then realising she'd forgotten to take off her apron. But she no longer cared about the trifling absurdities.

The sister unfolded her spectacles and fitted them carefully on her nose before picking up a sheet of paper to read its contents, then another. Purposefully done. Keep the girl in suspense.

'I haven't seen young Ben the gardener's boy around the last few days,' Emma said, hoping it annoyed the sister that she'd spoken and hadn't waited as she was supposed to.

'He's gone,' Sister Hyacinth said, looking over the rim of her glasses. 'There is another child in the asylum who has taken his place.'

'Where has Ben been sent?' Emma enquired, annoyance bubbling.

'I have secured the boy employment with one of our city's most prestigious families.'

For a price, Emma bet. For all that he'd been treated uncaringly here at the home, Ben would have been terrified to leave and unsure of what he was being sent to. All she could hope was that one day he got his bicycle. How many souls would she wonder about, care about and pine for? All of them from this horrid place.

'Your mother telephoned,' Sister Hyacinth said, removing her spectacles and placing them on the desk.

Emma's heartbeat rose. Had something happened to Dad?

'She wished to know what progress had been made with the child. I informed her of the adoption arrangement and she agreed it was a relief to know it will all soon be over.'

Emma waited. There had to be more. Her mother wouldn't care about the baby any more than she cared about the wellbeing of her daughter.

'Your mother suggested you stay on a further two or three weeks after the birth.'

Emma clenched her hands into fists. The prospect of more time here was possibly crueller than being sent in the first place. 'Why?'

Sister Hyacinth baulked at Emma's affrontery. 'The decision is ours to make and yours to abide by.'

'If my mother could just send the money for a train ticket, I could make my own way back.'

'You will stay until you have overcome your need to disagree with those who have charge of you and your welfare.'

Stay. For weeks. Even a few days would be nightmarish.

'Who will pay for my keep?' she asked, hopeful of a reprieve. It would be better to return to her hometown. Anything would be better than being forced to work and skivvy here.

Sister Hyacinth stood and leaned both hands on her desk. 'You will thank God and the sisters for your keep. You will pray for forgiveness.'

No, she'd be praying to get out of here. 'My time is coming soon. Can someone tell me what to expect at the hospital?'

Again, Sister Hyacinth studied Emma with deliberation before answering. 'You'll get what you get, Harper.'

'No-one has told me much about what happens during the birth.'

'The baby will be well tended throughout.'

'What about me? The mother.'

The sister's gaze was cold and sharp. 'You won't be the mother.'

The words were a knife through the heart.

Emma put a protective hand over her belly.

'Get on with your tasks,' Sister Hyacinth said. 'From now on, I shall be using Mandy Smith to clean and dust the office.'

* * *

'Harper, can you help me?'

'What is it?'

'I was doing the ironing,' Mandy Smith said. 'Cook yelled at me to fetch her a new apron but I wasn't thinking! I put the iron down on the ironing board and got distracted by a mouse running across the floor and burnt the hem of Cook's apron.'

'Give me two minutes to put this lot into the sisters' dining room and I'll come and see if anything can be done.'

'Oh, thank you, thank you! I just know they're going to beat me when they find out what I did.'

'There'll be no beatings. I won't let them find any reason to beat you.'

The sisters might taunt Emma, be mean to her, and even lock her in the linen room or tie her to a chair, but they would never do anything to harm the child. They would be guarding Emma's precious cargo and it gave Emma leeway.

'I didn't know who to ask for help,' Mandy said.

'Me. I'll always help you if I can.' Even if no-one else in Mandy Smith's life did. 'What's your real name?'

'I'm not telling you that!'

'I'm Emma. Emma Hatton. You can safely tell me your name. I won't let on.'

Mandy Smith gulped. 'Monica,' she said softly. 'Monica Stewart.'

Emma smiled. 'A beautiful name, Monica. Has anyone told you what a lovely smile you have?'

'Me?' Monica said, as though she thought Emma might be inebriated.

'Yes, you. I see how brave you are. I admire that.'

'Really?' Monica said, her gaze softening.

Emma was remembering Susannah of course, and the day the girl arrived, stalwart but bewildered. 'Try not to be frightened, Monica. I don't know much about what happens to us when they take us to the hospital but I'm going to tell you everything I do know. So you're more prepared.'

Monica's hands flew to her stomach. 'I've only got a month.'

'Me too. Perhaps we'll go on the horse and cart together.'

Fifteen minutes later, Emma hadn't been able to fix Monica's problem so she sent the girl off to do her next chore and went to Mrs Ross.

'Mandy Smith—her real name is Monica, by the way—has scorched Cook's apron. I hoped to fix it by cutting off the burnt bit and rehemming but it's a much bigger burn than I'd thought and Cook will notice the difference in the length.'

'*Mandy*,' Mrs Ross said in a quiet but firm tone, 'ought to be more careful with other people's possessions.'

'Help us,' Emma said.

After a moment of deliberation, Mrs Ross said, 'Come with me.'

Once in the laundry, after the housekeeper had viewed the devastation of the burnt apron, she lifted the iron from the wood stove and spat on the plate. It hissed. Then she moved to the ironing board, threw the apron across it and pressed the iron firmly onto the hemline of the apron, covering the initial burn.

When the smell of scorched cotton permeated the room, she looked up. 'I've had a little accident with one of Cook's aprons. I shall accept responsibility and advise Cook.'

Unexpected tears stung Emma's eyes but she blinked them away fast. 'Thank you.'

Helen Ross said nothing, although her expression was compassionate.

Emma turned, heading for the sisters' dining room so she could set the table for their evening meal.

'Emma.'

Emma halted, surprised by Mrs Ross's use of her real name.

The housekeeper returned the iron to the stove and clasped her hands in front of her. 'I understand that maybe your friend hasn't forgotten you—'

'She never would!'

'But you must learn to temper your passion. If you don't, you're going to be constantly hurt.'

Emma was holding the hurt inside her daily, wondering how she might manage afterwards. But she couldn't give any regard to the future because her thoughts returned time and again to the one event that loomed: losing her child. 'I can't think any other way but passionately, Mrs Ross. This is all so cruel.'

'Life can be cruel and what you're going through is possibly the hardest thing you'll ever deal with. The braver you are now the easier it will be in the future, should fate deal you another blow.'

Emma could only pray they weren't auspicious last words. All this time while her hopes had been flying on a breeze, while she gazed at dust motes and dreamed of finding enough stars in her world to make her feel secure, she hadn't seen the reality she'd worked so hard to master. Cassie would never forget their friendship, but she had gone. Sailed to America with only a memory of Emma to keep her company, never having received the letter.

Chapter Twenty-three

Emma and two other girls were standing at the foot of the staircase listening to Mrs Ross chivvy them to hurry up with the bed linen for the infants' asylum when Cassie walked through the front door as casually as though she'd arrived for afternoon tea. Eddie followed, sauntering into the home in his khaki summer service uniform, smoothing his hair after he took his cap off, holding it neatly folded in his strong, tanned hands.

Shock froze Emma to the spot. She could hardly take in the sight before her let alone believe it. Cassie wore the most incredible outfit. A deep rose fabric patterned with scattered petals in all shades of pink and a little matching hat, along with wedge-heeled shoes and a brown leather handbag with a golden catch.

'There she is!' Cassie said to Sister Hyacinth, indicating Emma. 'Emma Hatton. How lucky to have found her. We've had such a terrible journey. It's taken forever!'

'Not quite forever,' Eddie added, stepping forwards with a smile. 'But a fair while. It's good to meet you, sister. Lieutenant Edward Shea, United States Army Medical Corps.'

Sister Hyacinth frowned and didn't take his outstretched hand. 'It's not our custom to allow visitors, except on occasions where the parents of our charges request it and even then we are discerning about who our girls spend time with. It's not always good for the baby.'

'How caring of you!' Cassie exclaimed. 'Isn't that lovely, Eddie?'

'Who are they?' Monica Stewart whispered to Emma.

'Gosh, look at that dress!' Evie Pollock said. 'How many coupons would that take!'

'Hush!' Emma told them. She didn't want to draw attention to their presence because they'd be sent on their way. But she silently indicated her joy to Helen Ross: *That's my friend! She came!*

The housekeeper's expression warmed momentarily.

'I don't suppose we could have some tea?' Cassie asked, a slim hand at her throat. Emma caught sight of the brilliant diamond engagement ring—and so did Sister Hyacinth, going by the flare in her eyes. 'I'm parched after the dust on the streets. Aren't you, sweetheart?' Cassie added, throwing Eddie a smile.

'Tea would be welcome, Sister Hyacinth. If my wife and I can trouble you.'

Married! They were married. But what were they doing here?

Sister Hyacinth gauged Cassie for a few moments, her expression giving nothing away. 'Of course, Lieutenant Shea. I shall arrange it at once. Although I must reaffirm it is not our policy to allow the girls under our care any visitors except, on occasion, their mothers.'

'Oh, please do help us,' Cassie said. 'My husband and I are willing to offer a contribution to your charitable work if we could just see Miss Hatton.'

'We certainly are. Say, thirty pounds?' Eddie was already pulling a wallet from his back pocket. 'Would that suit, my darling girl?'

Cassie blushed. 'You're such a generous man.'

Emma swallowed hard, hoping the gulp wouldn't be heard. Thirty pounds! He was about to give away thirty whole pounds!

Sister Hyacinth took the money and held it firmly between her fingertips. 'I shall allow this visit but I must insist on accompanying you.'

'I'm afraid that wouldn't be acceptable,' Eddie said, still holding his opened wallet. He glanced at the money in Sister Hyacinth's hand. 'My wife and I must be allowed to see Miss Hatton alone.'

'Or else our journey will have been wasted, along with your precious leave,' Cassie said to Eddie with a despondent pull of her mouth.

Sister Hyacinth paused, clearly evaluating the situation of the fabulously attired young woman and the American officer with possibly a lot more money in his wallet. 'Very well,' she said, pocketing the notes in her habit. 'Just this once there may be a relaxing of the rules.'

Cassie clapped in glee and her big white diamond twinkled in the sunlight spilling in from the open door.

'Let us first have tea,' Sister Hyacinth said as she indicated her office with a thick-knuckled hand. There was a hint of a smile on her face now, something Emma had never seen before.

'Smith!' Sister Hyacinth barked. 'Help Mrs Ross bring tea for three to my office.'

Monica Stewart flew down the stairs and headed for the kitchens. Helen Ross hesitated only a second, then made her way after the girl.

Emma was still rooted to the spot, heart pounding. This could go either way. She had never known anyone to just turn up and demand to see one of the girls. Sister Hyacinth had taken the money but she wouldn't allow the visit until she'd questioned Cassie and Eddie thoroughly, getting as much intelligence from them as possible.

'Quick,' Evie Pollock whispered, 'Sister Peter's coming.'

Head in a spin, Emma stayed put, gritting her teeth.

'Come on,' Evie hissed. 'We can't stay here. I don't want to get into trouble and if you don't come with me, we'll both get a beating!'

Cassie and Eddie followed Sister Hyacinth into the office and Emma had no choice but to dash up the stairs with Evie.

She got to the second floor first and burst into the nursery, taking only a second to catch her breath. If they were being served tea, Mrs Ross would do it properly, so Emma had a bit of time. They'd have biscuits, or possibly fruit tarts. The tray would be set with doilies along with a little silver vase with a single-stemmed rose. The sisters adored their roses.

'What do you think all that was about?' Evie said, hand on her chest.

'I don't know.' Emma busied her hands with the first set of sheets. 'You do the far end of the room and I'll do the rest.'

She raced through the task, tucking in corners beneath worn mattresses and plumping thin pillows. She had never made half-a-dozen beds in such a short span of time.

She was supposed to head back to the linen room now. But not yet.

'Where are you going?' Evie asked as Emma ran to the door.

'Front hallway. Think I dropped a pillowcase.'

'Are you going to see that woman with the Yank? Who are they? What do they want with you?'

'I don't know.' Emma fled along the landing to the staircase.

'Wait for me!' Evie said, and ran after her.

They'd got almost to the bottom step when Sister Hyacinth's office door opened and Cassie and Eddie walked out, followed by the nun.

'Twenty minutes,' Sister Hyacinth said.

'Thirty,' Cassie said with a fluttering of her eyelashes, like a spoilt little woman with a husband who adored her, and nothing like the real Cassie O'Byrne.

Cassie Shea now.

Sister Hyacinth pursed her mouth, looking like she'd sucked on a rotten lemon. 'Pollock!'

Evie jumped then scuttled down the remaining stairs and ran across the hallway.

'Show our visitors to the library.'

'Yes, sister.'

'I'm Cassie,' Cassie said to Evie. 'What's your name?'

'Pollock.'

'I meant your first name.'

Evie shot a look at Sister Hyacinth. 'Pollock,' she said again, and turned for the library.

Emma gripped the banister, waiting for an instruction to join them.

'Harper. You have twenty minutes with these people.'

'Thirty!' Cassie reminded Sister Hyacinth with a sweet smile. 'And her name is Miss Hatton. Emma Hatton.' Cassie looked up at Emma, her eyes lightening and her lips widening in the wickedest smile Emma had ever seen her produce.

Emma's heart exploded.

Cassie. Cassie was here!

* * *

'Thank you, Evie,' Emma said. 'You can leave now. Close the door behind you.'

Evie glanced at the glamorous woman in the oppressive old library then backed out the door.

The library was suddenly swamped in silence. Emma turned to Cassie and drank in the sight before her. Cassie appeared to be doing the exact same thing before they dashed across the room and embraced. Cassie's body against hers gave Emma the sense of warmth and wholesomeness she'd missed so very much. The scent of her 7777 Eau de Cologne was almost suffocating since Emma had become accustomed to nothing but sweat and Sunlight soap.

'Oh my darling Cassie.'

'Sweetest Em!'

'I thought you might not have received my letter.'

'What a relief when I got it!' Cassie said, her hands gripping Emma as though she never wanted to let go. 'I didn't even wait to reply, I went straight to Eddie and told him everything you'd said.'

Emma closed her eyes, thankful for this moment like none before. 'I never thought I'd hear your voice again.'

'And here I am, turning up like a bad penny.'

Like a golden coin! Emma found a tremulous laugh as she pulled from the embrace but couldn't bring herself to let Cassie go completely in case she disappeared. 'I wondered if you'd forgotten me.'

Horror appeared on her friend's face. 'I've done everything in my power to find you! All this time. But I only got your letter five days ago. I moved out of the boarding house after we got married. I'm living with a respectable family Eddie knows—with my own bathroom, Em! Anyway, then I met a girl who still lived at the old boarding house and she gave me your letter.' Cassie took a breath. 'I went straight to Eddie. We've been telephoning the home every day this last week wanting to speak to you but the sister wouldn't let us. Before I got your letter I'd just wanted to know where you were so I could send you some money. I had no idea you were locked up like prisoners. I thought you'd get out to do some shopping or something.'

Emma put a hand over her mouth to stall the emotion welling inside her. Going out into the garden was the most they expected. As for shopping—a thing of the past.

'I'm such an idiot,' Cassie said remorsefully.

'No, you're not. You're wonderful.'

'I even telephoned the Colson house just before Christmas.'

'*Harry Colson?*'

'I had to get a message to your mother. It took some doing. Gosh, is that housekeeper of his a pain in the neck or what? In the end I demanded to speak to the man himself. But don't worry. I didn't say who I was, I simply asked if he could pass on my telephone number to your mother. I didn't tell on you. He didn't suspect anything.'

All the same ... Harry Colson. 'Did he get a message to my mother?'

'He must have. She telephoned me from a neighbour's house. I pretended we'd met at the Comforts Fund and was just enquiring after your health.'

'What did she say?'

'That you'd been sent away to do your war work in Brisbane. So I asked if I could contact you and of course she refused. Anyway, I've found you now! Eddie wangled a twenty-four-hour leave pass and we came straight to Brisbane by train. We have to go back tonight. Oh, Em! It's so good to see you. I've missed you so much. I was worried sick and no surprise. This place is a nightmare. I mean, what the heck is this?' She plucked at Emma's apron.

Emma couldn't help but squirm. She looked down at her apron and the skirt of her dress. Nothing more than a sack. Fitting for a girl considered a nobody. A worthless girl, apart from the child she carried.

But she pushed embarrassment away. There wasn't time. There were a hundred questions firing in her brain and the minutes were ticking. 'What happened in the office?'

'That woman absolutely drilled me! How can you put up with her?'

'It was a bit of a whirl,' Eddie said, stepping forwards from the spot by the door where he'd stayed while his wife and her friend became reacquainted. He looked somewhat bewildered.

'You're quite the actress, darling,' he said to Cassie. 'I could hardly keep up.' But he grinned and it was a welcoming smile. 'I thought she was going to ravage us with questions,' he told Emma. 'But Cassie took it all on the chin. Really, you should have seen her handle that woman.'

'What a rotten old cow,' Cassie declared, reminding Emma of Wynn.

'It's lovely to see you again, by the way,' Eddie said to Emma. 'I'm so sorry it's in these sad circumstances.'

'May I offer my congratulations on your marriage?' Emma said, returning the lieutenant's smile. 'I'm so thrilled for you both. Thank you for bringing Cassie to see me.'

He cleared his throat and opened his mouth to speak again but Cassie cut off whatever he'd been about to say. 'I love you, Em. If I could get you out of here I would, but it's not possible.'

'I know, my dearest friend. I know.'

'You're the bravest person. You will have my love and my heart always. Through all our trials, Em, we'll always know each other.'

Emma smiled but sensed something wasn't right.

'Darling.' Cassie turned to Eddie and tilted her head. 'Do you mind if I speak to Em alone now?'

Eddie took a step back, his cap in his hands. 'Of course. I'll get myself gone.' He turned for the door then swung around. 'I'll be right outside if you need me.'

'What's happening?' Emma asked once Eddie left the room and closed the door.

'Let's sit down.' Cassie led her to the armchair and made her sit while Cassie pulled the footstool over and sat on that.

'You've changed,' Emma said when Cassie looked up at her, eyes glowing.

'So have you.'

How they'd both grown up in the last year. In such extraordinary circumstances.

'How are you coping?' Cassie asked.

Emma wasn't, or hadn't been, until perhaps now. 'Let's not talk about me. I want to know all about you and Eddie. How was your wedding?'

Cassie scrunched her nose. 'Simple in the end. Quite small. Eddie only got a four-hour leave pass thanks to his obnoxious CO.' She produced a sudden smile. 'But it was *so* lovely! I looked a dream, I swear.'

'I bet you did. Mrs Edward Shea!'

'I put those daisies in my bouquet like I said I would. For you.'

Emma held onto the pain in her chest. How much had she missed? 'Thank you. I'll never forget you did that for me.'

'I missed you not being there, Em. I was so worried about you.'

Emma moistened her mouth. 'Now you've seen me and I've seen you. I'm so grateful for this. Did you get your visa permission to go to America?'

'Yes! I'm getting booked on a ship. I'll have to leave Eddie behind, of course, but he's insisting I get to Wisconsin as soon as possible and if I don't go now …' Cassie trailed off with an apologetic tilt of her head.

'You must go!' Emma insisted.

'Well …'

'What is it?'

'It's you, Em. Do you remember I said I wanted to take you with me?'

Emma took her friend's hand in both of hers, relishing the contact and the tenderness of her softened skin. If only life was one big Cassie O'Byrne adventure away. 'I'm so pleased for you, Cassie. You make my heart burst with joy. You'll take the memory of me with you and you'll never look back.'

'But that's just it.' Cassie glanced at the closed door and back to Emma. 'Eddie and I want to adopt your baby.'

Chapter Twenty-four

'We don't think we can take it without adopting it,' Cassie said, her words rushing. 'But if there's some way to get you to America after all this, maybe we could work things out. Eddie's all for it. He thinks it's appalling the way you've been treated.'

Cassie shifted on the tapestry stool, bringing herself closer. 'When we telephoned, trying to get hold of you, Sister Hyacinth told us it was their duty to care for you and we weren't even allowed to enquire as to your wellbeing. Apparently it's got nothing to do with your friends and the people who love you. She said the baby was going to be adopted out, that a family had been chosen and that was that.' Irritation flashed in Cassie's eyes. 'I'm not going to let it happen. It's not right.'

Emma couldn't catch her breath. Surely she was dreaming. She'd wake up soon—Sister Peter would ring the bell informing them it was half past five and they all had to get up.

'We haven't mentioned a possible adoption to the sister yet,' Cassie continued. 'We wanted to speak to you first. We'd never do anything you didn't want.'

But Emma's child was going to the Houlihans. Sister Hyacinth would never break that agreement. Not even for thirty pounds.

'I suggested we get you out of here and get you a room at a good guest house so you can have your baby and keep it,' Cassie said. 'Except Eddie said it wouldn't work. He said he'd thought it over and in a practical manner we could help for a while but then we'd be gone and you'd be fending for yourself. The war's not going to last much longer now.'

Emma released a sigh. Oh, to be free and to give birth in a real bed with proper help and no admonishing. But Eddie was right. She couldn't rear her child alone. Her family would shun her. Emma wouldn't get work and wouldn't earn a wage. Not with an illegitimate child. She'd have to move away from Queensland for a start or her mother would find her. She wouldn't put it past her mother to tell the whole neighbourhood the truth, just so she could slap down her daughter's pride while gaining sympathy for herself and the situation she'd had to bear.

'Em! Em!' Cassie said, shaking Emma's hands. 'You haven't said a word.'

Emma brought her focus back to her friend. 'I can't believe what you're saying,' she said, her voice barely above a murmur.

'Well, believe!'

Cassie's face took on a rosy hue borne from exhilaration and maybe a need to get her point across as fast as possible. 'It's a matter of filling in forms. I mean the adoption. Eddie says the baby will have to have our surname but we'll figure something out in the future.'

Emma could hardly comprehend the now, let alone the future. Shea. Not Houlihan. 'You'd do this for me?'

'I'd do anything for you! I'd stay if we could, but we just can't. Eddie's father has got him a job in a big hospital. It's an enormous promotion. Nothing like he could get here. His father is on the board of directors.'

'Oh, Cassie ...' Astonishment resided in every atom of Emma's body. 'Has Sister Hyacinth agreed?' Cassie would need a lot more than thirty pounds to secure Emma's baby and no matter how loaded Eddie's family appeared to be, Emma couldn't see them handing over more for someone else's child. Nobody in their right mind would do that.

'Em, I just told you, we didn't bring it up. We wanted to speak to you first. We'd never do anything you didn't want. Eddie's going to offer a hundred pounds.'

Emma choked on her surprise.

'I have forty pounds saved and I'll be putting that money to Eddie's if I need to. What do you think? Do you think it's possible she'll agree?'

Emma couldn't think about possibilities, only about what she knew. That the girls who'd already given birth cried through the night when they came back from the hospital. No-one in the dormitory asked them why, because everybody knew. The same thing was going to happen to all of them and not one of them truly knew what it might feel like to have a baby, then sob yourself into a state of panic when it was taken away and given to someone you'd never met and would never meet.

It would be different if Emma's baby was taken by Cassie. Even though she'd never know her child, her friend would. Emma might even learn of her child's progress if they kept in touch. She might get photographs.

'Emma Hatton, stand up at once!' Cassie said, pulling Emma from the armchair.

Emma trembled as she was tugged upright.

'We've only got minutes. You have to get real. Have you heard what I've been saying? I know it's going to be awful having someone take your baby but I can't think of anything else and neither can Eddie. Em! Are you listening?'

Emma roused herself and scrubbed her face. The considerations were overwhelming but it was an answer to a prayer she'd never contemplated making.

'How would it work?' she asked. 'You and Eddie will have your own children.'

'And yours would be our first. Until you get to us. Then we'll see what happens.'

Was Cassie saying they'd give the baby back? 'What if I can't make it to America?' There were a thousand reasons she might not travel. Poverty. Parental rule. A need to earn a wage. The war …

'Then your child will be our child forevermore. We'd tell it, Em. We wouldn't hide you away like your family has. We'll make your child proud to have you as its mother.'

'But Eddie's family … How could they possibly accept this?'

Cassie offered a smile that reached her green eyes. 'Eddie was adopted. So was his sister. We'd love your child like we will our own. He or she will be part of us and part of you.' Cassie laughed, although tears were now streaming down her cheeks. 'It's just what I wished for. I wanted to take you with me to America and now perhaps I can take a little bit of you with me after all.'

Emma closed her eyes as she fought her way through the incomprehension of it all. Why did life take so many turns? Why couldn't it be solid and dependable? Why had Emma Hatton fallen by the wayside and got herself into this trouble? And why had they given her all the blame?

'Did you think I wouldn't come to your rescue?' Cassie said. 'That I wouldn't help you?'

Emma opened her eyes. 'I never doubted it.' Not that she'd expected this kind of response.

'Listen to me, Em. The only other choice is that it goes to someone who might not love it. They already don't love it like I do. They just want it. I adore it.'

Emma adored it too. It was part of her, it was her whole world. But whatever the outcome, it would never be hers. It would be taken away.

'You'd do this for me if our situations were reversed. I know you would. You know this is the only way.'

Everything Cassie said was buzzing in Emma's head. Everything she'd offered. Everything she was prepared to do.

'Eddie says they probably won't let us meet again, even after the birth. He said we'll have to come to Brisbane to pick up the baby but that it's likely we won't see you—and I think I might be sailing within weeks. The thought of not seeing you again, of you not seeing me with your little one … it breaks my heart!' Cassie struck a hand to her breast. 'Em, darling. Do you agree? Can we ask the sister?'

Emma answered quickly and steadfastly: 'Yes.' It was the hardest and yet the easiest word she'd ever uttered.

Cassie stabbed a euphoric kiss on Emma's cheek then flew to the door and opened it.

Eddie stepped in looking as pale as a sheet and Cassie pulled him in as she closed the door. 'Yes,' she told him, smiling through her tears.

Eddie firmed his mouth, his emotion about the situation clear: concern, some anguish, but also relief. He took a folded handkerchief from the pocket of his trousers and handed it to his wife.

While Cassie blew her nose, Eddie strode towards Emma, hands outstretched. 'Emma.'

Emma had never known him well, only at dinner or sharing a drink after Cassie had been singing at one of the Comforts Fund's dances, but she wanted to throw herself into his arms.

He took her hands. 'This is what we want. Both of us.'

'I am so grateful.'

'We will arrange everything with the sisters. You mustn't worry. But I must advise you that it might be impossible for us to see you before Cassie sails.'

Emma nodded.

'The war will end sooner rather than later now, but it's likely I will remain in Townsville for some time. I just don't know. But as long as I am here in Australia, you have a friend.'

Every emotion was winging its way through Emma's system. Joy. Fear. Sadness. Gratefulness, most of all.

Eddie turned to Cassie. 'Darling, it's time. Sister Hyacinth is hovering in the hallway.' Turning back to Emma, he hugged her. 'Stay well, dearest Em. You're my wife's best friend and that makes you my friend too. I'll get word to you when I can.'

Once again, he strode to the door, a decent man, and in control now that the situation had been made clear to him. 'Two minutes, no more,' he told Cassie.

Emma's head swam. Everything was happening so quickly. An agreement had been made, another bond created and now there was only the deal to be struck with the sisters.

'I'll be sent home,' she told Cassie. 'That's where you can reach me. You will write?'

'As soon as I can. I'll write on the ship and when I land in America. I'll write every day, Em.'

And one day soon, Emma would receive the letters and she would know something about her child.

'I could be gone before I see you again,' Cassie said. 'Do you understand?'

Emma understood everything perfectly. Gone. Perhaps forever, and meaning this was their last goodbye. Tears ran down her cheeks and she let them fall. Had there ever been a more expressive and heart-wrenching goodbye? 'But you'll be going with a part of me, remember?'

Cassie held Emma's hand. 'Stay strong, Em. We were meant to meet and become friends. Now we know why.'

Emma put her arms around her friend and pulled her close. 'No matter what, you will live in my heart.' There was every possibility the sisters would refuse Cassie and Eddie's request, but how glorious to have known such a person as Cassie. A young woman willing to do the utmost for someone she loved.

'What shall we call it?' Cassie asked. 'What names would you like?'

Emma clasped her hands together. 'You choose.'

'No!' Cassie shook her head defiantly. 'This is your baby. You must choose.'

Emma licked her dried lips. 'Douglas.'

'And if it's a girl?'

'Grace.'

'Grace Emma.'

'Just Grace.' Grace Shea. 'In Latin, *gratia* means God's favour. I chose the name Grace because I hoped my child would be favoured.' Now, it was possible the child would know true kindness. 'I chose Douglas after my father.'

'I'll take care of him or her, Em. As if they were my own.'

'I know you will.'

The library door opened and whatever else they might have said would have to be told in letters.

'Darling.'

Cassie turned to Eddie then back to Emma. 'I love you, Em.'

'I love you too, Cassie. I always will.'

'Come what may.'

'Come what may,' Emma repeated softly. 'Thank you. I'll never be able to repay you.'

She stood frozen to the spot as Cassie left the room. Fifteen minutes she stayed there. Were they exchanging money? Were they signing the paperwork? Or were they making their argument while Sister Hyacinth disputed whether a hundred pounds was enough. How would Emma know what went through the woman's mind or how she calculated the price of a life?

When the library door opened, Emma discovered she'd been holding her breath. It came out in a rush and her knees almost buckled.

'I believe what you wanted has been arranged,' Helen Ross said.

Emma closed her eyes. It was done. Her child was going to Cassie.

PART THREE

Chapter Twenty-five

Blueholm Bay—June 1945

The Hatton house faced east and was bathed in winter sunshine all day. Leaning against the paint-worn balustrade on the small verandah at number eleven Herring Street, Emma watched the world go by. A world she once again inhabited. Katy Wheaton had a new puppy and two of her children were trailing in her wake, tossing a stick between them but not letting the dog get it, which was sending the pup crazy with frustration. Emma ensured she didn't catch Katy's eye as the family passed.

Three doors down, Mrs Jameson was out hanging the washing along with two of the younger of her brood of seven children. Not all the yards and gardens in Blueholm Bay were fenced but most had a marked boundary and everyone knew everyone and most of their business so it didn't matter that Mrs Jameson might be hanging out her smalls in full view of everyone because that's what they all did.

There was a true country-living atmosphere to Blueholm Bay but as it was only a mile's walk to the ocean there was an ever-present tang of brine in the air as people lived their lives and went about their daily business. But it wasn't home.

Emma lifted the note she held to read it again.

OPENED BY CENSOR

Miss E. Hatton
11 Herring Street
Blueholm Bay
Townsville

June 7, 1945

Dearest Emma,

    I'm sorry it has taken me this long to write but so much has been happening. Cassie was wretched at having to leave Townsville before she could see you once again, but I felt it wise she and the baby stay in Brisbane with the other war brides. No-one can predict what might happen next, or what restrictions might suddenly be put in place.

    The SS *Lurline* left Brisbane on June 3 as expected and should arrive in San Francisco on June 18. Cassie will be escorted by good relatives to my family in Madison and will write to you as soon as she is able. My parents and my sister are longing to meet her and the little one.

    If I can do anything for you while I'm still here, you must tell me. I will oblige your most simple wish if it is within my power to do so. I'm so sorry for everything you've been through but know that you are loved by my beautiful wife and therefore by me. As is the child.

    Yours faithfully,
    Edward Shea

It had been Helen Ross who helped birth her baby.

    Emma's waters had broken mid-morning in the dormitory and she thought she'd wet herself. Then the pain began. She begged Evie to fetch the housekeeper. Within what had felt like a ridiculously short time, and without much fuss, little Grace was born.

Mrs Ross allowed Emma ten minutes with her child before she went to inform the sisters. Ten minutes of pleasure with an overwhelming love building inside her moment by precious moment.

Cassie's baby.

Emma had been in the hospital for over a week after giving birth, then at St Philomena's for a further four weeks. But that wasn't only her mother's punishment: she'd bled after they'd taken Grace away and had continued to bleed. Her uterus hadn't contracted. Mrs Ross had had to make the blood stop. Emma had watched in horror as Mrs Ross frantically rubbed and squeezed her belly, expelling blood clot after blood clot with words of explanation and encouragement between shouts for someone to fetch the doctor.

She must have managed it, although Emma had passed out by that point. She'd probably been carried out of the home and onto the horse and cart by old Tyrell and the coachman.

When she came to she was in a hospital ward with a partition between her and the other mothers. The doctors weren't kind when they told her what had happened, neither did they fully explain why it had happened. But they had all seemed satisfied when they gave her their final prognosis: Emma could never again have a baby without fear of haemorrhaging.

So not one loss, but two.

* * *

'Maybe you should act a bit sicker,' Mum said a few days later.

Emma swung around, a peeling knife and a potato in her hands. 'Sicker?' Did her mother think she was anything but? She'd been slaving in the Hatton household every day, as she had at the home, but this time she was grateful for the labour, happy for her hands and mind to be occupied and dreading the time every night when she lay awake in bed, trying not to cry, trying to be brave.

'We could say you've got some disease,' her mother said. 'Everyone knows you're low of spirits after getting ill at Doris's in-laws' place.'

The townspeople had been given the new story of the in-laws without the couple having a first clue so much had happened to them. They had received help from another family member, so Emma's services were no longer needed. This was why she'd apparently fallen ill and was 'low of spirits', because she'd enjoyed her time with the in-laws so much and was adrift and bereft without their tender care. An emotional malaise that apparently frequently happened to young girls.

There had been a few questioning glances and enquiries but Emma and her mother stuck to the story without embellishing. Emma wasn't sure the townswomen took the lies to heart. They were utterly nonsensical.

'Being down in the dumps is plain on your face,' Mum said. 'You're the one with the fancy reading; what sort of disease could you get? Nothing contagious, mind. And stop standing out in the sun. The browner you get, the healthier you look.'

Emma might never recover. When she was sent from the hospital back to St Philomena's, she spent her time helping the other girls until she felt useless, much like Wynn must have felt as they dragged her out the door. So when she couldn't bear it any longer, she prepared to leave, even if it meant scaling a wall and walking all the way to Townsville. She had already packed her bag when Helen Ross came to the dormitory in the early morning darkness with whispered words of help and money for a train ticket home.

When Emma walked through the unlocked front door on Herring Street, her mother's face had showed surprise but there had been no questions. Emma slotted back into the daily grind with the ease of a silk strand slipping through the eye of a needle.

Germany had surrendered but the war hadn't ended and there were plenty of Yanks needing their laundry done, so Mum carried on working at Mrs Cosgrove's every weekday. Emma refused to go when her mother suggested she help. She might be remaining detached from each reality until she found more clarity on how to carry on, but one thing was certain. She was no longer a yes girl.

'The truth is, Mum, I've never been more unwell in my life.'

Mum grunted her displeasure. 'We have to find some real excuse for this depressing frame of mind.'

Real? Emma turned away. Perhaps the greatness of her loss would never die, never fade enough to carry on with a genuine smile and not the forced ones she occasionally produced for some of the neighbours.

'And I'd still like to know who that note was from.'

'None of your business.'

'You're still under my charge,' Mum said tartly. 'I hope you haven't got yourself involved with any of those girls at the home, if that's who the note was from. The nuns told me you weren't allowed to be friendly and that's the way it should be.'

'You know nothing about the place.' And Emma wasn't about to enlighten her.

'What about that girl who rang the big house wanting to know your whereabouts and creating a bother for me, I might add? I had to lie to a Colson. She said her name was Daisy. Said she was an acquaintance. Is that who the note was from?'

Daisy. It almost brought a smile. Trust Cassie to cover her tracks. Neither her mother nor Doris knew about the adoptive parents swap. Emma presumed Sister Hyacinth kept the one hundred pounds and gave the Houlihans some story about the baby dying while assuring them there were other babies being born, and that was that.

'You don't deserve a decent friend, anyway,' her mother muttered as she banged a pot and a frying pan onto the stove.

'Mum. I've prepared the veg and there's an apple pie in the food safe ready to go in the oven. Now let me get on with these potatoes or there won't be any mash for dinner.'

'You don't deserve a good man either,' her mother continued, desperate to throw as many stones at her daughter as possible. 'So don't go expecting one to pop out from the woodpile. Men want children and you can't supply them.'

Emma looked at her mother. 'That was heartless and I won't have you say it again.'

Mum mumbled something about it being the truth and Emma put the comment away in the furthest recess of her mind. Her mother's bitter words were more wounding than any she'd heard at St Philomena's.

'Why don't *you* pretend to be sick?' she said, throwing a peeled potato into a pot of cold water. 'Which means it's a good job your miserable daughter is home to look after you.'

Mum pointed a finger. 'Don't backchat me. I'll tell your father.'

'Go ahead. He won't do anything. He believes every bad thing you say about me.'

'How dare you!'

'Go write to him, Mum. Tell him whatever you want.' Emma dropped the knife onto the cutting board and walked out of the kitchen.

'Come back here this instant!' Mum yelled, but Emma kept walking down the dark hallway and through to her bedroom, slamming the door behind her.

She'd responded to Eddie's note, asking him not to write again until she found somewhere secure to receive her mail.

Emma didn't know how to go about this yet but if her mail came to Herring Street there was no guarantee her mother wouldn't get her hands on it first, and she wouldn't hesitate to open it.

And regardless of Eddie's generous offer of further assistance, Emma wouldn't ask him for anything. Not money nor help. She'd find a way to stand on her own two feet eventually, but holding his note next to her heart each night before she found sleep gave her comfort. Someone knew her truth, and maybe one day little Grace would know it too.

She pulled a cardigan from the chair by her bed and slipped her arms through. She'd go for a walk over the rickety bridge at the creek and try to extinguish the imagery in her mind of Cassie holding Grace, cooing words of love and watching how the baby's face changed every day.

All Emma had was a memory of the infant's smell, tender and fresh. She would never forget it.

* * *

Emma was used to feeling isolated, even when in company, and was uninterested in almost everything going on around her. But her mother's continuing heartlessness woke her to the necessity of not only living but of strengthening her resolve to get on with things.

It was a Saturday when she finally got the chance to put her idea into motion. She had a request to make of the Osbornes and she'd got out of the house without being questioned by her mother because she'd forgotten to pick up their tea ration. As she stood in the grocer's shop, crowded with as many goods and wares as a war allowed, she formed her words carefully. Her proposal was to have her mail addressed via the shop. She needed to send an address to Eddie quickly, before Cassie sent her letter because if the ship had docked on time she'd already arrived in America. But she wouldn't tell the Osbornes that.

'I have a friend,' she told them once the store had emptied of the few Saturday morning customers. A newly married friend who had sailed to America—a particularly interesting subject, because everyone knew someone who knew someone whose cousin, sister or neighbour had married an American or was about to. The friend would be sorely missed, and as she'd also had an injured brother a year ago and no other family in Australia, Emma knew she would be desperate to keep in contact with the few people she'd become acquainted with during the war but had left behind because of falling in love. This last part brought a warming to Mrs Osborne's eyes and a somewhat uncomfortable sigh from her husband.

'Can't your mother hold your mail?' he asked, the grey ends of his thick moustache getting stuck in the corners of his mouth as he spoke.

Fortunately, Emma didn't have to answer because his wife said, 'I don't see any difficulty with this.'

Emma darted her glances between them. They were in their early seventies and childless, but it hadn't stopped Mrs Osborne becoming an expert on all things pertaining to married life as well as the rearing of children or the straying of husbands. Many women in town would chat to her about their problems and Mrs Osborne always had an answer.

'It's likely we'll see a lot more of this type of thing in the future, Walter,' she told Mr Osborne. 'We must become accustomed to dealing with the unusual.'

'It just seems a little odd when …' Mr Osborne struggled through his lack of words, possibly knowing he'd already lost any argument that hadn't even begun. 'We're not a post office,' he finished gruffly.

'But who knows what we'll be doing when the war ends?' Mrs Osborne returned her gaze to Emma. 'I presume this will be an arrangement between yourself and ourselves only.'

Emma's heart beat wildly. 'It's not that I intend to deceive, Mrs Osborne, but I think everyone is aware that my mother and I don't always get along—'

'Indeed,' Mrs Osborne interrupted in a knowledgeable manner.

'I wouldn't like to add to her troubles by making her more anxious. My friend has married into a respectable and wealthy American family and perhaps my mother might find that a little uncomfortable, given that we have so much less—'

'I imagine she would,' Mrs Osborne said with finality in her voice. She and Emma's mother had been at loggerheads over one thing or another most of Emma's life, although they always remained neighbourly on the surface. 'Walter,' Mrs Osborne said, 'we will make arrangements to hold Emma's mail and we won't breathe a word of it to anyone.'

Mr Osborne scratched his head. 'Yes, dear.'

Emma thanked them both and was making her way out of the shop, almost blinded with relief, when she bumped into Harry Colson, practically knocking him over.

'I'm so sorry! I didn't see you there!'

'Gracious,' he said with a smile as he steadied himself. 'What a hurricane.'

Emma's face heated up.

'Emma Hatton, isn't it?' he said.

'Yes, Mr Colson. How are you, sir?'

'I'm well. And you? You're looking very well indeed, if I may say so.'

Emma couldn't answer for a moment as waves of anguish washed over her, as they did at the most unexpected of times. 'I am well,' she said at last. 'Thank you.'

'So, you made your sixteenth birthday and found freedom. And ... how old are you now?'

'I turned eighteen at the beginning of the year, sir.'

'Oh, don't "sir" me, Emma. I may still call you Emma?'

'Of course.'

'What are you doing with your time?' he said, a strong hand on his cane and looking for all the world as though they met every week and caught up on local news. She'd forgotten about him completely since she'd come back yet he'd been in her thoughts a number of times at St Philomena's.

'I'm at home.'

'And your parents? They are well?'

'Mother's getting by. We think my father's brigade is being relieved but we're not sure where they will be sent next.' Not that Dad had told them, it was Irene McDonald's brother who had written with the information. His letter had been heavily censored but everyone had become accustomed to sleuthing through blackened out words and reaching a conclusion.

'He's with the 11th Brigade, isn't he ... 31st/51st Battalion?'

'How did you know?' Emma blurted, surprised by his knowledge.

'Oh, I like to keep abreast of what's going on. At least your brother wasn't needed to fight,' he added after a quick intake of breath. 'Is he working?'

'The eldest two are looking for work.'

'I presume, like you, they had to leave school.'

Emma nodded, not wanting to go into detail. Joe was a young man now. He'd mended a few of the broken pickets on the front and back fences and fixed the canvas awning over the walkway from the kitchen to the laundry. He chopped kindling for the stove and talked incessantly of getting out of Blueholm Bay and finding a job. Simon, spurred on by Joe's newfound manly vigour, had informed their mother he too was leaving school.

Emma gave Harry Colson a smile of acknowledgement and made a move to leave.

He stepped sideways, halting her. 'And you? You've been home for some time, I believe.'

Emma turned to him, confused as to why he was prolonging the conversation. 'A little while.'

'I was surprised to find you not working, you see, but then I heard that you'd been ill.'

Emma paused. He would have been told about her malaise by any number of people, but perhaps he was suggesting she get a move on. She had been reluctant to get out and about. She wasn't allowed to look for work in Townsville so what else could she do? Milking the Colson cows was definitely not on her agenda.

'I do hope you're feeling better.'

'Thank you, I am.'

'It's just that I imagine a woman like yourself, a woman with your intelligence, would find life a little dull without employment.'

A woman. Like herself. How little he knew—thank God.

'All the jobs will go back to the men, of course, once they start arriving home,' he said, 'but I'm sure someone of your standing will find rewarding work. Something to keep that excellent mind ticking over.'

Heat crawled along the back of Emma's neck and she hoped she wasn't blushing too hard. 'I'm quite content at the moment,' she said, hearing the curtness in her tone but unable to do anything about it. He'd already questioned her far more than anyone else in town, and what right did he have to do that? 'I have a number of things to—' To what? Get over? 'To think through. Before I turn my sights to the future.'

'I'm sorry. I hope I haven't offended you.'

'Not at all, Mr Colson. You could never do that.'

'Yet I fear I have. Did something happen in Brisbane? I believe you were working for an aunt's in-laws?'

Confusion made her hesitate once more. Was he saying he'd heard rumours or was he being genuinely obtuse? Perhaps he remembered taking Cassie's telephone call. He must, because he'd got word to Emma's mother to instruct her to telephone Cassie—Daisy—about Emma's welfare. 'I was in Brisbane, yes. But the job didn't last.'

'I'm sorry to hear it. I'm sure you'll get by. Things will change for all of us now but life goes on ...' He trailed off. 'Well, I'll let you get along. Good luck,' he said kindly, and tipped his hat. 'I hope we meet again.'

'Yes. Thank you.'

Emma ought to ask how his sister was and if there was any news on her husband but didn't want to remind him of the secret he'd once asked her to keep, since she was keeping counsel on her own life. Her chest was tight with the humiliation of having to live with all these lies.

She made her way down the verandah steps and onto the road, ensuring she didn't look back. His words about her not having employment were sinking in faster than a lost boot in a sodden patch of quicksand. She wasn't ill. Not physically and not in the sense her mother meant. She was capable and intelligent as the man said, and though unlikely to be rewarded intellectually by the kind of job available for young women, especially in Blueholm Bay, she ought to be doing her bit for the war.

She drew breath when she reached her front gate and chanced a look at the grocery store when she heard Harry Colson's motor engine fire up. His insight had uncomfortably but instantly struck her to the core. From the moment she'd walked back through the kitchen door on Herring Street she'd had one goal: to get out of Blueholm Bay as fast as possible. It might not come to fruition soon but unless she got up and looked for the opportunity, it wouldn't happen at all.

Chapter Twenty-six

July 1945

Emma watched the townspeople do their bit, trying to get an idea of what she could do to help. She was determined not to work up at the big house with the cows; she wasn't yet in any frame of mind to work that closely with Ivy Williams and she'd likely end up causing a stupendous argument, the brouhaha of which would be heard all the way to the city.

On day three after her encounter with Harry Colson, inspiration struck.

'Betty, can I have a word?'

'What do you want?' Betty asked as Emma stood in front of her house on Whiting Court. Betty Soames was still friends with Katy Wheaton, although possibly not as brash or nosey, and she had the ear of a lot of women in town.

'It's about the vegetable plots you and some of the other wives are tending in your yards.'

'What about them?'

'Most of the wives are still working at Mrs Cosgrove's and the others are looking after the children. It must be hard work keeping up the plots.'

'Tell me about it,' Betty said. 'I'm either sweating over a copper or digging up potatoes.'

'I thought I could do it,' Emma said. 'Tend your yards while you're all out working, or busy with the children. I wouldn't get in your way.'

'You?' Betty said, looking sceptical, her nose crinkled as though there were a bad smell in the air. Emma ignored it. The women of Blueholm Bay had come to accept Emma's stand-offishness. It had become part of her nature, according to most.

'I could look after seven or eight yards on Whiting Court and Snapper Street alone.'

'What would you want in return?'

'Nothing. It'll be my war work. I'd be happy to do it. Would you have a word with the others and see if they agree?'

'They'll agree all right,' Betty said. 'When do you plan to start?'

'As soon as it's all arranged. I'll begin with your yard, if you like.'

'About time you did something,' Betty mumbled. 'Does your mother know you're offering to help us?'

'It's got nothing to do with her. It's my choice.'

Betty kinked her mouth. 'My, how times have changed.'

'Haven't they?' Emma agreed, deadpan.

So Emma weeded and picked vegetables from her neighbours' yards. There was no money of course, but at least it was a start and she was occupied.

She carted them to the Osbornes' grocery shop in a wheelbarrow. The Osbornes held all the town's vegetables and doled them out following a list which recorded every household's input and reward. Those who didn't grow their own vegetables bought them, and the money went into a fund for families going through hard times. Which they mostly all were, apart from a few in the outlying homesteads who were farming and selling their crops to the military.

Emma had furthered her initiative by suggesting they commandeer an empty block of land next to Betty's house and make it one big community allotment instead of using all the backyards. It could even be kept going after the war when the men came home. Emma thought the allotment might help to continue to feed everyone after the war, especially those families of the men who might not get work straight away, and it would also give the men a chance to regroup and recuperate from all they'd been through.

Over the following weeks, she put her efforts into getting a section of the land ready. It was wonderful seeing seedlings become small, fragile-looking young plants and she could hardly wait for them to bloom with their offerings. In the meantime, she'd uprooted and carefully transplanted rows and rows of veggies from others' yards into the allotment and they were doing well. It was backbreaking labour and so exhausting she was actually sleeping some nights.

She took the harvest from the allotment to the store three times a week. Today the wheelbarrow was filled with cauliflowers, onions and turnips. She was pulling another onion, gently brushing the warm, dry dirt from its skin, when a motor car tooted.

Harry Colson—and he was waving. He drove a Ford Super Deluxe, a big black shiny motor vehicle, its silver trims splattered with dried earth as he headed off the road and down the dirt track towards the allotment and Emma.

She stood, giving the merest acknowledgement with a lift of her hand, then wiped her hands on her shorts. She held her breath when he wound his window open as he brought the car to a halt at the edge of the allotment.

'Can't stop for long,' he said. 'Got an appointment at the bank and left my paperwork at home so had to return to get it. But I just wanted to say I've heard of your endeavours here at the allotment and I think it's a splendid idea. Good on you, Emma. That's the spirit.'

Emma stood in her grubby shorts and her brother's old shirt, frayed at the cuffs, earth beneath her fingernails and in the creases of her knuckles and knees. 'Everyone's helping out where and when they can,' she said. 'I'll pass on your praise. Thank you so much for taking the time to notice our little vegetable plot.'

'It's more like an enterprise. I knew you'd find something to do, although I admit I didn't expect you to do manual labouring. What an example you are to us all.'

Emma's toes curled inside her work boots, which were Simon's and too big, necessitating two pairs of socks so her feet didn't slip out as she marched around town with her wheelbarrow. She was also clenching her hands to stop them from moving to her head and her scruffy ponytail. 'I'm simply doing my bit, Mr Colson.'

'And we thank you for it. It puts my tiny vegetable plot up at the house to shame. But I'm mostly purchasing from your allotment these days so I hope the proceeds are useful to the good cause.'

'They are, thank you, sir, but it's not my allotment, it belongs to us all.' Emma gave him a stiff smile. 'I'd best get on,' she said, brushing the palms of her hands down her shorts once more.

'Actually, if you have a moment.' He got out of the car, turning to collect his cane from the passenger seat, along with a package he held under his arm. Books. He had books.

'I saw you earlier on my way through town and thought you might like these.' He rested his cane against his thigh and held out the books. 'Hemingway and a couple of others I've had hanging around.'

Emma scraped her teeth over her bottom lip as she withheld a need to check his shoes which must now be as dusty and grimy as her work boots. 'I couldn't possibly take your books.'

'I have other copies. You're welcome to these if you think you might like them. Really,' he said, practically thrusting the volumes on her. 'I'd like them to go to someone who will appreciate them.'

Emma took them, unable to refuse without creating a fuss. 'Thank you.'

He gave her a pleasant smile. 'Delightful to meet up with you, Emma. Makes me glad I left that darned paperwork at home after all.'

Emma couldn't find the words to thank him again for this unexpected gift. Her mouth had dried out.

He made his way back to his motor car and Emma turned her back when he reversed the vehicle up the track. She examined the books. *For Whom the Bell Tolls*, a Nancy Mitford and another Helen Simpson novel.

'Emma!'

Emma stilled at the sound of Betty's voice. She glanced at the Colson car then faced Betty.

'What did *he* want?' Betty asked.

'He didn't want anything. He was being polite.'

'Polite about what?'

'What do you think? The allotment, and what we're doing for ourselves. What else would he be interested in?'

'All right! No need to get touchy.'

Emma said nothing. Let the women think their thoughts about her being distant and tetchy and let them come to their conclusions as to why. So long as they never got wind of the truth.

'What's that he gave you?'

'Books. He thought we might like to read some. They're secondhand copies.'

'Christ, who's got time to read a bloody book? Oh, nearly forgot. Mr Osborne wants to see you.'

Emma frowned. 'Why? I was in there this morning.' She'd be back there in an hour or so.

'I saw him at midday. He said if I saw you to tell you he wants a word. He's got something for you.'

Goosebumps rose on Emma's arms. 'I expect he wants to hand over a list of preferred vegetables to plant. He sometimes does that after he's discussed it with Mr Jameson.'

'I don't care. Just say thank you or something,' Betty said, clearly disgruntled. 'I didn't have to pass the message on.'

Emma winced but didn't apologise and when Betty went on her way, she hauled in a much needed breath. There was only one reason Mr Osborne would want to see her: a letter had arrived and the wait was over. It had been weeks since the SS *Lurline* had docked in San Francisco.

She placed the books on top of the onions and pulled on her gloves. Picking up the handles of the barrow, she bounced the metal wheel over the ridges in the unsown part of the allotment and onto the packed earth towards the street.

'Very interesting,' Mr Osborne said ten minutes later, pulling at the end of his moustache as he, his wife and Emma stood over the wheelbarrow in the storeroom of the grocery store. 'A parcel from America. Never thought I'd see one out here.'

'Letters and parcels have been going to and from Australia and the United States for the entire war, Walter.'

'But not out here, dear. Not in Blueholm Bay.'

'And we'll remember to be circumspect about Emma's mail in future, won't we?' his wife said, taking the parcel off him and handing it to Emma, whose fingers were itching to get hold of it.

Mr Osborne accepted his wife's words with a sigh and went into the shop when the bell above the door tinkled.

'Sorry about his talking to Betty.'

'It's all right, Mrs Osborne. No harm done. Thanks so much,' Emma added as casually as possible while trying not to stare at the package as though it wasn't the most precious thing in the world. She'd expected an airletter but this was thicker and more like a small, flat parcel. It was practically burning a hole in her hands as she considered what its contents might be.

She yearned to get back to Herring Street and the privacy of her bedroom but first she had to empty the wheelbarrow. She rushed through the task, thankful there was little chance of bruising any of the vegetables as she practically threw them into their various boxes and baskets.

* * *

July 1945
Madison, Wisconsin

How do I begin, my darling Em?
    Firstly, forgive me for taking so long to send this but life has been incredibly demanding and not a little tiring.
    I've been in Madison for a month and we've been getting acquainted with everything that is new to us, most of which has been quite daunting but oh, so amazing.
    Anyway, here I am, in touch at last.
    I wrote so much on the ship and now I want you to have every scrap of paper or letter because they hold information about Grace and I know you will want every single detail of her.
    Oh, Em, she's adorable! I absolutely love her.
    It was Eddie who began my education into adulthood— bless him, he put up with so much from me, didn't he? As you did. (I know how unpredictable I can be.) But it is Grace who has made me a woman. I am simply not the same person now I'm with her. I am changed once again and give thanks for it all.
    The fuss Eddie's family made of us when we arrived! It was so beautiful. We were welcomed with such joy I cried for an hour.

I was lonely on the ship without Eddie. It was hard to leave him behind. The other women were a bit homesick too but we muddled through. All of us women plus over two hundred babies! When we got to San Francisco—I have never seen such big trucks in my life as I have here in America—there was a band playing 'Here Comes the Bride' and we all cried all over again.

Eddie's uncle and aunt were there to meet us. They were ever so good and now I'm in Wisconsin and I am happier than I ever expected. Apart from missing Eddie, and missing you.

I'll write again once we're more settled—what a whirlwind this has been! But I wanted you to know we are well and both thriving.

I hope you find joy in your life soon, my wonderful friend, as I have joy here, in my arms. My heart breaks to think of you alone but I know you'll get through and one day you will come visit us and we will make the biggest fuss of you!

Your forever loving Cassie

PS – I miss you dreadfully, Em. Please write back soon.

Emma squeezed her eyes closed, the letter held tenderly in her fingertips because she didn't want to crease it. She'd read it so many times in the last hour she worried the paper might rip. She'd read all the other letters Cassie had written on the ship a dozen times too.

She knew when Grace gave her first genuine smile that wasn't a burp. She knew Grace's eyes had turned from pale blue to soft hazel. She knew that she puckered her mouth and frowned when unhappy, and that she loved a little stuffed rabbit Eddie had bought her.

Grace was four months old and she'd only known the love of her real mother for ten minutes. But she had the adoration of her new mother and Emma was beholden to the Sheas, each and every one of them, for loving the baby.

Cassie's enthusiasm about her new life was a pleasure to read too and even though she mentioned Emma travelling to America, she hadn't reiterated the possibility of one day working things out regarding Grace. Emma wouldn't get the chance to leave Blueholm Bay any sooner than she'd get to Wisconsin so she wouldn't worry about that yet. There were already many concerns about whether she should even consider meeting the child let alone taking her. Neither would she think too deeply on anything else she'd hoped for from Cassie. Like a photograph, or a lock of hair …

Maybe it was too much to expect. Grace was in Cassie's arms and in her care and she was adored. It was more than Emma had imagined possible during the first months at the home.

She rose from the bed and pulled the large atlas from the bookshelf next to her bed. She concealed the letters within the pages along with the note from Eddie, slipped the atlas back onto the shelf and ran her finger down its spine. This precious book held her heart between its covers.

It was nine thousand miles to Madison, Wisconsin. How long would she have to wait for another letter? What news would it contain—and could she bear to receive it? Could she bear to watch her little girl grow up through the eyes of another? It was as though time had stopped for Emma since Grace had been taken from her.

Emma only felt the pain residing inside her.

Chapter Twenty-seven

February 1946

Emma dragged her attention from the light filtering beneath the hem of her bedroom curtains and pulled on thick socks. After lacing her boots, she tied the sleeves of an old and semi-waterproof jacket around her waist, ready to haul it on as soon as it was needed. The wet season was in full swing and it was muggy and humid, so she wore a thin shirt with the sleeves rolled above her elbows and the collar turned up behind her neck so as not to get too sunburned through the clouds.

She'd been home for nearly a year. The war was over—had been for months, since Japan surrendered following the devastation of the atomic bombs sent their way by the Americans. It was only then that her father had finally written. Emma hadn't been able to distinguish how he was coping from the few short sentences. Surely he was wanting to come home? Surely he remembered his youth and all he had taught his children? Returning home had to mean something to him now that all he had endured was at an end.

She opened the frayed curtains and glanced out the window to see the sunrise, taking a moment while the house was quiet to reflect on everything she'd achieved. Her patience with life and all it had thrown at her, along with her desperate need to escape her hometown, was starting to pay off. Not in any grand way, but she couldn't deny she was holding onto a sense of pride for her efforts.

She'd kept up with her work tending the communal allotment but just before New Year she'd leapt at another chance: paid employment. One of the local girls who worked part time in the Osbornes' shop had got engaged and handed in her notice. Emma had stepped up, dirty gardening gloves stuck in the back pocket of her shorts, dried mud on her leather boots, hair wrapped in a headscarf. She cited experience in invoicing and serving customers from her time at Gibson's and also the Comforts Fund.

Some of the women in town hadn't been too happy about her securing the position as they had daughters looking for work too, but Emma's good association with the Osbornes had undoubtedly swung the deal her way. She worked Mondays, Wednesdays and Fridays. It was a simple job for a woman with no expectations and she was more than happy to have it. She was still working three days a week at the communal allotment, including a Saturday now, but she was receiving a fair wage from the Osbornes so she could add to the Hatton household's income and also put a little something away for her future.

The Hattons genuinely needed the money Emma brought home—and more. Joe still hadn't got a job and was talking about moving to Cairns. Simon said he was going too. They had both got a lot tougher, with a fair amount of mean-spiritedness shared between them. Emma wasn't sure she even liked them any more. Will and Danny were still at school and she saw some gentleness in both, likely coming from Dad's side of the family.

And Emma? She just felt like the oddity in the family. Perhaps Dad felt the same way.

The only occasions she was extravagant with the money she earned was when she was paying for postage for letters to

America, and recently one to Helen Ross. Mrs Ross might know something about Wynn or Susannah, or any of the girls. She'd given Emma her address after slipping her the money for a train ticket home and without the sisters hanging over their heads, and with Emma having a private address at the Osbornes', the housekeeper might open up.

Emma could only hope. She longed to hear from any of the girls, but especially Wynn and Susannah.

Cassie wrote every six or seven weeks and the letters were beginning to hold more information about the wondrousness of her life in America than about Grace. Emma couldn't blame her for her enthusiasm.

She picked up the latest airletter from Cassie, received a week ago, and reread it.

You should see the lakes, Em. They're gorgeous and the best thing is, you don't have to go out of the city to visit one. I just love being in this city! Of course, with my Aussie accent, I stand out like a sore thumb but most people are enchanted to meet me. Who'd have ever thought!

The war is still going on even over here. We've got food and gasoline shortages (gasoline—listen to me! Becoming quite the American) and other things are difficult to get hold of because all the produce like ammunition and foodstuffs are going to the military. But on the whole, Eddie's family are pretty well off and we manage more than finely. If I'm truthful, we live quite grandly.

Now on to darling little Grace. Oh, Em! She's an absolute delight and she keeps me warm and content while we settle into our new lives. She's cooing and burbling, trying out her words. It's so adorable! We're going to throw a first birthday party for her next month and Eddie's sister will bring all her married women friends and their children. It's going to be such fun and

Grace will have the best day. So many presents and compliments, I bet. She'll be completely tuckered out by dinner time.

I'm going to dress her in the most gorgeous golden-yellow pinafore, with little puff sleeves on her white blouse. She'll look like an angel!

Emma attempted not to picture Grace in her mind. She was still longing for a photograph and wasn't sure why Cassie hadn't sent one, but perhaps her friend felt it best not to. Perhaps she thought it would be too painful.

Emma wasn't sure which was worse, knowing what Grace looked like or not knowing, although the only experience she had of the agony was down to the latter.

And yesterday we had some amazing news. Eddie is coming home!

Emma hadn't written to Eddie again after sending the short note advising him she could be reached via the Osbornes. She'd sensed it was better to let the man get on with his army medical work and not burden him with a reminder that his child back home actually belonged to a different mother. Now Eddie would soon join his wife and Grace's family would be complete.

Emma folded the letter without rereading the last paragraph where Cassie spoke of picnics on the lawn, shopping in the city and boat rides. Madison had two great lakes and Wisconsin had forests and plentiful farms. In some ways, Grace would grow up surrounded by nature and by water, just like Emma had. It was more than Emma could have wished for her little girl.

She reminded herself not to expect too many letters from Cassie in the coming months. Cassie would be concentrating on her husband, the man she'd had to leave behind while she travelled on her own with a newborn to a foreign destination.

They would spend time together before Eddie went back to work at the renowned hospital where his father was a senior board member. His parents or perhaps his sister might tend Grace so he and Cassie could have a few days away together to get reacquainted and seal their love once more.

Then one day, Cassie would get pregnant and Grace would have a brother or sister.

Emma shivered, a ghost on her bones.

Even if she had the opportunity, how could she take Grace from the only mother she'd known? The child would be three, four, maybe five or even six years old. She would have memories tucked inside her. She would have a routine and daily expectations. All of them with Cassie as her mother and, very soon, Eddie as her father. She'd have aunts and cousins she knew and trusted. Neighbours and play friends who spoke with the same accent she had.

Did Emma even deserve a photograph of the little girl? She already had more than Wynn and Susannah or any of the other girls from the home. She knew where her child was and that she was safe.

Yet Grace was the only child Emma would ever have and she'd had to let her go.

Putting Cassie's letter away in the pages of the atlas, Emma closed and locked her bedroom door with a key she deposited into the pocket of her trousers and headed for the kitchen, where she could hear her mother moving pots and pans and getting ready to cook the boys' breakfast. Emma's life wasn't too bad and she wasn't melancholy, not like she had been when she first came home. She was possibly just lonely, and a bit downhearted since she received Cassie's last letter.

'We all know the outcome,' Wynn had said one day while they were stuck in the linen room ironing a pile of the sisters' napkins, long before she'd decided she did want to keep her baby after all. 'We ought not to be so miserable. It's not as though we weren't told from the start exactly what was going to happen.'

'Yes, but this place and the treatment of all the girls who go to the hospital is nothing like I imagined,' Emma had said. 'I doubt it is to you either, so don't go saying you knew what it would be like. You're miserable too.'

'I didn't know and yes, I am miserable. Who wouldn't be? I'm just stating the facts now that they're staring us in the face. Unless we do something for ourselves and make some rash decision regardless of the outcome, what's going to change?'

Emma found a sad smile as the memory surfaced. How she missed Wynn and her straightforward talk.

'I miss too many people,' she said out loud, then put on a brave face and entered the kitchen. The road to recovery would be long but she would become stronger and until that day, she wasn't going to allow others to tread on her hopes or stamp on her grief.

Most of the time, when forced together, Emma let her mother talk or chatter on about whatever was bothering her. There was hardly ever a need to respond. But Mum had just received news from Irene McDonald's brother. There was talk of Dad's battalion returning to Australia within months.

'He'll be wanting a serious word with you when he gets back.' Mum's countenance was watchful and Emma knew she was about to get another verbal bashing. '*If* he can bring himself to mention the unmentionable.'

Annoyance rose at her mother's harrying, but she was worried about her father and what he would say. Her plan to get out of town, although a sensible one, hadn't come anywhere near to fruition and neither would it for some time. Dad might even turf her out of the house. That was a daunting prospect, given she had so little saved. Not even enough to find herself a place to board while she looked for employment in Townsville or elsewhere.

'I'm off to the allotment,' she told her mother as she divided her brothers' luncheon sandwiches between two plates and put them in the food safe.

'What about the boys' breakfast? I suppose I do that, do I? It is Saturday. My only day off.'

'No, it isn't, Mum. You have Sundays off too and you're not the only one who works a long week. I'll be back later.'

Without waiting for a response, Emma left the kitchen and headed out through the laundry walkway. The one thing that had escalated in the past months that had not been drowned in hard work was her temper. It would flare from nowhere and she literally had to bite her tongue. It was as though she was strung out on a wire too thin for its load.

Wrenching the empty wheelbarrow from between the house stilts, she frogmarched her way to the front of the house, down the garden path and out onto the street.

'Hello, sourpuss.'

Emma halted, taken aback. 'Hello, Janet,' she said, hopefully removing the bad-tempered expression from her face as Janet Jameson got up from the bottom step of her family's house and sauntered to the gate, shoving her hands into the pockets of her shorts. 'I heard yesterday you were home. For good?'

'Couldn't put it off. Arrived last night. I'm back to being a woman.'

'Can't say I blame you for being down about that. I read that women in the armed services are being advised to return to their traditional family roles and like it or lump it.'

'Too right we are. We're expected to go back to the kitchen and the bedroom as though we'd never been away doing useful work. So here I am. Waiting for all the expected to fall into my lap.'

'Did you love wearing your uniform?' Emma said, putting the wheelbarrow down and keen to hear more about Janet's war work.

'Did I ever! I'm so annoyed we're not allowed to stay with the WAAAF. We didn't even get paid as much as the men, although I tell you right now, we were doing the same work they did.'

'I bet you were.'

'Anyway, such is our lot. But I met a few good blokes from the RAAF. Still seeing one. He's Air Operations.'

'Did you do a lot of secret stuff?'

Janet winked. 'That would be telling.'

'How's your typing?'

'Fast. How's yours?'

'Non-existent. So what's next?'

'I'm faced with getting married, like every other bugger. Washing, child-rearing, ironing and cooking here I come.'

Emma didn't say anything. The only thing she had to look forward to was becoming a bitter old spinster.

'Still,' Janet said, 'it might not be so bad. He's a good man. Nice-looking too. Not that he's popped the question yet and he'll have to go back to Sydney once he's released, so I'm not sure what might happen.' Janet paused. 'What about you? You don't want to find a fella?'

Emma shrugged. 'Not really.'

'People are saying it's a bit odd you're still at home and don't have a bloke.'

'Not all of us want what others want.'

'I guess,' Janet said, looking unconvinced. 'I heard you've been getting acquainted with Harry Colson.'

Emma jolted. 'What?'

'People have seen him talking to you a number of times.'

'I'm sure the man talks to most people when he passes them in the street,' Emma said, getting somewhat peeved herself.

'Hope you're not setting your cap at him.'

'Don't be ridiculous!' Emma Hatton and Harry Colson—utterly preposterous.

'I heard he's coming out of his shell.'

'I wouldn't know anything about it.'

'What happened to the bloke in the war?' Janet asked with a frown. 'That Yank out at Mrs Cosgrove's.'

Emma didn't flinch, although her heart bounced. Nobody knew Frank's name or that he was already married with a child, so she played along. 'He'll go back to California, I expect. Find a girl and settle down.'

'Are you sad about that?'

'No,' Emma said, the response coming easily. 'He didn't deserve me.'

Janet grinned. 'Thought for a moment you were succumbing to my bullying. See?' she added. 'All it takes to put a person in their place is to tell them to back away, like you just did. So if anyone else says something about you and Harry Colson, tell them where to get off.'

'I bloody will.' Bad-tempered spinsters never smiled but Emma produced one anyway.

'Talking about gossip,' Janet said, 'you ought to know a few things.'

'There's always gossip going around.'

'It's about you.'

'What a surprise.' Emma didn't want to know what was being said about her but she would have to find a way to defuse whatever was being bandied around or it would get out of hand.

'It's the Wheatons, mainly,' Janet said. 'Katy and her gang of catty friends who have nothing better to do. They're saying the time you spent in Brisbane is a little odd.'

'I went to look after my aunt's in-laws. What's odd about that?'

'They figure your mum would never have let you go, considering she gave you a hefty workload and without you she'd be doing it all herself.'

'Janet, I'd been gone from Blueholm Bay for over a year. I was in Townsville once I turned sixteen, remember?'

'I'm just saying they're putting two and two together but it's not adding up to four.'

'Perhaps they ought to go back to school.' Emma lifted the wheelbarrow handles, gripping them firmly, and carried on walking, the wheel bumping along the crevices of grassy verge to hard-packed earth.

'Anyways,' Janet said, opening her garden gate and following.

Emma halted. 'Look, Janet. I don't care what's being said.' It was best if she kept to this particular lie.

'I put her straight actually.'

'Who?'

'Katy Wheaton. You see, I have this cousin in Brisbane.'

'You have dozens of cousins all over Australia.'

'The one in Brisbane has become useful.' Janet smiled. A cheery, friendly smile. 'He saw you in Brisbane, this cousin.'

If Emma's heart had bounced at the mention of Frank it now almost catapulted into her mouth.

'A few times, actually. Over the months you were there, I reckon he saw you just about every week.' Janet crossed her arms beneath her breasts. 'What was it he told me? Oh, yeah. He saw you going in and out of your Aunty Doris's in-laws' house daily.'

'You said he saw me weekly.'

'I meant daily. He lives near the in-laws. Coincidence, isn't it? He said he often saw you lugging your big shopping basket or washing the front step. He said he reckoned they were treating you like a servant. He said he didn't think they ever left the house in all those months, and he didn't think you ever got out to have any fun. Kept enslaved, you were, according to my cousin. That's probably why you've been so sick since you came home. You were worked to the bone by the old couple.' Janet shrugged. 'Well, I'm only guessing that's the reason.'

Emma shifted her stance. 'What's this cousin's name?'

'Can't remember. Not with all the cousins I've got. Andrew? Rupert? David? Anyway, he's a good one to have. I told Katy Wheaton all about him seeing you at Doris's in-laws' place and further advised her to stop throwing stones when she lived in a glass house. I said I knew about her little flings with the Yanks while her husband was in New Guinea fighting for King and country. Fighting for his family. For his darling wife back home, who was doing it hard.'

Emma's eyes widened. 'She had affairs?'

'Not that I know of,' Janet said, lifting a shoulder. 'But she coloured up quickly, so I reckon I stumbled upon some truth.'

'Well, then. Maybe Andrew Rupert David's reports have put paid to the ridiculousness of the gossip about me.'

'They probably have,' Janet agreed. 'I'll walk a ways with you, if you don't mind. I need to get my bearings again now I'm home. You know, get the lowdown on who's doing what and to whom.'

'Isn't it all the same as before we left?'

Janet shook her head. 'I reckon we've got a lot of change heading our way, Emma. It's best to know what might trip us up.'

Emma's world became just a little lighter. 'I noticed some of your mother's roses ought to have had a summer clean-up last month,' she said. 'They're getting a bit spindly. I might get the shears out later and give them a going over.'

'Thanks. Saves me bodging it.'

Janet couldn't bodge anything if she tried. She was too smart. Whatever she knew, or had heard, or had supposed regarding Emma's time in Brisbane, she was going to keep it to herself. She was keeping Emma safe. And Emma loved her for it.

Chapter Twenty-eight

June 1946

The next time Emma met Harry Colson she was standing on the Osbornes' verandah and the weather had taken a sudden turn from warm and dry to wet and windy. Rain dripped through the gutters and bounced off the ground, soaking Emma's headscarf and a raincoat that wasn't particularly waterproof in the first place. They hadn't had a downpour this hard since earlier in the year but there was something wild about the rain, and she didn't mind if she got drenched. It could hail for all Emma cared.

Her plans had taken a blow. She had clearly been dwelling too much on her supreme efforts to get on with things and had missed the realities right beneath her nose. She was no longer working at the allotment, for a start. The men were returning and a few had taken over the vegetable production, advising Emma she could get on with her own life now and let them do the backbreaking work. Presumably they meant she would prefer to be trimming a new hat or buying a new lipstick.

The problem was, she didn't have a life. Not one that mattered. Not the one she yearned for, where she was free. She still didn't have enough money to get herself set up in the city so here she was, being a good daughter and providing the household with money from her work at the Osbornes' and helping her mother out more than she ever had now she didn't have the allotment to escape to. It was as though nothing had changed after all and wasn't about to change any time soon.

'Hello again,' Harry Colson said as he stepped up and onto the verandah, an open umbrella in his hand and his fancy vehicle parked on the verge.

'Hello, Mr Colson.' Emma's mother was still inside the store, counting her ration coupons as she finalised her grocery order for the next week. She didn't trust Emma to do the entire shop on one of the days she worked at the Osbornes'. Emma couldn't understand why, since she managed everything else at home and actually worked in the shop.

Harry Colson shook his umbrella as he closed it to use as a walking stick. Then he tipped his hat, making a few drops of water trapped in the brim run onto the shoulders of his lined wool coat as he nodded at her basket. 'Shopping?'

It was a naïve and masculine observation but she forgave him because he'd never had to do his own shopping. Or cleaning. Or washing.

'It's an extraordinary day, don't you think?' he said.

'It's a bit wet.'

'Washing the cobwebs away.' A few strands of his slicked-down hair had escaped and blew across his forehead. The wind had given colour to his face, too. He didn't look the thirty-two years he owned. 'It seems ages since you stood in my garden looking forward to your sixteenth birthday.'

'Almost four years ago, sir.'

'We've all grown older. Maybe wiser. Or maybe not so much wiser, but rather more sentimental. Looking at, well, at people … I mean, certain people …' He cleared his throat. 'Sorry. Not sure what I was going to say.'

Emma kept her expression neutral as she wondered what he was referring to, why he would open up to her and how many people in town had already noticed. Rain or no rain, people had to go about their business and a few were out on the street. She took a small step back, clutching the basket in both hands. Janet's advice about gossip and whether or not she was setting her cap at him burned as indignation that she hoped wasn't also flushing her cheeks.

'I've seen you a number of times since we chatted about the allotment,' he said.

Emma hadn't been aware of his scrutiny other than the discomforting time he'd stopped to chat and hand over a few books, and another time when he tooted his car horn and waved. Vehicles were becoming a common occurrence in town and there had been two or three motor cars with regular visitors over the last months. Even the children didn't stare as much. There was Peg, bringing her vehicle out of the garage and visiting her family, and a few new business acquaintances of Mr Jameson, who was considering purchasing a van since his delivery business during the war had picked up considerably.

'I only saw you fleetingly,' he said. 'Twice or maybe three or four times. I didn't stop to chat, although I would have liked to, but time is often my foe these days. I have been wondering how you were so it's lovely to catch up.'

Emma licked her lips. Lovely to catch up? 'I haven't been at the allotment since some of the men returned.'

'Yes, well, you did a sterling job, Emma. A full wheelbarrow is monstrously heavy but you handled it remarkably well.' He stamped the tip of his umbrella onto the wet boards of the verandah. 'I've been giving a lot of thought to many things recently.' He cleared his throat again as though coughing away whatever he'd been about to say about his sentimental thoughts. Probably something about his sister. When the Allies liberated the prisoners of war in Germany, Squadron Leader Robert Allen had been one of the airmen flown to Britain. According to gossip, he'd had an extended stay in a London hospital, recovering.

'How kind of you to have given me your consideration,' Emma said, hoping to wrap up their conversation. 'I've been working here at the grocer's three days a week too. I help in all sorts of way but I'm also doing some bookkeeping for Mr Osborne now.'

'Yes! I heard you were working here,' he said. 'You don't work Saturday mornings?'

She halted an unexpected need to smile. If she worked Saturdays she'd be inside the shop now not standing around with a full basket. 'Just weekdays.'

'I have no doubt you could run the joint if you had to. Not that I'm suggesting the Osbornes' store is akin to a cheap bar!' he added quickly.

Emma choked on a laugh that rose from nowhere. 'I'm so sorry.'

He smiled. 'Don't worry. I don't suppose you expected me to say something so Americanised. I believe I'm considered a bit stuffy.'

'Not at all.'

'Oh, come on. I bet they all think I'm a little crazy or reclusive. I don't intend to be this way. I should try shaking off that boring mantle, don't you think?'

Emma felt a sudden affability towards the man. The capacity to make fun of himself was certainly not something she'd expected.

'I don't think you have to worry, Mr Colson.'

He moistened his mouth, looking keen to say something else, but Emma's mother came out of the grocer's, letting the door slam behind her.

'Oh, Mr Colson! How wonderful to see you in town!'

Harry Colson tipped his hat. 'Mrs Hatton. I hope you and your family are well.'

'Can't complain, sir, although we all have a bit of a moan about the rationing and such.' Mum was using her posh voice and Emma withheld a groan.

'Yes, it's still pretty rough, isn't it?' It was a stilted response and nothing like the way he'd spoken to Emma. Although why he might feel more comfortable conversing with Emma, she had no idea. Unless he felt sorry for her. The intelligent young woman stuck in boring old Blueholm Bay in the back of beyond.

'Your husband is due home soon?' he asked.

'We expect more of our men to return any week now, sir. We wives still waiting are on tenterhooks.'

'I expect you are. So much time lost.'

'Oh, I could tell you!' Mum exclaimed.

Emma saw a light of worry enter Harry Colson's eyes and thought quickly about how to extricate him. Mum would be making the most of this encounter once the rain stopped and she had the chance to chat over the garden fences, but if she caught wind of the approachable way he had been conversing with Emma there would be plenty of questions Emma had no desire to answer, either truthfully or with yet more lies.

'We must get on,' she said to her mother before turning to Harry Colson. 'So nice to see you again, sir. Do send our best wishes to your sister.'

'Excuse her,' Mum said. 'Some young women today, honestly, you'd swear they'd lived a whole life and had all the answers. What would you know about how we have to get on, Miss Smarty-Pants? I'm the mother here, not you.'

Emma inwardly cringed as Harry Colson cast a bemused glance her way. 'Let me take your bag, Mum. I'm afraid we'll have to make a dash for it.'

Emma grabbed the shopping bag, hung it and the basket over her arm and pulled her mother along by her elbow, leaving Harry Colson standing on the verandah still looking somewhat bewildered.

Ushering her mother across the wet street, she ignored her complaints about being told what to do by her own daughter, embarrassing a good woman of the town by being rude in front of a Colson. Emma would have dearly loved to tell her to shut the hell up.

'I tell you. Something's afoot!' her mother said not even a quarter of an hour later, having lost her earlier rancour after they had shed their wet raincoats and scarves and unpacked the groceries. 'I can't get over having seen him in town on a Saturday.'

'I expect he wanted to purchase something,' Emma said in a sarcastic tone that fell on deaf ears.

'Mrs Osborne says he's got a sweet tooth.'

'Well, there's your answer.' Emma was slicing onions while her mother put a pan of water on to boil for potatoes.

'He's been mooching around town a lot, recently. Pops into the Osbornes' quite often on a Saturday. I've never seen him, but others have.'

'How lucky some are.'

'They say he's coming out of himself because he's looking for a wife, although goodness knows why, after all these years a bachelor. He's got a damned good housekeeper. What more could he want?'

Emma imagined the poor man would want plenty of things. Was he aware his every move was being judged by the people around him?

'Doris said he's been to a few social gatherings in the city recently, which is almost unheard of. Believe you me, some woman is going to get a rosy future with all the money.'

She'd also be putting up with Ivy Williams.

Emma threw the sliced onion into the frying pan on the table. Maybe the new wife would get rid of old Ivy, or at least put her in her place. Ivy's tall tales about her wonderful life up at the big house, with all the trimmings and comforts she could wish for, were beginning to make everyone in town cross the street so they didn't have to listen to her.

'He's a catch, all right,' Mum said, looking around the kitchen as though she'd misplaced something.

'I thought you said he was dimwitted,' Emma remarked as she pulled the skin off another onion.

'That's as may be, but who cares, with that big house and the motor car? Emma—where are the beans? I told you to top and tail them.'

'Which is exactly what I did earlier. They're in the food safe.'

'When we'll get enough money to purchase a refrigerator, I don't know. It's your father's fault. He ought to have been working a lot harder before the war. We would have had much more to rely on while he was gone. I can hardly hold my head up in town some days. Everybody has a refrigerator!'

Emma cut through the onion, the knife hitting the board so hard it scored the wood. Not everybody had a refrigerator. They weren't the only poor family in town, just the poorest, but if she mentioned that she'd get the argument she'd been hankering for. She was no longer a yes girl but more often than not she kept her mouth closed, maintaining the balance of some supposed harmony while her blood boiled. Some days it was a hard thing to do.

When her mother left the kitchen, Emma closed her eyes. On days like today, when melancholy at her state in the world hit her in the gloomiest manner possible, she was almost ready to give up and give in completely. Yet she couldn't bear to imagine the rest of her life bleak and meaningless.

So she'd lost the allotment. So she was still fighting her way through each day. She had to learn to use the fear for her future and sorrow for her past as a means to independence instead of getting discouraged all the time, because hope for some better life continued to flicker, despite the knowledge that she'd never marry or have another child.

There were no tears left to cry about any of this, she'd shed them all. She might never be in a position to take Grace and the notion was fast becoming a fixture in her mind which hurt almost as much as it had the moment she'd handed Grace to Helen Ross.

Emma opened her eyes and glanced around the dull and outdated kitchen she'd known all her life. She was still here. Once again the last star in the night sky, left on her own come the rising of the sun. Wondering if there were any stars out there who would want her.

Chapter Twenty-nine

November 1946

Dad was back. He'd been home since July and four months later they were still waiting on him to return to his old self, to shift the haunting despondency in his eyes. Emma couldn't see how he might manage it.

'Cuppa, Dad?' she asked.

'Yes. Thanks, lo—' He halted. 'Thanks.'

Thanks, *love*. He no longer called her love but it was as though he forgot that he couldn't do that any more. Forgot that his wife had decided he should withhold fondness from his daughter. It broke Emma's heart. Not for herself, but for him. He hadn't castigated her once for what had happened although she'd heard Mum telling him to do it. He just listened to whatever his wife said without agreeing or disagreeing.

'Here you go,' Emma said, putting a mug of hot tea on the table in front of him. 'I've put in extra sugar, but don't tell Will and Danny.' Rationing was still in force and nobody could see an end to it.

Dad nearly smiled as he caught her eye. 'Life isn't what we expect it to be. But I trust you'll find your way forwards. As we all have to.'

'I know, Dad. Thank you.' He'd said the same thing a number of times and each time it was clear he forgot he'd already told her. She often wondered if he was talking about his own life and not his daughter's. Their roles had reversed now, Emma the parent and her father the child in need of attention. Emma tried hard not to feel concerned. She owed her father for everything he'd done for her when she was a child, but surely it wasn't fair she was the only one of his children to do the worrying, the nagging, the mollycoddling and the protecting? The only one who stood between the arguments he and her mother had, silent as they were on Dad's part. 'Want me to make you a sandwich?'

'No, thanks,' Dad said, not looking up. 'Might nip to Bohle.' He sipped the tea and sighed as the sweet warmth hit his lips.

'All right,' Emma said. 'But don't be late.' She turned and headed to the laundry, where the ironing waited. Mum and the wives no longer worked at Mrs Cosgrove's as the Americans had left for their homeland but Mum took in a bit of mending and, thanks to Doris talking to some of her friends, she was also doing some dressmaking. They needed the money, because Dad was dragging his feet about finding a job, and Joe and Simon had left home. They'd gone to Cairns in search of their fortunes under strict instructions from Mum to send money home as soon as they were able. Without their input for bills that had to be paid, Emma hadn't been able to save much more money for her future.

Emma put the two irons on the stove and gave herself a moment in the silence surrounding her. She couldn't live with her angry mother and hollowed-out father. She couldn't live without some happiness. Nobody could and nobody ought to. Although Emma knew that when she had enough saved to leave, money wasn't going to guarantee happiness so maybe what she needed most was a deep-seated rapport with another woman. A friendship that was alive and warm. Human touch.

Emotional contact. She wanted the ability to share something with another person who understood, like Wynn and Susannah would. Familiarity. Companionship. Cassie had only sent four letters since Eddie got home. Months with hardly a word from America. Emma missed the communication and the news about Grace, who would be an unbelievable two years old next March. She missed Cassie so much but their friendship would never again be what it was.

Helen Ross had replied to Emma's letter and they kept up an occasional correspondence but she hadn't known anything about Wynn or Susannah, nor any of the girls who had been at St Philomena's during Emma's time. Old Tyrell died last winter, and Cook was now retired. Mrs Ross was considering doing the same. Her older girls were married with young ones and they could do with their mother's helping hand.

Emma glanced at the ironing waiting to be done.

She had promised Wynn she'd find her, so why was she here, lost in contemplation while she ironed her brothers' school shirts? She should be thinking of ways beyond relying on Mrs Ross. There was the library in Townsville. She could visit and look through the telephone directories. There might even be some mention of a Poulson-Taylor in the New South Wales newspapers. Wynn would be harder to locate but she had to try. And she would need money.

She walked out of the laundry, checked her appearance in the hallway mirror and left the house.

'Good afternoon, Mr Osborne,' she said as she walked into the storeroom of the grocer's shop.

'You're looking bright and breezy. What can I do for you?' Mr Osborne asked, eyeing tomatoes in a box before picking up a vine brimming with the fruit.

Emma thought it best to cut straight to the chase. 'I wondered if you might like a bit more of my help in the store.'

Mr Osborne coughed and wouldn't meet her eye. 'Well now, not sure …'

'Yes.'

Emma looked around. Mrs Osborne had appeared from the shop.

'This is exactly what we've been waiting to hear. Isn't it, Walter?'

'Well now, dear, let's just—'

'We most certainly need your additional assistance,' Mrs Osborne said to Emma. 'I'm not normally the type to push people into something they're not ready for but I have been waiting for you to reach this decision yourself. Would full time suit?'

Gratefulness along with a large chunk of amusement filled the empty spaces in Emma's heart.

'Thank you. Full time would be wonderful.'

'I presume you'd like to start straight away? Say, Monday?'

'Monday would be excellent.' Emma paused, her throat suddenly dry. 'Although I might need a day off sometime soon.'

'A day off?' Mr Osborne said. 'You haven't even started—'

'Which day would suit?' his wife said.

Emma glanced between the two. 'Whatever day you think best.'

'We shall work it out next week. We'll also consider a more than suitable rise in your wages. Won't we, Walter?'

'Of course, dear. I was about to suggest it.'

Mrs Osborne stepped forwards with a smile that, although cursory, was tinged with warmth. She held out her hand for Emma to shake. 'We are delighted to have you on board, as they say in the navy. You're a hard worker, Emma, and that's what we need. Don't we, Walter?'

Mr Osborne pulled on the ends of his moustache. 'Welcome aboard, Emma.'

Chapter Thirty

Townsville—January 1947

The trip to the library had taken much more consideration than simply getting a day off from the Osbornes. Firstly there was the question of decent clothes. Emma had none to speak of since she hadn't left the confines of Blueholm Bay and had been disinclined to spend any of her hard-earned savings on material when the clothes she already possessed were perfectly fine for the jobs she'd been doing.

Secondly, Christmas and New Year had seen a rush of activity at the grocer's and Emma had worked additional hours as Mr Osborne had been under the weather, taking to his bed on a number of occasions. Plus, Mrs Osborne had developed some grand ideas—most of which infuriated her husband, who didn't like the thought of radical change—and had tasked Emma with reading all the newspapers from Townsville, Brisbane and further afield to see what was being sold.

Then there had been Emma's birthday, although nobody remembered it. The day she turned twenty had been the same as all the others but she didn't mind because she'd been busy, and useful.

But at last, here she was. In the city. Dressed reasonably well, thanks to Janet and a castoff lightweight flannel skirt and jacket, an updated old hat of Janet's mother's, a bolt of white rayon donated by Mrs Osborne for a blouse and her own sewing ability. She'd searched through the little intelligence available in the library, questioned the librarians to no avail and pored over telephone directories and a small collection of newspapers. Not a single Poulson-Taylor and, as expected, no Wynn Sinclair.

Disappointed, she stepped out onto Flinders Street and was immediately enveloped by the heat. She fanned herself with the old brown felt hat which she'd freshened up with some deep red velvet flowers. Then she stuck the hat under her arm and checked her wrist watch, worried to see how little time she had to get to the quayside as arranged with Mr Jameson, who'd given her a lift into the city.

'Hello! What a delightful surprise.'

Harry Colson. Emma dropped her hat, bent quickly to pick it up and settled it onto her head, hoping it wasn't at too jaunty an angle.

'What are you doing here?' he asked.

'I've been visiting the communal library.'

'No books?' he enquired, giving her a once-over glance.

'Not today.' Borrowing was, in essence, free, but people were required to pay a few shillings as a security. She'd have her money reimbursed once she returned the books, but parting with a shilling, even for a week, wasn't something she was comfortable doing. What would happen to her money if she couldn't get back into the city in time to return the books?

Harry Colson gave her a smile. 'I left the bank early. I've got some work to do at home.'

'I expect you're always occupied with business, whether at the bank or at home.'

'I try not to be when at home but it does creep up on me sometimes.'

Emma nodded, not knowing what to say next. There were people all around, on their way to or from wherever on Flinders

Street, and not one of them would be interested in the man and woman talking outside the City Buildings, but Emma was still uncomfortable. As though she were on show. The only relief was that they hadn't met up in Blueholm Bay, outside the Osbornes' again, where anyone passing would not only be keenly interested but would likely stop and stare. He had been into the store on one or two Saturdays but thankfully Emma had either been in the office with the bookkeeping paperwork or sorting onions in the back storeroom.

'How is your sister getting along?' she asked.

He paused as though considering his reply. 'Allen is sailing to Australia as we speak.'

'What good news!'

'Of course! But. Well …' He flicked his tongue over his lips. 'He spent a number of months in hospital in Britain after the poor wretches were flown from Germany.'

'Was he badly wounded in some way?' she asked, not bothering to suppress her curiosity. This had been gossiped about some time ago but nobody knew why Robert Allen had remained in hospital for so long.

'Not as you're imagining.'

'Oh?'

Harry Colson shifted his weight, resting it more heavily on his cane although he didn't appear to be in any discomfort, more like adjusting his position to get more settled. 'He was liberated from Belaria, a compound of Stalag Luft 3, according to what Cynthia's been told. It was built to contain Allied officers from the Commonwealth Air Forces. Apparently, he now speaks fluent German.'

'I expect they had so much time on their hands that any activity would have been welcomed.'

'It was probably more a necessity. It's a POW's duty to attempt to escape and it's our understanding Allen was the man who engaged the German soldiers when there was a need to put them off the scent of whatever his fellow prisoners were doing. Creating their escape plans. Digging tunnels. Making civilian clothes. Forging documents—train tickets, passes and the like. It was Allen's job to keep tabs on the Germans' movements.'

'So much,' Emma said reverently. 'They've been through so much we don't yet know about.'

'Cynthia has written to him, of course. He's responded, although not quite …' Harry Colson looked away for a moment. 'Not quite as she expected.'

'What do you mean?'

'He's in a poor way. He was undernourished, as they all were, but his left arm was banged up when he got shot down and it's still not right. They had to break and reset a bone and it didn't mend properly.' He paused briefly. 'It's more than just the physical ailments that concern me. He's been distanced from my sister in so many ways. I worry he won't recover.'

'Distanced?'

He shrugged. 'He was sent to Britain almost immediately they were married. Then he was captured and we had no idea where he was or if he was even alive.'

'Heartbreaking for your sister. She must have worried so much.'

'Terribly. But she tried her best not to get too downhearted.'

'That was brave of her.'

'I think perhaps there's more to come. More heartache. That's my worry, and I think it's hers too. These men are being sent back to the bosom of their families but they're changed men. Allen and Cynthia hardly know each other even though they've been married for close to five years.'

Emma almost reached out to put a hand on his arm but stopped herself in time. 'I can't condone those who expect our men to simply return home and carry on as though nothing has happened.'

'Exactly my thoughts,' Harry Colson said. 'You have a wise way about you, Emma. I always thought so.'

His eyes were brown, she noticed. Not dull brown, but with green flecks, which freshened them, like when the wind had lightened his features and the pelting rain had given his skin a healthy glow on that stormy day back in June outside the grocery store.

Emma lowered her gaze, self-conscious about her scrutiny of him.

'I expect your father has found it as difficult to adjust as many of the other townsmen who have come home,' he said.

Emma nodded but didn't want to divulge her father's true mental state. Not even to Harry Colson, who had a trenchful of sympathy for all the brave diggers. Admitting to him that her father was relying on beer to get through his days, while her mother chided him for absolutely everything, would be tantamount to admitting the Hattons were worthless after all, just the way everyone thought. Saying it out loud was an entirely different thing from living with it.

'Will you keep everything I've told you to yourself?' he asked. 'About my sister and her marriage.'

Emma looked up. 'Of course I will, Mr Colson. I shan't breathe a word.'

He smiled but there was a different query in his gaze now. 'Call me Harry,' he said in a mellow tone. 'It seems only fair since I call you Emma.'

Emma stayed as composed as possible. There was no way she could or would do that. 'I'd better not.'

He cleared his throat. 'I understand. Maybe just when we meet like this. Alone.'

He didn't understand at all. Emma wasn't likely to visit the city too often, and whatever he did around Blueholm Bay, everyone would be watching.

'Perhaps you'd like to visit me up at the house one afternoon this weekend?' he said suddenly. 'Have some tea.'

Emma gaped at him. Have some tea? Visit him? He must have lost all reason. Being polite—and downright friendly—to a Hatton, or anyone living in town, was a dangerous game to play. He had his reputation to consider.

'Mr Colson, if I can help you with something I'm happy to do so but otherwise I think it's best if … if perhaps we remain as we are. Acquaintances.'

He took a breath. 'That's the thing. I'm considering a number of changes in my life.'

'I presume you're thinking about moving to Melbourne to be close to family,' Emma said, eager to encourage him into saying whatever he was going to say so she could get on with finding her ride back to Blueholm Bay.

'Oh, God, no,' he said quickly. 'I'm quite happy where I am. No,' he reiterated, appearing a little sheepish, 'more like changes for hearth and home.'

He didn't say more but Emma thought she already knew. He was planning to get married. It shouldn't be a shock because he'd been gadding around the city attending social gatherings for practically the whole of last year, according to her mother. But receiving the news from the horse's mouth was something else entirely. She couldn't help wondering who he'd chosen and what she was like. Would she be attractive? A flower in his stark topiary garden? Or would she hold no bar with glamorous trinkets, preferring instead her tortoiseshell glasses so she could read him the latest articles from the newspapers as they enjoyed supper?

'Can I offer you a ride home?' he asked. 'I'm on my way now.'

Emma's eyes widened. Just the idea of arriving in town in his car made her gasp. She'd never live it down, and neither would he. 'That's kind of you but I've arranged to meet someone.'

'Oh, I see. Well ...' He tipped his hat, eyes somewhat glazed and seeming at a loss for words. 'I hope we'll meet up again soon. It was a joy to see you unexpectedly.'

Emma didn't know what to say, so she kept quiet.

He left, striding across Flinders Street where he paused momentarily as a van and a bicycle passed, tapping his cane on the ground in some rhythm that looked a lot like frustration. He continued to the other side of the road, his gait easy as though his leg neither troubled him nor gave him any pause for thought on what life had thrown his way. Did he regret not having been in uniform? Did he sometimes wish his life hadn't been different from other men's?

Emma let out a sigh, then trudged on towards her arranged meeting point with Mr Jameson, picking up the pace so she didn't miss him. She couldn't put her finger on why, but there was a definite deflating of spirit inspired by the news of Harry Colson's impending marriage. She could hardly call him a friend just because he spoke to her now and again, so she wasn't actually losing anything. But the town would change. The atmosphere wouldn't be the same. There would be a new Mrs Colson to bow and scrape to for a start. What else was he planning to change? The paintwork in the house, the furnishings, the rugs? If he was going all out for hearth and home changes it would definitely include his furniture and probably a lot of other amenities. Anything to make his new wife's life carefree and comfortable.

'Mr Jameson!' she called, breaking into a trot when she caught sight of her neighbour waiting patiently with his horse and cart. 'I'm so sorry I'm late. I got waylaid.'

'Not to worry, you're here now. Hop up, love, or we won't be home till after sundown.'

Emma pulled herself up onto the seat next to Mr Jameson and fixed her hat more firmly on her head, settling in for the trip home. *Call me Harry. Have some tea*—as if!

* * *

Emma hadn't given up on her dream of one day leaving Blueholm Bay, but she was perhaps becoming accustomed to the life she had. Although it didn't mean she had full control over her world because she didn't. Nor did it mean that she no longer yearned for the many things she didn't have. Like Grace.

> *Dearest Em,*
> *Can you ever forgive me? (You will likely have to for the rest of our lives. I am so thoughtless!)*
> *Eddie has told me off for not sending you a photograph of our little Grace. I can't begin to imagine what was going through my head. So to make amends, I'm sending five photographs and I hope you love them.*
> *She is such a bright little spark—very much like you.*
> *Does she resemble you when you were her age? Possibly not completely, but look at all that luxurious hair, although it has a tendency to curl, unlike yours (unless you use your hair rollers, of course).*

As Emma had suspected, it was as hard knowing what her child looked like as not.

The strangeness of it all was that she remembered the newborn, the fresh warmth and the softness of vulnerability. She didn't recognise the cherubic little girl with twinkling hazel eyes and a halo of dark blonde hair who was about to reach her second birthday, toddling on her own two feet, no doubt asking numerous questions of everyone around her.

One photograph in particular made a nauseousness rise in Emma's throat, because Grace didn't look like Emma. She looked like Frank.

Emma struck the thought away, refusing to be upset. But had Cassie noticed too? Is that why she'd been reluctant to send photographs? She hadn't been forgetful or shown a lack of judgement, but had been afraid of hurting Emma. Cassie was no fool and regardless of her self-deprecating humour about her thoughtlessness, she cared deeply about Emma—and very much so about Grace.

> *In other wonderful news—Em, I'm pregnant! I didn't tell you before because there was a bit of a problem and I kept fainting. I felt sure I'd lose it! But the doctor has told us we have nothing to worry about now and both the baby and I are doing well.*
>
> *We are all so excited.*

Emma looked up from where she sat on her bed in Herring Street and glanced around the sparse room. Soon, Cassie would send images of Grace sitting on a sofa with an arm around her baby brother or sister and after that there might not be so many photographs of Grace alone but always with a sibling or two. *Our little Grace* would become *our precious children*.

Emma clutched the photographs to her chest. With every passing week, month and year, it was more and more likely that Grace's fate was sealed. How could Emma contemplate taking Grace away from everything she'd known? How could she break the child's heart along with Cassie's and possibly Eddie's?

Her child was with another mother. Her child had a father. She had a family. How could Emma even build a relationship with Grace and what means would it take? She would have to be an aunt. A token aunt who never forgot birthdays.

She stood and put away the photographs and the letter then ran a fingertip down the spine of the atlas. Did she have a right to the child? Or should she, somehow, try to forget?

Grace was the only child she would have. The only baby she would give birth to.

How could she possibly ever let her go?

* * *

'Oh, it's you,' Ivy said, sniffing. 'I'll take a cauliflower and I'll have the usual tea. Be quick about it, I'm a busy woman.'

Emma smiled politely. *Three bags full*, she thought to herself as she went to fill Ivy's grocery demands. Mr Osborne hadn't been in good health since Christmas and his wife was often in the city speaking to other grocers about her plentiful notions for the future, as she was today, so Emma had stepped in to manage the shop. It wasn't as though she didn't know every aspect of what was needed. In many ways, she was running the joint after all.

'I suppose you've heard,' Ivy said. 'We're getting a new housemaid now things have settled down. One of Irene McDonald's girls is going to come up to help us three days a week. Quite grand we are up at the big house now. It's more like old times. There's me, the new house girl, two gardeners and a man to tend the animals. Plus we can get a labourer in any time we need one.'

We? Us? Emma placed the tea onto the counter and held out her hand for the coupons. 'How is Mr Colson?'

'What's it to you?' Ivy said, rummaging in her handbag for the tea coupons.

'I was just passing the time of day.'

'Well, I've got news on that score.'

'Oh? What might that be?'

'I'm not sure I want to reveal what I know. Not to the likes of you. You're a Hatton. Never had anything and likely never will.'

'I'm not sure I'd trust what you had to say anyway,' Emma responded pleasantly, albeit through gritted teeth.

Ivy sniffed. Emma went to get a cauliflower. She had the impression Ivy was dying to tell whatever it was she knew about her employer.

'He's going to be renovating the house,' Ivy said at long last.

Emma looked over her shoulder. 'Oh, that.'

'What do you mean "oh, that"? You know nothing about it.' Ivy shook her head, clearly believing Emma was playing funny buggers. 'He's going around with these men, measuring everything, saying that nothing has changed since his parents built the house. Saying it's dull. Saying he wants it freshened up. "Let's throw out the old and bring in the new," he says to me the other day.'

'Good heavens,' Emma remarked with a worried expression. 'I hope that doesn't include you, Ivy.'

Ivy paled.

Emma paused, mentally ticking herself off. At St Philomena's she'd struck a deal with herself to be as nice to Ivy as possible and try to make amends for her bad thoughts about the woman. But she was so damned snobbish and full of herself, it was an impossible task. Every saint out there would have trouble being nice to Ivy bloody Williams.

* * *

'I'll take a pound of sausages, a watermelon and our usual tea,' Ivy said a week later. 'I'll be returning in the next week or two for more expensive goods, so I'm hoping you'll have them to hand.'

'Depends on what they are,' Emma said. 'Can you give me a clue?'

'We're having a dinner party.'

'Who's we? I thought you were a single woman.'

'*We*,' Ivy said, as though Emma was slow on the uptake. 'Up at the big house.'

'Oh! You mean Mr Colson is holding a dinner party.'

'Well, of course I did. Who else would I mean?'

Emma went to get a watermelon. 'How are the renovations going?'

Ivy turned her face away, nose in the air, but her brow was furrowed. 'He's talking about installing a new kitchen.'

'Gosh, you'll have a lot of learning to do. There are all sorts of super electrical wares out there at the moment.'

'Perhaps I'll get him to employ you to use them all.'

'No, thanks. I don't want to work my fingers to the bone up at the Colson house. I'd rather dig ditches.'

'You wouldn't have a clue how to use all the fancy machines anyway. Your lot haven't even got a refrigerator.'

Emma drew a steadying breath and went to fetch the sausages.

'I don't need anything new in my kitchen,' Ivy said loftily. 'I can manage with the steam iron and the gas boiler, thank you very much.'

'But it's not your kitchen, is it? What if he buys an automatic washing machine?'

'He'd never do the likes! I've heard about those. You have to secure them to the floor or they bounce all around the room, smashing the chairs and the crockery. There's some lovely chinaware up at the house.'

'You might get a pop-up toaster then,' Emma said, wrapping the sausages and thinking Harry might like the idea of the newfangled toaster machine alongside his boiled egg each morning.

'I don't want one of them either. They sound as dangerous as the automatic washers. Popping,' Ivy said disparagingly. 'Whatever will they come up with next.'

Emma placed the wrapped sausages onto the counter next to the watermelon. 'You can't live in the past, Ivy, the world is modernising. It does this every so often. You have to move forwards. It's progression.'

Ivy snatched the sausages and thinned her mouth. 'It's Mrs Williams to you,' she said in a snarky tone, 'and I've progressed very well up until now. I've done enough progressing for a lifetime. I won't be progressing any more.'

Emma withheld a smile. 'When's the dinner party happening?'

'None of your business.'

'It will be if you want the Osbornes to supply some of the latest foodstuffs on offer. Mrs Osborne is in the process of acquiring a freezer cabinet so she can offer frozen peas and frozen cauliflower.'

Ivy adjusted her straw hat decorated with silk flowers that had seen so much sun over the years they'd whitened at the edges. 'I won't be asking for frozen anything. I'd never trust a frozen vegetable in a hundred years and neither should anyone.'

'They're quite the thing and have been for some time. I bet Mr Colson's dinner guests will know all about the new foodstuffs on offer, like the delicatessen items already available in the city.' Emma leaned an elbow on the counter, chin in her hand. 'What's on your menu for the dinner?'

'I haven't made up my mind.'

'Doesn't Mr Colson have a say?'

Ivy grunted. 'I was thinking of cutlets with a nice cake or tart for dessert.'

Emma wondered if that's what he ate once a week anyway and whether he'd interfere and ask for something new, which would certainly put Ivy out. 'Hadn't you better finalise your plans?'

'I've got another two weeks to give thoughts to my meal preparation.'

'I expect Mr Colson's sister and Squadron Leader Allen will be visiting,' Emma remarked, ensuring she sounded only vaguely interested.

'Cynthia won't be coming all the way up here,' Ivy said, perhaps forgetting who she was conversing with. 'She's in the family way.'

Emma's bad humour dissipated immediately. 'How wonderful!' Cynthia and her husband must be getting along very well indeed.

'What's it to you?' Ivy asked.

'I'm simply expressing my delight for a decent family.'

'Well, don't bother. Nobody in the family would care either way what you think.'

If only Ivy knew what Emma knew. That the renovation plans and the dinner get-togethers were all about impressing the would-be bride. Harry must have made his choice at last. Or perhaps he was simply in the planning stage, wanting to get it all done before she arrived.

'It's not the first dinner party I've catered for, mind,' Ivy said. 'His parents often entertained the hoity-toity. I've cooked for twenty people before now.'

'You have so many skills,' Emma said. 'Cook, washer woman, cleaner. You'll feel quite let down once Mr Colson gets married and his wife takes over the running of the house.'

'I beg your pardon?' Ivy said, scowling. 'Have you just insulted me?'

'Sorry,' Emma said, hand on her heart. 'I didn't mean to give you that impression.'

'Who told you he was getting married?'

Emma kept a straight face. 'Haven't you heard?'

'No, I have not!'

Emma tutted. 'And you living under the same roof.'

'You're having me on!'

Emma shrugged and let the issue go.

The bell above the door tinkled and Janet walked in.

'Hello, Ivy.'

'Hello yourself, and it's Mrs Williams to you.'

'Thanks, Ivy, I'll try to remember.' Janet stepped up to the counter. 'Why do you call yourself Mrs when you've never been married? I've often wondered about that.'

'It was the way of things in the olden days,' Emma said. 'No housekeeper could be a Miss, always a Mrs, whether they were or not. You've been in service all your life, haven't you, Ivy?'

Ivy stuffed the parcel of sausages into her shopping bag, undoubtedly squashing half a dozen in the process. 'I've had my chances. Mr Colson wouldn't be able to do without my help now, so that's that. Neither could his parents, which is the only reason I'm not a married woman myself.'

'Such a sacrifice,' Janet said. She was smiling but there was a deeper gleam in her eye than one of simply teasing cantankerous Ivy Williams. She looked a little smug, like the cat who'd got the lid off the billy and taken the cream.

'What's up with you?' Emma asked.

Janet took a deep breath, eyes sparkling, and held out her left hand. 'I've got news. I'm getting married!'

'Oh, Janet!' Emma darted around the counter to give Janet a hug. 'Congratulations! Who's the lucky man?' she asked as she admired the engagement ring, a sterling silver band with a Marcasite setting.

'That RAAF bloke I was telling you about ages ago. He went back to Sydney after the war but moved to Townsville a few months back. To get his hands on me, or so he said.' Janet grinned. 'The crazy thing is, he's got the same surname, so guess what? I'll go from being Miss Janet Jameson to Mrs Janet Jameson.'

'Never!'

'I'm not joking. It could only happen to me.'

Emma laughed. Two bits of good news. A baby for Cynthia and a wedding to look forward to. One Emma would certainly be invited to. 'Wedding bells all around us!' she said to Ivy with a smile.

Ivy snorted. 'I hope you won't expect butter and cream from the big house for your wedding banquet. We might have helped out during the war, but that's over now.'

'We? It was Mr Colson who helped out by giving away all his milk, wasn't it?' Emma said. 'I seem to remember it was Mr Colson who also handed over plenty of his ration coupons to those in town who were celebrating something like a wedding. I believe he also gave the couples gifts.'

Ivy sneered. 'I was talking to her, not you.'

'I can pay for my own wedding, Ivy,' Janet said. 'I've got a job. Not as glamorous as yours, of course, working up at the big house. But being a clerk-typist, at least I don't have to wear an apron every day.'

'Just think, Ivy,' Emma said with a brightening smile. 'You and I will soon be the only spinsters in town. Unless I leave, of course. Then you'll be numero uno.'

'Numero what?' Ivy snorted again. 'Don't forget my tin of corned beef,' she said as she struggled to get the watermelon into her shopping basket without dropping it.

'You didn't ask for one,' Emma said, wondering how the pound of sausages was going to fare beneath the weight of the watermelon.

'Well, I'm asking now, aren't I? And you'd better get it for me or I'll be telling Mr Colson.'

'Watch me fly to the shelf!' Emma said, giving Janet a wink.

'Nice work,' Janet said when Ivy left.

'Handling the old bat? It's not so hard. I quite like arguing with her. It thins the blood.'

Janet choked on a laugh. 'If I'd known you were so acerbic I'd have stuck around you more often.'

'I prefer to think of my responses to Ivy as witticisms,' Emma said with a grin. 'It seems less painful to provoke her if I think of it that way,' she added, remembering the day so many years ago when she'd almost sniggered out loud at Harry's reference to handling a cow when he'd come upon her in his garden, Ivy full of rage that a ragamuffin Hatton should be standing so close to Harry let alone talking to him.

Emma turned her face away from Janet and silently rebuked herself. Mr Colson, not Harry.

Chapter Thirty-one

May 1947

'That was Ivy again,' Mrs Osborne said as she came into the shop from the office.

'I couldn't help but overhear.' Emma brushed soil off her hands from stacking potatoes in a barrel. There was to be a second dinner party and Ivy was in a complete flap. The initial dinner had gone ahead without a hitch. The cutlets had been first class and the choice of either pink sponge cake or apple charlotte a decided success, according to Ivy.

But Ivy wasn't coping with this second meal. It was the third time in three days she'd telephoned Mrs Osborne with grocery requests, each of them different. Then she'd dash into town to collect the goods and scurry back without looking at anyone on the street, let alone talking up her position as she usually did.

'I told her to calm down and that I'd help in any way I could,' Mrs Osborne said.

'Do we know what she's cooking this time?'

'She didn't say, she only gave me the list.' Mrs Osborne took her spectacles out of her apron pocket and held them up in front of her face as she read the list in her hand. 'A pineapple, jelly crystals, potatoes, runner beans, onions, lamb without the bone and fourteen plums.' Mrs Osborne sighed and glanced at the rear door of the shop, which led to her home where her husband was upstairs, resting. 'How am I going to get it to her? She says she hasn't got the time to come into town. She was like a frazzled rocket with only half a fuse lit when she picked up her groceries yesterday. The woman might collapse with emotional exhaustion if I make her walk into town again.'

'I'll take it.'

'Would you, dear?'

Emma nodded. She felt bad about teasing Ivy in the last month and this was a way of appeasing her angst about it. It wasn't Ivy's fault she was a snobby nuisance. She'd been here through thick and thin with all of them for twenty-five years and she deserved some respect—and some help. If she'd accept it from a Hatton.

'What you need is a delivery boy,' she said. 'It might be another advancement you could consider.'

'You mean a regular boy to work for us?'

Emma paused as the idea took hold. 'I'm sure there are plenty of people in the outlying homesteads who would like their groceries delivered. You've got an old bicycle out in the back shed. There's nothing wrong with it except it needs new tyres and inner tubes.'

'They won't pay, Emma. They can't afford to.'

'But they wouldn't have to. It would be a free service.'

'Free? I don't think Mr Osborne would like that.'

'But you might gain more customers, and I believe the outlay for the boy's wages would be more than covered by the gain in profits. It's not really that far to Bohle either, if the boy was cycling. You might expand your customers considerably.'

Mrs Osborne tapped a finger against her mouth, undoubtedly giving the idea more thought.

'I'm sure if people knew they could get their groceries delivered free they'd start ordering more,' Emma said. 'It's a good marketing principle. They're bound to want to best their neighbours, and having groceries delivered would be deemed a posh thing to do. I bet they'd order a little something extra each time.'

'Good heavens!' Mrs Osborne said, putting her spectacles down and staring at Emma. 'I'm liking the sound of it already, but where would we find him? Most of the boys in town are still at school or desperate to get into Townsville to look for work.'

'You'd need someone full time, but in the interim my brother Will might be interested. He could only work after school and Saturday mornings, though. Perhaps it would be a bit like a trial run. Would you like me to ask him?'

'That would suit very well, if your mother were to agree.'

'Oh, I'm sure she will.' They needed the money and Will might enjoy doing a proper job. It would get him ready for his future.

Emma undid the ties of her bib apron and pulled it off her shoulders. 'Why don't I take that list off you and fill a basket for Ivy? I can get it up to her within the hour.'

Mrs Osborne gave Emma a satisfied look. 'Emma Hatton, what did we do without you all these years?' she said, making Emma blush.

* * *

Less than a stone's throw from the big house, Emma's heart began beating irrationally and her pace faltered. The prospect of visiting the Colson house was daunting, to say the least. The last and only time Emma had set foot inside had been when she'd telephoned Cassie and that memory conjured all sorts of recollections she'd rather not dwell on. It had been a pleasant walk though. She'd once found it all so boring but the truth was, the town and its surrounds were as lovely as a hidden gem. Once a person left the criss-cross of streets and the old wooden bridge, they were met with sandy shores, plentiful tracks sheltered by mangroves and the occasional boat ramp.

Making her way around the side of the house instead of marching up the front path, she stood on a paved area by the garage and the shed and gazed at the house. Ivy would be in the kitchen, her employer at the bank, so Emma had nothing to worry about. She wouldn't be discovered snooping as she had been all those years ago. The house had been built in timber, painted white, and was far larger than any in town. A lavish, sprawling home on tall stumps so the air flowed beneath, with deep shady verandahs all around, accessed via French doors. The roof was iron and the pitch steep and it was the epitome of the lifestyle Harry Colson was accustomed to: grand, yet with an open and airy feel. Almost welcoming in many ways. She wondered where he had his breakfast: in the dining room or on one of his shady verandahs, waking up to the day as he eyed his property and the beach that was so close Emma heard the rush of lapping water?

She turned to the garden.

Many of the taller topiaries had been removed, leaving only a few statuesque plants, tightly clipped. Others had been dug up and rested temporarily in large pots, their roots barely covered with soil. The gravel from years ago was looking a little dull and thinned, as though nobody had raked it for some time, and a long, straight pathway led to palms, wattle bushes and asparagus fern that fringed the Coral Sea a short walk away. Harry Colson was obviously making changes to more than his hearth.

It would all look lovely once finished. Although the straight path needed to be taken up and replaced with one that curved and meandered. Not that Emma would be suggesting that to the property owner.

She shifted the heavy basket from one arm to the other and made her way to the steps up to the kitchen. When she arrived at the closed kitchen door, she spun around on a whim, to take a look at the view. It was breathtaking. Such beauty. To have all this on your doorstep, an evocative view from every window. No wonder Harry Colson said he had no desire or intention of leaving.

Settling her features into a well-mannered but approachable expression, Emma rapped on the door with her knuckles.

The door opened with a squeak of unoiled hinges and Ivy appeared. 'What do *you* want?' she demanded, and immediately turned back to her kitchen.

Emma cast a glance around the room. Steam issued from several pots on the stovetop. 'I brought your groceries up,' she said as she walked in, basket in hand, pushing the door to behind her. 'Mrs Osborne asked me to.' It was close enough to the truth.

Emma put the basket onto the sideboard since the kitchen table was piled high with bowls and whisks and chopping boards full of potatoes, onions and half a loaf of bread with its innards removed, breadcrumbs strewn across the tabletop. 'Something smells good,' she said. Something also smelled burnt.

'This'll be the death of me!' Ivy proclaimed, swiping the back of her hand over her brow, which was red and damp.

'Can I help?'

'He's having another dinner party.'

'Someone told me. I must say, you are being kept busy. Are you sure I can't help?'

'He had one not a month ago,' Ivy said resentfully.

'I heard it went down well.'

Ivy eyed the shopping basket. 'Did you bring the jelly crystals? It better be raspberry. It's got to be raspberry!'

'Just as you ordered. What are you cooking?'

Ivy let out a disgruntled breath. 'He wants lamb stuffed with pineapple and I've got to do glacé plums for dessert.'

'Goodness. What a lot of fruit.'

'He's got a sweet tooth,' Ivy said distractedly. 'I'm going to have to cook the pineapple in that contraption or spend all afternoon cutting it up into tiny pieces.'

'I can do that. What contraption are you referring to?'

'A pressure cooker!' Ivy said, flinging a hand towards the stovetop. 'He bought me a pressure cooker! Who does he think I am, Merlin the magician?'

Emma stilled the humour creeping up from inside. 'Why don't you cook what you did last time? Cutlets, wasn't it?'

'Well, he likes his lamb, but I can't, can I? He's having the same guests. You'd think he'd want to have someone new over.'

'Perhaps he likes these guests.'

Ivy huffed. 'He's come up with these new recipes just yesterday and now he wants a practice run. I've got to cook it so he can taste it. He's never done this to me before.'

It seemed a little heartless of him but he was probably unaware of the burden his demands were placing on the only female in his household.

'What is it that's burning?'

'The pressure cooker! I don't know how to get the lid off.'

'You've done ever so well getting it going in the first place. Let's take a look.' Emma slid her arms out of the cardigan she wore and threw it over the back of a chair by the table.

'Get the lid off before it explodes!' Ivy said, flapping her arms as though she hoped to take off and escape through the kitchen window.

'We have to relieve the pressure first.' Emma picked up a long-handled fork and lifted the weight on the lid. Steam erupted from the vent, spewing an odour of burnt mush into the kitchen, causing Ivy to slap a hand over her nose and Emma to grimace.

'How did it do that so quickly?' Ivy asked, gazing inside at the burnt mess.

'It traps the steam from the water you put inside the sealed chamber. What was cooking?'

'Chopped onions for the stuffed lamb and beans as a side dish.'

'You're supposed to leave the onions whole, or only halved, and I don't think you're supposed to cook the beans and the onions together. How much water did you use?'

'Quarter of a pint. I can read!' Ivy said, indicating the instruction booklet on the counter next to the stove. 'It says there next to the beans! Cook for eight minutes.'

'It's a three, not an eight.'

'It's a what?'

'Never mind.' Emma smiled. 'Let's start again.'

Half an hour later, having dealt with the remnants of onion and beans, Emma had persuaded Ivy to continue the old-fashioned way—by hand.

'He's going to thoroughly enjoy his dinner this evening,' Emma said two hours later when they stood back to admire their efforts.

'But I didn't cook it, did I? You did most of it,' Ivy said unenthusiastically.

'Let's not tell him.'

'I won't be breathing a word of it! I have my reputation to consider. I intend to cook this meal more than twice between now and Saturday. That's what any respectable housekeeper would do.'

Emma thought Ivy's employer might be rather sick of pineapple lamb and glacé plums by the time Saturday came around and it served him right. *He* ought to try using the pressure cooker. That might give him a good insight into what it took to run his house and his kitchen.

At the sound of a motor car's engine, she stilled, wariness settling in her stomach as though she'd swallowed a rock. She shot a glance at the clock on the wall. She'd been here far longer than planned.

'It's him!' Ivy said. 'He's home!'

'But it's only five o'clock,' Emma argued, dumbstruck at the thought she'd lost all track of time. He didn't normally drive through town until six or after.

'He's been coming back from the bank early every day this week and the last,' Ivy said as she scuttled around the kitchen, picking up wooden spoons and whisks, saucepans and lids and dumping them all in the sink. 'It's the renovation plans—first the garden, and now this flaming dinner party.'

Emma peeked out the window next to the kitchen door. If she ran down the stairs and hid behind the shed or at the back of the garage, he wouldn't see her. Then she could leave as soon as he walked in through the front door.

'Get out! Get out!' Ivy shrieked. 'I can't have him thinking I've had guests over, making use of his rations.'

'He wouldn't object if you had a friend over now and again,' Emma said, grabbing her cardigan and thrusting her arms through. 'I'll get the basket later,' she said to Ivy as she fastened the bottom two buttons of the cardigan.

Dashing down the stairs from the kitchen verandah, she sheltered against the garage wall, waiting for a tell-tale sign of the front door opening and closing so she could make her way to town as swiftly as possible.

'I think we're both very different people to those back when we first discussed my garden.'

Emma spun around at the sound of Harry Colson's voice. He must have come out of the garage to view his topiary garden before heading inside—and he was without his cane.

'I'm delighted to see you,' he said, taking a step forwards. 'You're looking fighting fit. Actually,' he added, with an appraising tilt of his head, 'you're looking lovely.'

Emma's hand rose automatically to her hair. It had grown so long these last two years and this morning she hadn't bothered to curl her fringe or tie back the top section since she'd been working in the storeroom while Mrs Osborne served the customers.

'I was delivering groceries for Ivy,' she explained. 'She was a little busy in the kitchen to go into town to fetch them. She's got a lot of cooking to attend to.'

'Ah, yes! I'm having a dinner party on Saturday. Just a few people but rather VIP. Would you care to come?'

Good Lord, every brain cell in that intellectual mind must be fried. He'd lost all sense. Emma baulked as the thought of Ivy's face, dressed in her finest housekeeper's black, her white apron starched so much it would be like a board, as she thumped a bowl of glacé plums down in front of Emma before handing her a jug of cream and tartly informing her to pour her own.

'I don't think I'd fit in, sir.'

'Please don't "sir" me. Honestly, Emma, I thought we were friends.'

Emma shook her head in despair. He was kind, and quite the caring individual—apart from the pressure cooker purchase and the rush of new recipes he'd thrust on Ivy—but she had to make him understand this friendship, or whatever it was, could not proceed any further than it already had. 'I don't believe I would be the right match for your dinner guests.'

'Why ever not?' He stepped forwards once more. He had a limp but it wasn't particularly noticeable, unless he was hiding any pain he felt. 'There's one family in particular I'd like you to meet,' he said as he slipped his hands into the pockets of his charcoal grey jacket. 'My boss, actually. The owner of the bank. His wife and his lovely daughter are coming and I'd like Clare to have someone her own age to talk to. I'm trying to make the right impression on my employer,' he added with a grin. 'He can be a bit of a tyrant.'

Emma paused to take in everything he'd said. Clare. His prospective bride. Someone Emma's age. Someone left on the shelf by a lack of suitable men, all of them being at war and some of them not returning. Now Harry Colson was going to save her.

Emma doubted she was the tortoiseshell spectacles kind. She'd be intelligent, caring, very pretty and perhaps a little shy. A suitable match for him and Emma summoned every ounce of happiness for them. But she couldn't endure the imagined scene around the dinner table, even if such an absurd scenario played out. Watching Harry Colson do his utmost to impress Clare's father, unable to take his eyes off the young woman while Emma sat next to her attempting chit-chat. They would have nothing to talk about. Their lives were miles apart.

'I'm sure Clare will get along well with whomever you have around your table.'

'Oh, I bet she would. I'm not doubting it, I'd just like it if …' He paused, and looked over his garden. 'I've started taking up the topiaries,' he said.

'I noticed.'

'It's part of my plans to brighten the dull. What do you think?'

'I'm sure your efforts in the house and the garden will be excellent.'

'Actually, I meant me, not the house,' he said, his eyes on hers. 'I have something to admit, Emma. I have marriage on my mind.'

Of course he did. 'Congratulations.'

'Bit too soon for that.'

'Oh, I see.'

He smiled, rather whimsically. 'I'm not sure you do.'

Emma was confused. Should she nod in kindly understanding, or say something to lift his spirits? 'I wish you well, Mr Colson.'

A smile blossomed on his face. 'Thank you, Miss Hatton. We shall see.'

'Indeed,' Emma replied and shook herself out of her trance as she fastened one more button on her cardigan. 'I must be going.'

'I would offer to drive you back to town but I don't think you would allow it.'

Emma paused. 'No,' she said cautiously. 'It wouldn't be right.'

'Perhaps one day it would.'

Emma stared at him for a moment. It was as though her perception of him had grown without her realising. Without her putting a stop to it after all. His eyes and his smile were thoroughly masculine yet held a gentility. She didn't see the stuffy older man, as he'd laughingly referred to himself, she saw a man she would like to become friends with. She saw a virile man, probably a brilliant man. She saw the man Clare must see.

The man who deserved whatever happiness was there for him to take. Good luck to him.

Chapter Thirty-two

June 1947

Emma was rearranging displays of boxed and packaged goods in the Osbornes' shop window when news came to town that Cynthia Allen had died.

'That'll be the reason his second dinner party was cancelled all those weeks ago,' Mrs Osborne said. 'Because Cynthia was unwell throughout her term and he didn't want her to travel from Melbourne.'

'I heard it was because of Robert Allen,' Irene McDonald said. 'He was the one who was unwell, which must have troubled Cynthia as well as Mr Colson. Always had a lot of time for his sister, did Harry Colson.'

'It had to be because of her condition,' Betty Soames butted in. 'No woman as delicate as Cynthia has an easy time of pregnancy.'

'Show me one who's had an easy time,' Irene said drily.

'Well,' Mrs Osborne stated in a matter-of-fact tone, 'Cynthia didn't pull through at the birth of her child, regardless of her fragility or her position in life. Let that be a lesson to us all.'

Emma stepped down from the window, keeping her head bowed so she didn't meet the eye of any of the women in the store, not wanting to call attention to herself and certainly not wanting to be brought into the conversation. But poor Cynthia. What tragedy to strike, and how sad for her husband. Emma hardly remembered her apart from vague memories of a delicate hand holding onto a voluminous straw hat on her perfectly coiffured head as the young woman accompanied her parents on outings.

The town was subdued and plenty of people had already dug out their black armbands, wearing them out of respect for Harry Colson, who was making plans to travel immediately to Melbourne to arrange the funeral.

Imprudently, Emma wanted to go up to the big house to offer her condolences, or write a note maybe. But it wasn't correct to do either. She shouldn't be seeking him out, not even to offer comfort. He had his burdens to bear, as did Emma, and attempting to make the transition from acquaintances to friends was never going to work.

* * *

Sitting in her bedroom after her workday ended, her only place of refuge when in the house, Emma put her sympathy for Harry Colson to one side and turned her thoughts onto what to do about Cassie's latest letter.

Darling Em,

Look what I just found in an old suitcase. The forty pounds I saved while working as a hostess. I don't need it here so I thought I would send it to you. I'm sure it'll come in handy for something or other.

How is your work going at the grocer's? (Shame it's not a dress shop, but I imagine you're making do.)

Anyway, I'm wondering if you can afford to travel to America sometime soon. We'd love to have a visitor! Not that we're not busy little bees over here. Eddie's days are full at the hospital and I only have another month to get through and it's getting unbearably difficult because—guess what?

I'm expecting twins!

I know you'll be as shocked as I was when the doctor told me.

Honestly, I'm the size of a brick dunny. It's awful being this big.

Regarding your hopeful travel, if you need a bit more money we can send it. But only if you promise to spend it on a ticket to visit us. You wouldn't believe the life we live over here. It's so very different to Australia. You'd love it. And I have to say, I wouldn't mind having you around as a friend for after I've given birth. It's going to be an almighty change for Eddie and me, being used to only our darling Grace—

Emma pressed her lips together.

Cassie had fallen in love with Grace and Emma was grateful, but she was also reading between the lines. Regardless of the excitement in her letter, what Cassie wasn't saying hurt within like a physical ache.

The Sheas were giving Emma the chance to see the child and to make a decision about her future: take the child or leave her be. They would want to know what Emma's plans were, especially as there were soon to be two new babies in their family.

Emma stood and folded the letter. She hadn't told Cassie about the difficulties after the birth, nor that she couldn't have any more children. It hadn't felt right to upset her friend with yet more agony on Emma's part, and now, if she were to own up to the truth, Cassie would be more concerned that Emma would take Grace. The child Cassie had brought up. The child Cassie loved.

Emma did want Grace. How could she not? It was awful not knowing the touch of her child's hand. Not having the light of her twinkling gaze rest on her face. Not feeling the warm puff of her breath as she planted a kiss on her cheek.

She couldn't tell Cassie this either, because Cassie was pregnant and had already had problems. Emma couldn't make her life even more worrisome.

She squeezed her eyes tightly closed. She couldn't answer her friend. She couldn't make the decision about Grace. Not yet.

Not quite yet …

* * *

'Harry Colson's back,' Janet said as she blew in through the door at the Osbornes' in a rush of exhilaration. 'Just caught sight of him up at the house.'

'And Robert Allen?' Emma asked, her focus on the cash register she'd just tallied. That was the second time Harry Colson had been to Melbourne since the funeral and people were desperate to know what was going on. Emma admitted to having some interest herself. She'd even surreptitiously asked Will, who had been working as the Osbornes' delivery boy after school and on Saturday mornings, but he brushed off her casual enquiries with a retort that he wasn't going to do this job forever because he'd soon be a man and was already sick of carting around old women's groceries.

'Don't think he's here. I only saw the man himself,' Janet said. 'Ivy didn't know he was coming back today either. She's in a right state.'

'What were you doing up at the house?'

'It was my mother who made me go. You know my mum, always the charitable kind, but I have a sneaking suspicion she actually wanted to know what Ivy knew but didn't want to be seen as intruding. So she sent me.'

'What does Ivy know?' Emma asked, not expecting to get an answer.

'Exactly nothing.'

No. Harry Colson liked to keep his private business to himself.

'But I expect that will change sometime tomorrow morning now he's back,' Janet said. 'Someone is bound to go up there to snoop on the pretext of enquiring about Ivy's health. Irene McDonald, most likely.'

'Why would Irene go? Isn't her youngest daughter working up there three days a week?'

'Yes, but she's not nosey enough to ask. Although in this case, even I'm dying to know what's what.'

Emma bit her lip. It was a little odd. Something must be going on.

'Irene's girl just told me she's had enough of running and fetching for old Ivy too. Says she's not hanging around a mostly empty house being bossed by the housekeeper.'

'But there's no work here,' Emma said. 'What will she do?'

'What every other bugger does,' Janet said drily. 'Get married.' She sighed, then scrunched her face. 'Anyway, I came in here to let you know the latest but I think I was also supposed to get something.'

'Your mum usually likes a mixed grill for midweek. Lamb chops, kidney, bacon and sausages.'

Janet slapped the counter. 'I'll take double of each please. That way I won't have to remember it next week. Honest to God, it's got to be easier running my own household than that of my mother.'

'Roll on the wedding bells,' Emma said with a smile as she went to fill Janet's order. 'How are your plans going?'

'Mum and Dad want us to rent the little house next door. The one the Wheaton grandparents used to live in.'

'Is that too close for comfort?' Emma enquired, wrapping the sliced bacon.

'Everywhere in Blueholm Bay is too close for comfort but I'm used to it. It's my fiancé I'm concerned about.'

'Is he hesitating?'

'He says it makes sense to live cheaply until we've saved enough for a place of our own in Townsville. But my darling Mr Jameson might not like being so close to all my family members.' Janet drummed her fingers on the counter. 'I've warned him of what might happen and he's game to give it a go.'

'Good on him.'

'We'll see. Not convinced we'll stay as long as he's planning, to be honest.'

'While I've got you alone,' Emma said, putting the parcel of bacon down and leaning both elbows on the counter. 'What can I get you for a wedding present? I'd much prefer to give you something you'll like and not just another vase or a teapot.'

'Don't spend your money on me.'

'I'll do as I choose.' She'd be delighted to buy Janet and her fiancé a gift.

'Well,' Janet said, leaning on the counter, replicating Emma's pose. 'Because I think we might not stay here—a woman's place is by her husband's side and all that.'

Emma gave her a crooked grin. 'I'm sure you'll teach Mr Jameson the ropes.'

'It could be a stab in the dark but I'll give it a go. In case of emergency though, what I'd really love to have is a memory jar filled with things from Blueholm Bay. Something I can take with me if we do leave.'

Emma was baffled. 'A memory jar? What sort of things would you want to go in it?'

'Bits and pieces from the beaches. Pebbles and shells. Dried seaweed or leaves. You know what I mean.'

'What a beautiful idea,' Emma said, her mind already envisaging the jar. It wouldn't be an old jam jar but something purchased, maybe from a commercial supplier. A jar with an interesting shape, and it might have a cork stopper. 'I'll do it,' she told Janet. 'It would be my absolute pleasure.'

'Make up one for yourself while you're at it. Just in case.'

'In case of what?'

'Marriage.'

The smile on Emma's mouth stiffened. 'I'm happy as I am.'

'You can't be. Want me to find you a date? We could make up a double. You and Mr Possibly-Interesting and me and Mr Jameson. I'm getting sick of seeing your face around here all day every day. It's time to get off that shelf you've been sitting on.'

'Janet, I don't intend to stay here forever.'

'Good.'

'But I can't just up sticks. Dad's not working, the older boys are only getting occasional work in Cairns and the household needs my income.'

'You'd simply send money home.' Janet frowned. 'Any grocer would employ you with the experience you've got. What's got into you? Pull your finger out!'

'Stop yelling at me,' Emma said with a patient but pointed look.

'I'll yell as much as I want. There's nothing here for you, Emma. Nothing at all.'

Wasn't that the truth. But Emma couldn't say so because it would open an entirely new conversation about why.

She pulled herself back to the daily grind. 'What was I doing?' she asked.

'Lamb chops, kidney, bacon and sausages. You've only got the bacon so far. Get a move on or I'll be issuing a complaint.'

'Three bags full, Miss Jameson. Just remember who'll be left here to prune your mother's roses after you leave.'

Janet grimaced. 'Chances are I'll be here till I die—and so will you unless you're careful.'

'Truthfully, Janet, I can't think of a worse thing to happen. Believe me,' Emma said as she moved to the meat counter, 'I'll be gone from here as soon as it's possible.'

Or when she'd made a decision about America, and the child no-one knew she had.

Chapter Thirty-three

July 1947

'He'd only been back a week before galivanting off to Melbourne yet again,' Mum said.

Emma shifted on the armchair in the front room of the house on Herring Street, keeping her eyes on the long netting veil in her hands. Janet's wedding was happening later in the year but in typical Janet form, plans were already progressing. She'd borrowed a dress from a cousin and Emma's mother was tasked with doing the alterations. Emma was helping with the veil, which Janet wanted to sparkle, so Emma was sewing pearl-coloured sequins around the edge.

Mum was on the sofa with the skirt of the dress spread over her lap and down her legs. 'He went with not a moment's notice,' she said. 'Ivy knows nothing about what's going on. Irene McDonald's youngest stormed out the other day too. Got herself a job in Townsville at some hotel. Ivy says she's been left to cope with everything all by herself, just like she did throughout the war.'

Up until a few minutes ago they hadn't spoken except for the odd comment about tucks and pleats, and Emma had been reminded of the quiet evenings she'd spent alone at Doris's house, knitting or reading the *Daily Bulletin*, the lamplight soothing. Before everything had gone wonderfully well, and cruelly wrong.

'I expect he has things to do,' she said to her mother.

'Like what?'

Emma didn't answer, and thankfully her mother didn't pursue the subject, allowing Emma to continue with her own thoughts. She still hadn't been able to reply to Cassie's letter. It was harsh to make her friend wait but how could she respond when she didn't know what was best? She could use her savings to move to Townsville straight away and hope she found a job soon. Or she could stay put and use the money to travel to America.

There would be plentiful aftereffects for either choice. If she went to the city she'd never see Grace, because there wouldn't be enough money to travel. If she went to America she'd be opening up all her secrets. Whatever her decision, it was going to cause heartache and agony for more than one person.

The only good thing to come out of biding her time was the decision to buy Grace a present. Something Emma should have done a long time ago. Except she was stalling on that too. She didn't want to pander to the child with a lavish gift, because any present from Emma Hatton would need to reflect her take on life. A small, unsophisticated gift from the mother. The real mother.

So what to buy for a little girl who appeared to have everything? A little girl she'd only met once.

'Oh, I meant to say earlier. I've got you a job,' Mum said.

Emma looked up.

'Doris suggested it.'

'I have a job,' Emma said, frowning.

'I don't want you underfoot any more.'

'What are you talking about?'

'There's enough chatter about us all as it is, what with your father unemployed,' Mum said, stabbing the material with her needle. 'And here I am still coping with you.'

'Coping with what, exactly? Aren't you glad of the money I'm bringing in?'

'You can send some of your earnings home. I wouldn't expect you to send more than two pounds and seven shillings a week back here. I can manage on that. You can keep the rest.'

'How gracious of you.' Emma rested the veil on her lap. 'What is this job? Not that I'm saying I'll do it, but I'm interested to hear why you think you've got the right to go out and get me a job. I'm almost twenty-one, Mum. A grown woman. I can make up my own mind about the jobs I want to do or not do.'

Mum shifted the skirt of the dress. 'That's the uncanny thing. It's Doris's in-laws.'

Emma stilled, her senses spiking.

'They're getting on now and could do with a hand.' Mum bit through the thread and stuck her needle into the pincushion on the side table next to her. 'You'd live in and get all your food and they'd also pay you five pounds a week. That's a good wage, on top of everything else you'll get.'

'You cannot be serious,' Emma said, with little control over the fury rumbling within.

'It's not as though you'll ever prepare for your own wedding, is it? Not like Janet. The next sister down is about to get hitched too. What am I left with? You. Underfoot. Being miserable.'

'Miserable?'

Her mother shook out the skirt of the wedding dress and picked up the hem. 'This'll need unpicking. Janet's much taller than her cousin. Pass me the small scissors, would you?'

'Are you intent on destroying everything?'

Mum's expression hardened. 'Don't you dare talk to me as though—'

'I'll dare as much as I like. Do you really expect me to do the job you fabricated over three years ago when you hid me away, out of sight, out of mind? It was a despicable thing to do. Do you know what it was like at that place? Have you ever wondered? Do you know how many consequences it has for so many people?'

Mum pushed the wedding dress off her lap and stared at her daughter, her face full of bitterness. 'I don't want you here any more.'

'I do whatever I can to pull my weight. More than half of everything this household needs comes from my input.' Emma stood. This—this terrible idea she would work for Doris's in-laws—was an unbelievable suggestion. Did her mother have no empathy or compassion whatsoever? Had she never herself felt belittled or alone in the world with no-one at her side? 'Can you not just leave me be?' Emma said, her voice rising in pitch.

'Doris has already told her in-laws,' her mother said, outrage now replacing the bitterness in her expression.

'She had no right to do that. *You* have no right!'

'I'm not having you talk to me this way. Doug!' her mother yelled, getting up from the sofa.

'He's gone to the pub, Mum, remember? He's there most days. It's because he doesn't want to be around you. He'd rather walk all the way to Bohle than spend any more minutes in your company than he has to.'

'You ungrateful little—'

'You know nothing about gratefulness.' Emma was now shaking with anger. 'Nothing about love. Nothing about friendship. How could you do this, Mum? How could you have done *any* of it?'

Her mother started ranting, but Emma no longer heard the words. She'd been here before, had settled for second best at St Philomena's when she'd become acquiescent and almost reconciled with her lot before Susannah fell down the stairs and Wynn was locked in the linen room, and now she'd done it *again*.

She put her fingertips to her temples and closed her eyes as her own bitterness roared.

Three years ago the penalty for what she'd done had been to lose everything and she'd put all the will she possessed into moving on. Getting up every morning even though she was a broken human being. Every day, week, month, year, she had faced trials and more strife, hoping her plans would soon come to fruition, because they had to one day. They just had to.

And they hadn't.

No more. Absolutely no more. By staying here all these years, trying to help out while longing to leave, she had simply prolonged her agony. Her mother loathed her. Her father loved her but couldn't even say it. Will and Danny just thought of her as another mother, someone to get them food or put sticking plaster on their sores.

'I'm leaving,' she said, dropping her hands to her sides.

Her mother pulled her shoulders back. 'And where do you think you're going?'

'I don't care, but as soon as the Osbornes can replace me, I'm packing my suitcase and I'm not coming back. I'm getting out of Blueholm Bay. Do you hear me, Mum? I'm going. And I'm never coming back. *Never.*'

Chapter Thirty-four

To the dismay of Mrs Osborne, Emma gave her resignation notice the next morning. It was a Saturday, but Emma hadn't wanted to stall the inevitable. Better to get bad news out. Except she hadn't found the courage to do it when she arrived for work and had spent the whole two hours in agony until the shop closed.

Attempting to ease the responsibility for the angst the news caused, and having no wish to remain in the claustrophobic house on Herring Street where her mother was baking, her father drinking his fifth cup of tea and her brothers underfoot, arguing over a board game, Emma had changed out of her work skirt and blouse and had walked away from town, hoping to get her bearings.

The tide was out, the breeze gusty, and she was sitting cross-legged in the soft, dry sand, threading daisy chains, her back against a bank of vegetation. She'd picked the small yellow-headed wildflowers on her walk simply for something to occupy her. She would discard the chain, like everything else she had here. She was going to Brisbane to search for Wynn and if she couldn't produce a result, she'd head for New South Wales and look for Susannah.

She would find work. She'd beg for it if she had to, which was exactly what she should have done years ago. All this wasted time. She was furious with herself. But if there was a scrap of luck still out there somewhere, Emma Hatton might eventually become a woman who found contentment in the simplest of things. She had no expectations of more.

Only then would she find the courage to write to Cassie.

* * *

Some while later, Emma kicked off her shoes, leaving them and the flower chain on a rock, and wandered along the shoreline following the curve of the bay, delaying her return to town although it was already mid-afternoon. With the breeze more persistent now, she attempted to secure her hair back from her face and out of her eyes by twisting a red scarf she'd been using as a belt on her shorts and winding the band around her head, knotting it at the top. Within the last few hours she had settled upon a number of things she needed to do.

She was going to use the forty pounds Cassie had sent to buy a few things her friend might fondly remember and not be able to get hold of in America, like copies of the *Women's Weekly* and maybe her once favourite 7777 Eau de Cologne. She would also purchase gifts for the new babies, who were due any day. She would use her own money for this, and it was an easy task.

It was the gift for Grace that bewildered her. The child's bedroom in Wisconsin would be filled with plentiful stuffed animals and dolls dressed in pinks and cherry reds having tea parties with the dainty porcelain tea sets Cassie would have purchased. It would be best to send something simple, maybe something useful. But how would Grace think of this gift once she'd been told the truth? Would it be better to buy something expensive after all? This first present should be Emma's token. It would need to be a gift that spoke of her enormous love.

She rolled up the sleeves of her cotton shirt and pulled the shirt tail out of the waistband of her denim shorts to use as an apron to collect things for Janet's memory jar. She found uninhabited helmet shells, the odd pebble and piece of wood bleached by the sun and the brine—and a lucky find of a small piece of sea glass, washed smooth. She pocketed it in her shorts. She would keep it for herself.

Then she took the sea-washed glass from her pocket and popped it into her shirt tail. Why would she keep the sea glass for herself? Why would she want a memory from here?

'Hello! Emma—hello!'

She turned, the freshened wind whipping the long strands of her hair around her face as her heart slammed against her chest.

Harry Colson.

She'd wandered onto Colson Beach, oblivious to everything while in the midst of her thoughts. But here she was, in her bare feet, the sand cool and damp between her toes, with shells and pebbles sitting in the apron of her shirt and her midriff on show, trespassing on his beach in order to find some solace.

'I was collecting shells,' she called as an apology.

'I saw you,' he said, voice raised above the wind. 'I was on the living room verandah.' The tip of his cane was sinking in the sand.

'I shouldn't be here,' Emma said as he got closer. 'I didn't intend to wander this far and onto your beach.'

'It's not mine,' he said with a warming smile.

'It's Colson Beach.'

'A term used that suggests I own it.' He came to a halt a few yards in front of her and took a deep breath, indicating the effort it had cost him to walk this far across the shifting sand from his garden to the firm sand they now stood on. 'Which of course I don't. It belongs to Queensland.' He lifted the cane. 'Sorry about this. Can't quite make it across the beach without it and I didn't want to dawdle.'

Emma licked her lips and tasted salt. 'I'm so very sorry about Cynthia.'

He offered a sad smile. 'I was surprised you didn't visit me to see how I was getting on.'

'I thought it best to leave you be.'

'I would have welcomed your wisdom.'

'Mine?'

'Most certainly.' He gripped the handle of his cane more firmly. 'I'm so glad to see you. I was unsure how I might generate this meeting between us. I considered visiting you at the Osbornes' but felt it wouldn't have been a private place for us to talk. I also wondered if I should just knock on your front door.'

Knock on her— Good lord and all the saints. What could he possibly have to say that might have induced him to knock on the Hatton front door? 'Is there something I can do for you, Mr Colson?'

'I'm hoping so.' He gave her another smile but it was tremulous and faltered as he cleared his throat.

Emma cast a glance at the house, wondering where Ivy was and what she'd do if she peered out a window and saw her employer talking to Emma. The washing was on the line in the kitchen garden by the shed but Ivy wouldn't see it from the kitchen. Only the garden and the beach.

Harry Colson glanced over his shoulder at the house then back to Emma. 'Before I say anything more, I must tell you I am keeping the baby.'

Emma gawped. This was news indeed.

'I'm going to be bringing her up. We arrived home this morning, she and I.'

'Goodness. What a tremendous responsibility.'

'I'm aware of it.'

Emma could hardly take it in. 'And the child's father?' she asked, still clutching the hem of her shirt.

'Allen declined in health considerably over the last weeks and now he's not talking to anyone. He doesn't recognise me. I doubt he truly understands that Cynthia is gone and that he has a daughter.'

'How awful for him.'

'I engaged a nurse for him after Cynthia died, and one for the baby, along with staff to look after both, but I had to rush back there again a few days ago when I got news of Allen's complete decline. Anyway,' he said. 'There is something more I'd like to say. Something rather important and I would ask you please not to say anything until I am finished.' He studied the sand around her feet. Or perhaps he was staring at her toes, which were sinking into the wet sand as she scrunched them in order to stop herself from bolting.

'I have been thinking of my childhood and how lonely it was. Regardless of my parents being loving and able to offer me an excellent education and the means to continue using my intellect.' He lifted his eyes to meet hers. 'Yet, I have been considering options. Those of perhaps having a family to call my own.'

He had to mean Clare. He was going to want Clare to have a friend in town and Emma would be leaving. She immediately thought of suggesting Janet, who although upfront and not at all of the drawing-room chit-chat variety would be friendly towards Clare. Perhaps Clare might need someone like Janet. Someone who wouldn't mince words yet would never be unkind.

'In light of this,' Harry Colson said, thumping the sand with the tip of his cane once more, his gaze now intense, 'I am wondering if you would marry me.'

Emma blinked. 'If I would what?'

'I'm asking you to marry me. I would like you to be my wife.'

Emma released her hold of her shirt and stumbled backwards, shells and pebbles falling to the sand.

'Dammit. I'm making you uncomfortable. I knew this might happen.' He lifted his cane. 'Please be careful where you tread,' he said, indicating her feet. 'You're not wearing shoes.'

Emma shook herself, hoping to clear the shockwave coursing throughout her body.

'It can't really be a surprise, can it?' he asked. 'You must have guessed.'

'No!' she said, shaking her head.

'I like you, Emma,' he said. 'More than you yet know. I liked the young girl who stood in my garden almost five years ago, looking forward to her sixteenth birthday while milk slopped from the pails she was carrying. I thought you had an intelligence that was undoubtedly being neglected. You were also far too young, and I didn't have ...' He looked away, perhaps as he contemplated how to say whatever he was about to say next. 'I didn't have the kind of feelings for you then as I do now, I simply admired the young girl. But you are older today, you're a grown woman and I feel it is not inappropriate to offer you marriage.'

Inappropriate? It was beyond inappropriate, it was absurd. *Marry* him?

'I am about to be thirty-four years old,' he continued. 'Which you possibly consider quite ancient. I believe you are coming close to twenty-one?'

Emma pulled herself together and wiped her hands on her shorts. 'Mr Colson, I thank you for your offer and I am truly flattered, but it cannot be.'

'Oh? You have reached a conclusion so soon?' His expression changed from disquiet to awareness. 'Ah! It's the baby.'

'The baby?'

'Well, yes. You must be worried that I simply need a nursemaid.'

Emma shook her head, still trying to clear the confusion. 'What about Clare?'

'Clare?' he asked with a frown.

'Your employer's daughter.'

'What about her?'

'Well, I ... I presumed you and she ... I mean—'

'Good God,' he said. 'You thought I was going to ask *Clare* to marry me?'

'Well, of course I did! Why else would you have told me about her and how you want to impress her father?'

He threw his head back with a laugh. 'Here I am torn to shreds with anxiety about your possible answer and all this time you thought I was befriending you so I could divulge my romantic inclinations for another.'

'What else would I think?'

'My dearest Emma, I must explain.' He put a hand on his heart. 'My manager thinks of me as an eternal bachelor. Always there to work long hours. Never going out. I've been testing the waters for months now, attending parties and whatever, and the only way I could truly persuade him that I'm a man with a life of my own was to have him and his family at my home. I thought Clare might be a friend for *you*. I intended to inform her father of my desire to marry you—'

'No!' Emma said firmly. 'I can't let you go on. I am not the woman for you.' Unexpected tears burned her eyes. 'I am not the woman for any man.'

He dropped his hand to his side. 'Is it true?' he asked softly, the wind almost whisking his words away. 'The murmurs I heard from the women who came to attend my gardens and my animals during the war. That you may have been, shall we say, compromised?'

Emma's mouth fell open as the horror of his words struck her.

'I can see by your pallor that we have hit upon some truth.'

She stepped back, her hands flying to her cheeks. Why couldn't she speak? Why could she not show him the outrage sparking inside her? 'Mr Colson, whatever you think—'

'The truth is of no concern to me. I must state that strongly. However.' He paused, but only briefly. 'I would like to know if there was some repercussion that might impact us in the future. Is there a child?' he asked, then awaited her response as though he'd asked her if the sun rose every morning and set each evening.

'Yes,' Emma said in the barest of whispers. 'There is a child, but she lives in America.'

Again, he waited, his gaze bearing down on hers, but not in a remonstrating way.

'My best friend and her husband adopted her. I haven't seen her since she was born.'

'She's cared for? She's happy?'

'In the best possible way.'

'Do you yearn to see her? I imagine you must.'

Emma evaluated her response, not wanting to discuss her unhappiness. 'I am grateful beyond belief that she has found love in her life.'

'Then are we not free to be who we choose to be?' he said as though it had all been settled.

'I will never be free.' She wrung her hands with humiliation that this man had overheard gossip and had come to his own conclusions. The resurrection of shame almost swallowed her whole. The fact that he *knew*—that he had *guessed*!

'Nor will any of us be. Not truly free, but that is life. There is only the future. That is the only way out for any of us.'

'Nobody knows,' she said, 'only my parents and my aunt.'

'And now me.'

'The rest is just supposition from those who know nothing.'

'They never will know anything. Not from me.'

It took every ounce of courage to look him in the eye. 'You don't despise me? You don't want explanations?'

'I am very sorry for what happened to you and I don't wish to pry—in fact, I do not want to know the details or the circumstances unless you want to tell me, but I will never ask. I trust you.'

'Mr Colson—'

'*Please* call me Harry.'

Emma paused. 'What if I refuse you? What do I call you then?'

He considered this with an intake of breath. 'I presume you will go back to calling me Mr Colson.'

'And what would you call me?'

His eyes shadowed, a film of despondency entering his gaze. 'It's likely I shall manipulate situations whereby I ensure I do not see you and therefore shall not have need of referring to you by any name.'

Emma swallowed. 'Would you hate me?'

'How could I ever?' he said with a shake of his head. 'Not you. Not ever. And hate isn't a word in my vocabulary. One can find hatred in one's heart for another who has caused pain. One can see hatred burn in the eyes of others, but one cannot simply hate. It's a disposable word, an emotional release that momentarily illustrates our feelings. You hate a puppy when it chews a slipper. You hate the rain when you're dressed for a picnic.' He looked at her intently. 'Do you understand what I'm so ineffectively trying to say?'

Emma nodded. She didn't hate her mother. She didn't hate the sisters. She felt pity for them. She felt sorry for them. Neither did she hate Frank. Perhaps he too was paying penance somewhere in Kernville, California, with his wife and child.

'I have always been fond of you,' the man in front of her said. 'And I admit to being tremendously attracted to you these last few years. I think we are both alone in the world, Emma. Can we not share it together?'

'I can't have any more children,' Emma said, knowing this would halt the unbearableness of this incredible exchange.

He did pause, for quite some time. Then he produced his smile. The soft one, the slightest kink of his mouth, yet the smile reached his eyes and made his features radiate with care and consideration. 'I'm sorry for the pain you must feel. It must be agony. But it is you I wish to spend my life with.'

Emma shook her head. 'You can't expect marriage without wanting children.'

'I have a child. She's up at the house.'

'But you'd want your own.'

'Why?' he said with a simplicity Emma couldn't follow. 'I have my sister's child. There will be a child in my life. It's you I want to be with, Emma.'

'Are you saying love would play a part in this marriage?'

His eyes lit up. 'I cannot begin to tell you how much.'

Emma stared at him as a glimpse of a man she'd never thought existed began to emerge. He had empathy and compassion. Or perhaps it was just an understanding of how the world ticked.

'People will talk,' she said, and for the first time since the conversation had begun, she wanted to hear his answer. Wanted to listen to more of his argument.

'If we marry?' He shrugged. 'Of course they'll talk, but they will return to what they know and leave us alone.'

'My family are not …' What could she say?

'No,' he answered. 'They're not. Your family's interest will be keen to begin with but that will pass, along with the talk. Emma,' he said and stepped forwards until he was directly in front of her, a shell or two crunching beneath his shoes. He hooked his cane over his arm and held out his hand. 'May I?'

Emma lifted her hand and he took hold of her fingertips.

'Emma Hatton,' he said in a tone that held absolute sincerity. 'I shall not let anyone, not your mother nor myself, dictate your life nor any aspect of your life, should you marry me.'

Emma's fingertips seemed to be on fire. 'My parents—'

'Your parents will naturally gravitate back to that place from whence they came. For example, I cannot envisage them easily partaking of tea with us in the afternoons. They would be uncomfortable.'

It would be excruciating. Mum wouldn't be able to hold her tongue and she'd be sticking out her pinky when she lifted her cup from its saucer, quietly thumbing her nose at Ivy, who would have served the tea. Or worse, her mother would be closed-mouthed, feeling out of sorts sitting on a sofa in the big house, unused to it all and not knowing how to handle any of it.

'I wouldn't wish them to feel awkward or belittled. It wouldn't be fair.' Even though they had taken all fairness from their only daughter, Emma could not and would not throw disregard in her parents' faces even if she were given the opportunity. 'I would still need to see them,' she said. 'I would still need to know they were well. I couldn't give them up completely, not while I lived in the same town.'

'I agree. Of course we shan't give them up. On occasions we shall have tea in the garden instead of the house. At other times we shall visit them and allow your mother to produce her best cakes and tea sets and we shall be suitably impressed. Then we will return to our home, where our lives will be ours and ours alone and they will be satisfied they have done their bit. Which I'm certain they will. They will come to admire you, Emma. Eventually. We'll help them where we are able. Even perhaps in a monetary manner, so they are at least comfortable.'

'I don't want you to give them your money.'

'I shan't necessarily be giving it away. I have connections and I'm sure your father and perhaps even those brothers of yours might be found good, steady employment. So you see, they will feel enabled and independent and perhaps proud of their achievements. This gives people stability. A sense of worth stems from autonomy.'

There was a fluttering in Emma's stomach. A ripple of excitement. It wasn't his money—it would never be that. It was the calmness and affability that surrounded him which drew her. It was the protection she might receive should she become his wife. Which just half an hour ago would have been the most outrageous of thoughts, yet now …

'Would you like to see the baby?' he asked.

Emma was torn. He would never knowingly hurt her by reminding her of Grace and would likely be the sort to be agonised should he inadvertently do so. But had he genuinely thought this through? Or had receiving the baby into his care changed his perspective on his needs?

'Emma?' he asked again. 'Would you like to meet the baby?'

Emma drew a breath and looked over her shoulder to the ocean and the rivulets in the far distance, considering the lonely star in the night sky. The one that was looking for the other stars, just as she had been searching for people in her life who would stay by her side. So far in her twenty-one years, every good thing she'd been given had been taken off her. More recently, she had never imagined marriage would come her way and she'd had no intention of seeking out a mate.

Until perhaps now, when one had found her.

She brought her focus back to him. 'Yes. I would like to see the baby.'

* * *

'Mrs Williams, how are you?' Harry said as he slid his cane into the hallway umbrella stand by the front door. 'Everything all right?'

'Everything's as you left it half an hour ago, sir,' Ivy said, hawk-like eyes fully on Emma.

Emma had rolled down the sleeves of her shirt and buttoned the collar and cuffs while they walked across the sand to the house. They hadn't spoken, but she'd been aware of Harry's presence and the charisma emanating from him while she tried as surreptitiously as possible to make herself presentable. She'd run her fingers through her hair and tied it into a ponytail with the scarf and stuffed her shirt tail into the waistband of her shorts. Yet she was still barefoot, her shoes on a rock by the beach.

'Miss Hatton is here to meet the baby.'

Ivy's gaze shot from Emma's feet to Harry. 'Is she going to be the child's full-time nurse? I need to know, sir. There'll be more work for me with a nurse in the house, demanding hot water for warming bottles and washing nappies and the like.'

Harry cleared his throat. 'There's no need to worry about that quite yet. Emma, would you like a cup of tea?'

Emma was parched but there was no way she wanted Ivy Williams to serve her tea. 'No, thank you, Harry,' she said softly, knowing Ivy would be horrified at the use of her employer's first name. But everyone's life had changed in the last thirty minutes. No matter what happened next, there would be no going back without some sort of embarrassment or astonishment on everyone's part and Emma would never think of this man as anything but Harry from now on.

'I'm afraid it's still a bit dreary in here,' he said, leading her into the living room where the French doors were open and the hems of heavy floral drapes shifted slightly with the breeze. He picked up a stuffed-to-the-brim green velvet cushion from an ornate maroon-coloured settee, plumped it and placed it carefully back against the armrest. 'Cynthia told me years ago to get rid of the outdated furniture but I hadn't got around to it. Hadn't thought there was any need until I met you that day at the grocery store. The day it was raining hard and so unexpectedly. The day I first saw you in an entirely different light …'

Emma remembered every second but didn't say so. The day she first became aware of his warmth and affability. A person she felt some affection for.

'I've had some plans drawn up for renovations and I've had a lot of ideas but I haven't committed to anything in particular yet. Thought I'd wait until …' He smiled contritely then cleared his throat. 'Anyway, just wanted you to know that the house will not always be this dowdy.'

'It's a lovely house. It has character and charm. I'm sure whatever you've planned will suit perfectly.'

'You do?'

'Where is the baby?' Emma asked.

'Oh! She's here. Right here.' He moved across the room. 'I thought she might like the view from the open window during the day, so long as it's not blustery. Don't want her catching a chill, so I moved her pram into the corner while she was sleeping. Then I saw you on the beach and begged Mrs Williams to watch the child. She wasn't very happy about it,' he added, grimacing. 'I shall need to make it up to her.'

'You've been caring for the baby yourself? All the way from Melbourne?'

'Her nurse packed a bag with all the paraphernalia I'd need and gave me a quick lesson in bottle feeding and burping and all the nappy stuff. All the same, it was quite the journey.'

Emma bet it was, hardly believing he'd managed it without hiring a nurse to accompany him.

'She's amenable for a baby,' he said, moving closer to the cane pram, the hood raised so the sun and breeze wouldn't reach the child. A vastly different pram to the wooden boxed one her father had made that Emma had pushed her brothers around in. 'Not that I have experience of babies, but so far she and I get along well. I shall employ a nurse for her, of course. I can't take her to the bank every day. It wouldn't give the right impression.'

Emma suppressed a dazed smile. This was the self-effacing person she'd first got to know outside the Osbornes'. The person with a sense of humour he had no idea he possessed. The man who had actually considered taking the baby to his workplace and who had changed nappies all by himself in a train compartment. Or perhaps he and the child had flown from Melbourne.

'Would you like to hold her? She doesn't wriggle much, even when awake. Although I imagine that will change drastically once she starts crawling. What's your opinion?'

Emma followed him to the pram and withheld a need to peek closer at the small bundle wrapped in a woollen shawl, suddenly frightened she might cry at the first sight of this newborn child. 'I think it's amazing you're prepared to do all this for her.'

'She doesn't have anyone else.'

Emma looked up at him. 'It's wonderful that you love her.'

A smile tilted his mouth. 'You think so?'

'What's her name?'

'She hasn't got one yet.'

'Harry!' Emma exclaimed. 'She's six weeks old.'

He lifted a shoulder apologetically. 'I don't know what Cynthia would have wanted so I was thinking perhaps Maud after our mother. I just call her "little one" at the moment but it doesn't mean I don't appreciate or love her.'

Emma glanced at the child with her budded lips and strands of golden hair visible from beneath her dainty knitted hat. 'What about her father? Did he have a preferred name?'

'None that he mentioned. He hardly said anything to anyone and he didn't want to look at her, let alone hold her.'

'The poor little darling. Did your mother have a middle name?'

'Roslyn. It's also Cynthia's middle name.'

'Can you not settle on that?' Emma asked, looking up. 'Roslyn Allen. It's a beautiful name and I think it suits her.'

'You do? Well, that's settled. Roslyn. Yes, it is a lovely name. It's a relief, because I wasn't sure if Maud would set the right tone for her.'

'What tone would you like to set?'

'Oh, I don't mean I'm going to exercise paternal control over her or insist she does things the way I think she ought to. Not always, anyway. I had enough of that from my parents, as did Cynthia. No wonder she was pleased to marry Allen and get away from it all. I just mean I look at her sometimes—at little Roslyn—and see someone I've not yet met.' He frowned. 'I don't suppose that makes any sense.'

'It makes perfect sense. She's a new human being and nobody yet knows what sort of person she'll be. As a parent or guardian, you can only hold her hand during the tough times and make sure she gets through with knowledge, intelligence and learning.'

Harry's shoulders relaxed and the seriousness in his expression softened. 'What a lucky little thing she might be, to have all this wisdom at her fingertips.' He inhaled deeply. 'My only dread is that she might feel pain or sorrow from the life she's been placed into. The one she wasn't supposed to have.'

Emma put a hand on the pram, feeling braver as the baby moved her mouth in her sleep and uttered a meowing sound, as though she were dreaming. 'Have you noticed what a heavenly smile she has? She's going to be brave.'

'Really? You can tell?'

Emma nodded. 'I admire her already.'

He didn't speak for a moment but going by his expression, myriad thoughts were flying through his mind. 'You weren't given any support at all, were you?' he asked. 'As a young girl, I mean. You weren't given an opportunity.'

'I don't lay blame at anyone's doorstep.'

'I only pray I can do my best for everyone now at my door.'

He had both hands on the wooden handle of the pram and Emma put her hand over one of his. 'I know you will.'

He jolted and looked into her eyes, removing his hands from the pram and from Emma's touch. 'The thing is, I'm older than you, I realise that, and I'm a bit stuffy.'

'I don't find you stuffy.'

'It's not something I'm proud of,' he continued as though he hadn't heard her. 'But I'm aware others think of me that way. It's been my upbringing, you see. Incarcerated in libraries with my father as a boy, and in offices and business meetings as an adult.'

Emma had to halt another smile. 'You're a good man.'

'I do my best, but it never feels enough. I need someone's guidance. I once had Cynthia's but now she's gone and I'm the one left to guide her child and also care for Allen.'

'You'll cope, Harry.'

'Will I?' He ran a hand over his head. 'I wake up at night thinking about the baby and question what I can do for her to make her feel secure.' He straightened and placed his hands behind his back. 'It was hell spending the war at home when I wanted to be part of it. I didn't know what to do at first then, either.'

'It wasn't your fault.'

'But it didn't make me feel any less useless.'

'What did you do with your time at the bank?'

'Whatever I could to help people. Money was tight all round. I didn't want people to lose their homes, although some did. I persuaded my manager to overlook a number of things just so people could eat.'

'That was caring of you. I seem to remember it was your family who encouraged the growth of the town when you first moved here.'

'My parents were set in their ways, but never unforgiving. They loved each other very much and they wanted to give back. Not that I'm wanting any recognition for that. I simply mean they created a few decent roads in town and took the time to say hello to people.'

'You need to be proud of yourself and everything you and your family have done. You need to feel confident about what's ahead of you now.'

He gave her a sheepish smile and her cheeks warmed. 'What *is* in front of me? Not Roslyn, I know what I have to do for her.'

Emma glanced at the baby, her heart sore but swelling. 'Maybe I could hold her now.'

Harry stepped back. 'Please. Please do.'

Emma picked her up, heart pounding, but the baby was so tiny it was natural to hold her comfortingly against her chest. Not wanting Harry to see any emotion on her face, she walked to the window and looked out at the ocean, a hand on the back of the baby's head, not looking fully at her until the yearning to do so became overpowering.

Her skin was so pale and fine, like Cynthia's. 'What colour are her eyes?'

'Blue.'

'That might change. I've heard women say all babies are born with blue eyes.'

'Maybe they'll turn a dark chestnut like yours.'

Emma glanced at him. He was possibly the most caring man she had ever met or would ever meet. Roslyn was going to have a perfect life with Harry Colson.

Emma turned from the window and walked back to the pram.

Harry followed.

Emma lay the baby down and ran a gentle finger over her cheek.

'Do you like her?' Harry asked in a tone that suggested he was fearful of her answer. 'I almost wish she were awake so you could get to know her better.'

Did she like little Roslyn? No, she adored her. How could anyone not? The feel of her tiny body in her arms, the softness of her cheek against Emma's fingertip. The comforting baby smell she'd experienced with Grace. 'I like her very much.'

'You don't feel scared of taking on me and a child? I would understand…'

'Are you sure about this proposal?' Emma asked when he didn't continue, concern welling that he genuinely did need a handmaid to help him with his dreary furnishings and his new baby.

'I am very sure.'

It felt impossible, as though she were in a dream. 'Even with everything I've—'

'I am sure, Emma. Never more so in my life.'

'But I can't have children for you.'

'It's you I want.' There was a candid gentility in his expression, that of a real suitor. 'I've known few women, Emma,' he said softly, 'and some I was intensely drawn to. But never like this. I love you.'

Such a bold statement. Words she hadn't expected to hear in her lifetime. Emma could hardly draw breath yet beneath the bewilderment, her heart was beating in a way it had never beat before. It resounded in her ears.

He was a little older, yet the divide didn't feel cavernous and was already closing. But he needed to be told the truth. The absolute truth.

'I want to tell you about Grace. My daughter.'

'A lovely name.' He spoke calmingly and said no more.

'My best friend, Cassie, married an American medical officer and she came to the home for unwed girls where I'd been sent and she and her husband adopted my child. Without them doing that, I would never have known where Grace was. I have the chance to go to America to see her, but I'm scared.'

'I imagine you are. She's how old now?'

'Two and a half. The problem is she's been taken into the family and is loved by each of them. She's part of them.'

'So now you're uncertain. Do you visit or do you forget?'

Emma tried to subdue the emotion rushing through her. She would never forget. But to see Grace, to hold her in a hug. She desperately wanted it yet, frighteningly, didn't. 'She will be told the truth when she's old enough to understand but not too late that she might see it as a crime against her.'

'A crime? My dearest Emma—'

'Hear me out. Please. You need to hear all of it.'

He nodded, although he looked disconcerted now. Perhaps worrying about what the woman in front of him was going to say.

Emma clasped her hands in front of her. 'What I did by giving up my baby, what all we girls did—and plenty more women have done—wasn't necessarily our wish. Most of us would have kept our babies but we weren't allowed to. Giving them up would be seen by many people to be a shocking lack of care on our part.'

'Surely not everyone would think that?'

'They told us we were wanton. That we were despicable and that if we didn't give up our babies, we would become prostitutes and would no doubt soon be back with another illegitimate child on the way. They told us we would become sex starved—'

Harry held up his hand. 'I cannot hold my peace. Neither can I believe what you were put through.'

'That's because we were hidden away while others waited patiently for our babies to be born so they could be taken from us. We didn't matter, only the adoptive parents and the child.'

Harry inhaled, his eyes crinkled with concern. 'How can I help make it better?'

It was Emma's turn to pause and study the quiet, intelligent man in front of her. 'I have friends I met at the home. I'd like to find them.'

'Then we shall do so.'

'It won't be easy. We were given other names and mostly knew nothing about each other.'

'We'll discover a way.'

'You'd do this to help me?'

'I'd do anything for you.'

'And Roslyn? What will you tell her about her situation?'

'The truth. Right from the start. Her father is alive and we won't hide him from her, nor will we smother the memories I have of her mother. She will know Cynthia from my point of view, if not from her own.'

'You'd be like a real parent to her?'

'Of course! I wouldn't want it any other way.'

'What would she call you?'

Harry puffed out a laugh. 'I have no idea. I'm her uncle, but since I would be bringing her up, it doesn't sound enough.'

Emma understood. One of her choices was to be known as Grace's aunt, her mother's friend, until she was told the truth. Or until Emma went to fetch her.

She glanced at the baby in her pram. 'Roslyn had a mother and she still has a father, so perhaps Cynthia and Robert should remain Mother and Father. Perhaps you could take on a diminutive.'

Harry's smile grew warm. 'Which would be?'

'Dad.'

'Simple yet recognised universally. Dad.' He nodded. 'And what about Mum? Will she fit into the picture?'

Emma blushed, the heat flushing her cheeks as a shiver rode her skin. A pleasurable tremble, although unnerving in all its aspects.

'You haven't been able to answer me yet,' Harry said. 'My proposal. Would you like some time? Perhaps within a week you might visit little Roslyn and me again and give us your answer.'

'I can tell you now if you'd like me to.'

He stilled, clearly thrown. 'I'm fearful, but yes. I don't think I'd fare well over the next week. I would probably deduce the outcome and fall into despair by Wednesday.'

Emma attempted to again halt a smile. He truly had no idea how amusing he was.

'Do I make you smile? I think perhaps this is a good sign.'

'I do want smiles. I want lots of smiles.'

'I'm happy to oblige.' He took hold of her fingertips. 'Tell me what else I may give you. What I might do for you to persuade you to accept me and to make you welcome.'

'I think perhaps most of all I'd like to be valued.' She didn't pause before saying it—she didn't need to think about it or how he might react. It was her truth. 'But also loved.'

'Fine things to wish for. I would like love in my life too. Perhaps more than I ever thought possible. And if it helps in my plight, I am crazily in love with you already. Even more so now you have been at my side, in my home. You brighten this space, Emma. You brighten *me*. So feel free to give me your answer. I shall wear bad news if need be and I promise to never condemn you.'

Emma met his gaze, never having been surer about anything in her life except for the time she agreed to give Grace to Cassie. 'Yes, Harry. I will marry you.'

It was as though the awareness that shot through Harry reached Emma too. The spark, the tingling, the acknowledgement of intense communication between two people who had made the decision to join forces and manage the storms together.

Harry's grip on her fingers tightened. 'Thank you.'

Emma smiled tremulously while her heart thumped. 'It's all a bit new, Harry.'

'I know. And beyond my belief. May I kiss you now? Although we can wait. I can wait.'

Emma's smile faltered, not because she was embarrassed at having admitted her innermost thoughts to this man but because he'd taken them in his stride and it was unbelievable that she'd found a man who loved her and who was making her feel passionate the way a man and a woman should feel if they were considering marriage.

'Let's not wait,' she said, knowing she was blushing brightly while her heart beat madly. 'I would love you to kiss me.'

Chapter Thirty-five

Harry thought it admirable that Emma didn't want to give up her job simply because she'd accepted his proposal on Saturday and was in complete agreement with her on the matter. So here she was, Monday morning, back in the shop, working out her notice as originally planned until the Osbornes found a replacement.

Her parents had been told about the engagement on Saturday afternoon, Emma not sure whether to cringe or cry as she led Harry through the front door on Herring Street, but Harry had taken it all in his stride and, after the news had been told, had even taken her father to one side to ask his permission—not necessary, but so thoughtful.

That had left Emma alone with her mother who was in so much shock she'd been trembling and Emma had to make her sit down while she made her a cup of strong tea with three sugars.

Strangely enough, Emma had been more anxious about telling the Osbornes.

Mrs Osborne's eyes had been so rounded and her face so pale when Harry escorted her to the Osbornes' house early Sunday morning that Emma thought the woman might keel over. But Mr Osborne stepped forwards, patting his wife's arm before holding out his hand to Harry and saying, 'About time you settled down. I hope you'll look after her as she's looked after us.'

'I will,' Harry had promised.

With a sigh that was part contentment due entirely to Harry and part concern about the lack of customers—there hadn't been a single one since the shop opened and it was already gone nine o'clock—Emma continued dusting the shelves. Mr and Mrs Osborne were in the city. Mr Osborne had a doctor's appointment, which Mrs Osborne had said they couldn't get out of, but she was worried about leaving Emma alone to cope with …

With what was being said. Mrs Osborne hadn't needed to finish her sentence. Emma's engagement was being discussed, dissected, bandied around the quiet streets, behind closed doors or over backyard fences. She just didn't know what it was they were saying.

When at last the bell above the door tinkled, Emma held her breath.

'You sly old dog!'

Emma winced but turned to Janet. 'You heard then?'

'It comes up in conversation hourly since the news hit us on Sunday morning around eleven,' Janet said, moving to the counter. 'Just in time to disturb everyone's roast lunches and give the entire town indigestion. How long has it been going on?' she demanded.

'It hasn't,' Emma said staunchly. 'Until now.'

Janet peered at her for an age, then produced a grin. 'No need to panic. I believe you.'

Relief made Emma's shoulders relax. 'I wasn't sure what was going to happen. Nobody has been into the shop all morning.'

'They're still in shock and I can't blame them. Honestly, Hatton, you take the biscuit. I'm in awe of you. Harry bloody Colson!'

Emma smiled. 'I happen to be in love with him. Honestly, Janet. I love him.'

Janet paused, her expressing blooming from a grin to a glow. 'Well, bloody good luck to you. I can't think of a better nor more deserving person to gain some standing in the world and in life. I don't know what you've lived through but you got through it. I'm actually pretty proud to know you.'

Warmth surrounded Emma's heart. 'Thank you,' she said and quickly brushed a tear from her cheek.

* * *

It soon became obvious Katy Wheaton, Betty Soames and a few others had different opinions regarding Emma's news. But Emma simply nodded politely and walked on by, or filled their grocery orders while chatting about the weather or the continued rationing, not giving them an opportunity to make an untoward remark. Irene McDonald was speechless every time she saw Emma and appeared unable to say, 'I'd like my usual groceries, please,' so Emma had taken to packing Irene's shopping before she even came into the shop.

Most unexpectedly, Irene's other daughter, Lyla, who had driven an ice van during the war, had been hired by Harry as nurse for Roslyn. Only temporarily, because Emma was adamant she would do all the nursing and mothering once they were married, but Lyla had worked as a child's nurse in the city and was currently managing Roslyn, Harry *and* Ivy extremely well.

Dad was looking—dare Emma think it—happy. Or at least, she saw a sparkle in his eyes again, the one she remembered as a girl when he'd been so keen to have his kids walk in the bush with him, teaching them how to recognise the weeds growing between the trees and the plants.

As for life as Harry's intended, his kisses were divine, his arms strong but tender. When they first made love, alone in his bedroom while Lyla took Roslyn for a walk in her pram and Ivy was in Townsville buying a new frock for the wedding so she didn't let Mr Colson down, Emma hesitated, remembering the time in the air-raid shed.

Harry noticed. 'We can stop,' he said but she hadn't wanted to.

'It was a fleeting memory,' she told him. 'Nothing more.'

'Can we dissolve it? Can we make another memory to shadow it?'

'Yes, please, Harry.'

She was cherished and loved and best of all, she was useful. There was something to live for every day, every waking hour. Nothing her mother or aunt said would dissolve the newfound wonder building tentatively inside her. Nothing.

'I was thinking about the rest of the topiaries,' Harry said as they stood side by side at the bottom of the kitchen steps, Harry with his hands in his trouser pockets as he stared at his garden and Emma holding a basket of groceries they'd collected together and brought up for Ivy. The garden was just one aspect of the plans she and Harry would have to make, and her future husband was already casting his net of tactics and strategies wide. He'd had the telephone installed in the Hatton house so they could communicate with each other whenever they needed to in the frantic runup to their wedding day. The ceremony was going to be sooner than Janet's because Harry insisted on it being a matter of urgency. He was also teaching Emma to drive.

What they were going to do about Ivy Williams, Emma didn't yet know. How was Emma to make the housekeeper understand that she wanted to make the woman's life easier by helping run the house, and how to convince her of their ongoing appreciation for her?

'What about them?' Emma asked, shading her eyes with a hand as the sun poured over the ocean and up to the house.

'I know you loathe them.'

'Not really ... I mean they're ...'

'Artistic but lonely.' He turned, took the basket out of her hand, placed it on the ground and scooped her up in his arms. 'They're for boring old men. That's what you really mean. Let's get rid of them all.'

Emma laughed. 'You'd do that for me?'

'For you and Roslyn. The gravel can go too. She'll need a proper garden with grass and swings.'

'Can we have lots of flowers?'

'Absolutely. Whatever you want.'

'A meandering pathway to the beach instead of the straight one?'

'The path?' he asked, squinting at it. 'Are we sure it should meander?'

Still in his arms, Emma laughed. She would never make him plant a multitude of flowers if he didn't want them, nor dig up his pathway.

'Let's keep a few of the topiaries,' she said, settling her arms more firmly around his neck. 'We can keep them in stone planters by the back steps as an entrance to the garden, and two at the front door.'

'No, no. We don't have to.'

'I would like to. It would be a token of respect to your parents.'

He smiled. 'That is a nice idea. I would like it.'

'Then that's what we shall do.' Emma brushed back the hair from his forehead as he looked into her soul with his smile. 'You know something, Mr Colson? I fall for you more every day.'

'I love you more each second, Miss Hatton, so catch up sometime soon, would you?'

'I'll give it my all.' It would hardly be a chore.

Widening his smile, Harry settled her back on her feet and kissed her like he thought she might suddenly vanish.

Chapter Thirty-six

August 1947

On the eve of her wedding, Emma received an airletter from America. Cassie had given birth to two healthy boys and mother and sons were thriving.

> *They have not diminished our love of Grace, Em, I insist you know this. She is the most darling little thing and fills our hearts with joy with her sunny view on life even at her young age. People not only adore her, they respect her like only one other I know. Her mother.*
> *She is you, Em.*
> *She is you, my friend.*
> *I know she doesn't look exactly like you, which I've been afraid to mention before now, but your open heart and your intelligence reside within her and that is what I see.*
> *Thank you for sharing her with me and for trusting me with the life of something so precious to you. I hope I'm doing right by you. I love her as my own because she's yours. I sometimes think I love her twice as hard as my boys simply because your blood runs through her.*
> *Have you made a decision about her, Em? Are you coming to visit?*

I know you would have been thinking about it. I know you would have somehow understood my pathetic attempts to ask you.

But I must give you time to respond. I understand how difficult it must be.

You must get it right. You must do what you feel you have to. I will always love you, no matter what.

Emma folded the letter, the same sensation of gratitude and grief overwhelming her the way it always had when she received news from America, but far more poignantly this time, given Cassie's plea.

There was also a photograph enclosed. One of Grace, an innocent smugness in her sweet and crooked smile, her hands intertwined on her lap, her shoulders hunched in pride as she sat between her baby brothers as though unbelieving of what she'd been presented with.

How beautiful she was.

What sentiments and words Emma would use when she replied to Cassie's letter, she didn't yet know. She would need to first recuperate from the ongoing tornado of happenings, but she would send the gifts she'd purchased for Cassie's boys along with the silver bracelet she'd bought for Grace. She'd asked the jeweller to attach tiny porcelain daisies. Her first gift to her child. Given with undying love. It wouldn't be the last.

For the twins she'd bought cuddly koalas and silver egg spoons because she didn't want to favour Grace above the little ones she already thought of as her nephews.

Emma put the letter and photograph between the pages of the atlas which she then carried to her suitcase that held all her frugal belongings. It would be taken up to the big house tomorrow morning, before she married Harry.

* * *

'I always said she'd bring you luck,' Doris said, sipping her tea, pinky raised.

'You did no such thing,' Mum replied, slamming the teapot onto the table.

'This is better than two ten-pound notes,' Doris argued. 'You've got the telephone, there's a brand-new refrigerator on its way via Mr Jameson's delivery van and Doug's found a job at Mrs Cosgrove's tending the cattle and the chickens. He's good at that sort of thing, always has been.'

It hadn't been anything Harry had done to secure Emma's father a job. It had been Dad who had gone to see Mrs Cosgrove early the next morning, after he'd been told of his daughter's engagement. He'd then sought Emma out and told her he was doing it for her, so as not to be a fool of a man, like he had been all this time. He hadn't said more and Emma hadn't prolonged his embarrassment except to say thank you and that she understood.

'It's a casual job, Doris. We don't know how long it will last, since old Cosgrove can't be expected to live much longer and her chickens and cows will go to her girls.'

'They won't want them. They'll be looking at getting married.'

'And their husbands will tend the livestock. It'll be a living. The men won't give away money handed to them on a plate and neither will they want to pay someone to do work they can do themselves.'

Doris huffed, settling her cup on its saucer with a clink. 'At least you're getting a refrigerator at long last.'

'But where I'm going to put the washing machine I don't know.'

'It's more than you ever contemplated, Miriam, don't try to tell me otherwise.'

'I've not taken anything from him,' Mum said sternly, referring to Harry in the only way she did these days: 'him', never Mr Colson or Harry, although he'd asked her to call him that. 'And neither *will* I take anything from him. It was our Emma who purchased the refrigerator and the washing machine with her savings.'

'But he put in the telephone.'

'I only accepted because of his insistence.'

'Well, of course, Miriam. I wouldn't have thought otherwise.'

Emma was content to let them bicker as she cut slices of a chocolate Kentish cake for their supper. Doris had once again taken to visiting regularly, three times a week since Harry proposed. While the women chatted about the arrangements for the wedding at a Presbyterian church in Townsville tomorrow at three o'clock—thank goodness the day had almost arrived because living at home with the Hattons' sudden rise in status was somewhat trying—Emma took out the sewing basket and resumed her task of attaching a gold clasp to the short veil she'd already embroidered with delicate white flower heads. She'd purchased the clip on a trip into Townsville with Harry so they could buy their wedding bands. He'd given her his mother's engagement ring, the most valuable of possessions, stunningly expensive yet relatively simple in its design and she'd been pleased to accept it. One day Roslyn would have it. It would be her family heirloom.

Much as Ivy hadn't wanted to let Harry down at his wedding by wearing a drab old frock, neither had Emma. She agreed to have one made after Harry suggested it, knowing she'd have little time to sew a wedding dress with everything else going on. Deep inside, she was pleased she would look her best for him, and for herself. Her savings were almost gone but she didn't care. She didn't need anything more that money could buy.

Harry had also given her a silver sixpence to put in her shoe.

A sixpence! How big a part had a simple sixpence played in her life? It was apt she'd marry him with one in her possession.

She would keep it, perhaps tucked beneath their mattress like a good luck charm.

She had something else silver, a locket given to her by Harry as an engagement present, which Emma intended Grace to have one day as part of her Hatton inheritance. She also had something borrowed—an unused handkerchief from Janet, who else? She didn't have anything blue yet but perhaps Harry wouldn't notice. Emma was arranging her own bouquet of wildflowers and greenery she'd picked along the wayside, much to her mother's consternation. But Emma insisted it was what she wanted.

'Betty Soames,' Mum said, interrupting Emma's thoughts. 'She's taken Emma's job at the Osbornes'.'

'Does she need the money?' Doris asked.

'We all need the money out here. Unlike some I could mention,' Mum answered, nodding at the new hat and leather boxed handbag next to Doris's tea plate.

'Oh, that's right. Criticise me for getting somewhere in life.'

'It's your husband who got somewhere, not you.'

'That's an outrageous thing to suggest! I've helped him in every way I can. He doesn't make friends easily, Miriam, and I do. Friends who count, I might add.'

Emma kept her focus on the net in her hands, wondering if she should step up and put an end to an argument in the making.

'Anyway,' Doris said, shifting on her chair so hard the legs scraped on the floor. 'If it wasn't for me, Doug wouldn't be wearing a smart three-piece suit for the wedding tomorrow, would he?'

'I accepted the loan of your husband's suit because I'm trying to save money in any way I can. I've had to dress the boys, too.'

'Didn't stop you going out and buying a new frock though, did it? I wasn't going to have my brother dressed in his army uniform while you shone at his side in your fancy dress.'

'I made that frock myself. From fabric purchased with money I earned myself.'

'Money you wouldn't have earned if I hadn't stepped in and found you the ladies who wanted their clothing altered.'

Emma was about to stand when Mum spoke again.

'I've done as much for my husband as you've done for yours. Perhaps more so, since Doug always had so little, so I'll thank you to stop belittling me. Don't think you can come out here after the wedding, expecting me to take a break from my workload and bake you a cake, because it won't be happening. You can bring your own cake if you want one and you can make your own damned tea, too.'

Mum rose from the table and pulled at the hem of her cardigan. 'Now excuse me while I get ready for bed. I've got a lot to do tomorrow.'

'Mum,' Emma said pleadingly, hoping to get her mother and aunt onside again before Doris left.

'As for you,' Mum said as she turned and eyed her daughter. 'At least there's no need for me to have that little chat with you. The one mothers of clean daughters need to have regarding their wedding night. You already know what's what.'

Emma took a steadying breath. 'That was mean and undeserving.'

If her mother heard, she didn't respond, she simply walked out of the kitchen and towards her bedroom. Emma sighed. Her mother had been given every opportunity to fit in with the arrangements. She'd even been good with Ivy, settling the woman down as she fussed about the banquet, which was to be catered so Ivy could attend the wedding without having to work.

'She's upset,' Doris said, picking up her hat. 'It's a reminder. She was having you before she got wed. Doug did the right thing at the time.'

The veil in Emma's hand slid out of her fingers. She bent to retrieve it from the floor before it got marked. 'What are you saying?'

'Not sure he would have proposed at all, if you want my opinion,' Doris said, giving Emma a know-all look. 'But she got herself in the family way, didn't she?'

All the consideration and attempts of appeasement Emma had been utilising for everyone in her family over the last weeks disappeared in a flash of anger. 'Surely your brother had a hand in the matter.'

Doris shrugged. 'Some women have a way with men, that's all I'm saying.'

Emma rose and carefully placed the veil on the seat of the chair. 'I trust you will not mention this to anyone and that you will never refer to it again. Certainly not to my mother and *never* to my father.'

'I won't be saying anything. Miriam goes on about her reputation but I have mine.'

'So why tell me?'

'I thought you needed to know.'

'Did you think the same when I got into trouble? It didn't appear that you gave tuppence for my feelings. You're a selfish woman, Doris, and I may not be able to forgive you for what you just told me for some time.'

Her aunt stared, open-mouthed, clearly shocked her niece would speak to her in such a manner.

'You can let yourself out,' Emma said. 'We'll see you at three o'clock tomorrow.' She collected her veil and the clasp and walked out of the room.

In her bedroom, she put the veil on the chest of drawers then attempted to still herself and the tumbling thoughts. Her wedding dress hung on the back of the door and her handmade bouquet was in a vase next to her bed. She was shaking so much she had to lift her hands and stare at them, willing them to stop quivering.

Whatever her parents' relationship had been like when it first began or what their marriage had entailed or how they'd felt about each other, she might never know. Drudgery over the years had undoubtedly changed both of them. Yet it was her father's position, being the man, that dictated the ensuing hardship and overall existence of his wife.

For perhaps the first time in many years, Emma's heart went out to her mother.

* * *

'Dad?'

Emma stepped tentatively into the front room where her father sat, yesterday's *Bulletin* open on his lap, his head fallen forwards on his chest.

He woke when she said his name again and, bleary eyed, shuffled to sit up straight.

Emma went to him and knelt at his side, her hands on the armrest.

'I've got the suit,' he said. 'I'll happily wear it. I think your mother's going to look pretty smart too. Made herself a dress. Always did have a way with her needle.'

'Yes, she did.'

'Is there something else you need?' he asked. 'Because I'm not sure I can give it to you.'

Emma smiled. Whatever their faults, she would forgive her parents. 'I don't need anything from you, Dad. I just want to know if I have your blessing.' It would be the greatest gift, the best he could give her.

He looked her in the eye for a long time before answering. 'Did you ever think there would be a day when you wouldn't? I'm proud of you, love.'

Emma's eyes brimmed with tears. 'Thank you. For all you've taught me.'

'I don't know about that, but I wish you happiness.'

'I think I've found it.'

He nodded. 'Good luck to you both.'

Emma stood and kissed the top of his head. 'No pub tonight.'

'No, no,' he said quickly. 'Not tonight. Best stay alert. Don't want to embarrass you.'

'You won't, Dad. You never have.'

'Goodnight, love. Pleasant dreams.'

'Goodnight, Dad.'

Closing the door to the front room behind her, Emma went down the hallway and knocked on her parents' bedroom door.

A few moments later it opened, her mother staring at her.

'Do I have your blessing?'

'Do you need it?'

'I'd like it.'

Her mother didn't respond and Emma persisted. 'Can we not see eye to eye? Just a little.'

Mum sniffed, holding herself taut and not meeting Emma's gaze. 'I have something for you.' She turned and went to her dresser, producing a folded piece of silky cream fabric. She shook it out, revealing a petticoat slip with sapphire-coloured lace on the darted brassiere top and the hem of the flared skirt. 'I understand you don't have anything blue.'

Emma took hold of the delicate straps and stared at the design, cut on the bias so it hung beautifully. 'You made this for me?' she asked incredulously.

'We might not follow all British traditions out here but when a Colson gets married to one of us, we need to step up.'

Emma looked at her mother, bemused.

'You have my blessing,' Mum said. 'I can't say otherwise or I wouldn't be seen as a good mother.'

Well. A typical response from her mother but it was a start. Perhaps a mending of ways wasn't too distant.

'Now you'd best get some beauty sleep,' Mum murmured. 'Tomorrow will be a long day.'

'Goodnight, Mum, and thank you for everything you've done for Harry and me.' Emma held the slip against her and gauged her mother a moment longer before turning and leaving the room.

Tomorrow would indeed be a long day. So many people would be there, the church packed. There was even a reporter attending from the *Daily Bulletin* and, sometime next week, everyone in Townsville would be reading about the wedding.

Emma thought it unlikely she'd get a wink of sleep.

Chapter Thirty-seven

TOWNSVILLE DAILY BULLETIN

WEDDING
COLSON – HATTON

St Mark's Presbyterian Church was the picturesque spot chosen for the wedding on 3rd August at 3 pm of Miss Emma Hatton, only daughter of Mr Douglas Hatton and Mrs Miriam Hatton of Blueholm Bay to Mr Harold Colson, also of Blueholm Bay, only son of the late Mr Henry Colson and the late Mrs Maud Colson, both previously of East Horsley, England. Rev Stephens officiating.

The bride made a beguiling picture as she entered the church on the arm of her father. Mrs Dawn Jameson presided at the organ, ably playing the 'Wedding March', her daughter Miss Janet Jameson one of the bridesmaids alongside Miss Clare Forsyth, both dressed in lovely frocks of flecked cotton voile with full skirts and delicate floral arrangements in their hair.

The bride wore the palest cream embossed satin, cut on classical lines. The skirt flowed from the hipline into a short but beautiful train. Tiny buttons secured the pointed cuffs over the hands and the back of the bodice and the very latest in long sleeves set off the simplicity of the gown. A dainty veil of embroidered net was caught in a coronet of clustered white silk daisies attached to a delightful heart-shaped golden clasp. The bride carried a bouquet of wildflowers and sprigs of greenery, made most capably by the bride herself, bound with long cream ribbons, their tails curling to her feet.

The groom was attended by the brother of Miss Clare Forsyth, Mr Dominic Forsyth, as best man. Mr Peter Jameson, fiancé of bridesmaid Janet Jameson, served as groomsman along with two younger brothers of the bride, Master William Hatton and Master Daniel Hatton.

The reception was held in the Colson gardens in Blueholm Bay and was a charmingly enjoyable occasion for all. Mr Dominic Forsyth aptly presided as master of ceremonies while the bride's mother, dressed in teal green relieved with white accessories, received the guests alongside her husband and Mr Duncan Forsyth, owner of Forsyth's Bank.

The happy couple will reside in Blueholm Bay.

Chapter Thirty-eight

September 1947

If she'd thought herself ready to be second best, living a quiet, simple life alone—and content to do so—Emma had been very wrong. Her wedding day was the moment she truly appreciated herself and everyone around her. The day a love bond had been sealed of the type she hadn't anticipated. That of husband and wife. Of mother and daughter, because she'd insisted Roslyn be present.

Lyla held the baby, smiling smugly at Irene, who insisted on sitting next to her nursemaid daughter in the row behind the groom's friends and business colleagues. At the reception, the baby had been passed around and cooed over by just about everyone and Emma was relieved when she started to get cranky so she could take over, cuddling her until she fell asleep.

Now here Emma was, living in the big house and waking every morning to the sound of the ocean lapping on Colson Beach, as she still privately referred to it.

When the telephone rang she put her napkin onto her empty breakfast plate and walked into the hall to answer it. But Ivy had got there first.

'Is that for Harry? He went to fetch his briefcase from the study.'

'It's for you, *Mrs Colson*,' Ivy said, putting the telephone receiver onto the hall table.

Ignoring the belligerence in Ivy's voice, which she had come to know well, Emma gave her an encouraging smile. 'Thank you.'

It was possibly one of Harry's colleagues' wives, although it was early at just gone seven thirty. Emma was having to learn how to behave with a diverse range of people. It was a little tiring, attempting to fit in, but she persisted for Harry's and Roslyn's sakes.

'Emma Colson. Can I help you?' she said when she picked up the receiver.

'It's me. Janet. Sorry, but I haven't got time to visit in person.'

'Janet! What a relief! I thought it might be yet another invite to dinner with yet more people who don't really want to know me. Some are just being nosey. You know, is she a poor wretch who got lucky or—'

'Emma, listen. Your mother just got a telephone call at my mum's house.'

'But she has her own telephone.'

'My mum gave your mum this person's telephone number but your mother is refusing to return the calls. This person rang twice this week and she just telephoned again.' Janet took a breath. 'I didn't bother going for your mum this time because it's *you* this person wants to speak with, not your mother.'

'Me?'

'Someone called Susannah Poulson-Taylor.'

Emma stilled as her skin prickled in a rush of shock. Susannah?

* * *

'You mean one of your friends from the—'

'Yes,' Emma said, interrupting Harry. 'Susannah. It's unbelievable.'

'Darling, what wonderful news. I'm sorry we haven't yet got around to searching for your friends.'

'We have been a little occupied.'

'And now I've got to dash,' Harry said, hugging her quickly. 'Got a meeting with Dominic and his old man.'

'Of course.' Emma straightened his waistcoat and adjusted the chain of his fob watch so it sat neatly.

'Where's Roslyn?' Harry asked. 'Still upstairs?'

'Asleep.' The baby had spent an uncomfortable night, which meant so had Emma and Harry, Lyla having been dismissed with a decent monetary thank you and an excellent reference. 'Harry, I'm going to give Ivy the day off. I don't want her listening in to my conversation with Susannah. It would be awkward.'

'Want me to do it?'

Emma pulled a face. 'I have to manage this myself.'

'She'll come around eventually. She's in shock, that's all. She'll be good in a few months.'

Emma thought it might be more like years. Ivy loathed it when Emma entered her kitchen to help. She didn't want Emma's assistance setting the table, nor boiling the eggs nor making toast. She didn't see the need for *Mrs Colson* to strip the bed and hang out sheets.

Yet Emma persisted. The woman worked way too hard and although Harry said they'd employ a young girl to come up to the house a few days a week, Emma resisted. She wanted to manage her home and do the necessary work herself. What else was she to do except tend Roslyn and paint her nails while the baby slept?

'Got to go,' Harry said, plucking his keys from beside his empty coffee cup and kissing Emma on the lips.

'Have a good day,' Emma told him.

'You too,' he said with a wink. 'I hope it's an excellent day.'

'I have a feeling it will be,' she responded, a twinkle still in her eye.

'Oh, sorry, sir, I was just wanting to remove your breakfast plates.'

Emma turned to Ivy. 'Thank you, Ivy.'

'Have a lovely day, Mrs Williams,' Harry said as he sailed past her towards the door. 'May the wind be at your back.'

'At my what, sir?'

'He was being silly,' Emma explained after Harry left the room.

'Mr Colson has never been silly in his life! Not even as a boy.'

'No, I just meant—oh, never mind.'

'Should I collect the breakfast dishes now?'

'Yes, please, Ivy. How wonderful of you to recognise our needs without us even asking.'

'I've been recognising needs around here for twenty-five years.' The housekeeper took a tray off the sideboard and began piling the crockery and cutlery with more force than was necessary.

'Yes, of course you have, I just—' Emma expelled her breath. What *was* she going to do about Ivy?

After Roslyn had been fed, changed and settled in her pram in the living room, drowsy and full, Emma headed for the kitchen. Once in the hallway she pulled her shoulders back, reminding herself she was a capable woman and could deal with just about anything thrown at her. Including Ivy bloody Williams.

'Mrs Williams,' she said with a smile as she entered the housekeeper's domain. 'Why don't you take the day off?'

'The day what?' Ivy said.

'The day *off*,' Emma repeated, casting a glance around the pristine kitchen.

'Does Mr Colson know you're giving me the day off?' Ivy asked, wiping her wet hands on a towel slung over the sink. 'I don't know if he'd want me to take a day off.'

'He thinks you're working too hard and so do I. It can't be easy catering to us, but woman to woman, Mrs Williams, I have to admit we can't cope without you.'

Ivy appeared flabbergasted at the sudden and clearly unexpected praise. 'Well, I ... I ...'

'Exactly! That's what I thought too. You're being overworked and it's not fair, so from now on you shall have not two days off a week but three. Starting with today.'

Ivy pulled on her earlobe. 'I wouldn't mind a few extra hours but I'd have to know it was all right with Mr Colson.'

'It's perfectly fine. I asked him.'

'And he gave you his permission?'

Harry's permission? It was easier to agree, so Emma nodded. 'Where's your jacket and hat?'

'Behind the laundry door but I'm not sure I want a day off. I haven't finished the washing up yet.'

'I can do that.' Emma located the jacket and hat. She put the hat on the kitchen table and shook out the mauve box jacket so Ivy could slip her arms through.

But Ivy didn't.

'Didn't you strike up a good acquaintance with the Forsyth cook?' Emma asked. 'Perhaps you could visit her.'

'I did enjoy my acquaintance with her at the wedding,' Ivy said. 'Quite an important family yet she didn't have too many airs and graces.'

Clare's family. Emma had met the young woman with some trepidation before the wedding when Harry advised she might make a good second bridesmaid, but Clare had been delightful. Young and brimming with joy, eyeing all the unmarried men in the room and definitely not Harry's type. Clare would want parties galore when she eventually found a man to fall in love with.

'Why don't you nip into Townsville to see her? Spend a few hours catching up on gossip and new recipes. Have you got enough money?'

Ivy blanched. 'I beg your pardon? I always have enough money. I save some of my monthly wage. I'm quite used to making do, thank you very much, *Mrs Colson*.'

'Monthly?' Emma said with a frown. 'That's no good. You need to be paid weekly.'

'I make do with what I've got.'

But it wasn't good enough. The woman needed money each week so she didn't have to worry. 'I shall ask for Harry's permission to pay you weekly.'

Ivy thinned her mouth as she thought about it. 'It would help, I suppose, if you believe he's likely to agree.'

'I know he will. So Townsville it is,' Emma said and shook Ivy's jacket. 'What a lovely jacket. Very smart,' she said when Ivy slipped her arms through. 'Where's your handbag?'

'Left-hand drawer of the sideboard. Do you mean you want me out all day?'

'Of course. It's your day off and that means the entire day as well as the evening, if you like.'

'Who's going to slice the ham for dinner?'

'Me,' Emma said with another smile, which was slightly more difficult to produce than the first. 'I'll do it while Roslyn is still down and I'll also do the salad to go with it. If I can remember how,' Emma added with a genuine grin. But the subtlety of the witticism was lost on Ivy.

'I always add tomatoes,' Ivy said. 'Mr Colson likes them.'

'Yes, I know.'

'And I use lettuce hearts. It looks fancier.'

'I shall do the same.'

'I don't add anything to a salad other than grated carrot and the tomatoes. This is not a cafeteria in the city. We don't produce American, Dutch or anything foreign in a salad and never have. A dollop of mayonnaise goes into the porcelain jug. The small one, mind, and the mayonnaise must be home made.'

'Got it. Don't forget your hat,' Emma said, indicating the straw bonnet with the faded fabric flowers on the kitchen table.

'I might occasionally add some apple rings to the salad,' Ivy said knowledgeably. 'Since it's ham.'

Which sounded like a Venetian salad but it was best not to say so.

Emma went to the sideboard to retrieve the handbag, a worn leather affair which might have once belonged to Harry's mother. Next step—buy Ivy some new clothes and accessories without appearing overbearing or keenly charitable.

'I'm going to telephone Mr Jameson and let him know you're walking into town,' Emma said as Ivy settled her hat on her head. 'He doesn't go into the city before mid-morning. He'll give you a lift there and back in his new van.'

'I haven't said I'm taking the day off yet.'

'But you're already kitted out and ready to go,' Emma said, offering the handbag.

Ivy grabbed it and held it close, possibly appeased about her worth in the household, but undoubtedly still suspicious about being given a day off out of the blue. 'Things would be different around here if his parents were still alive.'

'I know. But they're not here.' And Emma was. She went to open the kitchen back door. 'Have a lovely day, Mrs Williams!'

Ivy stepped outside with a sniff of the air, as though she expected it to be different to any other morning. 'I shall return before dinner time.'

'And we shall look forward to seeing you. Bye!' Emma said cheerily when Ivy stomped off towards the stairs.

Closing the kitchen door and leaning against it, Emma threw her head back in exasperation. This had to get easier.

* * *

Ten minutes later she was alone in the house, Roslyn sleeping peacefully in her pram, which Emma had pulled into the hallway so she could keep an eye on the child. Fingers trembling, she called the exchange and asked to be put through to the number Janet had given her.

'Hello? Is this Susannah?'

'Harper! Is that really you?' Susannah laughed heartily. 'Emma Hatton, I've had the devil's own job tracking you down!'

Emma was momentarily stunned to hear Susannah's voice. She sounded as classy as ever but there was also a newly acquired maturity in her tone. So many questions that needed answers crowded Emma's mind. Where to begin? 'It's wonderful to hear your voice! How are you?'

'Quite independently wealthy, actually. Which is how I found you.'

'What on earth happened?'

'Long story, but in a nutshell my grandmother left me a lot of money and my father didn't tell me. When I found out, I challenged him. Gosh, he didn't like it one bit, but I was fuming! Honestly, my parents practically hid me away when I got home. I spent months doing nothing but embroidery. Then one day when they were out, I had to entertain my father's lawyer's assistant. He'd come over to discuss my inheritance and whether or not we intended to invest. I swear, Emma, that was the minute I changed. It was the moment I grew up.'

Emma understood. She'd had a similar experience at St Philomena's. 'So how did you find me?'

'I hired an inquiry agent. He wasn't much good until he read about your wedding in the Townsville newspaper but he could only get his hands on two telephone numbers. One was that of the bank and I didn't want to telephone your husband, because he'd want to know who I was and how I knew you.'

'He knows everything.'

'Oh, gosh, how wonderful. He sounds a decent sort.'

'He is.'

'The other number was that of your bridesmaid and the woman who played the organ, so that's who I telephoned.' Susannah took a breath. 'And at long last, here we are, chatting like we've never been apart. I might pay the agent's last invoice after all. I threatened not to.'

Emma smiled widely. 'I told you how brave you were! Now look at you fly.'

'It's terribly refreshing!' Susannah said.

Emma settled herself, moving the receiver from one ear to the other. 'So are you partying and meeting lots of young people?'

'I'm not keen on any of that. I'm looking for something positive to do with my life.'

'Good for you.'

'Oh, and I found Mrs Ross the other day.'

'I've been in touch with her too! She helped me so much.' Emma glanced at the pram where Roslyn was still sleeping.

'Do you remember Ben the gardener's boy?' Susannah said. 'He's boarding with her.'

'Ben?' Emma frowned, never having expected to hear about the lad ever again. 'How come? Sister H sent him away.'

'Mrs Ross found him wandering the street. The poor wretch got sacked from his job. She told me he doesn't do very well. He's a simple lad, not unintelligent, but reserved. She said he's scared of practically everything around him. Vehicle horns, delivery trucks, even bicycle bells and horses and carts.'

'Poor Ben.'

'She got him another job but the same thing happened so now he's living with her and assisting around her house and also the homes of her married daughters.'

'What can we do to help?'

'I guess we can try to find him another situation. One he might take to.'

'I've got an idea,' Emma said, perking up. The Osbornes. Will was still aggrieved to be carrying old women's shopping baskets and Dad had told him if he finished his schooling he could work with him at Mrs Cosgrove's. Ben might fit the mould perfectly if Emma could persuade everyone involved, including Ben, to give it a go. The young lad might get his bicycle after all. 'But let me think more about it,' she said before taking a steadying moment to gather herself, hoping what she was about to say wouldn't be too intrusive.

'Darling Susannah, you've done so well tracking people down. You astound me, truly, and I can't help but wonder if you'll also try to find your baby.'

'It's impossible. I haven't the first clue where they took him. I wasn't told the family's name. And what could I do about it, anyway? I can only pray he's well and is loved.'

'How do you know it was a boy? Mrs Ross told me and Wynn you didn't know.'

'I discovered it at the hospital. Some nurse was talking and let it slip.' Susannah paused. 'I named him Michael, Emma. In my heart, he's Michael.'

'Oh, darling.'

'And you? Gosh, I'm sorry to ask. I know it's upsetting.'

'Grace. I named her Grace.'

'Did she go to the family you told us about?'

Emma shifted her weight from one foot to the other. 'I hope you won't resent me, but no, she didn't. My best friend and her husband adopted her. She lives in America. I have photos.'

'Oh, you lucky thing!'

'Yes. I am.'

Neither spoke for a moment.

'What am I saying? Of course you're not lucky. Neither of us are. We've both lost our babies.'

'Perhaps I am more fortunate, though.'

'Did you get to see her before they took her away?'

Emma relived the moment Helen Ross put Grace into her arms. 'Mrs Ross was there. She let me hold her for ten whole minutes. I was able to kiss her and tell her how much I loved her.'

Susannah choked on a sob.

'I'm sorry. I've made you cry.'

'Will there ever be a time when we don't?'

Emma shook her head. 'No. There never will be.'

'Hold on,' Susannah said. 'I have to get a handkerchief.'

Susannah blew her nose, sniffed some more then came back on the telephone. 'I'm looking for Wynn too, but no luck yet. Do you have any idea where we can start?'

We.

Friendship. Emma's heart filled.

'I might have an inkling. She told me her parents and brothers lived not a mile from St Philomena's.'

'Well, that's something to go on.'

'I didn't know where to search for either of you, I haven't been able to get into Townsville much if at all in the last few years—and I've only just got married.'

'I'll put a new man on it. Honestly, the last one was useless unless he was pushed and prodded.'

Emma grinned. 'Susannah, you are so changed.'

Susannah laughed. 'For the better! Now, tell me all about your husband. Who is he? I hope he's truly deserving of you or he'll be answering to me.'

Emma glanced at the pram in the hallway and its precious cargo. 'Darling, there is so much to tell you.'

* * *

A week and a half later, Ben was on the train from Brisbane and Harry was preparing to go and meet him.

'Harry, you'd overwhelm him.'

'I can't imagine how and someone's got to get him to Blueholm Bay.'

Emma put a hand on his arm. 'Believe me, you would. It's best if I fetch him.' Ben hadn't stalled once about moving to Blueholm Bay, he'd accepted Emma's proposal as soon as she explained what his job would be, what the town was like, that he'd be boarding with the Osbornes in a small room off the storeroom they were converting to a bedroom just for him and that Emma would be around to help him with whatever he needed.

'Very well. I'll pop into the Osbornes' to meet him sometime next week instead. Would that suit?'

'Thank you, darling.'

'How are the Osbornes?'

'They're monitoring Walter's heart but it's not anything to worry about at this stage. He's under doctor's orders to laugh more and have some fun.'

'Is that a possibility?'

'Mrs Osborne thinks so. She told me having Ben living with them would give them both a kick in the backside.'

'Does the good lady need one?'

'I think she's delighted to have a young man under her care. It'll put years on her life, I bet.'

Susannah was planning to visit soon too and Emma couldn't wait to see her. To take hold of her hands, to hug her. It was such a blessing to be in touch again after so much had happened in their lives.

There was no trace of Wynn as yet. She was out there, somewhere. Being brave and smart and becoming the someone she deserved to be. *One day, Wynn, we'll find you.*

'What time is Ben's train getting in?' Harry said now.

'Midday.'

'How will you get there?'

'I'll ask Mr Jameson for a lift.'

'Don't do that. Here.' Harry threw her the key to the Ford. 'You drive me to the bank then you can drive into the city again this afternoon to collect Ben. I'll cadge a ride back with Mr Jameson when I finish work. I want to chat to him about his new loan anyway. I've had some thoughts on how he can expand even more.'

Emma stared at her husband, not hearing a word he said about the business proposition while the key to the Ford burned a hole in the palm of her hand. Drive the Ford Super Deluxe? Completely on her own, all the way to the city and back? Twice in the one day?

'Thank you, Harry,' she said, as excitement overrode trepidation. 'I'll do that.'

'Emma,' he said, his tone sombre. 'Don't forget you have one more task, and I think you ought to do it soon so we can make any arrangements we need to.'

'I know. I will do it.'

She couldn't put it off any longer. She had to write to Cassie.

'But first,' Harry said on a more uplifting note, 'you're going to drive into Townsville and pick up a young lad who will at last be getting his own bicycle and a place to call home. I presume he can ride a bicycle.'

Emma's eyes widened. 'I have no idea.' She hadn't thought about it but now she did, how would Ben have learned? Not at St Philomena's and not at his employment as a gardener's boy. 'Oh, gosh,' she said with a worried look at her husband. 'What will we do?'

Harry did his best not to laugh. 'I shall teach him.'

'Can you ride?'

'Of course I can, I just don't. But I will now. Picture the scene: me on a bicycle, my cane strapped to the front basket and everyone in town standing on the street in disbelief. Still. Needs must.'

'Harry,' she said with a grin. 'You have changed my life.'

'I think it's you who has changed mine,' he said, pulling on the hem of his waistcoat.

'Harry?' Emma asked when he made a move to leave. 'Is it all right to be happy?'

He studied her then came closer and took hold of her hands. 'Yes, my darling. We're a family. Don't ever forget that. Come what may, we will charge at life together, Roslyn and Grace coming first in whatever way is necessary, but you and I will always be a family.' He kissed her. 'You *have* made the best decision, Emma. Don't doubt it.'

Chapter Thirty-nine

Townsville

Emma arrived safely at Townsville train station in plenty of time to get Roslyn out of the Ford before Ben's train pulled in.

'I got here then,' he said when they met, Emma wanting to hug him but thinking he might not care for such close contact. Mrs Ross had ensured he looked scrubbed up and bristle clean. Even his work boots had a shine and there was strength in his shoulders and in his shy smile. He blew out a somewhat bewildered breath and glanced around the busy platform. 'Lots of people here, aren't there? It's just like it is in Brisbane.'

'It's quieter in Blueholm Bay. Have you got everything?'

'Everything I own. Mrs Ross gave me this,' he said, proudly holding up a battered holdall so Emma could study it. 'It belonged to her husband when he was a young man. He was a sailor back then. It's been all around the world, this holdall.'

'She must be very proud of you to give you something of her husband's.'

'I did my best to repay her for what she done for me,' he said as he followed Emma towards the exit, sticking close. 'First time on a train, now first time in a motor car,' he said when they got outside, goggle-eyed as he viewed the Ford. 'This is living, Miss Emma.'

Emma nodded, warmth for the lad burgeoning. 'Indeed it is, Ben.'

'She's a cheery little thing, isn't she?' Ben said, wiggling his fingers above Roslyn's head and making her scrunch her face in a smile. 'Never seen so many cheery little kids. Mrs Ross's grandkids, they all smile. Most of the time anyways. Not like at that place.'

Emma cleared her throat before heading into a conversation she had to have. Mrs Osborne didn't know about St Philomena's but had been told that Ben had been in an orphanage all his life and that Emma had met him while doing charitable work in Brisbane. When her aunt's in-laws gave her a few hours off, of course.

'Ben, about that place. I don't think it's wise for either of us to mention it. It's not that I'm trying to deceive anyone, and my husband knows I was there, but no-one else does.'

'Oh, that's all right. Mrs Ross gave me a talking to before I left. She said the same. She said it's time to get on with the rest of our lives and that perhaps some folks might not understand about the place.'

Emma's heart filled. 'Thank you, Ben. You're a smart young man. You'll go far.'

He grinned in appreciation, but his smile faded suddenly. 'I shan't ever utter the name of the place,' he told her sincerely. 'I'll never forget that honey sandwich you pinched for me, Miss Emma. Not ever. I don't even want to remember the place except for that.'

Emma smiled. 'Thank you. And I can promise you one thing. Life is about to get a lot better.'

'I reckon you might be right. I saw the other one a few times.'

'The other what?' Emma said as she held Roslyn in one arm while opening the passenger door so she could pull the seat forwards and place the child in the baby basket on the back seat.

'The tall one. The one who helped you rake the leaves.'

Emma paused, goosebumps rising. 'Wynn?' she asked. 'Are you talking about Wynn?'

'That's her name!'

Emma straightened, Roslyn still in her arms. 'Where did you see her?'

'She was on the street around the corner from Mrs Ross. Didn't speak to her. Thought I'd better not. Anyway, she was always in a hurry.'

'How often did you see her?'

He shrugged. 'Two, three times, maybe more.'

'Was she ...' Emma could hardly speak the words. 'Was she with someone?' *Did she have a pram?*

'On her own. Heading into some welfare place.'

* * *

'Susannah!'

'Hello! Did the scrawny scamp arrive safely?'

Emma swallowed the moisture that had gathered in her mouth and had been there practically all of the last two hours as she settled Ben in with the Osbornes, drove home, fed Roslyn and helped Ivy bring in the washing before she found time to herself to telephone Susannah.

'He did, and he's not so scrawny any more. He's now having tea and cake with the Osbornes. Susannah—'

'I bet he's wolfing it down. Do you think he's going to be all right?'

'I believe he'll be more than right.'

'Tell the Osbornes to feed him apple pie. Honestly, it's the best. I have my cook bake one every week.'

'Susannah!' Emma interrupted. 'I think we've found Wynn.'

Silence, but the emotion rushing down the telephone line was palpable.

'Oh, God,' Susannah said at last. 'Where?'

Emma explained about Ben seeing Wynn outside the office of some welfare place.

'Does this mean she needs help?'

'I don't know.'

'I'll get my man on it straight away. He's already in Brisbane.'

Emma closed her eyes. 'I hope she's all right.'

'Of course she is!' Susannah paused. 'And if she's not, we're here for her.'

* * *

The inquiry agent hadn't had a whit of trouble discovering where Wynn was once he'd been given the intelligence needed to find her. Emma stared at the scrap of paper now in her possession. A scrap she'd torn from the bottom of a receipt for material for new curtains in the living room, hastily scribbling down the telephone number Susannah had given her. Wynn's telephone number. Susannah had said it should be Emma who first contacted her.

Could this really be Wynn? She was employed by some relief agency and Emma could only imagine what Wynn was doing working for these people. Or why.

With fingertips tingling, she picked up the receiver and got through to the exchange.

The ringing went on forever and Emma bit into the tip of her thumb as she waited.

Then it stopped.

'Wynn Sinclair. Before you say more you need to know I'm already running late, so if you could make this quick I'd be grateful.'

Emma paused for only a second after hearing her friend's voice. 'Wynn,' she said softly. 'It's me. It's Emma.'

Chapter Forty

Blueholm Bay—October 1947

Since Emma couldn't give Ivy a day off every time something important happened in her life, she packed a picnic basket and a flask of coffee and took her visitors to the beach. Roslyn was asleep in the kitchen under the watchful eye of the housekeeper, who had unexpectedly taken a shine to the child, although she continually reminded Emma that Roslyn was Miss Cynthia's baby.

'What an utterly delightful house,' Susannah said, holding onto her summery straw hat in case the breeze whisked it away. She'd slipped off her sandals, as had Emma, but Wynn was still in her sturdy flat lace-ups, standing at the base of a large palm tree, hands behind her back as she studied the ocean.

'Nice view, Hatton.'

'Thanks.'

'Better than the one out of my boarding room window,' Wynn said. 'That's just a brick wall.'

Emma held back a smile, one that kept forming no matter what she had to do, whether it was changing Roslyn's nappies, listening to Ivy's disgruntled comments about how things used to be or sweeping and mopping the many verandahs. Once Wynn had discovered Susannah was intending to visit, she got time away from her work and now here they were, with as many sandwiches between them as they wanted to eat, although Emma wasn't hungry and suspected the other two weren't either.

'So what are your plans?' Emma asked Wynn as they sat on a picnic blanket beneath the palm tree. 'Tell us more about what you've been doing and this course you're so intent on.'

Susannah twisted her hands together. 'How do you feel being on the opposite side of the table?'

Wynn's baby had been taken off her. She thought it might have been a girl, so she'd named her Susannah as she'd said she would. She'd been sent home, spent a week recovering then had walked out and found herself a job. She was working with a relief agency dealing with family welfare and had come across plenty of girls who found themselves in the same position.

'Strangely enough, I don't feel too bad,' Wynn answered. 'I get to see a lot of girls, although always with the welfare woman.'

'What do you do?' Emma asked. 'How do you let these young girls know you're on their side?'

'I slip them some acknowledgement of what's happening to them and whatever comfort I can.'

Emma inhaled the freshness of the air and tasted the salt. 'Bless you, Wynn. You make me proud.'

'Could I slip them some money, do you think?' Susannah asked, making Wynn's smile widen and her cheeks bloom.

'Keep your money until I find a way to really make a difference.'

'It's yours when you want it.'

'And ours,' Emma said. 'Harry and me. We'll help in whatever way we can.'

'If you're in the midst of all this information,' Susannah said, 'will you try to find your little Susannah?'

Wynn shook her head.

'Are you sure?'

'Emma, I'll never find her. Neither will Susannah find her son. They're lost to us. There's no paper trail we can readily get our hands on. We weren't given a copy of the birth certificate so we can't prove we even gave birth. They seal the certificates and we can't get hold of them. So, where the hell would we start? Nobody at the homes or the hospitals would speak to us. Nobody wants to know or become involved.'

'It's like we've been forgotten,' Susannah said with a frown.

'We weren't meant to be remembered,' Wynn said. 'We were supposed to be invisible. And anyway, with you two it was your mother and your parents who were your guardians, and they were the ones to sign consent for you to relinquish your babies. With me, my mother took over, stating I was delusional for wanting to keep mine even though I was nearly twenty-two and should have been able to make my own decisions, so she was allowed to sign my child away.'

'But our babies are out there,' Susannah said, leaning forwards, 'and in our hearts.'

Wynn smiled. 'Damn right they are.' She moved, curling her legs and resting her weight on an outstretched hand on the blanket. 'I do feel sick to my stomach some days, but there's a lot at stake, so I keep going. There are people who are doing their best to change things but they're not getting anywhere in a hurry.'

'It will take time,' Emma said quietly.

'It'll take years, Hatton, perhaps decades. But I've plenty of years left in me.'

'I'm terribly impressed,' Susannah said. 'I couldn't face these poor young girls like you do. I wouldn't know what to say.'

'I don't get the chance to say an awful lot and I can't give them false optimism. I just want them to know somebody cares.' Wynn moved again and pulled up her legs, wrapping her arms around her knees. 'I do what we call fieldwork. I walk into the homes of the poor and tell them what's what. There's no other choice for them unfortunately. It's the same with the unmarried pregnant girls and the welfare women who insist on their nice little chats. Did you know,' she said, looking up, 'that the number of illegitimate births in our state alone doubled during the war? Nearly seventeen hundred recorded in 1945.'

'That's the year ours were ...' Susannah didn't go on, instead folding an arm around herself.

'Taken,' Wynn stated. 'Born and taken.' She glanced at Emma and smiled tenderly. 'Yours too. Grace was taken.'

Emma shook her head. 'It was different.'

'But no less painful.'

Emma thought of Cassie, Grace, and of the letter she had to write.

'Do you think you'll *enjoy* this kind of work though?' Susannah said to Wynn. 'Because if you're only doing it to help others, I shall worry about you every hour.'

'Dearest Susannah, I probably won't enjoy any of it but I intend to change things in whatever small way I can. One day, I'll do something about it. I swear I will. From what I know so far, most women leave this work after they get married and certainly don't continue once they've had children.'

'A woman's place is at her husband's side,' Emma said, remembering what Janet had said after she'd been forced to give up her uniform. Although thankfully Janet and Peter were a happy couple.

'Not for me,' Wynn said. 'I'm never getting married.'

'Nor me,' Susannah said firmly. 'Not ever.'

'Oh, come off it. You're the type to have three husbands.'

'Wynn,' Emma admonished.

'She's probably right,' Susannah said. 'But what fun it might be to get divorced not once but three times. Imagine my family's horror!'

'And this diploma course?' Emma asked Wynn.

'Well, that's the exciting bit. There are less than a hundred properly qualified social workers in the whole country and I'm getting the chance to be one more.' Wynn's eyes were alight. 'There's a two-year diploma course, but not in Queensland, only New South Wales, Adelaide and Melbourne. So I settled upon Sydney.' She rolled her eyes. 'It was the only one of the three universities that would take me, actually.'

'When are you going?'

'Early next year.'

'You can live with me,' Susannah said. 'Say nothing!' she added, holding up a hand. 'I insist you live with me.'

'I accept.' Wynn grinned. 'Generally women who do this diploma are from a much higher social background than me so being able to give them your grand address will work in my favour.'

Susannah's eyes widened.

'Don't be daft,' Wynn said, kinking her mouth. 'I'm joking.'

'But it might actually help,' Susannah replied in earnest.

'Oh, God, what have I started? Come here, woman.' Wynn scrambled up and pulled Susannah to her feet before embracing her in a hug so hard Susannah had to let go of her hat, which fell off her head and onto the sand, tumbling along the beach as the breeze took it.

Emma laughed and ran to get it before it got a soaking in the ocean.

'Thanks,' Susannah said as Emma secured the hat beneath the blanket. 'It was fairly expensive but, more importantly, I like it.'

'I'm not surprised.' It was a complicated affair of straw, ribbon and fabric flowers. Quite the becoming accessory when perched on Susannah Poulson-Taylor's wispy blonde hair.

Wynn put an arm around Susannah's shoulder. Emma made it a circle.

'We really do have a lot in common, we three, don't we?' Susannah said.

'Incredibly, I agree,' Wynn answered.

'We were meant to meet,' Emma said. 'Maybe to offer comfort to each other.'

'We will be friends *forever* though now, won't we?' Susannah asked.

'Yes,' both Emma and Wynn answered firmly.

Susannah smiled. 'Come what may?'

'Come what may,' Emma said, thinking of the pact she and Cassie had made. Whatever trials or troubles they were to face, friendship was the way through.

Chapter Forty-one

Blueholm Bay—October 1947

Colson Beach,
Blueholm Bay,
Townsville

Dearest Cassie,

The sun is out, the sky blue and the air cooler after days of humidity. The sun is warming my bare shoulders and the soles of my feet as I lie on the beach on a bright blue towel scribbling you this letter. And guess what, my darling friend? There's a baby next to me, sleeping and sheltered by a large umbrella.

I'm smiling at your shocked response to this news, so let me tell you why and how before you explode with your guessing.

Remember the man with the twelve cows and the big house? I married him. Just last month.

His name is Harry, in case you've forgotten—and Cassie, I'm in love with him. Truly in love, like there is no other love in the world that anyone could possibly experience. I realise how ridiculous that sounds but I can't find enough words to explain. My love for him is as deep as the ocean, and all the other tried and tested clichés.

I am now Mrs Harry Colson. Emma Colson.

Harry's sister died in childbirth and that's how Harry became guardian to the gorgeous little Roslyn, whom we're bringing up as our own. Her father is alive but unable to cope with life after the ravages he experienced during the war. So we will be Mum and Dad for her in place of her own.

How similar suddenly our lives have become, yours and mine.

Thank you for the photograph of Grace with the twins. She is absolutely beautiful. My hair was the same when I was her age, thick and unruly with curls that suddenly disappeared when I turned eight. Perhaps it will be the same for Grace.

And your boys! So like Eddie in looks but there's a marvellous bubbliness in their eyes and the curve of their smiles that tells me they have a little bit of Cassie O'Byrne in them. I'm betting they'll be a handful! But an absolute delight. How could they be otherwise when they belong to the Shea family?

And now I must tell you about the decision I have made. It was not an easy one to come to, apart from the fact that you make it bearable for me. As does your whole family.

Cassie, I gave you a piece of myself. I entrusted Grace to you when I had no other choice and you have loved her unconditionally. I will never be able to repay you. Except for one thing: I cannot take her away from you. It would rip your heart to shreds, I know it would, and it would be so hard on the little girl to be removed from the only family she has known. So I wonder if you would keep her safe and warm and loved for me?

Perhaps Harry and Roslyn and I might travel to Wisconsin one day to meet all you wonderful Sheas. I will break down in floods of tears when I at last see her, but I'll have Harry with me. My strength, as I hope I am his.

In the meantime, even though she will know the truth when she's a little older, I will be like an aunt to Grace. When you do tell Grace the truth, please tell her that she is in my heart, that she was from the moment she took her first breath and that she will remain in my heart forevermore. Love abides by time and deeds, sad and happy. A love like this cannot be broken.

I find I can't write more now as tears are stinging my eyes. But I will write again—soon.

Take care of your beautiful family, Cassie, as I can now proudly and happily say I will take care of mine.

We will never be apart now, dearest friend. Not ever. We will always be one.

Your loving and eternally grateful,

Em.

When Harry came home from the bank later that evening, Emma had supper waiting.

'We shall travel to America one day and you shall meet Grace,' he said as they stood side by side by the open French doors in the living room after Emma told him she'd mailed her letter.

'I'll cry a rainstorm.'

'I'll bring handkerchiefs.' Harry put a reassuring hand on her shoulder. 'You haven't let her go, Emma. Never think it. You've given her a wonderful life.'

Emma bit into her lip to halt the tears that threatened.

'Just think,' Harry said with a tender smile. 'Roslyn and Grace might one day become friends. They'll have a lot in common. They will both know a different set of parents to the ones they were born to yet they will both know love.'

Emma nodded. She would protect Roslyn with her life. Roslyn would never know heartache if Emma could help it. As Cassie would ensure the same for Grace.

'Do you think Robert will ever know Rosyln? Truly know her?'

'Not as we do. What are your thoughts?'

Emma wound her arms around him and rested her cheek on his chest.

'What's all this?' he asked as he embraced her. 'Is it Grace?'

Emma shook her head. 'I know Grace will be cared for, and that I will always be a part of her life in any and all ways I can be. It's just that you ask my opinion and listen to my answer, even if it differs from yours.'

'That hasn't always been the case for you, has it?'

'It is now. That's what matters.'

Harry spun her around to face the window. 'This is all ours to share,' he said, his breath warm against her face as he spoke.

Emma felt the balm of contentment surround her. It was a new sensation and she was still vulnerable to its influence. She would never accept that the things she'd experienced had been normal. Nor would she accept the cruelty. But thanks to the friends she'd met along the way, she had got through. They had helped shape the woman she was.

As had Harry.

'Harry,' she said as she turned to him, 'you won't understand this, but I've found my way to the other stars. The ones I thought had left me behind.'

His eyes brimmed with tears, which she was surprised to see. 'You have many good friends now. People who love you. People who admire you. I wonder if perhaps ...'

'If what?' Emma asked, almost fearful of his answer.

'I wonder if you will be content to stay here,' Harry said. 'With only me and Roslyn.'

Emma smiled as she lifted a hand to his cheek. She had a house by the ocean to tend, a child to care for and a good man at her side. All of it in Blueholm Bay, the small oceanside town she'd spent so many years longing to run from.

'Harry,' she said gently, 'you brought me home. You and Roslyn *are* my stars.'

Acknowledgements

Thank you, my close writing fraternity friends. Your friendship and the sustenance that friendship gives me means so much.

Thank you, HarperCollins and the Harlequin team, for the continuing support.

Thank you, Nicola Robinson, my commissioning editor, for the perceptive and expeditious way you work. You take my breath away.

Thank you, Kylie Mason, my story's editor. What you showed me was possible filled all the senses.

Thank you, Julia Knapman, senior editor at Harlequin, for all you do and for your skilled work. It was such a delight to work with you once again.

Thank you also, Annabel Adair, my proofreader, for your exceptional attention to detail.

To everyone who has had a hand in producing or supporting *Daughter of the Home Front*, I thank you. From the bottom of my heart.

talk about it

Let's talk about books.

Join the conversation:

facebook.com/harlequinaustralia

@harlequinaus

@harlequinaus

harpercollins.com.au/hq

If you love reading and want to know about our authors and titles, then let's talk about it.